"WHAT I WOULD LIKE YOU TO DO," JAMEY SAID, "IS UNDRESS FOR ME . . .

Take your time. I have never known your body, Christina, except in the darkness.''

She raised her head.

''Show me your body, Christina.''

''I shall not!''

''And why not? Are you not my wife before God?''

''I have sworn certain oaths, and I shall keep those oaths. If you take me, it will have to be by force.''

He never moved. ''Do you not suppose I will do that? Do you not suppose I can bend you to my will, whenever I wish it? I will have you, Christina, every day for the rest of my life. I have made myself this promise, and I will keep it, as I have made all my other promises come true.''

BROTHERS AND ENEMIES

DANIEL ADAMS

A JOVE BOOK

BROTHERS AND ENEMIES

A Jove Book / published by arrangement with
the author

PRINTING HISTORY
Jove edition / December 1982

ISBN: 0-515-05854-8

Jove books are published by Jove Publications, Inc.,
200 Madison Avenue, New York, N.Y. 10016.
The words ''A JOVE BOOK'' and the ''J'' with sunburst
are trademarks belonging to Jove Publications, Inc.

PRINTED IN THE UNITED STATES OF AMERICA

BROTHERS AND ENEMIES

Chapter 1

"Land ho," came the call from the fore-topmast, and William Grant leveled his telescope with a sigh of relief. In the spring of 1761, the war in which Great Britain—with the aid of the Kingdom of Prussia on the continent of Europe—was seeking to carve for herself the greatest colonial empire the world had ever known was already six years old, at least on the North American continent, where the first shots had been fired on the day Braddock's regulars had been cut to pieces at Fort Duquesne. And if, since Wolfe had taken Quebec for the British two years before, the French navy had been almost driven from the sea, their privateers were still to be found on the western side of the Atlantic Ocean.

Presumably he was growing old, Grant thought with a twist of his lips. In 1755 he had been but forty-five himself, and this had been a new land, with a new life to be made. Since he had only fled Scotland because of his involvement with Bonnie Prince Charlie's desperate, romantic adventure in '45, he had hardly been sure which side he was on, here in America, the British or the French.

But now he was past fifty, with a good ship under him, all

1

paid for, and a smiling wife and daughter waiting for him at
home, and two strong sons to support him—and recurring
chest pains to make him wish to enjoy his sea-stolen wealth
rather than consider mixing it with authorized pirates. The
noonday sun was shining from the low hummock of No Man
Land Island, with Martha's Vineyard looking altogether larger
in the background. Nantucket Island itself was in sight to
starboard, and before him the Muskeget Channel into the
Sound. Here was fresh reason for caution; the French were
not William Grant's only enemies.

For his wealth was largely sea-stolen. And if he was by no
means the only New England sea captain who chose to evade
the outrageous British Navigation Acts, which insisted all
trade to and from the colonies should be carried in English
ships and should first touch at English ports—regardless of
the absurdity of carrying sugar from Jamaica all the way
across the Atlantic and then back again to disembark it at
Boston—he was one of the most successful. He knew his
name was high on the list carried by every revenue man, and
if he also knew that the *Gaspee* was the only revenue cutter
on this entire coast, from time to time she came looking even
to Nantucket Island.

"You'll take the helm, Jack," he said quietly, still studying the approaching land through his glass. "And harden in
that mainsheet," he called.

For the *Lodestar* was a brigantine; square-rigged on her
foremast, she carried a huge fore and aft mainsail on the
aftermast, to enable her to point closer to the wind than more
conventional craft, and now she was heeling as she cut through
the calm seas to the light northeasterly breeze, gaining another half a knot as Jack Grant closed his fingers around the
spokes of the wheel. At twenty, Jack Grant—christened
Jonathon—was already six inches taller than his father; he
possessed his mother's height. But his features, long and
thoughtful, with a suggestion of a future cragginess about the
big jaw and nose, and his straight black hair, were all inherited from William Grant, together with his skill as a helmsman; he seemed to have spent all his life at sea. And although
he could scarcely remember Scotland at all—he had been

only five when the Grants had stolen away from Dumfries just before the arrival of Butcher Cumberland's redcoats—he displayed his pride in his nationality by the tam-o'-shanter he wore in place of the more usual woolen cap used by the rest of the crew.

William Grant could relax; his ship was, literally, in good hands. But he was a careful man, and he swung the glass left and right and came to rest on the eastern edge of Martha's Vineyard, eyes screwing half-shut. "Jamey," he muttered. "Jamey boy, you've young eyes. Take a look on the larboard bow."

James Grant stood beside his father and leveled the glass. Two years younger than his brother, it was equally obvious he was William Grant's son, although his features, especially his eyes, reflected an altogether livelier temperament than Jack's somewhat thoughtful character.

"Did you not see a mast?" William Grant asked.

Jamey shook his head. "Not a thing, Father. There's nothing there." He gave the telescope back with a grin. "No revneue cutter, at least."

"Maybe. But you'll check the hold anyway, Jamey. Take Dutton. Make sure that timber hasn't shifted, that all those sugar bags are properly concealed."

Jamey Grant shrugged, and slid down the companion ladder from the quarterdeck into the waist of the little ship. "Open up that hatch, Dutton."

The big bosun, standing at the bulwark to watch Nantucket Island rising on the starboard bow, laboriously crossed the deck and began releasing the battens on the hatch leading to the hold. "You've lost something, then, Master Jamey? Are we carrying less cargo, maybe, then when we set sail?"

"You'll watch your tongue, Ned Dutton," Jamey said, "or I'll have it out."

He was much slighter than Dutton, and certainly not much more than half the other man's age, but there was no mistaking the menace in his tone, and Dutton, who had sailed with the Grants for several years, had had time to see the young man's temper at work.

"Just a joke, Master Jamey," he said, opening the hatch. "Just a joke."

James Grant swung himself into the gloomy pit of the hold. Here he stood on neatly stacked logs of timber, the official reason for the *Lodestar*'s voyage down the coast to the Carolinas. But if there was no other cargo to be seen, there could be no mistaking the sickly sweet smell of the stored sugar, the nostril-tingling scent of the rum and molasses which lay in the bottom of the ship, beneath the wood. No revenue officer would have any difficulty in identifying what was there, or in calculating where the goods must have come from.

"Whew!" Dutton sat in the hatch and peered in. "If they catch us, we'll hang. And for what? Trading with Englishmen?"

"You'll have to ask King George about that one," Jamey agreed. "English goods go to England first—that's what he says, Ned Dutton, so he can collect his duty." He smiled. He had a singular smile, one which seemed to light up his entire face but which at the same time contained an almost sinister private delight, as if only he understood the true substance of the joke. "Even if he knows we're not likely to put up with it."

"So them Boston merchants will pay a fortune for West Indian sugar and West Indian rum, by the time it gets here from England. They'll still come to watch us hang, though, even if we're doing 'em a favor."

"We'll not hang." Jamey Grant climbed out of the hold. "We can outrun any revenue cutter in these waters. We'll not hang."

"It'll happen one day," Dutton grumbled. "All it takes is a snapped halyard, a worn shroud. It'll happen."

"Not to me, Dutton." Jamey sat down beside him in the hatchway. "I'm not sailing in this crate again. Once we unload this cargo, the revenue men can cry for me."

Dutton frowned at him. "You'll not sail with your dad again?"

"He's got Jack. Now there's a real sailorman. He doesn't need me, Ned. I'm for South America."

"The Dons don't take to strangers, Master Jamey."

Jamey Grant continued to smile. "The Dons ain't what

they used to be either, Ned. I'm after gold. El Dorado.
Maybe you've heard the name."

"A legend."

"It's there, Ned. I've read Raleigh and those others. It's
there and I aim to find some of it, Dons or no Dons. I'm not
spending the rest of my life running away from revenue men.
One day I'm going to be so rich I'll come back and buy
Nantucket Island." Once again he smiled his secretive smile.
"You want to come along, Ned Dutton, and make your
fortune?"

With perfect judgment of distance the last foresail was
handed, and the *Lodestar* ghosted alongside the crowded
wooden dock. Mooring lines were thrown and made secure,
and the brigantine bobbed quietly against the heavy plaited-
rope fend-offs which protected her topsides, while the crew
ran the gangway ashore and the spectators eagerly hurried
aboard.

"Pa, Pa!" Mary Grant was sixteen, the youngest of the
three Grant children, small and dark, and never to be a
beauty, but attractive in her bubbling vitality. "You're early.
Oh, I'm so glad you're early, Pa."

William Grant hugged her close while Jack leaned over for
a kiss. "And where's your mother?" William asked.

"She's home, Pa. She's poorly."

"What's that?" He released her, only to see her swept
from her feet by Jamey.

"Oh nothing serious, Pa. Dr. Armstrong says it's just a
cold on the chest. But he reckons she should stay indoors.
And we've a visitor," she added mysteriously.

"A visitor? Why . . ." he turned away from her to greet
the rather florid man who was at that moment clambering
down from the gunwale. "Good day to you, Mr. Butler."

The customs agent wiped his neck with a spotted handkerchief. "What's your cargo, Captain Grant?"

"Timber from Wilmington, Mr. Butler. My holds are full."

"And nothing to declare."

William Grant smiled at him; they were old friends. "Not a
thing, Mr. Butler, save maybe a present for Miss Lizzie."

"I'll have it now!" Lizzie Butler cried, dropping down beside her father. Like her father she was inclined to plumpness, but in her it took the form of soft curves that complemented her soft golden hair. The crew of the *Lodestar* abandoned completing the furling of their sails to watch her as she held out her hands. "Well, Jack? I'll wager you've forgotten me."

Jack Grant was flushing as he squeezed her white fingers. "I've dreamed of nothing else these past three months," he said.

"Nothing else than what?" she demanded, and presented her cheek for a kiss. Although they were not yet officially betrothed, their love was smiled upon by both families.

"All of you," he whispered, and felt her fingers tighten on his.

"You'll come to supper, Jack," she whispered in turn.

"Tomorrow, Lizzie," he promised. "Mother's poorly, I'm told. I must get home."

"Now!" she said fiercely. "Please, Jack. It's terribly important."

He leaned back to gaze into her face. Despite the vivacious smile, her eyes were solemn.

"I must get ashore," William Grant was saying. "You'll come along, Jamey . . . Mary. I'll be back later, Dutton."

"Oh aye, Captain," Dutton said with a wink.

"Billy Grant." John Atkinson, Nantucket's leading merchant, was waiting for William at the foot of the gangplank. "You've had a successful voyage?"

"I think so, Mr. Atkinson."

The two men clasped hands, which allowed them to step close together. "And when will you be unloading?" Atkinson asked in a low voice.

"Midnight for the special," Grant said. "We'll start on the timber tomorrow."

"Midnight," Atkinson agreed. "My people will be here." He smiled past the sea captain at Butler. "It'll be a fine night, Mr. Butler. Good day to you, sir."

"Give Mother my love," Jack Grant said, "and tell her I'll be home soon."

"So you're running off with Lizzie," Jamey said with a sly smile. "Ah well, I'll get to the tavern soon enough."

"Whatever are they up to?" Mary Grant asked, linking her arm through Jamey's as they hurried up the dock, and down the street between the neat rows of weather-beaten wooden cottages. "Off to the Butlers' before even going home. Important matters, indeed. You don't think? . . ." she gazed at her brother with enormous eyes, her cheeks flushed.

"My God, what a thought for a lass of sixteen," Jamey said, and pinched her arm. "And I can tell you she's not. I doubt Jack ever even bundles with her. Sure as Satan he'd not know if she has a mole on her fanny."

Mary gave a nervous giggle and squeezed him closer. "Jamey, have you ever . . . well, *been* with a girl?"

Jamey looked down at her. "Why do you suppose I spend so much time at the tavern? I'm no toper, Mary my girl. But some of the women there, why, they'd sell their souls for a penny."

"Oooh." She gave another shiver. "The thought of it."

"Well, don't think about it. Time enough for that when a girl gets married. If you ever let a man at you, Mary lass, I'd kill him."

Her head swung, and her eyes again became enormous. He had neither raised his voice nor changed his expression, and yet she could have no doubt that he meant what he said.

"Flora?" The Grant cottage was only one street removed from the dockside, and William Grant was already hurrying up the front path and throwing open the door. "Flora? You're not well."

Flora Grant wore a shawl, even indoors, and smiled at her husband somewhat wanly. "Just a chill, Billy. But the better for seeing you."

He kissed her forehead and her mouth, then looked past her at a huge mountain of a man, with sun- and wind-burned cheeks and a prizefighter's features, who stood in the corner. "What's this?"

"An old friend, Billy. Don't you remember Mr. Conybeare?"

William Grant slowly released his wife, allowing her to be

hugged by Jamey in turn, and stared at the big man.
"Conybeare? Not Arthur Conybeare?"

"The same, Billy," Conybeare said.

"By all that's holy," Grant said, and held out his hand. "I
thought you were dead."

Jamey looked at his mother with raised eyebrows.

"He and your father escaped Culloden Moor together,"
Flora explained. "Tracked clear across Scotland together,
with a redcoat behind every bush. Your father was wounded,
and would never have survived the journey without Mr.
Conybeare."

"But you'd not take ship with us," Grant said.

"Aye well, I was younger then." Conybeare grinned.
"But I went to sea anyway. I was impressed by the British."

"The Navy? By God, there's ill fortune."

Conybeare shrugged. "I'm still alive. And wishing to give
it up. But not the sea, Billy. I reckon it's got into my blood.
And I've heard tell there's a mighty successful skipper sailing
out of Nantucket."

"Ha!" Grant shouted. "You've a berth, Arthur. Oh aye,
you've a berth. I'll make you mate, that I will. After the lads,
of course. You've not met my younger son, Jamey?"

Jamey shook hands, his expression slightly contemptuous.
"It's my pleasure, Mr. Conybeare," he said. "You'll excuse
me, Ma, but I've some people to meet."

"At the tavern?" Flora Grant could not keep the disap-
proval from her tone.

"Well," Jamey said. "I'd not sit in on a reminiscence—
I've nothing to add. I'll away to my friends."

"You'll have more ale, Jack," Mrs. Butler invited. She
was an older edition of her daughter, plump and good-natured,
and her table was the best in Nantucket, as was her company.
But not tonight. She talked as vivaciously as ever, smiled and
served the food, asked about the Carolinas and the weather
her future son-in-law had experienced—and kept glancing at
her husband for support. She did not receive a great deal.
Peter Butler chewed slowly and rhythmically, cleared his
throat noisily, and said little.

Neither did Lizzie, also concentrating on her meal and only occasionally smiling at Jack with a soft flush. Well, he thought, it's as plain as a pikestaff what's in the wind. They've had an offer from someone else, and now it's up to me.

He gazed across the table. Marriage, to Lizzie Butler. It was something he had looked forward to for all of his life, it seemed, without ever really considering what it would entail. They were friends. Since she was only a year his junior, they had been friends all their lives, had learned to sail together, had fished and walked and climbed trees together. She had always been far more of a sister to him than Mary, who was nearer Jamey's age. And in time, as they had grown older, they had held hands when walking out, and last year for the first time he had kissed her mouth, a mutually shy explosion of affection and uninformed desire. Marriage to Lizzie would enable all those desires to be fulfilled. And it would be a happy marriage, because they had always been happy together. He liked her cooking; it was nearly as good as her mother's. And she understood the sea, which was essential for a seaman's wife.

There was sound business sense in the idea as well; having the customs agent as a father-in-law would make life that much easier.

"I won't have any more, thank you, Mrs. Butler," he said, and returned Elizabeth's smile. "I must get home to my mother. You'll have heard she's ill?"

"A cold, I believe," Mrs. Butler said. "You'll give her my best regards, Jonathan. But there's nothing the matter with her a good night's sleep won't cure."

"She'll not have that with Billy Grant home from three months at sea," Butler remarked, and flushed as the others turned their heads. "A jest, only a jest."

"Nonetheless, I must get home to her," Jack said. "But if you'd spare me a moment, Mr. Butler, there's a matter I'd like to discuss before I go."

Butler turned his heavy gaze on him. "A matter?"

Jack mentally cursed the heat he could feel in his cheeks.

"Of some importance, at least to me, sir. And, I believe to you and your family as well."

"Oh, aye," Butler remarked, leaning back in his chair.

"Well then, we must leave the men to it," Mrs. Butler decided, getting up. "You'll assist me, Elizabeth."

Lizzie hastily scrambled to her feet and hurried behind her mother.

"You'll take a cigar?" Butler offered.

Jack regarded the brown tube. "I never have before."

"Aye well, then it'd be a waste to start on these," Butler agreed, replacing the cigar in its case.

Jack finished his mug of ale. He had not supposed it would be so difficult. "The fact is, Mr. Butler," he said, "you'll have been wondering, well . . . Lizzie and I have been friends for so long . . . well. . . ." He paused, hoping for some assistance, but Butler appeared to be having trouble in lighting his own cigar, and was not even looking at him. "Well," Jack went on, "you'll have been wondering what I've had in mind."

Butler leaned back in his chair again, his head wreathed in smoke.

"My prospects are good," Jack hurried on. "You'll know that Father isn't intending to remain at sea more than another year or two. He feels he's getting a little old for it. I'm to be master of the *Lodestar*." Again he paused, more hopeful than before. But Butler continued to peer at him through the smoke. "That's a good position for a young man," Jack explained. "I'll be able to afford a house of my own, Mr. Butler. Lizzie won't ever want for anything. You've my word on that. Of course I'll be away for a few months at a time, but she's used to that already. She'll not mind."

Butler cleared his throat and sat up. "You're asking for Lizzie's hand in marriage," he remarked.

"Sir? Well, yes. Yes, I am, Mr. Butler."

"You're young to be thinking of marriage," Butler said.

"Well, I'm twenty years old," Jack protested. "And I wasn't thinking we'd get married tomorrow, Mr. Butler. There'd be the betrothal. I just wanted to reach an understanding. With you, and Mistress Butler. And Lizzie, to be sure."

"Young," Butler said again. "There's a lot of water to flow by before you can think about marriage, Jonathan Grant. Oh aye, a lot of water."

Jack was becoming irritated. "I'm prepared to wait for as long as you think fit, Mr. Butler," he said. "I only want to reach an understanding."

"We'll reach an understanding when the time is right, Jonathan," Butler said. "It ain't right this minute. There's no hurry. Lizzie is just a girl. You're just a lad. And there's . . . well, there's time."

Jack stared at him, watched him push back his chair and get up. "So I'll bid you good night, Jonathan," he said. "I'm for an early bed. And no doubt you'll be wanting the same, just home from the sea. Besides, there's your mother to attend. You'll want to spend some time with her." He paused in the doorway to glance over his shoulder. "While you can, to be sure. Good night, Jonathan. Good night."

The door closed, and Jonathan was left alone, gazing at it impotently. He was too surprised to be really angry, but he could feel the anger lurking at the edges of his reasoning. Someone else *had* asked for Lizzie's hand, and Butler had decided this upstart was a better bet than a Grant. Some moneybags from Boston, no doubt, in Nantucket looking for West Indian sugar. Well by God, he thought, his big hands curling into fists . . .

"Ssssh," Lizzie Butler cautioned, entering the room from the kitchen doorway. "You're to go. Pa says so."

"Well, I've a thing or two to say to him."

She put her finger over her lips, held his hand, and kissed him on the cheek. "You must hurry."

"So you've decided against me too," he said bitterly.

She frowned at him. "Against you, Jack? I'll never be against you. I'm trying to help you. Pa would help you too, if he dared. But he can't."

It was Jack's turn to frown. "I don't understand a word you're saying."

Now she had grasped his arm, was half pushing him toward the door. "It's a deadly secret," she whispered. "The revenue cutter."

He checked. "What! . . ."

"She's moored in the next bay. They're laying for you, Jack. For all of you. There's been a tip."

"A tip? By Christ . . ."

She shook her head. "Losing your temper won't help. There's been a tip, and that's it. They knew you were expected back this week, and they've been waiting. They know too that you'll unload at midnight, because you always do. They're laying for you, Jack."

"Is this your father's doing?"

She shook her head. "No. I swear it's not. But they told him what was going to happen."

"And he'd not pass it on to me?"

"He dares not. Don't you understand? If he did, they'd know. He'd lose his living. But I couldn't let them take you, Jack. Listen to me. Harry Petersen has a small sloop. The revenue men don't mean to move before midnight. You've time to get down to the beach and put to sea. You'll make Martha's Vineyard easy. Or even the mainland. It's settled weather."

"And what then?"

"Well . . . you're a seaman. You'll find a berth."

"And you?"

"Well . . ." Again there was hesitation, this time accompanied by a flush. "Maybe someday, after this has blown over . . ."

"After Father and Jamey have been hanged, you mean. And after the *Lodestar* has been confiscated."

"You can't help them now, Jack. You can only save yourself."

"The devil I can't." He freed himself and yanked open the door.

"You can't fight the revenue, Jack," she begged. "There're too many of them. And even if you succeeded, you'd be a pirate."

"And what'll I be if I just run away?" he asked. "A cutpurse who's deserted his father and brother. If a Grant is to hang, Lizzie, then we'll all hang together." He took her arms and pulled her against him, kissed her on the lips, forcing them apart with the passion of his embrace, touching her tongue, truly possessing her with his mouth for the first time in his life.

And the last, he thought ruefully.

"Maybe I'll come back," he said. "One day. When King George's men are gone."

Jack Grant threw open the door of the inn and blinked into the smoke-filled interior. It was still daylight outside, but the lamps were lit in here, and there was a large company, drinking and smoking, laughing and exchanging stories, turning their heads to look at the newcomer in surprise, for Jack was not a habitual customer.

He spotted Ned Dutton easily enough, as well as several other of the *Lodestar*'s crew, made his way through the tables and past the somewhat blousy women who attempted to attach themselves to his arm, and tapped the bosun on the shoulder. Dutton, engaged in drinking beer, with a woman seated beside him murmuring into his ear, turned his head with a grunt.

"Where's Jamey?" Jack asked. "He's not gone home already, has he?"

Dutton blinked at him. "Mr. Jack?" he asked. "You're wanting a drink, man?"

"No," Jack said. "I'm looking for my brother."

"Ah well, he's not here."

"I can see that," Jack pointed out, with as much patience as he could muster. "Has he left?"

"Well, no," Dutton said. "He's being entertained, you might say."

"Where?"

"Upstairs, I reckon."

Jack glanced at the stairs, then at the other men in the room. He knew most of the people in Nantucket, at least by sight, and there were no strangers to be seen. On the other hand, someone had tipped off the revenue men, and the culprit might well be here now. And Ned Dutton was no great keeper of secrets. Jamey had to be alerted, though.

"You finish your drink, Ned," he said softly. "And don't have another. I've something for you to do."

"What's that?"

"I want you to find all the others you can and go along to my father's house. Quietly, now. It's a surprise."

"A surprise?"

"For Father," Jack said. "We're to give him a surprise present. You go along there, Ned, with the others. I'll catch up with you, soon as I get Jamey."

He ran up the stairs, looked along the corridor, and heard a woman giggle from behind the first door. As he reached for the knob, a hand touched his shoulder, and he swung around to face Johnson, the landlord, who had followed him up.

"There'll be no trouble, Mr. Grant," Johnson said. "Your brother's old enough to know what he wants."

"I'm not looking for trouble, Mr. Johnson," Jack agreed. "But I must have a word with Jamey."

He opened the door and gazed at the bed in consternation. It was a warm June evening, and Jamey and his companion had not troubled to get beneath the covers; it was the first time in his life that Jack had seen a woman naked.

Her name, he recalled, was Annie Sweet, and she was at least ten years older than himself, much less than Jamey. She was also larger than either of them—a vast expanse of pink and white flesh.

At the sound of the door opening she had pushed Jamey off her. Having recovered from her initial alarm, however, Annie did not seem to be the least embarrassed. "Why, Jack Grant," she said. "Have you come to share, then? It'll cost you another shilling."

"Jack?" Jamey rolled over and sat up, reaching for the blanket. "For God's sake . . . you'll not tell Father about this?"

"Get up," Jack said. "And hurry. Get dressed. Is there a back way out, Mr. Johnson?" He turned to the landlord, who, intent on keeping the two brothers from fighting, was hovering at his elbow.

"There is, Mr. Grant," he said, "if you'll tell me what you need it for."

"My brother and I must get home," Jack said. "But privately. You've no objection, I'm sure." He glanced at the woman again. "I'll pay you another shilling to stay where you are for the next hour, Mistress Sweet."

"Now look here," Jamey said. But he was reaching for his pants as he spoke. For all his pretended contempt for his brother, experience had taught him a healthy respect for Jack's fists.

"Just hurry," Jack said, and threw the coin on the bed. Annie Sweet seemed to uncoil as she reached forward; Jack stared at her heavy breasts in fascination. Jamey had been enjoying all of that, and Jack doubted it was for the first time. While he . . .

Jamey pulled on his boots. "I'll see you later, Annie," he said. "Now Jack . . ."

"Come on," Jack said, and closed the door behind them. "If you'll show us the way, Mr. Johnson."

"Along here," Johnson said. "There's a back staircase. There's no trouble I hope, Mr. Grant?"

"None involving you, Mr. Johnson," Jack called back, running down the stairs.

"Maybe you'll tell me now what this is all about," Jamey panted.

"I wonder it's worth it," Jack remarked.

"Well . . . three months at sea. We're not all monks like you, Jacko."

"She's hardly better than a whore," Jack said.

"She knows what it's about," Jamey said. "But you didn't drag me out here for a lecture, I hope."

"The revenue cutter is in the next bay," Jack said, hurrying up the street behind Dutton and the twelve other crew members, who were loudly discussing the possible reasons for their being so urgently recalled to duty. "And they've men ashore, waiting for us to start unloading."

"Revenue men? By Christ, what'll we do?"

"Tell Father, for a start. You'll wait here, Dutton," he said, pushing his way through the men to reach the door of his home. "I'll be back in a moment." He went inside and embraced his mother.

"Jack!" she cried. "I thought you were never coming."

" 'Tis lucky I delayed," he said, and frowned at the stranger standing at his father's side.

"This is an old friend of mine, Jack," William Grant explained. "Arthur Conybeare, my elder son, Jack."

"A pleasure, Jack," Conybeare said, and held out his hand. "I remember you as a babe."

Jack nodded, squeezing the offered fingers. "Well . . . could I have a word with you, Father?"

"Fire away."

"In private."

William Grant glanced from his wife to his daughter to Jamey, waiting in the doorway. "You can say what you have to in front of Arthur, Jack. He's shipping with us next time out."

"If there is a next time out," Jamey said.

Jack hesitated, but time was getting short. "There's to be a revenue raid," he said. "Tonight, when we're unloading." He glanced at Conybeare once again. "There's been a tip."

"A tip, by God," William Grant cried, leaping to his feet.

"Oh my God." Flora Grant was overtaken by a fit of coughing. "What'll you do, Billy?"

"Do?" Billy Grant asked. "Do?"

"What if we simply don't unload?" Jamey suggested.

"Then they'll search the ship anyway," his father said. "They're only waiting in the hope of catching our buyers as well. But they'll settle for us if they can't do better. By Christ, to know what to do!"

"Put to sea," Conybeare recommended.

The Grants stared at him.

"Put to sea," Conybeare said again. "Your brigantine has the legs of that cutter. Then you can decide what to do, either dump your contraband or come back here when the cutter's gone. She won't hang around very long."

"To sea?" Flora Grant cried. "But they've only just come home."

"It's the only way," Conybeare insisted. "I'll come with you, Billy, that I will."

"You're right," William Grant said. "It'll only be for a

couple of days, Flora. As Arthur says, they won't waste their time around here when they see we've gone. Aye, that's the ticket. We'll put to sea and give them the slip.'' He threw his arm around his wife's shoulder. ''Only a few days, my sweet. It'll be better than losing the *Lodestar,* and maybe us into the bargain.''

It was nearly dark by now, but all Nantucket seemed to know what was afoot. Windows were opened and heads peered out as the fifteen-man crew of the *Lodestar,* accompanied by Conybeare, hurried onto the dock.

''Haste now,'' William Grant said, and looked at the sky to determine the wind direction. ''It's offshore. We're in luck. Just cast her free, and we'll get sail on her as we drift out.''

''You'll stop there, Captain Grant,'' a voice said.

They halted, Jamey's foot already on the gangplank, and seemed to huddle closer together as they faced the naval officer, who had a dozen bluejackets at his back. ''I've a warrant to search your ship.''

Jack realized they had been hiding all along in the warehouse immediately opposite the *Lodestar*. He cursed himself; he should have checked that first. But a quick count told him there were only twelve of them. And there was nothing to lose now. He glanced at his father.

William Grant was still undecided. The officer drew a pistol. ''You'll not resist a king's warrant.''

Conybeare gave a roar and hurled a stone. The missile struck the officer on the shoulder, and he half turned with a grunt of pain, dropping the pistol.

''Scatter them, lads,'' Conybeare shouted, ''and then we can get to sea.''

Dutton gave a cheer which was echoed by Jamey Grant, and the sailors ran forward.

''Arrest those men,'' the officer shouted. ''I want the Grants. Arrest them.'' Having regained his balance, he abandoned any attempt to find his pistol—it had been kicked aside in the rush of the *Lodestar* sailors. Avoiding the flying fists, he made for William Grant, still standing irresolutely by the gangplank. ''I arrest you, William Grant,'' he said, putting his hand on the sea captain's shoulder, "in the name of the law . . ."

"No you don't," Jack snapped, coming to life, and pushing him aside. "Get on board, Father."

Someone struck him a searing blow across the back of the head and he realized that the revenue men were armed with belaying pins, heavy wooden spokes normally inserted into matching holes on the sides or around the foot of the masts of a ship for the purpose of securing sheets and halyards. The force of the blow sent him staggering and he fell to his hands and knees, turned as the sailor aimed a kick at him, threw both arms around the man's legs, and brought the man heavily to the ground alongside him. For a moment they wrestled, but Jack was the more powerfully built, and with an extra effort he pushed the man away. As they both rose to their knees, Jack struck him a swinging right-hander on the jaw which sent him arcing backward. Jack reached his feet in time to watch his father grappling with the revenue officer, still at the foot of the gangplank, and suddenly fall away from a punch himself, teeter for a moment on the edge of the wooden dock, and then fall. The sound of the splash as he entered the water was accompanied by the dull thump of his head hitting the side of the ship.

"Father!" Jack shouted, and dashed forward, only to be checked by another sailor appearing in front of him, belaying pin swinging. Jack caught the blow with his left hand, struck the man in the stomach with his right, but mistimed the punch and did not fell him. They closed, Jack trying to force him away. "There's a man drowning over there," he shouted, but his assailant did not seem to hear, or to care. It was several seconds before Jack could hurl him aside and reach the dockside, to stare into the black water between the ship and the dock and to see Conybeare swimming clear of the piles, holding the unconscious William Grant under the shoulders.

The fight was over. The revenue men had either fled for help or were lying on the ground. The officer had disappeared. "Over here," Jack bawled. "Give us a hand." He climbed down the nearest ladder and caught his father's collar as Conybeare, puffing and grunting, brought him up to the rungs. "Is he . . ."

"He's alive," Conybeare said. "But just. Haul him up."

Jamey had found a length of rope, and this was fastened around William Grant's body and secured in a bowline knot. With a dozen men heaving on the end, he was lifted from the water and stretched out on the dock; gasping for breath, he opened his eyes.

"Thought I was done for," he grunted. "Oh aye, thought I was done for."

"Conybeare fished you out, Pa," Jamey said.

"Arthur?" William Grant struggled into a sitting position. "Why, man, 'tis the second time my life is in your debt."

"Then there's naught to be remembered," the big man muttered in embarrassment.

"Oh aye? I'll have to pay you back one of these days, and that's for certain. Here's my hand on it."

Conybeare grinned at him as he squeezed his fingers. "Until then, Billy, we'd best get to sea. That revenue officer will be back with more men."

"What do you reckon?" Conybeare asked. With Jack and Jamey he stood at William Grant's elbow, waiting while the captain scanned the shore through his telescope. After two days at sea, they had returned within sight of the island and now lay rolling in the long Atlantic swell, hove to into the light southeasterly wind; the breeze was warm and gentle at the moment, but combined with the swell, it offered a reminder that as June came to an end the western ocean was liable to suffer the destructive tropical storms called by the old Indian name of hurricanes.

"Can't be sure," William said. "If she's still in that bay round the corner, then her topmasts will be hidden by those trees. We'll wait until after dark, then put in closer and send a boat ashore. That'd be best. For the time being, we'll stand off again. No point in letting them know we're about."

"Sail ho," came a call from forward. "Coming up from the south."

The Grants hurried to the other side to peer at the approaching three-master, square-rigged and blunt-bowed. Once again William Grant leveled his telescope. "That's a man-of-war," he said.

"British or French?" Jack asked.

"In these waters, she'd have to be British."

"A man-of-war?" Conybeare muttered. "By God, there's a stroke of ill fortune."

"Naught to concern yourself with," William Grant said reassuringly. "She can't know anything about Nantucket. She's on patrol, that's all. We'll just stand out to sea as if we'd not a care in the world. She's got no interest in us. Man those halyards now, and get under way."

The crew responded eagerly, casting nervous glances at the approaching frigate, freeing the sheets to bring the *Lodestar* off the wind and send her beating down the coast, as if headed for New York.

Jack Grant stood at the rail and watched the black and yellow hull approach. Her broadside gunports were closed, and there was little activity on her decks; since she was running at very nearly the speed of the wind, her huge white ensign hardly fluttered.

"A warship," Conybeare muttered at his elbow. "By Christ, but I hate the sight of the things. I served on them, you know. Impressed, I was. Hard times, I can tell you. Christ . . ." his voice took on a new note as he pointed, and Jack looked at a puff of black smoke drifting into the air above the frigate's forecastle. The sound of the explosion reached him a second later.

"Only a blank shot," Jack said. "They're wanting us to heave to."

"Heave to?" Conybeare asked. "By Christ . . ."

"Back those yards," came the call from William Grant. "Heave her to."

Conybeare ran across the quarterdeck. "You don't intend to stop for her, do you? She's out for men."

It was the habit of the Royal Navy, whenever they were shorthanded, to stop merchantmen and take by force as many seamen as were needed.

"I'm not going to argue with a frigate, Arthur," William

Grant said. "She'll not get any out of us. I'm shorthanded as it is, and my men have tickets of exemption from service." He smiled grimly. "They're all married, with children, save my officers." He clapped his friend on the shoulder. "And if you've been paid off, you've naught to worry about either."

Jack went amidships to supervise the rigging of the ladder, and watched the longboat dance over the gentle waves toward them. She was manned by half a dozen seamen, and there was a smartly dressed lieutenant in the stern. "Ahoy there, the *Lodestar,*" he called as the boat approached. "What port?"

"Nantucket," William Grant replied. "Bound for New York with timber."

"You'll receive us, sir," the lieutenant said, and the boat came alongside as the crew shipped their oars. The naval officer came up the ladder, leaped over the gunwale, and saluted. "Martin Beresford, sir."

"William Grant." Grant shook his hand. "You've seen no frogs?"

Beresford smiled so tightly it was difficult to imagine his ever laughing outright, or even indulging in humor. "None, sir. We've seen to that, in these waters."

"Good news," William Grant said. "Good news. You'll wish to see my manifest?"

"I doubt it would interest me, Captain Grant." Beresford turned to look at the crew, who had gathered in the waist. "Are these all your people?"

William Grant stood at his shoulder. "Aye." Conybeare had apparently gone below.

"A likely lot," Beresford observed. "And every man a competent seaman, if I know my Nantucket traders."

"Why yes, that is so," Grant said. "And every man necessary to the ship, Lieutenant. She takes a deal of working."

"Hardly," Beresford disagreed, "in settled weather, and with a short voyage ahead of you. I'll tell you frankly, Captain Grant, I need four of your men."

"Four? Why, sir, that's impossible. And besides, my men all have tickets."

Beresford leaned over the side. "You'll come up, cox, and

bring Fleming with you. In time of war, Captain Grant, tickets can be disregarded. Without my frigate, sir, these waters would be swarming with French privateers, and you know that as well as I. But if we're going to fight the French, sir, why, we must be fully manned. I'll have four of your men." He faced the crew. "Line up there."

"You'll not let him take us, Captain Grant," Dutton said. " 'Tis not legal."

"If he must have someone," said another man, "give him Conybeare."

There was a sudden silence as the crew of the *Lodestar* exchanged glances. Beresford slowly turned back to William Grant.

"What was that name, Captain Grant? You've a man named Conybeare on board this vessel?"

Grant frowned at him. "That's no concern of yours, mister. He's been paid off, and he's past the age for impressment, anyway."

"Conybeare," Beresford said again, and glanced at his coxswain, just climbing over the rail, accompanied by a very large sailor. "What do you think of that, cox?"

The coxswain grinned. "It'll be the one, sir. That's not a common name."

"I'd formed the same opinion," Beresford agreed. "I'll see this man, Captain Grant."

"Now you listen to me, mister," William Grant said, his face starting to redden with anger. "He's done his time, and he's older than I am. You've no right . . ."

"Are you proposing to argue with a king's officer in time of war?" Beresford's voice was quietly menacing.

"He's right, Billy." Conybeare came up the companion hatch. His shoulders were bowed, and he suddenly looked far older than his age. "Not under the guns of his ship."

"Arthur Conybeare." Beresford's tight-lipped smile made him resemble a wolf showing its teeth. "Now there's a pleasant sight. Served his time, has he, Captain Grant? I've a surprise for you."

"You mean you know him?" Grant asked.

"Know Conybeare? There isn't a Navy seaman on this

coast doesn't know Conybeare," Beresford said. "Oh aye.
Served his time? He's served his time in irons, if that's what
you mean. A more mutinous dog I have never encountered.
He belongs to a sister ship of ours, Captain Grant, and was
under arrest for striking an officer when he broke out. Taking
him back is going to be a pleasure. You are going to hang
from the highest yardarm we can find, Conybeare. But before
that, we're going to take every last strip of skin from your
back. Over the side with you."

Conybeare hesitated, glanced at William Grant, and then
went to the rail without a word.

"You can't let them take him," Jack whispered. "He
saved your life."

" 'Tis the Navy," William Grant muttered.

"God damn the Navy!" Jamey Grant shouted, and in a
sudden bound he leaped forward, grasped Beresford by the
arm, twisted it behind his back, and drew his seaman's knife.
He held the point against the lieutenant's ear.

"For God's sake," William Grant shouted.

"You, sir," Beresford gasped, "are a pirate. You'll hang
beside Conybeare."

Conybeare himself had stopped at the rail and now turned,
seeming to shed all the extra years in a moment. "I'll not
forget this, lad," he said.

"Aye, but we're *all* scuppered now," Ned Dutton said,
watching the cox, who together with the seaman Fleming was
waiting for some order from his officer.

"Get him off me," Beresford said, trying to look down at
the knife blade, grimacing from the pain at having his arm
twisted. "Get him off me, and I'll take only him and
Conybeare."

"You can't, Father," Jack said. "Not Jamey."

William Grant seemed to awaken from a deep sleep. "Aye,"
he said. "Put them below."

"Down there," Jamey said, pushing Beresford toward the
hatch cover to the hold, while Jack beckoned the other two to
follow.

"They'll blow us out of the water," Dutton protested.

"Their ports are closed," Conybeare said. "They never

expected trouble. And we're hove to into the wind. If we free our sheets we'll be out of range before she can even wear ship. This vessel can outbeat any square-rigger."

"Aye," William Grant said. "Free those sheets. Haste now."

Beresford turned at the top of the hatch and looked over his shoulder. "And where will you go? Are you mad, man? You'll be a pirate. They'll catch you in the end for certain, and you'll hang." He looked at the crew. "You'll all hang."

"Aye well, it's been an unlucky week, to be sure," William Grant said. "But we'll take our chances. Get them below and free those sheets. You'll take the helm, Jack. You're the best we have. Show those Navy boys what you can do."

Jack Grant wrapped his hands around the spokes of the wheel, waiting to feel the weight of the ship, as Dutton drove the men forward to free the sheets. It had all happened so quickly that they, like himself, he supposed, were reacting instinctively to the commands they were given without truly stopping to consider the results of their actions. Several of them were married, as was Father. And as he had soon hoped to be. But after today, would they ever again be able to show their faces in any British territory?

That was assuming they survived this day.

Now the wind was filling the sails even as Jamey and Conybeare replaced the hatch over the hold to secure Beresford and the sailors. From alongside there came alarmed shouts from the other seamen in the dinghy as they felt themselves being dragged along.

"Cast those fellows off," William Grant shouted, pounding his fist on the gunwale. He was suddenly swept with excitement, and Jack, watching, recalled that his father had spent his entire youth in Scotland fighting the English.

Wind fluttered against Jack's face, and the *Lodestar* heeled onto the port tack; clearly it would pay to pass as wide of the frigate as they could. He tightened his hands on the wheel and glanced to his left, where the warship was only just awakening to what was happening. Officers had run to the rail to level their telescopes at the brigantine; others were pointing at the dinghy, now cast adrift and falling behind. But the *Lodestar* was gathering speed every second.

"Come on," William Grant shouted, climbing into the lower shrouds in his excitement. "Come on. Give her all she has, Jack. All she has."

Jack watched the foresail flapping and allowed the ship to fall a little further off the wind. Now heeling several degrees, she began to race through the calm water. "Harder in," he commanded, and Jamey ran forward to help the crewmen haul on the sheets, the ropes which were attached to the sails to adjust their trim; for working to windward the *Lodestar* needed her square sails to be set as near as possible fore and aft—they might not assist the thrust given by the mainsail and the jibs, but at least they would not hinder them.

Once again Jack glanced over his shoulder at his father, still pounding the rail, at the dinghy, tossing in their wake, and then at the frigate, a hive of activity as British seamen clambered into the rigging to flatten in *their* square sails and attempt to bring the ship around in pursuit. And now the huge black-painted gunports began to flop open to reveal the ugly snouts of the cannon as they came poking out.

"Ah, they're smart," Billy Grant shouted. "They're quick. They're good, Jack. But we're better, eh? By God!"

The oath resulted from an explosion at the frigate's side, which was immediately followed by several others. Water spumed around the *Lodestar,* but the guns had been too hastily aimed for accuracy. Nonetheless it was nerve-wracking to be under fire. The crew gathered forward to chatter among themselves, and Jamey came hurrying aft, followed by Conybeare.

"Those were close," Jamey shouted. "I'd not thought they could load and fire that quick."

"They're the best in the world," Conybeare said grudgingly.

"But we've got the heels of her. We've . . ." William Grant's exultant cry died in a choke as he fell back from the rail.

"He's been hit!" Jack released the wheel and ran to his father's side.

"Can't have been," Jamey shouted, kneeling beside him.

" 'Tis a seizure," Conybeare said. "The excitement . . ."

With cries of wailing fear, Dutton and the crew came aft as, lacking a hand on the helm, the *Lodestar* had turned into the wind and now lay stalled, only just out of range of the warship. And once again the guns boomed to send water spewing into the air just astern of them, while now the frigate was completing her slow wheel into the wind to begin her pursuit.

"The helm," Jamey begged. "For God's sake take the helm, Jack, or we'll all hang."

Jack stared into his father's face; the red had suddenly disappeared and the flesh was now quite gray. He got up and grasped the wheel. "How is he?" he asked.

The crew had gathered on the quarterdeck and stood behind Conybeare and Jamey as they lifted William Grant's head, patted his hands and cheeks. The rumble of the frigate's guns were forgotten, as was the flying spray; in any event, the *Lodestar* was now pulling safely out of range.

"He's dead," Conybeare said. "It's my fault. But for me . . ."

"That's nonsense," Jamey said. "He'd not have had it any other way." He got up and stood beside his brother. "Would he, Jacko?"

"No," Jack said, staring ahead, over the bow, at the sparkling blue water. The sea had been his father's life, and his own life, so far. And he had died at sea, and quickly. There was a blessing. But how to tell Mother? How could he even get word to her?

He realized they were all looking at him.

"What'll we do, Mr. Jack?" Dutton asked. "What'll we do? We're outlaws. What'll we do?"

'What'll we do? Jack thought. What a problem to have to face. He was only twenty years of age. He had grown up in considerable comfort, and some security; the hardships which must have accompanied his childhood, as Father had gone off to fight for Prince Charlie and then had to flee for his life before Cumberland's redcoats, were too distant to be recalled. In Nantucket life had been good, their smuggling only adding a dash of excitement to the humdrum business of trading up and down the eastern seaboard. He had looked for nothing else, save marriage to Lizzie Butler and a home of his own and children. . . .

And eventually command of the *Lodestar*. Now it was his even sooner than he had anticipated. *What'll we do, Captain Grant?* And there could only be one Captain Grant.

He squared his shoulders. "So we're outlaws," he said. "That's what Father decreed, and that's what we'll have to be. We'll find somewhere to live, and then we'll send for our families. We have the ship, after all. We'll always earn a living."

"Where?" Dutton asked.

Jack chewed his lip. The Americas were divided into British, French, Spanish, and Dutch colonies. And Great Britain, as usual, was managing to be at war with all the other three. To go anywhere would be to risk confiscation of the ship and imprisonment, while to visit a British island was to risk a hanging. Where indeed?

"We'll find somewhere," Jamey said fiercely, and to his surprise Jack saw that tears were running down his brother's cheeks. "We'll find somewhere. Jack will take us somewhere."

Chapter 2

~~~~~~

"You'll hang, Jack Grant," Lieutenant Beresford remarked with obvious satisfaction. "You'll all hang," he added, looking around him at the crew. "If you don't drown first." He pointed at the sky. "Ever seen clouds like that, *Captain* Grant? That's a hurricane cloud, that is. Ever weathered a hurricane, *Captain* Grant?"

"I wonder you don't throw him over the side and let him swim ashore," Jamey remarked. He waited with the crew of the dinghy, bobbing on the long swell—another portent of bad weather.

"He'd get there," Conybeare said. "Not even the sharks would try digesting him."

"Make haste." Jack swept the horizon with the glass, paying particular attention to the low hills of Barbados, three cables to the west. In his anxiety to avoid the frigate, or any other British ship, he had stood well out into the Atlantic. This was the best course south in any event, as his navigation told him; from Barbados both wind and current made northwest, and the old saying was that a ship could sail from Barbados to Jamaica in seven days but would require three weeks to beat back. They had taken no more than three weeks on the voyage down from New England, about twice the distance. In all that time they had seen not a ship, or land, having made a gigantic dogleg to take themselves clear of the Bahamas and Cuba before setting down to the south, still outside the arc of the Windward Islands. That they had made Barbados at all was quite a feat of navigation, he thought with some pride; his father had taught him well.

Besides, it had given him time to digest the loss, and come to terms with the realization that he was now head of the family. Time to recover from his grief, and attempt to plan a future. But here he had had little success, because for all that time he had had to bear the gibes and threats of Martin Beresford. He had tried to treat the man as a gentleman, had released him from the hold and invited him to dine aft, and sleep there as well, to consider the entire episode as the fortunes of war. But the officer remained a bitter and vengeful man, as much from humiliation as from anger, Jack imagined.

But *he* would carry the game through to the end. He raised his tam-o'-shanter. "Good fortune to you, Mr. Beresford," he said, "and to your people. We'll not meet again."

Beresford smiled at him as he swung his legs over the gunwale. "Oh we will, Captain Grant. Be sure of that. If it takes me to the end of my days, we'll meet again. You'll come back, Grant, looking for your loved ones in Nantucket. We'll meet again."

"If you harm a hair on my mother's head," Jack said, "or my sister's, Beresford, we *will* meet again, and I'll kill you even if I do hang for it. Now get off my ship before I listen to my brother and make you swim."

He watched the dinghy pulling for the shore and made another sweep with the telescope. The *Lodestar* was at her most vulnerable; although he had carefully selected the scarcely populated and harborless Atlantic coast of the island, there was almost certain to be a British warship in Carlisle Bay, the anchorage for Bridgetown in the west, and were she to come creeping around the headland now, with Jamey and six others on the beach. . . . And they had to fill the water casks while they were there; the ship was at the end of its supply.

"You've a lot on your mind," Conybeare observed. He had slipped easily into the role of second mate, apparently not at all concerned at taking orders from two young men hardly more than one-third his age. He had proved a good companion too, and a sober, God-fearing man. If only, Jack thought, I could get over the feeling that he is a bearer of ill fortune. With his appearance their life had fallen apart. What must Mother and Mary be thinking, as three weeks had passed and not a word? But they would hear soon enough, once Beresford was ashore. What then?

And what of Lizzie, magnificent, golden-haired Lizzie? Her promise to wait for him had been somewhat half-heartedly delivered.

"Maybe too much, for one so young," Conybeare went on, as Jack had not replied. "I'd help, if I could."

"And I'll ask for your help, Arthur, when I reckon it can be given," Jack agreed.

"You've nothing planned? We've sailed for three weeks now. There's scarce enough biscuit for another long spell. But you've said not a word."

"Which doesn't mean I haven't thought about it," Jack said. "But our destination was not something to discuss while the Navy men were still aboard. 'Tis only a few days' sail from here to the South American coast."

"Brazil? That's Portuguese territory. And the Portuguese are thick as thieves with the British."

"It's a big country, I've heard tell," Jack said. "With a lot of empty coastline."

"So we'll comb beaches for the rest of our lives? 'Tis also a place of vast forests and savage Indians and a fever that reduces a man to bones in days. And a government that doesn't welcome outsiders, even if they weren't outlaws. Brazil's no place to make a future, lad."

"You'll be suggesting we turn pirate next," Jack said.

"It's worth considering," Conybeare said in a serious tone. "Every man's hand is against us."

"And we're armed with two swivel guns to repel boarders," Jack said. "We'd be the terror of the ocean."

"Many a famous captain began with far less."

"And the last of them was hanged forty years ago," Jack pointed out. "You're fortunate, Arthur. You have no family, no ties. The rest of us need somewhere to settle, somewhere we can fetch our loved ones to. I'll hear no more talk of piracy."

Yet the uncertainties of the future hung above him like a dark cloud. Nor was Jamey a great deal of help, when the matter was discussed between them that very evening.

"Make land wherever you choose," he said, "and let me off. I've had all the seafaring a man can stomach. Brazil's as good as the next place, as far as I'm concerned. So they have forests and Indians—so does New England. But they also have gold. El Dorado is in South America, Jacko, and that's where I was determined to go anyway. The City of Gold. Gold is what counts in this world, Jacko. If you have enough of it you can cheat the gallows of any crime. Even Beresford won't be able to touch us if we come home with our pockets jingling; we'll just bribe the judge." He pointed at the eastern sky. "But whatever you're going to do, do it quickly."

Dutton was also alarmed. The weather, always hot in these latitudes, had now lost its normal humidity, and the breeze had dropped to just a whisper out of the east. The sky above was still blue, but enormous black clouds filled the eastern horizon, seeming to pile one on top of the other like huge, threatening boulders.

"That's a storm on its way, Mr. Jack. You can take my word for it," Dutton said. "We'd best seek shelter while we can."

"Where, without a wind to get us there?" Jack demanded. "Our friend Beresford will have reached Bridgetown by now, and he'll be raising the dead against us. Anyway," he added, desperately trying to recall everything his father had ever told him about the weather, "hurricanes don't blow south of Barbados."

"We ain't south of Barbados yet," Dutton grumbled. "And they don't draw no lines on the map either."

"Nonetheless, by making south we'll know we're headed away from it," Jack insisted. "Just in case, though, we'll make all secure."

By dusk the wind had dropped altogether, but this was common enough. Far more disturbing was the fact that the lights of Barbados remained just visible to the west, and the way in which the clouds gradually spread over the sky. Reckoning that the wind would have risen by dawn, Jack left Conybeare on watch and turned in, to lie in his bunk debating with himself whether to shorten sail now or hope that by carrying full canvas he could work sufficiently far south before the wind got above gale force. He no longer doubted for a moment that there was going to be a blow.

An uneasy doze was ended by the splatter of rain on the deck just above his head. He rolled out of the bunk and reached for his heavy canvas smock and hat, then gave Conybeare, who was snoring on the other bunk, a nudge; Jamey had taken over the watch. Jack scrambled up the companion ladder and emerged into the deepest darkness he had ever experienced. The lights on the island had disappeared and there was not a star to be seen; he guessed that the cloud cover must now be complete.

The wind had freshened and had backed almost due east, a clear indication that the center of the storm was still ahead of them. On the other hand the direction was excellent for the *Lodestar*'s purpose, and she was bounding along on a broad reach. The only discomfort was caused by the driving rain, which stung faces and hands and made it difficult to see.

Dutton was on the helm, with Jamey beside him. "We must be making ten knots," he shouted. "She's creaming along."

Jack peered over the side at the waves hissing away from the hull. Further off he could just make out the crests as the seas started to form white horses. As yet the waves were not very large, about six to eight feet from trough to crest, he estimated, but he felt fairly sure that they were already within the circumference of the storm.

"I'll take her, Dutton," he said. "You get the watch on deck and shorten sail."

"But we're doing fine," Jamey protested. "There's not a drop coming on board."

"It's going to freshen," Jack said. "We'll have wet decks soon enough."

"Your brother's right." Conybeare had joined them. "Better to reef too early than too late."

Dutton hurried forward and began bellowing down the forehatch. When Jack took the helm, he immediately felt the weight of the ship as she fought to turn up into the wind, a characteristic of any well-found vessel, especially when overcanvased. But now the breeze was backing even more, to the northeast, and steadily increasing; spray was starting to fly and then without warning the *Lodestar* seemed to fly off a crest and land on another with a shuddering crash which knocked all the speed off her. Jack had to spin the wheel desperately to stop her broaching, slipping sideways into the following trough, to be rolled over by the next wave.

"Get forward," he shouted to Jamey. "Tell them to hurry. I want her reefed, and all the square canvas down."

Jamey nodded and ran forward to join Dutton and the crew; some clambered precariously into the rigging to furl and secure the square sails, while others pulled on the sheets to trim the yards and spill the wind from the canvas. Even so, handing the sails was clearly not possible while the *Lodestar* was hurtling downwind at twice her normal speed. Jack looked over his shoulder, was momentarily appalled at the way the seas astern had built in only a few minutes, chose his moment, and wrenched the helm around to bring the ship up into the wind.

Instantly the wind's force seemed to double, and the seas revealed their full menace. Clouds of spray came over the bow, which kept pointing skyward and then dropping into the following troughs with a series of sickening lurches. But most of the noise was caused by the flapping of the sails, which slammed to and fro as the wind was spilled; now the crew found it relatively simple to clew up the yards.

Jamey came aft, having to hold on to the lee bulwarks as a wave broke amidships, flooding the waist deck with green water; Jack estimated that the wind was already up to gale force.

"Do you want the jibs reefed down?" Jamey gasped, climbing the ladder to the poop and shaking water from his head and clothes like a dog.

Jack hesitated. But clearly he was still carrying too much sail to risk running off before the storm. His father had always brought the ship to a stop when the wind reached forty knots, and he estimated it as not far off that now. Hurricane winds were at least thirty knots stronger than an ordinary gale, but there was no other way that he knew of to face the weather which was clearly on its way.

"Take in numbers one and two," he agreed. "And back the number three. Then I want the mainsail reefed to the third cringle and sheeted in hard to windward. Hurry now, Jamey."

From above came the first flash of lightning; it cut the night in two, leaving Jack blinking, and the accompanying peal of thunder seemed to shake the ship. The *Lodestar* was gathering way again, far too fast; the sickening rolling had diminished, but now she was charging the crests, her bow going up and up and up, until it was impossible to stand on deck without holding on; then would begin the terrifying slide down the other side, down and down and down until it seemed that the ocean had no bottom. And all the while they faced the fact that the next wave was there to be climbed again, assuming the ship survived. For the long bowsprit invariably thrust itself into the huge, towering green wall, and hundreds of tons of water came crashing down on the fore-deck, causing the boat to shudder, burying the men working there up to their necks, setting up a force which it seemed impossible to surmount—and yet the *Lodestar* always came up again, tossing the remnants of each wave aft as flying spray, pointing her bowsprit at the lightning-torn sky as she began her next climb. She would, Jack knew, do this forever as long as she had masts and sails. His worry was that by carrying too much canvas he would lose one or the other, or both, and be left wallowing in the troughs, to be rolled and smashed by each breaker. Thus he heaved a sigh of relief as the two larger jibs were brought in, and the mainsail reefed—

lowered for a third of its height and tied down with stout line, passed through the eyelet holes in the sail itself, and secured around the boom. Now the ship could be hove to: the remaining foresail and the greatly reduced mainsail were sheeted, or made fast, one to starboard and the other to port, so that as one sail filled and the *Lodestar* gathered way, she was checked by the other sail filling in turn; she forged ahead only very slowly, and the motion became much easier.

"That was nicely done," Conybeare said. "She'll be all right now."

Jack watched the breaking waves, some fifteen to twenty feet high, he estimated, and listened to the howling of the wind. It was now almost due north and still backing—shifting counterclockwise, so far as he could decide. There was a lot worse to come; his experiences reminded him that a backing wind always eventually veers, or reverses its direction, and always with greatly increased force.

"I hope you're right," he said. But there was nothing more to be done at the moment. Hove to, the ship was as safe as she could be, and he could send the crew below to the warmth and relative dryness of the forecastle, and even lash the helm in order to join Jamey and Conybeare in the aft cabin.

"All's well that ends well." Jamey remarked.

"It ain't even begun yet," Conybeare said.

"How far off Barbados are we, do you reckon?" Jack asked.

Conybeare shrugged, bracing himself against the heave of the cabin. "Thirty miles."

"Not far enough," Jack said.

"It's a small island," Jamey pointed out. "Chances are we'll miss it."

"If we stay afloat that long," Jack muttered. For he could *hear* the wind increasing, as he could feel the ship's motion becoming more violent. Even halted she was hitting the waves far too hard, slamming her wooden timbers into the almost solid water with such force that he felt sure they would eventually split. "We'll have to run off," he decided.

"That's suicide," Conybeare protested. "You'll never hold her."

"We'll slow her down," Jack said. "Take off all sail—we'll run dead before bare poles. That'll take us south, away from land as well."

"*You'll* hold her, downwind, under bare poles?" Jamey asked.

Jack nodded. "And let's get to it, or she's going to open a seam and go down like a stone."

Jamey went forward to get the weary crew on deck again. Conybeare came aft with Jack to lash him to the helm, so that he could not be washed overboard. By now it was midnight, but the lightning—each flash followed by a deafening peal of thunder—was so continuous that there was almost no darkness. The waves were terrifyingly huge mounds of water, thirty feet and more in height, and capped by another ten feet of seething foam.

The screaming of the wind was so loud it was impossible to shout against, while the air was filled with so much flying spray it was difficult to see even as far as the bowsprit. But the crew knew what they had to do, brought in the storm jib and then dragged down the remains of the mainsail to lash it to the boom. The *Lodestar* immediately fell away into the next trough, a sickening roll which landed her almost on her side, while Jack fought the helm to take control. Slowly she came around, and then he had her before the wind, running off with the great combers rushing up astern to toss the boat forward, hurl her into each succeeding trough with rib-shattering force.

"She'll not stand up to this," Jamey bellowed, arms wrapped around a backstay as he refused to desert his brother.

"We're still going too fast," Jack agreed. "We've got to take way off her, slow her down."

"How?" Jamey bawled.

Jack chewed his lip as he wrestled with the wheel, fighting to keep the brigantine from broaching.

"A sea anchor," he shouted with a sudden inspiration. "Break out all the rope we have, and tie one of the foresails into them to form a loop, then pay them out astern. And make haste!''

Jamey made his way forward to summon Ned Dutton. Conybeare was already there to assist, and with half a dozen seamen to help them they huddled against the flying spray and the breaking seas, to secure each end of the triangular jib to a length of mooring warp, made the ends of the warps fast to cleats on deck, and then threw the sail over the stern and slowly paid out the ropes.

Immediately the *Lodestar* commenced to lose speed, as the sail filled with water and began to act as a check. Now she was much more manageable, her principal danger the risk of being pooped, having a wave actually catch them up and break on the stern. This indeed began to happen regularly, but after the first couple of times, when his heart seemed to leap into his throat as he was buried up to his waist in foaming water, Jack realized that so long as not too many of the hundreds of gallons of water on deck found their way below, the ship was in much less danger than she had been. He worried mainly about Jamey and the other men, who were constantly being swept from their handholds by the surging water. So he sent everyone below, with orders to batten the hatches, and remained by himself, strapped to the wheel, fighting the rudder while great rivulets of pain began to run up and down his arms and lodge in his shoulders. He prayed so long for the dawn and for some abatement in the wind that he could not believe it when, just as the first fingers of light began to drift across the sky, he realized that the thunder and lightning had ceased and that for at least ten minutes no water had broken on deck.

Exhausted, soaking wet, yet filled with immense satisfaction that ship and master should have survived so well, he allowed his head to droop, and actually dozed off for a few moments, to be awakened abruptly by the sound of an exploding cannon.

Jamey and Conybeare were on deck in a moment, followed by the crew from forward.

"Cannon," Jamey shouted.

"Or more thunder," Conybeare suggested.

"It was cannon," Jack said, wiping a salt-caked hand across his eyes. "Release me, and get those warps in."

He felt confident in giving the order, for while the seas were still huge, they had definitely moderated, and the wind had dropped. But what a scene met his eyes as he looked into the dawn: nothing but white-streaked water and chaotic waves for as far as the eye could see, while the sky remained totally obscured by the heavy cloud cover, which every few minutes sent a vicious rainstorm whistling over the morning; during the height of the storm he had been unable to tell the difference between the rain and the flying spray.

"He's done in," Jamey said, gently releasing the ropes holding his brother.

"It was a mighty performance, helming through all that," Conybeare agreed. "Take the helm, Dutton. Keep her downwind. That's safest. 'Tis your bunk for you, Jack Grant."

Jack shook his head as he watched the sailors slowly reeling in the warps holding the sea anchor. "We must find that ship," he said. "Listen."

The cannon had exploded again, and from close at hand. "Haste with those warps," he shouted.

But it was an enormous relief to be able to stretch his exhausted, taut-muscled limbs and clamber into the lower shrouds to look across the sea. A telescope was useless, since the height of the waves limited visibility to about a quarter of a mile.

"We'll never find her," Jamey shouted, standing beneath him at the rail. "Here. Take a swig of that."

It was hot broth laced with brandy, and tasted like nectar. Jack could feel the heat coursing through his veins, restoring his energy. Once again he peered across the windswept morning.

"There," he shouted.

The *Lodestar* had mounted a crest at the same moment as the vessel in distress, and for a brief moment Jack could see a dismasted hulk wallowing low in the water. She was a considerably larger vessel than the brigantine, but had clearly not been as expertly handled.

"I see her," Jamey said as they sank into the next trough. "But you'll never lay alongside in this swell, Jacko. We'll both end up with a hole in the side."

Jack looked forward; the trailing warps had all been brought in, and Conybeare had already set the storm jib. The ship was gathering way.

"We'll have to use the dinghy," he said. "You'll take her."

"In this?"

"We can't just desert them," Jack pointed out, and climbed down from the shrouds. "I'll take the helm again, Dutton. Prepare to launch the boat."

Dutton also peered over the side, pessimistically, but no member of the crew was going to argue with their young captain after he had brought them successfully through the storm. The dinghy was unstrapped from its chocks amidships, and the oarsmen climbed in. Jamey took the tiller while Dutton settled in the bow, armed with a boathook and a throwing line. The dinghy was swung up on the halyards, and out over the side, while Jack chose his moment and turned the *Lodestar* up into the wind. Instantly she came to a halt, once again facing the mammoth crests, and in that instant Conybeare gave the signal; the falls were let go, and the boat splashed into the sea.

"Pull!" Jamey shouted, both hands tight on the tiller to guide the little boat away from the side of the ship. "Pull!"

Jack had put the helm down, also to increase the gap between the two vessels before the dinghy could be smashed against the *Lodestar*'s sides. Now the oars bit into the water, and the boat surged away. The moment the shelter of the larger vessel was lost, the spray started to fly, together with the occasional splash of green as they slid down the next trough, once again immense when viewed from water level. But Jack, with his customary skill, had maneuvered the *Lodestar* to within a hundred yards of the stricken ship, and Jamey could clearly see the group of people gathered on the strange ship's poop, just as he could also make out the tangle of spars and rigging lying alongside, where apparently all three masts had come down together to form a series of jagged wooden barriers which could easily pierce the boat. But haste was imperative: he could tell that from a glance at the bow of the ship, which was awash, suggesting that she had opened a seam below the forward waterline and would not float for very much longer.

"I'm going to try for the counter," he yelled to Dutton. "Pull, lads, pull."

They sank into a trough, then emerged onto the next crest, seeming to hang immediately above the ship. Desperately Jamey dragged on the tiller while the oarsmen, facing aft but realizing their danger from the expression on his face, redoubled their efforts. The boat surfed down the side of the wave and came under the stern of the ship, where several willing hands reached down to seize and secure the rope thrown by Dutton. A stream of quite unintelligible words was directed at the Americans.

"Use your hook," Jamey shouted. "Keep us off." He looked up at the poop, realized there were women up there as well as men, and shouted, "You have to come down the rope."

A man leaned over the taffrail. "English? You are English?"

"Near enough," Jamey said, not prepared to argue the point at this moment. "For God's sake, hurry, senor." For he could now see the ship's name, *Gloria Dei*, carved on the stern, together with the port of registry, Lisbon.

"Of course," the man agreed. He was an extremely distinguished-looking gentleman, with crisp black hair and a neat beard, and although he was obviously concerned by his situation, he seemed by no means frightened. "Christina," he said, and then reverted to Portuguese.

The dinghy surged upward on the next crest, almost level with the poop deck, as the sinking ship dipped over lower into the water, and Jamey gazed at the girl being pushed to the rail and realized that he had never in his life seen anyone so beautiful. Perhaps it was a result of exhaustion and the long night's battle against the storm, but in her midnight hair, torn and tangled by the wind, in the trace of slender white calf that was exposed as the breeze whipped the skirt of her gown when she lifted her leg over the rail, and most of all in the composure of her face, each exquisite feature—high forehead, small straight nose, delicate lips, pointed chin, and glowing dark eyes—revealing her determination to conquer fear and fatigue for this last time, he knew that he had achieved at least one of his ambitions, in discovering that perfect woman of whom he had hitherto only been able to dream.

In an agony of suspense and anticipation he watched her lift her other leg over, allowing him a tantalizing glimpse of underskirt, still held around the waist by the English-speaking man who must be her father. Her small white hands closed on the rope, and she was released to swing down to the bobbing dinghy, which at that very moment was picked up by a larger than usual wave and pushed away from the ship's side. The rope tightened as if jerked by a giant, the girl gave a terrified scream as her hands were torn loose, and she plummeted into the water.

The two other women on the poop also screamed, and her father gave a despairing cry. The girl had gone straight down, and when she reappeared she was some fifteen feet astern of the ship, while from the way she was beating the waves it was obvious to Jamey that she couldn't swim.

"Get those other people off the ship," he snapped at Dutton, and jumped over the side, to be immediately picked up by the next swell. But the waves were breaking less regularly now, as the wind continued to diminish, and a couple of strokes—he was a powerful swimmer who had learned his art in the cold waters and strong currents off Cape Cod—brought him to the side of the drowning girl.

"Easy now, easy," he said, reaching for her armpits. She turned her head, and there was no doubt that she understood him. For all her fear, and her gasps for breath, she immediately relaxed and allowed him to roll her on her back and begin the slow swim back to the boat; only his legs propelled them, since he was holding her by the shoulders, and he shook his head to free himself of the long black hair that drifted away from her. Already, he saw, her lovely small face was starting to regain its composure.

Something struck the water beside him, and he realized that

Dutton had thrown him a rope. He was able to guide the girl's hands to it, and a moment later they were alongside and she was being dragged to safety. Willing hands were also there to help Jamey, and he sat in the bottom, against the girl, reaching for breath, only now remembering how exhausted he was, and facing the distinguished-looking man who was kneeling by his daughter and addressing her in Portuguese, of which Jamey understood only the name Christina, repeated several times. But Christina was able to reply and reassure her father, for he now seized Jamey's hands and pressed them between his own.

"You have saved our lives," he said. "You may be sure, senor, that for as long as I live I shall always be in your debt. You have the word of Pedro Alonso de Sousa e Melo, viceroy of Brazil."

Chapter 3

She lay in a strange cabin, on a narrow bunk bed, wrapped in unfamiliar blankets. Her head throbbed and her throat ached; her chest and stomach seemed filled with air which was threatening to lift her from the mattress and spin her up into space.

She had no recollection of being rescued, save that of powerful fingers on her arms and in her armpits; she could still feel them, was undoubtedly bruised. And of a man, lean and strong, shouting at her, telling her to be calm, and she would be safe.

A dream? She opened her eyes, gazed at deck beams close above her head, and closed them again when the feeling of being about to drift into space grew unbearable. She could use her experience of having felt like this once before to remind herself to lie still and breathe, slowly and evenly, and eventually all would be well.

She had been eleven at the time of the earthquake. That had been six years before, in 1755, when Lisbon had been laid flat in ten seconds. It had been very early in the morning, and she could remember lying in her bed and suddenly waking up, her nostrils choked with dust, her ears deafened by the most tremendous rumble she had ever heard. She remembered too the horror when she had attempted to move and found that she could not. Yet there had been no pain, only a realization that things could never be the same again, not for her or for many other people. It was only afterward that she had realized it would be tens of thousands of other people for whom nothing would ever be the same.

Understanding of what had happened had come to her slowly then, as she had put her hand down, first of all, to discover her mattress but no bed, only stone beneath her, and then up, to touch the lathes lying across her legs and thighs as if she were strapped in. Which indeed she was. She could also smell wine and sewage and realized that, however incredible it was, she had somehow fallen from her dormitory on the third floor of the convent, right through the chapel and the schoolroom and even the reception hall, to arrive in the cellars, and that her fall had probably shattered both the communion wine and the good wine, for Mother Superior was fond of her glass; evidently the drains had been shattered too.

After the rumble had died as quickly as it had arisen, there had not been a sound. Throughout the convent, in which there had been, seconds ago, thirty-one nuns, forty-seven servants, and twenty-four young ladies—each one belonging to one of the noblest families in the land—all sleeping, some snoring, there was now absolute silence. And this in the center of one of the greatest cities in Europe, where even in the middle of the night the quiet was punctuated by the calls of the watch. Now, of them all, it seemed that only Christina Maria Theresa de Sousa e Melo was capable of sound.

She had screamed. It was not something she was used to doing, for she had been a pampered child. Christina Maria Theresa, as the first-born in her branch of the de Sousa family— related to the great Pombal himself—had always been important, a young lady for whom a great marriage would have to be arranged, who would have to learn to take her place at court and no doubt in Her Majesty's bedchamber, but who would nevertheless also have to learn to take her place behind her brother, whenever he might arrive. Then year after year had passed and candle after candle had been lit and prayer after prayer offered, and still Mama had done nothing but miscarry, until even the miscarriages had ceased, and Papa, a man who recognized no obstacles in the pursuit of what he considered best for the de Sousas, had been forced to realize that not even he could brook the will of God. Then Christina Maria Theresa had suddenly become the most important thing in all the universe for the de Sousas. She was the heiress, and only through her husband, and her children, could the de Sousa wealth and, far more important, the de Sousa power, be transmitted to future generations. And now she lay pinned to her broken bed in the cellar of her convent, afraid to move for fear of dislodging the hundreds of tons of stone and rubble which must be hovering above her, able to do nothing more than wait, with as much composure as she could manage, for what might happen next.

Afraid even to scream again, both because the noise had seemed so strange issuing from her lips, and because it had been followed by a fall of dust and pieces of plaster onto her head.

At least she had been used to waiting. All her life had been spent waiting—for tutors to school her, for maids to attend her, for Mama and Papa to receive her, for something to happen which might possibly disturb the absolutely even, absolutely predictable course of her days. She had never doubted that something would happen, and had been prepared to wait; she was not by temperament a rebel, like some of her schoolmates, who had indulged in delinquency merely because even to be whipped by Mother Superior meant a break in the monotony of their existences. But for a de Sousa e Melo to be whipped was unthinkable; Christina had preferred to put her faith in the future, even at ten.

And now something had most definitely happened. And not only to her. Waiting had required a supreme act of will, especially since the silence had at last been broken by the trickle of water, and she had recalled that the cellars of the convent were below the level of the Tagus River, and that the retaining embankments must also have been destroyed by the cataclysm. To this danger from beneath had soon been added an even greater danger from above, as she had begun to inhale smoke and had become aware of a tremendous amount of heat. It seemed to be a question of which fate got to her first. But she had reasoned that a girl does not fall fifty feet through a collapsing building and survive only to be drowned or burned alive. Whatever Mother Superior or Christina's confessor or Mama herself might say about the inscrutability of God's purposes, Christina had no doubt at all, deep in her heart, that she and *He* had a private understanding. It had been one reason why she was prepared to wait.

For two days. She found it difficult to believe, now. And everyone else had found it difficult to believe, then. When they had found her, she was lying on her mattress with river water swirling gently around her thighs and shoulders, gazing up at them. She had said, "I'm very hungry."

She imagined she had become the most famous girl in all Portugal. Her Majesty herself had had her sit beside her to recount, as best she could, what she had thought about during those interminable forty-eight hours. She hadn't told her the truth, of course. Her thoughts during those hours when she had known she might die had explored avenues and considerations and desires she had always rejected in the past, and were entirely between herself and her Friend and Savior. But the mere fact of her survival had been enough.

And now she had survived again, when by all the laws of nature she had been even more irretrievably lost, because she could not swim a stroke. She hoped, vaguely, as she fell asleep again that God would not continue to test her this way.

"They were scoundrels," Pedro Alonso de Sousa e Melo explained. "Absolute wretches. And scarce to be regarded as seamen, Captain Grant. They lost their heads the moment we lost our rudder, and wished only to abandon the vessel. And when Captain Naranha attempted to explain to them that they would be far safer staying with the ship, they mutinied. Would you believe it? One of the villains struck poor Naranha on the head with such force that it split his skull. Then they came aft. I will confess to you, Captain Grant, that I thought

our last moment had come, and that indeed we were about to
suffer dreadfully. I was thinking of the ladies, of course.''

"But you resisted them," said an alien voice.

"Oh, indeed. And when they saw our swords and realized
that even my brave Christina was prepared to sell her honor
dearly, why, they left us alone and launched the boats instead. They deserted us, Captain Grant. Left us to our fates. I
tell you, sir, when I find them, and find them I will—''

"I doubt you'll do that, sir," said the strange voice. "I
would estimate your captain's warning was correct. No small
boat could have survived in those seas of last night. Your
mutineers are all dead, Don Pedro. I'll wager on that.''

The words played around Christina's head, made her realize that she had not been sleeping after all. She understood
what was being said, of course, because so intimate were
relations between Portugal and England—with almost all Portuguese trade, whether with Europe or the Americas, in the
hands of British merchants—that English was taught as a
matter of course in the schools, and fluency in the language
was regarded as essential for anyone who would aspire to be
an aristocrat.

But what words they were: *all dead*. Again she recalled the
horrors of not only the past twenty-four hours, but of six
years ago. After she survived the earthquake, there were
some old women about the court who suggested that she was
cursed rather than remarkably fortunate.

And then there had been her betrothal—the greatest day of
her life. She had been fifteen, was still regarded as the
miraculous sole survivor of the convent of Santarem, a young
lady who quite apart from her family and her fortune would
make, by reason of God's blessing, the perfect wife for any
man. And in addition, as she well knew—because Aunt
Malina, her duenna, never tired of reminding her—she was
quite the loveliest creature in all Portugal. Her husband would
have to be truly a man to match everything she would bring to
his bed—whatever that might mean—because neither Mama
nor Aunt Malina had ever been the least forthcoming on the
subject, and in view of the fact that Mama's retirement to
Papa's bed had always been followed, a few months later, by

agonizing pain and the loss of a great deal of blood, the whole thing sounded the worst part of a woman's existence, and not in any way connected with the emotions she had managed to enjoy in utter solitude, in the convent cellar.

But the husband—there was an important subject, and not least to her, for although she had every intention of abiding by Papa's wishes, she could not but reflect that life would be so much more pleasant, more exciting, more enjoyable, were he to choose someone reasonably her own age. She had the example of her own parents to set before her. Papa was only four years older than Mama, and according to Aunt Malina, there had been many whispered predictions that such a match could never be happy, especially when it united a third cousin of the queen with an upstart; the de Sousas e Melo had risen only as *their* first cousin, the marquis of Pombal, had risen, but the fact was that he himself had been a nobody only a dozen years before, had attained the position of first minister of Portugal and dictator of every aspect of the nation's life only because of the remarkable—and absurd, as his enemies would have it—favoritism of King John.

But they had been happy, and their happiness had survived all the tragedies and disappointments that had accompanied their failure to have a proper family.

More important even than that, they had decided on happiness for their only daughter, and her chosen husband had been Don Miguel de Castro, who, in his looks, his youth, his gallantry, his prowess as a soldier, and his utter charm, had filled roughly the male role at court comparable to Christina's female position. The decision that two such dazzling luminaries should marry had been blessed by Church and crown as well as by nobility and gentry, and even cheered in the street by the common people. The marriage had been intended for the day after her sixteenth birthday, and by now, she realized with a start of dismay, she should have been a mother.

Instead, Miguel de Castro had fallen from his horse and broken his neck.

Her grief had been extravagant, partly because of the extravagance of the grief all around her, which would have left any acceptance of the tragedy on her part as an indication of

unfeeling coldness. But in fact as she had never done anything more than touch Miguel's hand, and since she *had* been
distinctly bored as he had regaled every company in which he
found himself with the minute details of his latest athletic or
military triumph, and in addition as she still treasured her
private relationship with God and *knew* that whatever He
decided was for her personal benefit, she had been far less
distraught than Mama and Aunt Malina, or even than Her
Majesty. As for what came next . . . she had been aware
only of a distinct feeling of relief that she would not actually
have to undergo any of the agonies of being a wife for
another year or two, at least.

And perhaps even longer than that, for Papa, more upset
than any of them as he considered that wherever he had
turned his every dream had literally turned to dust, had
approached his illustrious cousin and had been rewarded with
the viceroyalty of Brazil. A meager post to be sure, because
according to the experts the colony was not what it had once
been. In the two hundred and thirty years that the Portuguese
had laid claim to, and had exploited, this vast area, roughly
as large as all Europe, one of her tutors had told her, they had
used its wealth to build themselves colonies in other places,
in Africa and in the Spice Islands and even in fabled India.
But the amount of gold being returned from the mines of
Minas Gerais had been steadily dwindling over the past thirty
years, and there was a considerable body of opinion in Lisbon
which was suggesting that since the British handled all the
carrying trade anyway, it might be more economical to hand
the whole great empty forest over to them and let them do
what they could with it.

Pombal had not agreed, and neither had Papa. At least part
of the drying up of the Brazilian revenue, according to Papa,
had been because of increasing governmental supervision,
high tariffs, and restrictive laws. Pombal was not prepared to
relax the government's stake in the colony, but he also felt
that the situation could be more profitably handled by one
viceroy instead of half a dozen local governors, and by a man
who, while tied to his employer's side by birth as much as by

inclination, would be able to decide what should best be done to restore the Golden Age of Brazil.

It had been terribly exciting. As Mama had said, a few years in Brazil would enable her to forget, and if Christina had not been entirely sure she wanted to do that, because life was composed of memories and she would not forego a single one of them, the journey had promised a whole new series of experiences, and therefore memories, to content her in her old age. Sailing out of the Tagus had been the most memorable day of her life, with the whole huge Atlantic in front of her, an unending carpet of gently undulating blue, the most splendid sight she had ever beheld.

But that had been before the storm and the mutiny. Was she, after all, cursed? Doomed to attract disaster wherever she went?

Her eyes flew open in alarm, and Aunt Malina, seated beside her, gave a cry of joy.

"She is awake. The child is awake. She'll live."

Faces crowded around the bunk: Mama, pale and anxious, also absurdly wrapped in a blanket, Papa and Father Luis, and the other members of the viceregal party who had survived, all disheveled and anxious, but alive, and delighted to see their idol once again restored to life.

And with them, another face. The face she remembered, even if vaguely, which had been close to hers in the water, which had commanded and reassured her, while strong brown hands plucked her from the fury of the waves, and which now held a smile.

"This is Captain Grant, my dearest Christina," Papa was saying. "He commands this ship which has so providentially come to our rescue."

Christina slowly sucked air into her lungs, discovered that her tongue would move. "My life is in your debt, Captain Grant," she whispered.

"Not mine, alas, Dona Christina," Jack Grant said. "It was my brother plucked you from the sea. Jamey."

Christina could not believe it. The man who had spoken was not her rescuer? And then she turned her head and she saw another face, one she remembered not vaguely but exactly, because of the eyes, which she would never forget even if she lived to be a hundred. And those eyes were more intense than ever, determined to convey the man's innermost thoughts to her; never had she experienced such intensity in a gaze.

Jamey Grant lifted her hand from the blanket and kissed her knuckles. "If I die tomorrow, Dona Christina," he said, "I will have succeeded in living beyond my wildest dreams."

"By the evidence of your own navigation, Captain Grant," Pedro Alonso de Sousa e Melo pointed out, "Pernambuco lies not more than two days to the southwest. Now, sir, your situation as regards food and water is parlous, and rendered the more so by this sudden accession of a dozen people to your ship's company. And of course I am also in great haste to land somewhere in Brazil. So it would appear to me that the course of action which must most recommend itself to us all is to land there."

They sat at dinner—Christina's parents, her Aunt Malina, Father Luis, and their two hosts, the Grant brothers. The other man, Conybeare, was on watch, and their attendants were of course fed separately. In the small aft cabin of the *Lodestar* the seven of them were forced to huddle absurdly, to Aunt Malina's obvious concern as she watched her charge unavoidably rubbing shoulders with Captain Grant, Christina dressed only in the remnants of her nightgown and dressing robe, now dried, and with a borrowed shirt over that. She knew she must look ridiculous, as did they all—a company of castaways who only forty-eight hours before had worn silk and satin and dined from silver plates. But they were alive, and the storm had passed; the seas had dwindled into a long, low swell. The food might be an odd assortment of stale biscuits and dried fruit, and instead of wine they might be drinking quite foul tasting water, but they were alive and in good hands. It was not merely the fact of having been rescued. The Grant brothers exuded such an air of competence, of determination, and of modesty, that she was already prepared to concede that they were the two most remarkable men she had ever met.

Not that Jack Grant appeared truly to appreciate that he was sitting with his shoulder against that of the darling of all Portugal. He was a man who, for all his confidence, took his responsibilities seriously.

"Then Pernambuco it shall be, Your Excellency," he said. "I have already made the necessary alteration in course."

"Capital," Don Pedro said. "And I am not insensible that the delay may be costly. Your ship carries timber, does it not? That is not, as I understand it, a commodity which is scarce in Brazil, but I will happily purchase your entire cargo at whatever price you care to name."

"I should not dream of permitting it, Your Excellency," Jack said.

"Well at the very least, my dear Captain, you will permit me to see to the refitting of your vessel. My dear sir, my family and I owe you our lives. I will tell you frankly, sir, that were you to decide to use Brazil as a market, or even as a home, I should be delighted, and you may be sure you will have the support and the power of the viceroy at your disposal in whatever direction you should direct your ambition."

He leaned back in his chair, flushing in his own excitement, smiling at Jack Grant, who allowed himself a moment to glance at his brother. Jamey was watching Christina.

Christina herself had been well aware of his gaze throughout the meal, as she had been aware of it during almost every minute she had spent on board this vessel. No indifference there, like his brother's. Aunt Malina, at least, had perceived that too. Then what of Christina herself? Here was someone as far removed from the languid, listless Portuguese men with whom she had spent her life up to now as was the burning sun fom the deadened moon. And he was young, hardly a year older than herself, she had been told, talented in his chosen profession, and full or ardor . . . and he had saved her life. That he would also be as difficult to handle as a wild pony was something her instincts kept telling her. But was there anything more marvelous than a wild pony in full flow?

And he had saved her life.

And had a brother in whom she could perceive almost every human virtue.

"Your offer does you great credit, Your Excellency," Jack

said. "And I honor your desire to repay my crew and myself for assisting you. But, sir, if I may make the point, it was but a turn of fate that we happened to be in such a place at such a vital moment. I am sure you will agree with me that we must all thank God, rather than any human agency, that we came together at such a time."

Don Pedro smiled at him. "Admirably put, Captain Grant. Yet I am conscious that it was *you* God sent to my rescue. Nor would He have me forget it, either."

"Are these young men, then, true members of the Church?" asked Father Luis.

"We are Christians, if that is what you mean, Father," Jamey said. "Although we are Presbyterians rather than Papists."

"Presbyterians?" Dona Inez de Sousa exclaimed in alarm.

"I have no doubt, Dona Inez," said her husband, "that these most gallant young men are as devout in their belief, certainly inherited from their parents, as we are in ours."

"Nevertheless, Don Pedro," the priest pointed out, "residence in Brazil is forbidden to anyone not of the Catholic belief, as you well know."

"A governmental policy," Don Pedro insisted, "which is subject to exceptions, in exceptional circumstances. I do not see how men such as Captain Grant and his brother can bring anything less than great credit to the colony. My invitation stands, Captain Grant."

"Then, sir," Jack said, "I must beg leave to inform you of our exact situation, lest you would prefer to reconsider."

For the first time Jamey Grant looked away from Christina, sitting bolt upright as he gazed at his brother in alarm.

"Are you then criminals, sir?" Don Pedro inquired, still gently smiling.

"Exactly so, sir," Jack said. "If you would listen."

As indeed they all did, to the story he had to tell.

"A remarkable tale," Don Pedro remarked when Jack at last fell silent. "And a tragic one. My heart bleeds for you two young men, who have lost your father in the hour of his fullest strength and power. And at your long separation from your mother and sister. But that at least can be remedied. My word is law within Brazil from the moment I land. No English warrant can ever touch you or your families there, my friends. It will not be a difficult matter to arrange for the removal of your mother and sister to the altogether more rewarding climate of Rio de Janeiro, which is where I am to establish my viceroyalty. As for yourselves, why, it will be a pleasure to establish you in regular trade between Rio and Lisbon. If you would consent to sail under a Portuguese flag, I can promise you that no English man-of-war would ever dare arrest you.''

Jack frowned at him. ''You would help us despite all, Your Excellency?''

''Despite what, my dear Captain Grant? You have confessed to breaking the English Navigation Acts. Sir, I will tell you that those laws are pernicious deterrents to free trade, upon which in my opinion, and in the opinion of my government, the entire future of the world is to be based. And upon what are *they* based? Only upon the equally pernicious maritime supremacy which Great Britain has managed to establish these last hundred years, a maritime supremacy which is directed only to the aggrandizement of Britain herself, and which you, to your eternal credit, have seen fit to challenge. Sir, I salute you.''

Jack could only stare at him, while Jamey produced a handkerchief with which to wipe his forehead.

Don Pedro leaned forward. ''When we get to Pernambuco,'' he said, ''I shall, as I have promised, see to the refitting of your vessel, but just sufficiently to allow us to proceed down the coast to Rio. I would arrive at the seat of my government in no other ship than this, Captain Grant. I wish the world to know of my gratitude, of my friendship, of my determination that you and your brother shall form a part of the growing empire that I have been sent to govern. Then, sir, I shall send for your mother and sister, and I shall inform His Majesty's government at Whitehall of my actions, and that I have taken you under my protection, and that the best course they can undertake is to grant you and your crew a general pardon for your acts. Believe me, they value their Brazilian trade too well to defy us for long.''

"I am overwhelmed," Jack said. "Now, Your Excellency, it is I who owe you more than I can ever repay."

"I wish your friendship, Captain Grant. My entire family wishes your friendship. That is all the repayment I desire." He turned to Jamey Grant, seated at his elbow. "And you, sir. You have contributed nothing to this conversation. Are you prepared to sail beneath the flag of Portugal? Or are you content merely to follow your brother's lead?"

Jamey Grant smiled at him. "It has long been my intention to give up the sea, Your Excellency, at the earliest possible moment. I am a landlubber at heart."

"Well then, providing your brother has no objection, I will find you a post ashore."

"Simply give me a permit to seek gold, Your Excellency."

Don Pedro frowned at him. "Gold? Those days are behind us, Master Grant. Brazil, they say, has been dug dry of the precious metal."

"Brazil is probably the largest colony in all the world, Your Excellency," Jamey said. "But give me the permission to *look,* and I will find your gold for you." He smiled across the table at Christina. "And for myself."

With exclamations of interest and pleasure the crew of the *Lodestar,* and their illustrious passengers, clung to the bulwarks to see the bulk of the sugarloaf mountain rising out of the calm sea, to peer at the lagoon of Guanabara beyond, so studded with islands, to admire the immense stretch of white gold sand which curved to the south, to stare at the squat bulk of the fortress which commanded the narrows and the cluster of houses which huddled close to it for protection. The beauty they had anticipated; they had been told of nothing else at their previous port of call, Pernambuco. What they had not expected was the welcome, for the bay was alive with craft of every description, from a stately man-of-war through a cluster of merchantmen to a host of small craft, sailing to and fro, firing blank shot, and flying every flag they possessed and various other bright pieces of cloth; the news that their viceroy had not after all been drowned at sea and was on his way to them had been sent down the coast by fast sloop.

"This will be a great country," Don Pedro said, standing with his wife beside Jack on the poop as the young American conned his ship toward the harbor; the Spanish party had been equipped with new clothing in Pernambuco, and were at last dressed as Portuguese nobility again. "All it needs is government."

"And people," Dona Inez suggested.

"To be sure. Christian people. What do you think of it, Jack?"

By now he seemed to regard the Grant brothers almost as the sons he had never possessed.

"It's the biggest place I ever saw," Jack confessed, realizing that to sail from Pernambuco to Rio had taken him as long as it would have from Nantucket to Savannah. Of course this coastal strip was backed by impenetrable forests and tall mountains, according to the books Don Pedro had brought with him, and then by the Spaniards, much as New England was bounded by the Appalachians and then the French; but here the Spaniards were much further away.

"And we must keep them there," Don Pedro had said during one of their after-dinner conversations. "That is part of the task that has been set me."

Part of the task he would be happy to share, Jack thought, for the Spaniards would only be kept at bay by making the colony into an ever growing, ever prosperous community, and for that the essential was trade. He could hardly believe his fortune, to have become the friend of such a man. To have such a future to look forward to. To be able to send for Mother and Mary—for this the viceroy had promised the moment they landed—and for Lizzie as well.

Would she come? Of course she would, if marriage to a successful sea captain, who was a friend of the viceroy as well, lay at the end of it. If only Father had lived to see both his sons well launched upon their lives.

Both his sons? Jack glanced away from the helm and down into the waist, where Jamey was standing close to the girl. Jamey invariably managed to be close to her whenever she was on deck, although he was of course required to share his conversation with the ever present Aunt Malina. But today even the duenna was neglecting her duties in her excitement at seeing her new home for the first time, and was crowding the rail with the rest of the viceregal party, leaving the two young people standing isolated by the mast, also gazing at the approaching land, and talking. At least, Jamey was talking, and the girl was listening. She was more beautiful than ever in her deep blue brocade gown—however hastily it had had to be altered to fit her—and with her hair braided and carefully arranged. Jamey had plucked a mermaid from the depths of the ocean, and had undoubtedly fallen for her. In which case, Jack reflected, he was showing a great deal of common sense in choosing exploration of the country's interior rather than remaining in Rio de Janeiro, however much *he* might personally regret the decision which would rob him of his most trustworthy aide for a very long time. But since a viceroy's daughter who was also related to the queen of Portugal was as far above him as was the sun in the sky, Jamey was undoubtedly doing the wise thing in turning his back on her.

But, Jack thought, he would give a great deal to know what he was saying to her, so animatedly.

"Forests," Jamey said. "And mountains. And Indians. North America has them all, Dona Christina. And no guaranteed wealth, either. I think I will do better in Brazil."

"And I am so happy that you have decided to make it your home, Jamey," she agreed, "as it is to be my home too."

"I understood your father to say that his term of office would not exceed five years."

"That is probably correct," she said. "But I think he means to take some land for himself and remain here. My parents have not been entirely happy in Portugal."

"And you?"

She turned her head. Having heard of the death of her fiancé, of her remarkable survival of the earthquake, he was inclined to ask questions like this, but always Aunt Malina had been standing at her side to reply, whenever she supposed her charge might be embarrassed, or even too interested. But Aunt Malina had drifted out of earshot.

And so, *was* she interested? If only she could be sure exactly how a woman should be interested in a man. He was exciting. There it was. Whenever she heard his voice she twisted her head to watch him and to listen to him, and to catch the smile he would be sure to direct at her. Whenever he went aloft, hand over hand with such confident casualness, her heartbeat seemed to double in a mixture of envy that she could not climb beside him, and fear that he would one day miss his hold and come tumbling to his death.

It was that interest which was framing her reply, with the instinctive coquetry of a woman in the company of *the* man.

"I do not think I have ever been truly happy anywhere," she said. "At least there is a possibility, here in Brazil."

His eyes glowed, and she realized that she was being very cruel, even to suggest affection for him. For all Papa's gratitude, these two young men were really nothing better than sailors. Jamey would probably not even know how to sit a horse, much less bend a knee or dance a quadrille. As for the requirements of being a husband of a de Sousa e Melo . . . but the very thought was bringing a flush to her cheeks. She bit her lip.

"Then you will be happy in Brazil," he said.

"You are a fortuneteller?" she asked, anxious to cover her confusion.

"I am a man," he said, "who is determined to dedicate himself to that end."

"You?" she asked. "But—"

"Is it not my right?" he asked, allowing his hand to drop over hers and give it a gentle squeeze. "I saved your life. In many a society that would make you mine, utterly and irrevocably."

She gazed at him, realized her mouth was open, and hastily closed it.

He smiled at her. "Of course I cannot make such a claim on you, Christina. Nor would I. I shall earn you."

"That is impossible," she said, and bit her lip again.

But he was not abashed. "You think so?" he asked. "Oh, you are the daughter of a viceroy, and I am mate of an ancient tub. Your father has millions at his disposal, and I have nothing. But I will not always be destitute, Christina. You may believe that. Listen to me. I am going to find gold here in Brazil. Gold such as no man has ever dreamed of. Entire mountains of it. I know it is there. I have heard of it, read of it, dreamed of nothing else ever since I can remember. El Dorado. That is my goal. It may take me a year, or even longer. But I shall find it. Have no doubt of that. And when I return, I shall be the man your father is seeking for your hand.''

"Jamey!" she cried in alarm.

"Oh, I will do it properly," he said. "I will approach him and ask for you. I will be a gentleman, Christina. Even a Portuguese gentleman. I require only one thing from you. Your promise that you will wait for me, for at least two years. Just that." His hand tightened on hers. "After all, I did save your life.''

After supper, she delighted in retiring to her bedchamber, and after being undressed by her maid and having prayed with Aunt Malina and officially been seen to bed, her mosquito netting pulled tight to resist the advances of the hungry insects which teemed in this climate, she delighted, too, in going out onto the balcony and gazing west, where the sun would have set a few hours before.

The idea of Brazil, of Rio de Janeiro itself, had been so exciting. She had devoured her father's books on the subject, had anticipated not only the country itself, but also its multiracial inhabitants, its Indians and its mestizos—half-white and half-Indian—its Negroes and its mulattos—half-white and half-black—and its several intermediate mixtures.

But there was no excitement in these people, borne down as much as Europeans were by the combination of heat and humidity and poor food; for never had she known such a monotonous and unhealthy diet, composed as it was almost entirely of manihot flour and tough, stringy beef, varied only by fish, with never a green vegetable to be seen.

Yet there had to be more to the country, she was sure. And it must lie out there, to the west. Out there were those impenetrable but apparently gold-filled forests which so occupied Jamey's imagination. Nothing would alter *his* intentions, not even the long discussion Papa had made him have with the governor of Minas Gerais, who had come last month to pay his respects, and who had quite categorically stated that all recent efforts to discover fresh seams of gold in the province had failed, and of course all the already established mines were under government control, and not even the viceroy could grant permission for private working—even supposing it might be worth it; the supply had dwindled to a trickle.

"But Minas Gerais is only a province in a land as large as an empire," Jamey had said.

"It would take an army to penetrate the forests of the Matto Grosso or the Amazon," the governor had said. "And even then the chances of success, much less survival, are small. You have no idea what lies out there, Senor Grant. Forests so thick that men standing a yard apart do not know the other is there, and so luxuriant that a path cleared this morning is grown more than six feet high this evening. Snakes as long as a ship. Alligators hardly smaller. Poisonous spiders. Savage Indians, whose only pleasure is killing intruders, after abusing them most shamefully. And above all, the deadliest of climes, where it either rains so hard that a man is literally crushed into the earth, or the sun burns down with an intensity that can turn his brain. Believe me, senor, if there is gold out there, it will stay there until the end of time."

"Had Columbus considered *his* ambition in such a light, Your Excellency," Jamey had replied, "not one of us would be sitting here tonight."

And the governor had made a face to suggest that he, at least, still regarded the discoverer of America as a reckless madman.

But nothing would dissuade Jamey from his purpose, and even Don Pedro had been forced into reluctant admiration. Once *his* support had been announced, volunteers had not been lacking, among them even Ned Dutton and Arthur Conybeare from the *Lodestar* itself. Tomorrow some fifty men, with their mules and their food supplies, would begin the journey beyond the limits of Brazilian power, in search of their El Dorado. Maps were scarce, and no one knew for sure where the mythical City of Gold lay, assuming it existed. But it was in the north, hard by the great river the Spaniards had called the Amazon. No one, indeed, knew precisely where the Amazon began, or where it emptied into the ocean; the northern shores of Brazil, and those of the adjacent Guyanas, were said to be haunted by sandbanks and shallows so far offshore that the sea was mud-brown for some hundreds of miles before the land could be reached. There was a Brazilian outpost on that northeastern coast, the town of Belem, lying where the river Tocantins joined the Para to debouch into the mud-stained Atlantic, and some geographers claimed that the great Para itself had to be an offshoot of the Amazon, which—basing their theories on their knowledge of the Nile—must have several exits.

But no one had ever successfully explored that maze of sandbanks and shoals. On such maps as were available the great river looked much closer by land. That it was largely unexplored land was, in Jamey's opinion, all to the good. Unlike the average Portuguese, who wished only enough acreage upon which to farm, and advanced into the interior only as it became necessary, Jamey wanted to explore, to go where no man had trod before, and to grow rich. His plan was simple in the extreme. He reckoned that by heading north, across country, he must eventually come to the river. From there he would find the city. For him it was as simple as that.

And only Christina knew the true force that was driving him on. She believed that he *would* find his city, and would come back the richest man on earth. She had never met any man, she had never even heard of any man, with quite such a determination to succeed. But what would happen then? She had given him no promises, and she did not believe he had truly expected her to. He had been satisfied to have had the chance to tell her his feelings. But whenever he and Jack came to the viceregal palace for supper, which was often, since Don Pedro far preferred their company to that of the stiff-backed Portuguese nobility who had managed to secure colonial posts or large land grants on which to farm their cattle and grow their sugar cane—and who all clearly regarded a de Sousa e Melo as a total upstart even if they were anxious to be gracious to his royal wife—the look in Jamey's eyes bespoke his feeling of possession.

She wondered that she was not offended. Not even Miguel had ever dared look at her like that. But Jamey Grant was not Miguel de Castro, and besides, he had saved her life. Undoubtedly he had been sent by God especially for that purpose. So to marry him might be to drive Mama wild with anger, cause Her Majesty to banish her, even make Papa unhappy, but if it was the will of God, then it would happen. She could take refuge in the thought that a decision could be postponed for a year or two; Papa was unlikely to produce any of these creoles as a possible husband in that time, and by then she would be more sure of her own mind.

Then what were her feelings now? She could love him. There was no doubt about that. But since she dared *not* love him, she did not, at the moment. It was even possible to feel a sense of relief that he was leaving for a while, removing the necessity to consider the matter at all—although she wished it had been possible to say a proper goodbye. He had been toasted and wished the very best of fortune, and had then departed with his brother. True, he had gazed at her across the table throughout the evening, but then this was his habit. And now, unless she rose very early in the morning, she would not see him again for several years.

As if she wanted to! But perhaps . . . if only it were possible to come to a decision.

The gentle whistle took her by surprise. And there he was, standing beneath her balcony.

The ground was some twenty feet beneath her, but she could see his face quite clearly in the moonlight; he was looking up at her, smiling that crooked smile of his. She felt a warm glow spreading through her chest. He had, after all, come back to say goodbye, and it was quite a bold feat, for the viceregal palace was well guarded.

But it was probably not a bold feat at all for Jamey Grant.

"You should not have come," she said, taking refuge in cliché.

"I had to. Christina, are you alone?"

"Well, of course," she said. "I am supposed to be in bed."

"I hoped you would be. Ssssh, now."

She watched the trellis of vines and roses which decorated the side of the house begin to move, leaned farther over, and to her consternation saw him beginning to climb.

"No!" she cried. "No. You must not."

"Ssssh," he cautioned again, coming up the wall, hand over hand, as he would climb a mast at sea. Before she could think what else to say or do he had swung a leg over the balcony, only inches away from her.

"You are mad," she said. "Think of the danger."

"No danger," he said. "I have climbed further than this."

"And suppose the trellis had broken? Or a guard had come along?"

"I'd have climbed faster." He smiled at her. "But if I stay here, Christina, I might well be seen."

Once again she hesitated, glancing over her shoulder to the darkness of her bedchamber. No risk of his being seen in there. But no man had ever entered her bedroom, except her father and her confessor.

Her confessor. She would have to tell him of this.

But Jamey Grant had saved her life.

And while she had been debating he had swung his other leg over the rail and had taken her hand. "Say you're not angry with me."

"Angry with you? How could I be?"

"And you have not yet promised." His fingers were tight on hers, slowly drawing her closer.

"You know I cannot."

"But you will wait."

Their bodies were almost touching, and now he had her other hand as well. This was really quite absurd. And there was no possible *way* in which any of it could be confessed.

But she was aware of a slowly rising excitement within herself, aware that her heartbeat was wild and her body suddenly seeming to contain too much blood, while her brain was spinning around and around, sending her senses with it.

She dared not admit—for she had never felt anything like it before—the tingling of her nipples, the enormous wanting that seemed to be spreading through her groin, the certainty that he was about to kiss her, that she wanted him to kiss her. Her lips parted before his, unintentionally, as she was drawing breath, but when she would close them his tongue was between, and seeking hers, stroking around hers, his breath mingling with hers, while his hands slid up her arms, carrying the sleeves of her negligee with them, all the while bringing her closer, until she was crushed against him, feeling his body fitting itself to hers, his hands now sliding around to hold first her shoulders, and then slipping lower, down the arch of her back.

Desperately she freed her mouth, got her hands between them, attempted to resist. But she dared not speak. To speak would have been a lie. Because she did not wish him to stop. Her body had cried out for a rising tide of delicious passion like this ever since she could remember. With the appearance of Miguel, she had supposed she would find it—until she had discovered that he was so consumed with his own importance and his own beauty that he would never pay sufficient attention to hers, never grant her the true ecstacy she had *known* must be there . . . and which *was* there, for Jamey's strong fingers were sliding over her buttocks with incredible softness, beginning a long shiver of desire.

Now she had to speak, but when she opened her mouth he kissed her again, and at the same time his fingers tightened and she was lifted from the ground, his hand sliding between her legs, carrying her negligee and nightgown with it, and then her entire body seemed to become a single swell of passion. Mosquito netting brushed her hair, and she realized that he had carried her across the room. And suddenly she knew her danger. "No," she said as his mouth slipped from hers. "No. We cannot. Jamey. . . ."

He kissed her again, while pulling the netting free. She sat, and then lay, pushed back by the incessant loving of his mouth and his body. She gazed up at his face, wishing she could see more clearly, wishing that *he* could see more clearly, could more properly understand the beauty that he was possessing. His hands had left her bottom and were now at her ankles; they came sliding up her legs, carrying the nightdress with them. No one had ever touched her like that, except herself, and even then she had known it had to be sinful.

But how could it be sinful, if they loved? Because now she knew that they did. That this was the man, the feeling, for which she had waited all her life.

And besides, he had saved her life. As he had said, in many cultures this would make her his, to do with as he wished. What a delicious thought that was, to be utterly possessed by a man like Jamey Grant. There was simply nothing else she wanted at this moment, or could ever want, she supposed.

But he was gone. She opened her eyes in alarm, and sighed with relief as she saw that he was still there, but half out of the bed, as he tugged at his clothing. And she lay before him, her nightgown about her waist. Instinctively she reached for it, to push it down, but he saw her movement and was quicker than she, lowering his head to kiss her pubes while still removing his clothes. She gave a gasp of mingled delight and alarm, and brought her knees up, only slowly to lower them again, her body rocking to and fro as it seemed to develop a will of its own.

What happened after was only an extension of this kiss. How she wished she had felt more, had been able to look, to see, to understand what he was doing, what he was like . . . but the kiss, the soft touch of his tongue sifting through the curly hair, had completed her soar into heaven seconds before he was ready. She knew only that he was lying on her, that he was kissing her mouth, and working his body against hers, and sighing, and then gazing at her, their lips almost touching, his eyes bright in the darkness.

"You'll wait for me, Christina," he said. "You'll wait for me."

There was no greater pleasure than walking her horse along the huge sweep of white beach which the Indians called the Copacabana, early in the morning, while the sun still hung close to the eastern Atlantic, at this hour just warm enough to dispel the mist. Here she was alone, accompanied only by her groom, who kept a discreet distance, and of course by Aunt Malina, who no longer rode, but preferred to sit in an open carriage, already sheltering beneath a huge parasol, already preparing to feel enervated and exhausted.

It was a feeling which Christina herself anticipated, come ten of the clock, and one which concerned her less on her own account than because of her parents' suffering, and because, even more, of the thought of Jamey forcing his way through the jungles and across the prairies, also subject to the extremes of the climate. She reasoned that it could not be merely the heat that plagued them so; Portugal was very little cooler, at least in the south. But Portugal was at least subject to sea breezes to drive away the miasmas, and Portugal was *not* subject to the cloying dampness, the tremendous rainstorms which whipped across this land, making trees bend before their force, rattling on wooden rooftops like pebbles thrown by a giant, encouraging, it seemed, the development and voracity of the hordes of fine ants which infested everywhere, eating everything from clothes to wood until they left a mere shell; and leaving many a man, too, she suspected, nothing more than a shell, ready to collapse at the first tentative push.

And did they also reach the brains? Or was that something entirely more sinister? A combination of altogether too many subtleties to be understood until it was too late. It was a condition, she had early concluded, that was endemic to the Indians, who appeared as fine, even noble creatures, certainly handsome in many ways, but afflicted with a dreadful, perpetual lethargy which left them happiest when doing absolutely nothing. Certainly they sought nothing except food and, since their contact with the Portuguese, drink. The African slaves were hardly more energetic, save when they were driven to it. But this depended to a large extent upon the energy of their masters and mistresses. And here the deadly debilitation of the climate showed itself most clearly. So many of these men must have left Portugal, their hearts and their minds aflame at the thought of a new world, of fortunes to be discovered, empires to be seized, immortality to be won, only to find that by stooping for an instant to secure some of the creature comforts of life, mainly the joys of a woman's arms, be she Indian or Negro—there were no white women available for the average colonist—they immediately became the victims of their conquests' lazy lack of concern with anything more pressing than the wherewithal to purchase a glass of wine.

Even for those who gloried in their families and their backgrounds, who sought to maintain the exclusiveness of their blood by bringing their women with them across the ocean, who *huddled* away from the contamination of the tropics, there was that certain fact that a glass too many of wine, taken in the midday heat, would send them into somnolence for the remainder of the day, with each day building upon the last until all life became centered in a precious couple of hours at dawn and after dusk, and business dwindled into a succession of tomorrows which never came. This torpidity affected even the viceroy, for all his determined energy. Certainly it had reached his wife and her cousin, Malina, whom Christina called "aunt." And his daughter? No, Christina vowed fiercely to herself, not while she could think like this, could recognize the dangers as well as the pleasures of not having enough to do.

And the Grants would not be affected, either. Jack was the fortunate one, as he himself recognized, in that he was nearly ready for his first voyage to Portugal. There could be no risk of mental and physical stagnation when he had the sea airs to blow through his brain; in the six weeks since his brother's departure he had worked as hard as ever, refitting his ship, eager to be away again, disappointed only in that there had been no word from his mother and sister, or from his fiancée back in Nantucket, but certain, with the eternal Grant optimism, that word of their imminent arrival could only be days away.

And therefore, Christina reasoned, there could be no risk for Jamey either, as he plodded through forests and across rivers, up and down mountains, driven by his ambition, by his determination to return and claim his bride.

In a spasm of near anger she wheeled her horse and walked it back toward the waiting carriage, little spurts of sand flicking away from its hooves to disperse in the dawn breeze, the gentle Atlantic rollers now whispering at her back. She recognized the temptations, in her case increased and made more dangerous by her isolation. She now supposed that on that night six weeks ago she had been mad. She was Christina Maria Theresa de Sousa e Melo, not some tavern girl. Her body, her mind, her name, her very existence, were there to be worshiped by some aspirant to greatness, not to be seized and enjoyed by a lusting appetite.

But it *had* been enjoyed, and by them both. There was the point. And Jamey Grant had never known the immobile grandeur of the Portuguese court, or any court for that matter. She was a black-haired nymph he had plucked from the sea, and from that moment she had been his, in his eyes. And in hers? Hardly less. How she wracked her brain, day after day, in an effort to remember everything that had happened to her that unforgettable night. Quite without success. She had even attempted to write it down, in the form of a diary, in the hopes that she might extract more from the memory than was possible, and accomplishing little, had hastily burned it, because the little was in itself damning. Only that kiss, so wanton, so obscene, so almost blasphemous, she sometimes thought—and so utterly the most delicious thing that had ever happened to her.

Confession had been out of the question. Therefore the original sin, which was perhaps expiable on grounds of passion and gratitude, had been compounded into a guilt which gnawed at her conscience every waking moment and during quite a few nightmares as well. And was compounded by her *refusal* to regret what had happened, what she had permitted, by her determined belief that God was the sole arbiter of her fate, and that He had caused her to be saved by a man who had been capable of bringing her passionate dreams to a proper conclusion.

Here was arrogance upon a scale she had never supposed possible. Were Father Luis to suspect even a fraction of her thoughts, she doubted he would rest content without prescribing a penance. Often she simply avoided him by retreating to the privacy of her bedchamber or even to her bed. No one appeared to find her new habits strange, since they had all began to behave similarly.

But she had the sense to understand that the climate and the humidity and the insects were also playing their parts. She found it difficult to enjoy food, and for nearly a month now had scarcely had a glass of wine; its very taste could set her stomach to rolling. It was affecting her digestion, in that she was often overtaken by great waves of nausea which left her quite unable to stand. And most serious of all, it was affecting her as a woman as well, in that her monthly flow had been absent these past weeks. She conceived of herself as shriveling up inside, as so many of the white women in the colony seemed to have shriveled, and was obsessed with the fear that Jamey would come back to a dried-up stick, and would turn away.

She was instantly reassured, though, whenever she looked in her mirror. Even viewed with the most skeptical eye, her beauty had never been more blooming. She was careful not to expose her complexion to the sun, remained indoors whenever it was hot, wore a broad-brimmed straw hat for riding even in the early morning, as now, and used a variety of salves and ointments, brought with her from Lisbon and recommended by other ladies who had experienced the tropics. Thus her cheeks were pinkened only by heat, and by health, despite all her internal disorders.

"Haste, haste," commanded Aunt Malina, fanning herself vigorously. "You are perspiring."

Christina looked down at herself, at the bodice of her habit, clinging damply to her neck and shoulders; even her right knee, hooked high on the horn of her sidesaddle, was showing clearly through the layers of petticoat, most unsuitable garments for this climate, however much they were required by custom and modesty. But in fact she perspired at the slightest movement. As did Aunt, for that matter. Or even Mama.

"Then I *shall* make haste," she decided, and kicked her horse into a canter down the road, her groom hurrying be-

hind, and the carriage hurrying behind that. Her route took
her close by the rear of the fort, where the sentries clustered
to look down at her, as they did every morning, then along
the next stretch of beach, moving always into the shadow of
the towering height of Acacar, which the locals called the
sugarloaf mountain, dominating the narrows, and thence left,
skirting the green waters of the bay of Botafogo, where the
barracoons and warehouses and docks clustered, and where
the *Lodestar* lay amid several other vessels—but, surprisingly, not being worked this morning.

From the docks she entered the town itself, through streets
of surprising width when compared with those of Lisbon, but
entirely lacking in paving or drains, or any regular mainte-
nance, so that when it rained the earth dissolved into water-
filled potholes often more than a foot deep, or when, as now,
the weather was dry, the dust swirled from her horse's hooves,
settling on the clothes and faces of those passersby unfortunate enough to be on foot, carrying with it the effluvium
arising from the bloated body of a dead cat thrown carelessly
at the side of the road.

Yet Rio was saved from squalor by the luxuriant growth of
trees which shaded it and gave it beauty, the red-flowered
Poincianas that blazed with color, many-trunked banyans,
protruding from street corners like ancient fortifications, stout-
branched tamarinds whose podlike fruits, adored by the Negro
children for all their lip-twisting tartness, threatened to brush
the hat from her head. Here were the residences of the whites
and creoles, two-storied wooden houses dominated by their
enormous verandas and open-shuttered windows, and then the
square, where the huge cross formed a focal point, facing the
cathedral on one side and the viceregal palace on the other.
Here the sentries, regulars in tight white breeches and blue
jackets, blue and gold tricorne hats and smart white leather
equipment, stood to attention, while in the courtyard beyond,
a cluster of grooms and maids waited to assist her down, to
hold parasols above her head, to surround her with their
chatter, which seemed distinctly muted this morning. And
among the horses being held before the staircase to the vice-

roy's private apartments she recognized that of Jack Grant. At seven o'clock in the morning?

"There has been some disaster," she said. "What is Captain Grant doing here so early?"

"He speaks with your father, Dona Christina," said one of the maids. "It is an urgent matter."

Christina frowned at her ar   then hurried up the stairs and along the corridor in long strides, boots crisp on the wooden floor.

The doors to her father's study were closed, but the major domo hastily opened them at her approach; the viceroy's only daughter was not to be challenged.

The doors swung in, and she gazed at her father, leaning forward, at, amazingly, her mother, still in an undressing robe and weeping, at Jack, seated in a chair to one side, his head in his hands . . . and at Conybeare, standing before the desk and twisting his hat before him.

"Conybeare?" she cried.

They all turned their heads.

"Christina, my dear," Inez de Sousa said, "there is sad news."

"Conybeare," Christina said again, more quietly. She must not betray either herself or Jamey. But Jamey . . . "What has happened?"

The big seaman sighed. "Terrible it was, Miss. Terrible."

"Rapids," Den Pedro said. "Unexpected rapids."

"But what *happened*?" Christina cried, her stomach seeming to turn to lead.

"They tried to shoot these rapids," Jack said miserably, his shoulders bowed. "The lead boat struck a rock and capsized, and the others followed."

"Terrible it was," Conybeare said. "Terrible. There we were, upside down, swimming for our lives . . . I've spent twelve years at sea, Your Excellency, and I've never seen water like that. Boiling, it was."

"You mean it was hot?" Inez de Sousa asked.

"No, no, ma'am, but it was just white, bubbling and rushing. There weren't no man in the world could swim against that. I was the lucky one. I was able to hold on to the upturned boat, and I just clung there, Your Excellency. I thought I was done for. But eventually I came to shore.''

"And the others?'' Amazingly, Christina's voice was quiet. But the entire room seemed to be spinning.

"Well, miss, like you might suppose, I did what I could. There were people there, on the shore. Some priests had a mission just down the river, and they helped, with their Indians. Without them I'd have died myself. We found poor Dutton and a couple of the others. All drowned. But the main group, why, they was just swept away. The priests said that river don't usually give up its victims. It travels so fast, you see, miss, it sweeps them along.''

Slowly Christina sat down; the major domo had thoughtfully placed a chair for her. "And Jamey?'' she asked.

"We didn't find Jamey,'' Conybeare said. "Oh we looked, miss, we looked.''

She discovered her father standing beside her, his hand on her shoulder. "It is a great tragedy,'' Don Pedro said. "And for you as much as anyone, my dear child. He saved your life. But you may be sure that he died as gallantly as he lived, on that day. And he was doing what he most wished. Our grief must go out to poor Jack. First a father, now a brother, separated from his mother and sister . . .''

"I must return to the ship,'' Jack Grant said, standing up. " 'Tis an unlucky family we have become, to be sure. Ever since . . .'' He gazed reflectively at Conybeare. "You'd best come with me, Arthur. Work is the best remedy for grief. You'll excuse us, Don Pedro.''

But what of me? Christina wanted to scream. What of me? He was your brother, but he was my lover. He was my fiancé. He was my *man*. The second man to whom she had attached her life. But since no one knew, no one cared especially for her feelings.

Suddenly she knew she was going to vomit. She leaped to her feet, ran out of the office and along the hall, up the stairs to her room, threw open the door, reached for the slop pail that waited beside her basin and ewer, and knelt on the floor, the bucket in her arms.

"You poor child," Aunt Malina said. "You poor, poor child."

Christina raised her head, and her aunt wiped her face with a handkerchief soaked in eau de cologne. "Now come and lie down," she said, "and we will decide what is to be done."

Christina crossed the room with difficulty; the floor seemed to be surging up and down. But her brain was swinging even more wildly. "Do, Aunt Malina? Do?"

She was lying down, the pillows heaped beneath her head, and with a wave of her hand her aunt was dismissing the anxious maids, but not speaking again until the door had closed behind them.

"Do," she repeated firmly. "I only wished to be sure."

A great feeling of helplessness seemed to be overtaking Christina. "To be sure?" she whispered.

"Who it was who came to your room that night, Christina," Aunt Malina said. "Do you not suppose I knew of it? And of what you had done? Do you not suppose there was blood on your linen the next day?"

"Oh my God," Christina whispered. "Oh my God."

Aunt Malina got up, walked to the window, looked out at the morning. "What was I to do, child? Tell me that? My instincts were to hurry to your mother, to have you whipped until you confessed the name of the man, to disgrace you forever . . ."

"It would have been your disgrace as well," Christina said.

Aunt Malina turned. "Do you really suppose that would have mattered to me?"

"No," Christina muttered. "No. I am sorry, Aunt Malina."

Her aunt sighed. "But then I thought, what is done, is done. It cannot now be undone by a whipping. To have betrayed you to your mother would only have compounded the dreadfulness of what had happened. And besides, I think that even then I knew who it had to be. Your reaction to the news of his death has only confirmed that."

Christina sat up. "I loved him, Aunt Malina."

"And he saved your life."

"No," Christina insisted. "I mean, yes, of course he did.

But I did not yield to him merely out of gratitude. I loved him. I love him now. As he is dead, I shall never marry. So we shall carry our secret, you and I, to my grave as well. I doubt it shall be long delayed."

Aunt Malina came back to sit on the bed. "And what of the child?" she asked.

Christina could only gape at her.

"Do you not realize that you are pregnant, Christina?"

"But—"

Once again Aunt Malina stood up, restless. "You have missed your time of the month. You feel sick a great deal of the time. And yet you are obviously as healthy as you have ever been." She shrugged again. "What was I to *do,* Christina? I could only wait, and pray for the young man to come back, or for you to lose the child. I thought perhaps, riding every morning . . . it has happened before. But you are too strong for that. Now, however—now you *must* lose it." She sighed. "But I do not see how that can be done without the knowledge of your mother." Her smile was twisted. "So, the disgrace I sought to avoid for us both will now be redoubled. A convent for you, I suppose. And for me . . ." another sigh.

"Lose it?" Christina stared at her. "If I am pregnant, it is Jamey's child. It will be all of him that I will ever possess now."

"And you will have it, and rear it? Listen to me, child, that thing in your belly is a bastard, a perpetual reminder, a perpetual advertisement, of your crime. It might have been possible, by careful choosing, to marry you to a man either so ignorant that he would not understand about virginity, or so much in love with you he would forgive. But no one on this earth is going to forgive you for having an illegitimate child. Think of the disgrace it will bring on your family, on your very name. No, no, we must go to see your mother immediately and throw ourselves on her mercy and let her make the necessary arrangements. She will undoubtedly wish to send you back to Portugal, perhaps to your old convent. If the miscarriage were to take place at sea, then no one would know of it. It can all be arranged. I know about these matters. But I am very afraid that—"

"I will not lose the child," Christina said. "I will kill myself first."

"Now, Christina, having hysterics will not help." Aunt Malina attempted a smile. "Five minutes ago you were preparing to die in any event."

"That was before I realized I was pregnant," Christina said. "If it is so, then Jamey and I are married in the eyes of God just as much as if we had been married in a church. I will have this child, and I will rear him, and in him I will find my happiness."

Aunt Malina frowned at her. "And how do you propose to do that? You are seventeen years of age. Do you suppose your father will even consider such a nonsensical idea? And who are you going to set against your father, to support you? He is the viceroy. There is not a soul in Brazil who will not bow to his command."

Christina gazed at her. "I know of one," she said. "At least one who will know what to do. And I will do whatever he wishes. We will go to see my mother, Aunt Malina, after we have gone to see Captain Grant."

Chapter 4

~~~~~~

"There was nothing I could do," Conybeare said miserably. "Believe me, Jack. Jamey was in the lead boat, I was in the second. When we went over, it was all so quick I couldn't do nothing more than hold on."

"I understand that, Arthur." Jack stood at the head of the gangplank and looked down into the waist. Word had already spread of the disaster to the expedition, and work on the *Lodestar* had stopped immediately; he had dismissed the crew as well as the stevedores for the rest of the day. Now the ship looked as dead as everything else. And wasn't it dead? His entire life had been centered on this ship. He had watched her being built as a small boy, had sailed on her maiden voyage, had not been much over fourteen when he had grasped the wheel for the first time. She was as much a part of him as his family—but she was also a part of the family. Because when he had first sailed upon her, there had been Jamey jumping up and down at his side, and Father giving the commands, gruff and confident, just as there had been Mother waiting for them to dock, with Mary jumping up and down at *her* side.

He could have said much the same thing only six months

ago. And now . . . Mama would have received his letter. In the news that he and Jamey had survived, at least, he had hoped that she and Mary would find some solace for Father's death. That they would wish to pack up and join them in Brazil he had not doubted. Don Pedro had already arranged for the necessary funds to be placed at their disposal.

And instead they would be coming to yet another tragedy.

He sighed, and climbed down into the waist of the ship. He had also written to Lizzie Butler. But here he did not even expect a reply. The optimism with which he had viewed the future six weeks ago had quite disappeared, and he recognized that Lizzie's roots were too firmly set in New England, and on the side of the law. She had proved her affection for him in the warning she had given him; it would be too much to expect her to abandon home and family and friends and reputation to become the wife of an outlaw, even one who had landed on his feet.

And *had* he landed on his feet? Had any of them, really? Cast away in a strange country with a debilitating climate, to dwindle and die?

"If there'd been anything I could do. . . ." Conybeare said.

"There was nothing, Arthur." Jack paused at the top of the companion hatch. "You'd best go home and get some rest."

Conybeare stared blankly at him, and Jack remembered that the big man had no home; he had left the ship to accompany Jamey upon his desperate adventure, while the rest of the crew had all found themselves women ashore, be they pure Indian or mestizo, Negro or mulatto. Jack had encouraged them all to write to their wives, and the viceroy had promised to support them too with money, but he doubted that any of the men really wished to regain their legal families, when so much uninhibited dusky beauty was available.

"Well then," he said. "Take to your bunk, Arthur. You'll be first mate of the *Lodestar* now."

He allowed his father's friend to go below, and went onto the poop and to the taffrail, to stand gazing at the still water aft of the vessel, while the sun began to beat down on him with its usual pitiless intensity. He raised his head at the sound of hooves and frowned at the sight of the phaeton which was hastening down the dockside, driven by a sweating groom. In the back were Christina de Sousa and her duenna, and neither had changed their clothes, so far as he could see, from when he had been talking with them an hour previously, after their morning ride.

He ran down the ladder, went to the gangway as the carriage came to a halt in a flurry of dust.

"Dona Christina?" His frown deepened. The girl had been weeping, that was obvious. For Jamey? Well, he had saved her life, and they had undoubtedly been friends. She was also more disheveled than he had ever seen her since the day Jamey had plucked her from the ocean, and her cheeks were bright with what he might almost have thought was a fever. "Dona Christina?"

She was already halfway up the gangway; he caught her at the waist to swing her down onto the deck, hastily did the same for her Aunt Malina. The duenna's face was grim; she lacked the excitement of her charge.

"What has happened?" he asked.

"I must speak with you," Christina said. She glanced at her aunt. "I must speak with you, Jack. It is most urgent." She made for the companion hatch.

"Conybeare is down there sleeping," Jack said. "The poor chap is entirely done in."

Christina hesitated, once again glancing at Aunt Malina.

"We do not need the cabin," Aunt Malina said. "Captain Grant can receive us up there, on the deck. I doubt there is anything he can do for us anyway."

"There is. I know there is." Christina climbed the ladder to the poop, moved to the outer gunwale, farthest from the dock, and turned to face Jack. The pink in her cheeks had deepened, and she was breathing deeply. It occurred to him that she was the most lovely creature he had ever seen.

"If I can help you, Dona Christina, be sure that I shall," he said. "You have but to tell me what you wish."

She gazed at him, and the rosy flush spread from her cheeks down to her neck. Once again she glanced at her duenna.

"Between us," Aunt Malina said, "we seem to have managed to destroy ourselves. With some help from your brother, to be sure."

"From Jamey? But . . ." Jack looked from one to the other.

"Before leaving on his madcap quest," Aunt Malina said, spitting the words almost like a snake, "your brother managed to seduce my sweet girl."

"To . . ." Jack stared at Christina.

"And now that he is dead, Christina is with child," the woman went on.

"With . . ."

Christina came to life. "That is not true at all," she said. "I mean . . ." She bit her lip, and her flush deepened. "I am with child, Jack. And it is Jamey's. But he did not seduce me. We loved each other. He came to my bedchamber to say goodbye, and . . ."

"Your *bedchamber*?"

"Well . . . we could meet nowhere else. Not properly."

"Properly," cried Aunt Malina.

"Hush, Aunt Malina," Christina said. "We loved," she repeated, as if trying to convince herself. "And he saved my life. I belonged to him. He said so."

"The scoundrel," Jack said. "So to take advantage—"

"He did *not* take advantage," Christina shouted, careless now of being overheard. "What do you take me for, some halfwit? I . . . I knew what was happening. What he was doing. What I was doing."

"But . . . you knew you could not marry," Jack said helplessly.

"Not then. But when he returned from the Amazon, with his pockets filled with gold. When he discovered El Dorado—"

"You really believed he would find El Dorado? I doubt any such place exists."

"It does exist," Christina said fiercely. "Jamey knew it did. Everyone knows it does. Your own Walter Raleigh knew. Jamey has read his work."

"Raleigh was a dreamer, and lost his head for it," Jack said. "But even supposing it does exist and Jamey had been able to find it, do you suppose your father would have given permission for you to marry?''

"Yes,'' she said. "Yes, he would. Jamey would have been wealthy. He could even have been given a title. For heaven's sake, only two generations ago the de Sousas were nothing. Nothing at all. And now the marquis is more powerful even than the king.''

Jack sighed, and decided against reminding her that those who have recently arrived at greatness are even less likely to accept parvenus than those established for generations.

"And what of his religion? Supposing he possessed one,'' Aunt Malina sniffed.

"That does not matter,'' Christina insisted. "We were blessed by God. I know we were,''

"Ha,'' Aunt Malina snapped.

"Well—'' Jack began doubtfully.

Christina caught his arm. "Aunt Malina says we must go to Mama and tell her what has happened. But I'm afraid they'll take away my baby,'' Christina said. "I know they will. If they even let me have it, they'll still take it away. I'll not let them, Jack. It is my baby. Mine and Jamey's. It's all I shall ever have. Please, Jack.''

He gazed at Aunt Malina. "I'm not sure what you want me to do,'' he said.

"It'll be your nephew, Jack, or niece. You could take me away. Just as you fled Nantucket. You could take me with you when next you sail. No one would know. I won't be showing for another two months at least, Aunt Malina says. I could come on board and you could take me away. I don't mind where. Just somewhere to have my baby, to bring him up. Just somewhere, Jack.''

Jack shook his head slowly.

"It would be madness,'' Aunt Malina said. "And criminal. You would be fugitives all your lives. Is that what you really wish to be, Captain Grant? You must be able to see that she is suffering from an excess of grief. That she is really out of her mind, at least temporarily. Heaven knows I don't want to see her hurt. I believe she did love your brother, and I will do all

I can to intercede for her with her parents, but you must see that what she proposes is out of the question.''

Jack continued to gaze at the girl. The most beautiful creature he had ever seen. And she had lain naked in Jamey's arms. He supposed that what she had been telling him was only now reaching his true understanding. Mad and criminal. That summed up Jamey accurately enough. In his insensate lust he did not care whom he hurt, or what were the likely outcomes. Jamey had never loved anyone in his life. He *had* seduced this lovely girl, however easily he had managed to persuade her that she had been a willing partner in his crime.

And now this fabulous creature was, like Jack himself, cast utterly adrift, at least for the moment. He could agree to sail away with her. She would have her child, and then she would have no one to turn to but himself. She would be his, irrevocably. All that beauty. All that exciting anxiety to live, and love. She would love him, eventually, because there would be no one else *for* her to love. They would sail the seas together . . . and eventually they would die together. Rather sooner than later, with every man's hand against them, either in a storm at sea or hanged from the same gallows.

Christina watched his face. No doubt she could read the thoughts racing through his mind.

"Please help me," she said. "I'll do anything you ask if you help me."

Criminal madness. He was no better than Jamey. But she was his already, if he had the courage to reach out and take. And *his* crime could be dressed up in the guise of chivalry.

If he dared. But did he dare do anything else? And would he not hate himself throughout his life if he did not follow his instincts now?

"Your aunt is quite right," he said.

Slowly Christina's mouth sagged into an *O*.

"But I can, and will, help you," he said, "if you will let me."

She frowned at him.

"It was my brother's fault you are in this condition," he said. "And as you have said, it is my nephew that you carry.

We are all Grants, Dona Christina, and I am prepared to take responsibility for my family. If it would please you, my lady, then I would ask for your hand in marriage myself.''

The frown deepened, the mouth formed another *O*. "Marry . . . you?" she asked.

"That is absurd and impossible," Aunt Malina said. "How can she marry you?"

"Because she carries my dead brother's child. Because I can be a husband to her and a father to the baby, where no one else would suffice."

"You are a penniless sailor," Aunt Malina declared. "You are not even Catholic."

"I am Don Pedro's friend and savior," Jack said. "With his help I shall not always be poor. As for my religion, well . . . one is much like another."

Christina stared at him with enormous eyes. "You would change your religion for me?"

"A man who can do that has no religion," Aunt Malina insisted.

"Then Christina can teach me to believe," Jack suggested. "Christina is Don Pedro's daughter. He would do much to avoid having to shut her in a convent." He lifted Christina's hand to his lips and kissed her fingers. "It is *your* agreement that I require, my lady."

Her eyes came to meet his, little pools of uncertainty.

"Marry *you*?" she asked again.

Don Pedro clasped his hands under his chin and stared at the young man in front of his desk. "I cannot believe it," he said. "I cannot believe what you are telling me, Jack."

"Do you realize the enormity of what you have just confessed?" Father Luis asked. There was nobody else in the room, Jack having requested a private interview.

"I treated you as a son," Don Pedro said. "I have given you a home, and money . . . I am bringing your mother and sister out here to be with you . . . I have grieved with you over the death of your brother . . . and this is how you repay me? By seducing my only daughter?"

"You should be hanged from the highest gallows in Rio de Janeiro," Father Luis said.

Jack let them have their say. He had anticipated some such storm, and that it was actually blowing was a good sign. His nerve had not failed him before, either when opposed to revenue men or the Navy or the hurricane; it would not fail him now.

But now they had both paused for breath. And it was as necessary to be hard, and even cruel, in his lies as it had been to bend before their verbal assault. For if he were to fail now, then he was indeed a castaway. But if he were to succeed, the future could be golden beyond his wildest dreams.

With a woman who did not love him? And perhaps never would? But also the most beautiful woman he had ever seen, who would be *his*. It was only necessary to keep remembering that.

"I understand your anger, Don Pedro," he said. "I can only hope and pray that you will understand something of my point of view. I know nothing of courts and gallantry, nothing of kings and viceroys. I saved your life, and the lives of your family, the life of Christina, not because you were the viceroy of Brazil, but because you were a human being in distress."

"And you would trade on that for the rest of your life," Father Luis remarked.

"By no means, sir. I am but attempting to explain how I felt about you. Because of our meeting, I had supposed we were friends, in a manner that would cut across differences in rank or religion or background. True friendship does not admit of such barriers. Certainly Christina felt as I did."

"She is only a girl, of whom you have taken shameful advantage," Father Luis said.

Jack continued to gaze at Don Pedro. "A girl with whom I fell in love," he said. "Love also does not admit of barriers, especially when it is reciprocated."

"And would it not have been more admirable to have come to me to speak of your love," Don Pedro asked, "instead of sneaking into Christina's bedchamber like a thief?"

"My actions were dictated by circumstances, Your Excellency, and also by Christina herself. She doubted that our love would be accepted by you, in the beginning. It was, in any event, necessary for us to meet, and discuss, and plan, and dream, sir, of the future we both desired, and how could this be done, save clandestinely, because of the rules imposed by your society? Once a clandestine meeting was possible, and arranged, well, sir, we are both young, and ardent, and very much in love.''

''And foolish enough to assume that your guilt could remain a secret,'' Father Luis said.

''Why yes, Father. We did assume so. But I for one have no regret that it did not. I did not welcome the role of thief which was thrust upon me. I accepted it to humor the woman I loved. But now, sir, why, I can boldly approach you and ask for Dona Christina's hand in marriage.''

''You have the effrontery to ask for Dona Christina's hand in marriage?'' Father Luis cried. ''You, an upstart sailor, dare to aspire to the hand of a Sousa e Melo?''

Jack returned his gaze. ''As the Sousas e Melo once accepted my hand, sir, to survive a watery grave.''

The priest stared at him, brows drawing together in an angry scowl.

''You are an incredibly bold young man, Jack,'' Don Pedro said, speaking quietly. ''But then I knew that from the moment I met you. No doubt I am as guilty as anyone, in not foreseeing the probable results of such boldness.''

''You cannot possibly consider agreeing to such an insulting proposal, Don Pedro,'' Father Luis said. ''It would mean condemning Christina to a life of degradation and misery. I cannot permit it.''

''*You* cannot permit it, Father?'' Don Pedro inquired.

The priest flushed. ''The Church cannot permit it, Your Excellency.''

Don Pedro sighed. ''The Church will *have* to permit it, Father. What would you have me do? Execute or imprison or exile the man who saved all our lives? Force Christina to destroy this child, a mortal sin which might also cost her her life, and then lock her up in a convent for the rest of her days? Would either of those courses not condemn me as a barbarian? You have known Christina from childhood, Father Luis.

She has had a strange, a unique life. You know as well as I that she is possessed of an almost mystical belief that God is watching over her every step, her every thought, that she is in His hands far more than in mine, or those of the Church.''

"That is close to blasphemy, Your Excellency.''

"It is close to true religion, you mean. Certainly there is nothing we can do that will change her opinions. To take her child would only earn her hatred. No convent would contain her, should her instincts tell her to flee.''

"Is that an argument for never imprisoning criminals?'' Father Luis demanded.

Don Pedro sat up straight. "My daughter is not a criminal, Father. Neither is this young man. They are two people who met in the strangest of circumstances, and loved, and wish to continue loving. It will cause a scandal, certainly, but my family has survived scandals before.''

"You mean you will agree to their marriage?'' Father Luis was clearly horrified.

"I can see no alternative. It will be put about that I have acted out of gratitude for Jack's having saved our lives, and . . .'' He gazed at Jack. "In the certainty that he intends to make his home here in Brazil, and share with me, with us all, the responsibilities of making this colony grow.''

"You have my word, sir,'' Jack said.

"Then the marriage must be celebrated immediately, before Christina's condition is obvious.''

"And when the child is born, in seven months' time?'' Father Luis asked.

"There will be whispers. But no one will *know*,'' Don Pedro said.

"Now I owe you as much as you owe me, Your Excellency,'' Jack said. "But I never doubted that you would deal with me as a man, rather than a viceroy.''

Don Pedro gazed at him. "I can only pray that I do not live to rue the day you plucked me from that ocean,'' he said, "as I feel inclined to do at this moment. And you have as yet no cause to thank me. My consent to your marriage, and my forgiveness of your crime, rests entirely upon Christina's signifying that everything you have told me today is the truth, and that marriage to you is the thing she desires above all else in this world. Father Luis, you will be good enough to ask my daughter to attend me here.''

Now he could do nothing but wait, as he had waited, lashed to the helm of the *Lodestar*, for the storm to do its worst. If she had appeared to understand what he was offering her, had appeared to realize there was no other practical course for her to follow, her initial reaction continued to burn its way through his brain. It was his brother she loved. And as her father had said, she was a unique personality, and once she had given her love, she would not easily deviate.

That he could love her, that he *would* love her, was certain. But what then would be his fate? It had been the thought of her, the sight of her, the sudden desire to possess her, that had led him into this subterfuge in the first place. But could he possibly be enough of a villain to carry his plan through to its obvious conclusion? And could Christina, understanding nothing of his doubts, knowing only that he was a man and she a woman and that marriage would mean the surrender of her body to him?

Her face was composed. She had changed her clothing, now wore a loose house gown. Her hair was also loose, and trailing past her shoulders.

''Sit down, Christina,'' her father invited.

Slowly she lowered herself into the chair before his desk. Jack stood to one side of her, Father Luis to the other.

Don Pedro also sat down. ''You will know what Jack has just been telling me,'' he said.

She nodded slowly.

''You are prepared to confirm his story?''

This time the movement was even more reluctant.

''You are pregnant?''

''Yes,'' she said, her voice no more than a whisper.

''And he visited you in your bedchamber?''

The briefest of hesitations. ''Yes.''

''Do you have any understanding of the wickedness of what you have done?''

''Yes,'' she said.

"But you love him."

Christina started to turn her head, to look at Jack, and then straightened it again. "Yes," she whispered.

"And in your eyes that condones all crimes."

"Yes," she said more boldly.

"Even that of not confessing to Father Luis?"

She brought her head up. "I confessed it to God."

"Do you suppose He will listen to a confession unless it is made through His appointed intermediary?" Father Luis asked.

"I confessed it to God," she repeated stubbornly.

"And do you have any doubt that I should imprison you both for the rest of your lives?" Don Pedro asked.

She met his gaze. "You have that power, Papa."

"But if you were given the opportunity, you would wish to marry Jack?"

This time there was no hesitation. "Yes," she said.

Don Pedro gazed at her for some seconds, while Jack's heart seemed to swell. She *was* unique. In the most mysterious of fashions, God had given him the most marvelous creature on earth. *God* had done that, as she had known, not the devil. Must he then become a gentleman, at the expense of being a man?

"Very well," Don Pedro said. "I am prepared to permit this marriage, providing it is celebrated immediately." He glanced at Jack. "You will have to convert to Catholicism. Have you considered this?"

"I have, sir."

"And you are willing?"

"I am, sir."

"Ha," remarked Father Luis.

"Well, then you will undertake your instruction as from today, with Father Luis." Don Pedro frowned at his daughter. "You do not seem very pleased."

"I am overwhelmed, Papa," she said.

He pushed back his chair and got up. "Well, you had better come along with me and confront your mother. You as well, Jack."

"With your permission, sir," Jack said, "I would like a moment alone with Christina."

"That is quite impossible," Father Luis said.

"Oh come now, Father," Don Pedro said with a sad smile. "They appear to have been alone together before, from time to time." He went to the door. "I should be obliged if you would join us as soon as possible," he said, and left the room. Father Luis gazed at Jack for a moment, his expression pure venom, and then he too left, closing the door behind him.

"I had not known you would be so completely successful," Christina said. "I was preparing myself for the worst. But my father likes you very much. Had you been born a Portuguese hidalgo, I suspect he himself would have suggested you for my husband. Now that his hand is forced, so to speak, why I think he is secretly delighted."

"Are *you* delighted?" Jack asked.

"Of course." she said, at last looking directly at him. "It means . . ." She bit her lip.

". . . that you can have your child, and live a normal life," he said. "It also means that you will be my wife."

She did not lower her eyes. "I understand that." She smiled. "It is very important for a mother also to be a wife."

Jack drew a long breath. There was no necessity to say another word. And yet he knew he was going to.

"I would like you to know," he said, "that my marriage to you will be as *you* desire it, Christina. Your son I will treat as my own. This I swear. Your body is *your* own, and I will not trespass. This too I swear."

A faint frown gathered between her eyes. "A marriage must be consummated. A wife must be a wife or there can be no marriage, only bitterness. I would have no bitterness between us, Jack."

"I would take no woman to my bed without love," he said. "I will wait for your love."

She gazed into his eyes for several seconds. Finally she said, "Then let us go and convince my mother that we *do* love."

The cathedral was crowded. This was no massive stone edifice dedicated to the glory of God and of the imperial power as was to be found in so many of the Spanish colonies, for that was not the Portuguese way, but rather a smaller, altogether more humble church, dedicated to God alone, and not intended as an indication of the wealth and power of the community which worshiped Him there.

But this was a wealthy community. Again in remarkable contrast to the Spanish colonies, these men, and those of their women who had accompanied them to the tropics, had not sought merely gold, had not immediately rejected this land to return to their homes across the ocean the moment the precious metal had become scarce. They had come to live, to *colonize*, and they had found their wealth far more in the richness of the soil, the enormous estates which were theirs for the taking, than in the dwindling mines of Minas Gerais. Nor were they entirely pureblood, any longer. Again with the easygoing Portuguese approach to moral and social attitudes, there had never been any stigma on those who had chosen to seek wives from among the often beautiful Indian maidens they had discovered here in Brazil; as the occupation of at least these coastal areas had continued for better than two hundred years, some of these mestizo families were now in their sixth generation, handsome, brown-skinned men and women, as wealthily well bred as any who thronged the courts of Europe and, Jack supposed, a good deal better bred than the majority of the inhabitants of New England, with their courtly manners and their elegant conversation.

To most of them, no less than to most of the Portuguese nobility, a de Sousa e Melo was an upstart, but since this one was their viceroy, they had come flooding into Rio to witness the marriage of his only daughter—to an American sailor. No doubt, Jack supposed, he was sadly disappointing them, as he stood at the altar in his red velvet coat, with its matching waistcoat and knee breeches, his gold buttons and braid embroidery, his white lace-edged shirt, the ruffled white pigtail wig which apparently went with such an ensemble and had to be worn on such an occasion despite the heat, his white silk stockings, and his black leather shoes with their jeweled buckles. He should have been wearing a pigtail and earrings, a bandana instead of a tricorne hat. He had not recognized himself in the mirror this morning, and had been afraid to step out of doors, to risk the gazes of Conybeare and the crew of the *Lodestar*. He could only now take comfort in the realization that most of the other men in the church were dressed with similar splendor, and indeed his best man, Christina's cousin, a young officer in the garrison named Thomas de Carvalho, selected for this august position by the viceroy himself, was even more magnificent; *his* suit was in cloth of gold.

The ladies competed in the dazzling colors of their gowns, the twinkling stones of their rings and their necklaces and their brooches, and, in a manner superior to anything any man could offer, in the gleaming shoulders and bosoms which fought against the scant restrictions of their decolletages. Seeing so much beauty, so much poise, so much sheer femininity, inhaling so much perfume, listening to so much rustling of silk and taffeta, whispering of voices and fans, which challenged even the gentle music of the organ, left him consumed with an anxious impatience to behold his bride, to feel her beside him, to know she was there. For in the past month he had seen her only three times, and on each occasion in the company of several others. And, he realized, they had *never* spent a private moment together, except for that hurried conversation before they had faced the tears and the swooning of her mother.

There had been too much to do. She with her dressmakers and her instructions, and no doubt in reconciling Dona Inez to what had happened, he with his tailors and *his* instructions, both in Portuguese manners and in the Roman faith.

Did this bother him? He did not honestly think so. And besides, if he was undertaking so gigantic a lie, what did one more matter? He was reminded of a tale he had once been told, of a man who had sold his soul to the devil in return for ten years of wealth and power. Well he had sold his, in exchange for the possession of two arms and two legs, a pair of breasts and buttocks, a slender waist and a mane of magnificent hair, a beautiful, determined face, as well as, he had no doubt, an irresistible, passionate sexuality—all of which had previously belonged to his brother, and must still belong to his brother in memory, and none of which he had any guarantee would ever belong to him. The devil, he thought, must be pleased with his bargain on this occasion.

But these were hardly proper thoughts for a bridegroom. For suddenly the music swelled to a crescendo, the rustling grew louder as heads began to turn, the church to fill with incense as the choir slowly came up the aisle and debouched into their stalls. He would not turn his head, but remained staring straight in front of him, at the various priests who filed beside the altar, at the bishop, resplendent in his purple robes and his mitred cap, until he felt her hand on his arm. Only then would he allow himself to look down and reassure himself as to just what he had secured.

It had been decided that she would wear virginal white, regardless of the facts of the matter; Don Pedro had considered there was no point in adding to the gossip which had already spread about the pair. Her hair, braided and secured on her neck but allowed to peep from beneath her white cap in a fringe, appeared almost as a decoration and did nothing to detract from the pure beauty of the face, the serious contemplation with which she regarded the world, the disturbingly abstract expression that so often dominated her eyes, suggesting that that world she beheld was nothing more than an antechamber, and not a very interesting antechamber, to be endured until she could reach the privacy of her own mind, her own thoughts.

And will I ever be admitted into that inner world? he wondered.

He scarcely heard the service, nor did he understand much of it, as his progress in Portuguese was slow. He was too conscious of the small fingers gripping his, of her scent seeming to rise to envelop him as she breathed, of the slight touch of her thigh as she knelt beside him before the altar. He seemed to move in a dream, as if perhaps hoping that by so doing he might be able to find his way into the dream world in which she so obviously existed.

Then it was out into the suddenly bright, and hot, sunshine and the cheers of the crowds who had assembled in the square, restrained by the blue-coated soldiers. The bridal party walked through the throng, followed by their guests,

and into the viceregal palace itself, where flags and bunting
hung from every beam, where the main dining table groaned
beneath the enormous weight of food arranged upon it, where
the minstrels were already gathered in their gallery, sawing at
their violins, where there were more blessings to be undergone. Two hours must be spent in the reception line, shaking
or kissing the hands of people he had never seen before,
although not all their names were unfamiliar to him, bound up
as he now was in the carrying trade to and from Lisbon. Here
today were the Coelhos from San Paolo, descendants of the
famous Duarte Coelho, the first Portuguese nobleman actually
to cross the Atlantic with his family, to make a new home for
himself, thus setting the example for all the rest; and with
them the Ramirezes from Bahia, and the da Cunhas from
Minas Gerais, and the de Carvalhos from Rio—the family of
his best man, who themselves claimed relationship to the
great marquis of Pombal and thus to the de Sousas themselves—
and the da Silvas from Pernambuco. From all these the smiles
were wintry and the gazes intense; there was not one of these
great families who had not seen, in the arrival of a viceroy
with an unmarried daughter, the best of opportunities for their
own sons. Thus there was not one, Jack realized, who would
not regard this American adventurer with hatred.

But there was nothing any of them could do about the
situation and, the handshaking and hand kissing completed,
their menfolk clustered around to talk to, and at, the bridegroom, for they nearly all spoke English, to ask pointed
questions about his background and antecedents, his estates
and his family wealth. He forced himself to reply with the
simple truth, reasoning that he could only appear more dubi-
ous were he to attempt to suggest a nobility which did not
exist, and all the while he wished that he could have them on
the deck of the *Lodestar* in a hurricane—because then they
would find out who were men and who were not.

But at last he was once again united with his bride, as they
stood at the head of the table and listened to the speeches,
extolling the beauty and splendor of Christina, the gallantry
and prowess and inevitable rise to prosperity of her husband,
and drank the toasts and cut the many-tiered cake, and here,

for the first time, he realized with a start of surprise and indeed dismay, he was required to kiss his wife: a chaste kiss, a touch of lip upon lip while the assembly clapped its approval, a disconcerting hint of the problems which lay ahead and were momentarily coming closer.

As they sat down to a sumptuous lunch he found he could again sit next to Christina, with Dona Inez on his other side, tearfully reconciled to the catastrophe which had overtaken her family. They were served vast quantities of turtle and beef, washed down with port and sherry wines and topped with madeira, all far more fortified than any French equivalent, which, combined with the food and the buzz of conversation and the rising heat, soon had heads drooping, the bishop going so far as to snore openly.

Jack ate little, and so did Christina. But they both took more than one glass of wine, sufficient to isolate themselves from the surrounding noise, insufficient to send them into careless inebriation like their guests. Thus when he looked down at her, he found her looking up at him and raising her glass to him with a smile.

"I love you, Christina Maria Theresa Grant," he said, enjoying the sound of the name. "I think I must have loved you without knowing it from the moment I first saw you. And I shall love you all my life. Do you believe that?"

But her gaze was suddenly clouded with a frown. All her life, for a seventeen-year-old mother-to-be, was too great a chunk of the future to be digested in one reply.

And then she was away, as was he. He was rushed to a changing room by a horde of now definitely drunken men, whooping and cheering as they tore his finery from his shoulders, smothered him in pomade and eau de cologne, and dropped a nightshirt over his head, all the while passing the most ribald of comments on his obvious unpreparedness for the coming encounter. That they might wish to remain to see at least the opening skirmish had not previously occurred to him. What to do? And immediately he realized the reason for much of Christina's pensive nonacceptance of his promise; unlike him she would be perfectly well aware of the marriage customs of the Portuguese nobility.

But it was too late now, as he was already being half led and half carried along the corridor and up a flight of stairs to the next floor. Here there was a far worse ordeal to be endured; those women who had not actually been able to gain access to the bridal chamber had gathered, eager to greet the groom, to pull his head aside for a kiss, to seize his hands to press against bosom or cheek, and to send their own hands questing into the flapping nightshirt as they screamed their inebriated joy.

Then they were at the door, upon which imperious knuckles rapped, to have it opened only a crack.

"Who's there?" asked a young woman, the sentence ending in a huge giggle of laughter.

"Your lord and master, come to claim what is his," was the reply, and with another shriek of mirth the door was thrown wide, and Jack was propelled into the room. Like all the rooms in this palace, the bedchamber was an enormous vault, high ceilinged and spacious, to permit air to circulate freely. Since it was still but three in the afternoon the shutters stood wide to allow what breeze there was to enter, but there floated in as well the enormous racket from the square, where the Negro slaves and the Christian Indians, given a holiday on this great day, were beating their drums and cymbals and blowing their flutes. The mosquito netting was still secured to the tent of the great tester, leaving its occupant exposed to the inspection of everyone in the room. Christina sat up against the cambric pillows, her hair spread around her like a black shawl. She wore a linen nightgown which came primly to her neck, and the sheet was folded across her stomach.

Her face was, as ever, composed and slightly watchful as she gazed at her husband, still being forced toward the bed.

"In with him," they shouted. "In with him."

The sheet was torn back, exposing Christina's ankles and feet, and the men gave a roar of delight. Jack was lifted bodily from the floor and laid on top of her, while in the same moment the sheets were whipped back over the pair of them and the pillows were pulled away. Christina's head went back onto the mattress with a thump, and his came down on top of hers, their cheeks clashing. But this only seemed to amuse the spectators the more, as they leaned forward to slap him on the shoulders and backside. He discovered his mouth against her ear. "My darling," he whispered, "I did not mean this. I did not know."

"Yet must you not fail them," she whispered in return, "or they will spend the day here with us. Nor will they be fooled," she added urgently as he commenced to work his body on hers in the semblance of passion.

Desperately he reached down, to find the skirts of the nightdress and pull them up. The crowd cheered. His own nightshirt was about his waist, and he could feel the warmth of her thighs against his. Yet the entry took him by surprise, it was so easy; he was harder than he had ever been in his life. With another wave of alarm he realized something that had never occurred to him—*he* was the virgin of the pair. And passion was mounting, as he had dreamed of such a moment for so long. With desperate anxiety he attempted to control himself, withdrew at the last moment and collapsed on her stomach, their bodies cemented by the still spurting semen.

Of which, happily, the crowd was unaware. That he had climaxed was obvious, however, and now Aunt Malina could at last drive them from the bedchamber, follow them to the door herself, and turn to smile at her charges and blow them a kiss before leaving them alone.

For some moments he remained still, afraid to move, afraid to raise his head and look at her, to face the reproach that would have to be in her gaze no matter how she had been forced to accept what custom had dictated.

Yet it had to be done, and soon he became uncomfortable. He pushed himself up, allowing the sheet to slide off his back, got out of bed without looking at her, went to the washstand, filled the basin from the china ewer, and washed himself, still with his back turned. But listening all the while to the rustle of movement.

"Leave some for me," she said softly, and at last he turned, to step backward in delighted consternation. For rather than soil her nightdress, she had taken it off altogether, and stood before him in utter beauty, her slight, still slim body superbly adorned with rounded pink-nippled breasts, and lower with a thatch of silky black hair, now glistening with water as she washed herself with the tremendous concentration which was her most attractive characteristic. Her legs and thighs were slender, her feet small and as perfectly shaped as the rest of her. And her midnight hair, loosed from its braids, fell to her waist.

She dried herself. "Why did you withdraw?" Her head was still bowed.

"I . . . I had done you enough injury," he said. "And besides, the baby . . ."

"Would not have suffered. I have consulted Father Luis on this matter." At last she looked at him, half smiling. "Now there must be a technical question as to whether or not the marriage has been consummated."

"I entered you," he said.

"Yes," she turned away from him and looked at the window. "What a tumult. They will keep it up all day and far into the night. And if we close the windows they will make even more noise."

"And we will suffocate," he said, keeping his hands at his side with an act of will.

"Yes," she said, and returned to the bed, to sit there, feet still resting on the floor. "I have never seen a man before," she said.

"But . . . Jamey . . ."

She shook her head. "It was in the dark, and we were not naked."

He frowned at her. "Do you mean it was only once?"

She nodded. "The night before he left. Would it have made any difference if you had known that?"

"No. None at all." His heart began to pound. Here then *was* something which he could claim for himself alone. Nor had Jamey possessed her any more than he now possessed her, for if she had not seen him, then his memory too must have been clouded by clothes and darkness. He took off his nightshirt and dropped it on the floor.

"You are very strong," she said. "Such muscles. But—"

"Also very spent." He sat beside her. "Which is all to the good, when I look at you."

Her eyes were more solemn than ever.

"You have naught to fear," he promised. "What happened this afternoon was forced upon us. I shall not intrude again. If you will just let me look at you from time to time, I shall be content, for I will have seen the most beautiful creature in the world."

"Do you then find me beautiful?" she asked.

"More beautiful than anyone I have ever imagined."

"At the table you said you loved me."

"I do. I will not lie to you, Christina. When I realized that you . . . had given yourself to my brother and that you were turning to me for help, I lusted after you. I have known no women intimately before you, but I have dreamed often enough. And I am not a good man, in my dreams, my lusts. But knowing you, understanding you, I realized how criminal I was being."

"You have saved my reason," she said. "Without you they would have shut me in a convent. Certainly they would have taken my child. I would have gone mad."

"You are my brother's wife, in all but name," he said. "I could do nothing less than protect you."

She frowned at him. "And you love me as your brother's wife?"

"No man could love you, Christina, save as what you are."

She got up, took a few steps toward the window, and half turned.

"I do not know about love," she said. "I know that you and your brother were two of the most splendid men I have ever met, and not merely because you saved all our lives. If I turned more toward Jamey, it was because he showed his feelings for me, he told me of them. But I do not know if I loved him when he came to my room that night. Yet he was being himself, Jamey Grant, a man at once more exciting and more . . ." Her shoulders rose and fell. "How shall I say it? A Portuguese gentleman might have come below my window, but it would have been to sing to me. He might have loved me, but he would never have told me so in words—he would have written me poetry. Jamey came to touch and to hold, and tell me in words what he felt, and what he wanted. He came to possess me. I think I knew that then. And I fell to his assault. Because it was the most exciting thing that has ever happened to me." She turned back to face him. "And I am not forgetting either the earthquake or the hurricane."

"He behaved like a scoundrel," Jack said.

"He behaved like a *man*. And then, then I tried to love him, because I felt that I must. I felt married to him, as you say. I could not allow myself to feel otherwise. I think . . ." She bit her lip.

"Go on," Jack said.

She sighed. "I think he is still the most exciting man I have ever met. But he is dead."

"And now you are prepared to settle for second best," he said with a touch of bitterness. And utter unfairness, as he immediately admitted. It was he who had proposed marriage.

Christina had not taken offense; he found it difficult to envisage her doing so. "Now I wish to start again," she said seriously. "And thanks to you I am being given that chance, without sacrificing anything of what I may remember, or have received." Her hand slid over her stomach. "Thus I am beginning my married life with extreme gratitude toward my husband, to whom I already owed my life. Is that not promising?"

He waited.

"He is also a man I have discovered to be kind and gentle and chivalrous, as well as brave and strong. I do not suppose there can be any *better* man in the world. I do not suppose my father could possibly have selected a better husband for me, however noble his title or ancient his family. I count myself the most fortunate woman in all the world."

"But love is a different matter." It was his turn to sigh. "I do not ask it of you, Christina. I will never do that. You have my word."

"But I will ask it of myself, Jack." She came back across the room, knelt beside him, her hands on his thighs, her breasts against his legs. "Because I wish to love you. And I know I shall. I ask only your patience with me. Not with my body, but with my mind. I wish to be your wife in every way. Thus I will learn to love you the sooner. But love me, Jack. Take me and love me. Make me happy. Give me joy. And I will give you joy in return. That is my oath to you, Jack Grant. That I will give you joy in return."

Chapter 5

"There, Mother, is it not a magnificent sight?" Jack threw his arm around Flora Grant's shoulders as he pointed at the sugarloaf, which seemed, from this distance, to rise directly out of the calm sea. "It marks your home."

"It is certainly remarkable," Flora Grant agreed, and Jack glanced hopefully at his sister. Mary at least was more excited, but there too he saw much uncertainty, much apprehension in her gaze, in her very movements.

The fact was, he had come to realize early on this voyage, they were now strangers. He had never imagined it would take three years for them to come together again. He had underestimated the slowness of the mails, which was at least partly due to the war with the French, and the length of time that the war would drag on. He had underestimated the desire for vengeance on the part of the British government, who despite the applications of the viceroy of Brazil, even when supported by his famous and powerful cousin in Lisbon, had steadfastly refused to pardon "the pirate Grant," as they described him, or to relax their Navigation Acts to permit the pirate's family to travel directly from New England to South

America. So passages had had to be arranged from Boston to Bristol and thence from Bristol to Plymouth and thence from Plymouth to Lisbon, each one attended by delays and bad weather, before the second, and far longer, Atlantic crossing could be undertaken. He did not doubt they had sometimes wondered if the entire upheaval had been worth it, especially after the news with which he had had to greet them in Lisbon.

It had, of course, been worth it. For Lieutenant Beresford had not been slow to publicize exactly what had happened on board the *Lodestar* that June day in 1761. Fortunately, the news that her husband had died and that her sons had undoubtedly been lost in one of the worst hurricanes to hit the Caribbean for several years had almost immediately been followed by the arrival of Jack's letter, but life had been hard enough for the next year, as Flora Grant had been delayed and humbugged at every turn by officials hoping that at least one of her pirate brood would attempt to return to Nantucket for her. For Flora, who had accepted her husband's smuggling as a gentle aberration, but who had never dreamed of a life outside the law once they had settled in the safety of Nantucket, this had been a terrifying experience, as Jack could recognize. It certainly accounted for his sister's continuous nervousness, for his mother's watchfulness, especially when taken in conjunction with their several long ocean voyages—Mary had never been to sea in her life, and Flora only once, during the flight from Scotland, pregnant and accompanying a husband with a price on his head.

And yet, Jack had come to realize early on this voyage, they had not changed so much. It was he who had changed, and they who were feeling like strangers. They had known a boy whose only art was the handling of a ship, and even that skill was only exercised with his father nearby. Otherwise, the Jack they remembered had been very much an innocent in the world of men and women. They found it hard to reconcile that memory with this broad-shouldered, sunburned man, who had now made the voyage from Rio to Lisbon and back eight times, who wore cambric shirts instead of homespun, who in Lisbon had had conversations with the great marquis of Pombal himself, who drank sherry instead of ale, and who even, from time to time, wore a sword. And who was a Roman Catholic. The very thought was anathema to a devout Presbyterian, and if the Grants had never been particularly devout while William Grant lived, Flora had found a considerable solace in attending the kirk since his death. In vain Jack had attempted jocularly to explain that Portuguese Catholicism contained nothing of the Spanish strictness. His acceptance into the Church had depended entirely on his ability to say the Hail Mary and the right version of the Lord's Prayer, to be able to recite the Apostle's Creed, and to cross himself. Flora and Mary had still found it difficult to become reconciled. In Jack's company they had stepped into a world with which they were totally unacquainted, and, he thought as he left their side to guide his ship through the narrows, they were about to enter an existence even more remote from anything they had expected.

The arrival of the *Lodestar* in Rio was always an event, for she was by far the most reliable means of sending goods and letters across the Atlantic; driven hard by her captain, she even maintained a certain schedule—the weather would have to be abnormally bad for her ever to be more than a week late. Added to that was the fact that she sailed with the viceroy's blessing, invariably carried his mail and official dispatches, and Jack's principal problem was which requests for space on board to refuse. Indeed he had already laid the keel of a new ship, which by the end of this year, he hoped, would take her place beside the *Lodestar,* could he but find competent seamen to crew her and a master to navigate her. Jack Grant, mate, had become Jack Grant, shipowner.

Now his approach had been signaled from the fort, and the dockside was crowded with people, slaves as well as owners. Arthur Conybeare, left behind to superintend the building of the new ship, towered above the Portuguese and the Indians as he strode up the gangplank. Here was a reminder of the past for Flora and Mary, but Conybeare also had changed; he wore a poncho and a broad-brimmed straw hat, and was so sunburned that he looked like an Indian himself. He was closely followed by the priest, who glowered at them ill-temperedly, even if he knew that, as Protestants, they had already been given the necessary clearance by the viceroy to land and take up residence.

Then there was a ride in the carriage through the city, to the outskirts and thence to Copacabana, for it was here that Christina had decreed her house should be built. And for the two women, more cause for concern appeared as they viewed the three-story mansion, with its deep verandas on every floor, its storm shutters neatly bolted back, its retinue of Negro slaves to greet them, contented-looking people, for Jack Grant was an indulgent master, and then, its mistress, standing at the top of the wide front stairs to welcome her mother-in-law.

He had possessed no portrait on board the *Lodestar* to show them, and any man will describe his wife, to a relative who has not met her, as beautiful and accomplished. Thus they had not, perhaps, truly prepared themselves for the woman with whom they were to spend the rest of their lives. At twenty Christina had reached her true beauty, which was but enhanced by her third pregnancy, only just beginning to show. She wore her hair up, as a European lady might have done before donning her wig, but in the tropics wigs were not in use, and instead she crowned her head with a white mantilla, the lace folds of which dropped past her face to either side to enhance the purity of her features. She awaited their arrival like a queen surrounded by her court, for little James, already standing sturdily at two years old, waited on her left, his Negro nurse immediately behind him, and baby William waited in the arms of another nurse, while Christina's two dogs, European mastiffs, panted obediently at her heels.

It was far too great an extension of imagination to suppose that this magnificent woman could possibly own to the name of Grant, possibly share her son's bed every night; Flora Grant stopped halfway up the steps and had to be urged on by Jack's hand on her arm. But she could hardly doubt the evidence of her own eyes as to their love, in the way they embraced, the slow warmth of their kiss, the eager squeeze of their fingers as a wife welcomed her husband home from an ocean voyage. Flora was overwhelmed by her own embrace into those sweet-smelling, aristocratic arms, and took refuge in dropping to her knees to embrace James.

"What a splendid child." She held him at arms' length. "Do you know, Dona Christina, he looks just like my Jamey did."

She raised her head as there was no immediate response. But Christina had summoned a smile. "No 'Dona' for you, Mama Grant," she said, and helped the woman back to her feet. "And why should he not look like Jamey, since he is a Grant?"

"Poor Jamey," Flora said, her course becoming tansparently clear; if Jack was lost to her, in his growth to manhood, in the splendor of his wife and her relations, she would spend the rest of her life in remembering Jamey, gay, charming, headstrong, belligerent Jamey. "I dream of him, you know. I cannot believe he is really dead. I *do* not believe it. I will not believe it until I am shown his body."

"Dear Mama Grant." Christina linked arms with Flora to walk her into the house. "It is three years. Even if he had somehow survived the capsize, he would have returned by now if he were alive. Besides : . ." She looked across Flora's head to Jack Grant, who read her meaning well enough.

If Jamey was alive, then God have mercy on them all.

In its slow approach to the water's edge, the tapir betrayed its innate caution, its suspicion of every ripple on the water, every shiver of every blade of grass. A cowlike creature, it was no predator itself, but rather lived on grass and roots which it unearthed with its powerful snout. Large and powerfully muscled, it feared only the most aggressive alligator, the most meat-starved jaguar; even the great constricting snakes, the anacondas and the boas, seldom attempted to digest quite so massive a meal.

Yet today the animal could scent danger, knew it lurked, without being able to discover where, without being able to identify its source. Here was a new menace that had entered the rain forests, a new terror, and yet water had to be drunk.

In the instant that it lowered its head to lap at the quiet brown liquid, the tapir stood absolutely still, and died.

The shaft of the arrow struck it just below the ear, with deadly accuracy, in the very place where the brain could immediately be penetrated; the animal dropped like a stone, only its head making a splash as it entered the water. Instantly the man left the shelter of the long grass and bounded across the soggy, muddy ground, discarding his bow as he ran. It was the dry season and the river had dwindled to less than half its normal flow; this was all to the good, since it also meant that the alligators would be in hibernation, waiting for the rains to return to awake them for another year. The hunter would be uninterrupted in his work, except by his mate.

They made a strange contrast as they knelt by the beast, far too heavy to be dragged to dry land and therefore having to be dismembered on the spot; besides, they could only carry a fraction of the meat. Thus their razor-sharp knife sought rib and shoulder and thigh, slicing through muscle and joint, removing the legs altogether.

The blood that stained their arms to the shoulders made little difference to the woman with her easy skill. She possessed copper brown skin, had lank black hair, short, heavily muscled legs, a long, somewhat plump, and disturbingly hairless body, concealed only by a hide apron which was less an indication of modesty than that she considered herself to belong to the man. Her heavy breasts sagged and her face was immobile, with heavy cheekbones seeming to rest on the thick jaw, compressing the wide lips into an expressionless line. Only the eyes, as black as her hair, darting to and fro as she sliced into the meat, indicated the alertness of her brain, just as her hands, wielding the knife, and only occasionally flicking at the flies which had immediately gathered above the carcass, showed a lifelong intimacy with the business of remaining alive, here in the most treacherous country in the world.

The man's movements were more deliberate, less anxious, just as they were less practiced. He had survived three years in this eternal swamp by determination rather than instinct, by a relentless application to the skills of existence where every man's hand was against him, and every woman's too, except for this one, as well as every living creature's claw and tongue and jaws and sting. That he would not have survived without the woman he was prepared to admit, at least to himself. It was not necessary to admit it to her, for she was well aware of it, and seemed content that it should be so, although from time to time he found that difficult to believe. Because if she was a long way from his ideal of feminine beauty, he must be equally unattractive compared to her ideal of male handsomeness, with his shaggy beard, which he only cut with a knife when it threatened to hamper his movements, his sun-leathered skin, which was still inclined to blister from time to time, and with his initial ineptitude at woodcraft. He had not even possessed the superior height so often to be found in the white man when compared with the forest Indian. Only in his amazing agility was he clearly her better.

Her name was Cali, so far as he could understand it, for even in three years they had progressed no further toward each other's languages than grunts and an occasional word—and without her he would certainly have died within a month of the disaster at the rapids. His memory of that month was dim; it was too mingled with the unforgettable journey that had preceded it. On the morrow of that tumultuous night with Christina, the night which had seen the realization of his dreams—all that would follow was merely consolidation—the expedition had left Rio in the flotilla of small boats which had been awaiting them, and crossed the Bay of Guanabara, leaving the city and the sugarloaf always astern as they had navigated the archipelago of islands which thronged this land-locked sea, until they had arrived at the Porto de Estrella marking the mouth of the River Inhomerin.

Here a convoy of seventy mules had waited, a tremendous caravan which had subdivided into groups of seven to negoti-ate the difficult trail and river crossing. Soon they had come to the boundary of the captaincy, where Minas Gerais began, and had had to produce their passes from the viceroy to avoid paying the duties to which all nonedible items were subject, and which were the biggest barrier to the development of Brazil as a single homogeneous colony. Then they had taken the treacherous road upward into the Mantequiera mountains, escorted now by a squadron of the Minas Dragoons, part-time soldiers whose main responsibility was to look out for diamond smugglers, but who were not above requiring a bit of bribery from even a caravan traveling under the auspices of the viceroy himself; by now Rio was a very long way away.

They had reached the high plateau at Igreja Nova, one of the earliest mining towns, where they had been beset by hordes of mulatto prostitutes, once among the wealthiest of their kind but now dwindling into destitution as the mines were worked out and their clients moved farther afield. Beyond the town the forests and the craggy peaks suddenly ended, and they had entered a prairie of gently undulating hills, mostly bare of trees and relatively pleasant to traverse. All had seemed optimistic, with the treasures of the Amazon basin only perhaps another few weeks away and the peaks of the Serra de Espinhaco already in sight. Here were the real gold mines of Minas Gerais, a series of shantytowns huddling close to the ore-bearing streams. Then, almost without warning, they had found themselves in the remarkable township of Vila Rica, sheltering beneath the peak of Itacolumi, and so high that it was often isolated above the clouds, subject to freezing nights and burning hot days. Here was a wonderworld, after the emptiness of the plain, where elegant two-story houses clung to the steep streets and flowers and vegetables, almost unknown on the steamy and termite-ridden coast, abounded. And here too were the evidences of the wealth which had been extracted from the surrounding valleys, churches in which all decoration and every chalice was made of beaten gold.

But here too were the limits of civilization; this was the true beginning of their adventure. From the northern foothills of the mountain range the San Francisco River ran north, into the province of Bahia, but the Amazon lay northwest, across the valley of the River Doce, where the Aimores Indians, whose reputation for ferocity had reached even the coast, were to be found. Now the faint hearts had spoken up, insisting that there was sufficient gold to be picked up in the mountains, however illegally, to make a return visit to

Igreja Nova well worthwhile. He and Conybeare had had to bully them into continuing across the plains once more, down into valleys and up onto another plateau, promising them that the Amazon was only another week away. They had seen little of the Aimores, which had added to their confidence, but by now they had seen enough fever and snakebite and scurvy to convince them that they would earn whatever they managed to bring back from the City of Gold, even if they avoided any conflict with the Indians.

And in time they had come to a river, rushing due north, onto which he had been incautious enough to launch his tiny force, having observed the ease with which the Indian dugouts negotiated the waters with which this vast country abounded. And for several days all had been well, until they had arrived at the mission. The priests had been pessimistic about their chances of proceeding much farther by water, and indeed about their chances of proceeding much farther at all. Out there, they had said, pointing to the northwest, is the Matto Grosso, the great forest. There is nothing, they had said, but snakes and alligators and savage Indians and death. He had been at pains to discount such talk to his already nervous people, pointing out that many would have laid wagers against their reaching even this far.

But the priests had been right, as he had understood in that tumultuous moment when his canoe had been seized by a force beyond human control, and a moment later he had been in the water, and his entire life had been ripped away in teeming disaster, causing all that had gone before, all that was happening now, to come together in a long rush of confused catastrophe.

He only knew he had been in the water for a very long time, whipped onward by the ever increasing current below the rapids, desperately clutching a paddle which was his sole means of support—he had had sufficient intelligence to understand that not even Jamey Grant would have been able to swim in that turbulent millrace.

Then had come the fall. He had not known it for what it was then, had understood only that there was a tremendous roaring sound, and an eternity of dropping through watery space, and then nothing. Yet he had survived. He supposed that for all his lack of consciousness he had somehow fought for life, used his arms and legs, and, incredibly, come to the shore. It was then that true uncertainty had begun. He had no idea how long he had lain on the bank of the river, half in and half out of the water; the proximity of the fall had at least ensured that he had been untroubled by either alligator or snake or piranha fish—any of those who had found themselves in the neighborhood had also been swept over the lip and had been far too concerned with their own safety.

He had no real idea of what had happened after that. His brain had been clouded with disaster. His expedition had come to a frightful end, and apparently he was the only survivor. The sensible thing for him to do was to follow the river back upstream, to the mission they had passed the previous week. But to do that would have been to admit his failure, to acknowledge that all of those who had insisted the jungle would prove too much for him had been right, and to accept that, by his own standards, Christina would remain out of his reach forever.

He did not remember actually making a decision. He had needed food and, armed only with his sheath knife, had sought it in the forest. He remembered eating berries, and vomiting, just as he remembered chewing bark. He remembered actually seizing some unsuspecting monkey and tearing it apart to stuff the raw meat down his throat, and again vomiting at the sight of the carcass, so like a human child's, lying on the ground.

At that moment he had known he was going to die, as he should have died in the river, a certainty confirmed when there had been a sudden hiss and a violent movement beneath his feet and a searing pain in his leg, immediately to be replaced by utter numbness. Then he had fainted, had only dimly been aware of the excruciating agony of his own knife biting into his tortured flesh, of the feeling that every last ounce of blood was being drawn from his body as tremendously strong lips had been applied to the crisscross incision to draw out the poison.

Then had come true unconsciousness, and raging, agonizing

fever, and the wildest of dreams, and eventually, a splatter of
water in his face to awaken him, screaming, supposing he
was still in the grip of the river, with the waterfall about to
carry him to tumbling death. Through the rainstorm, the
terror, the exhaustion of fear and illness, he had stared at
Cali, bending over him, raindrops pouring from her face and
hair.

She had, so far as he had been able to make out, been
pursuing him for several days, perhaps equally uncertain of
her ultimate intention. She was an outcast, driven from her
tribe for some crime he had been unable to ascertain, but
which had certainly been heinous, since it had cost her her
husband and family. Thus she had wandered into the forest to
die, as was the requirement of her people, and instead had
come across this white-skinned creature. He had no doubt that
her instincts had been to destroy something so strange—he
had seen her instincts at work often enough since. But that he
was of a species like herself, and a male version of it, had
soon occurred to her, and she subscribed to that primitive
belief which held that for a woman to survive she needed the
company of a man, however unlike any other man she had
ever known. Besides, he also knew that he was not entirely
inept. His ability to shin up a tree—there was no tree in the
world tall enough or bare enough to compare with the mast of
the *Lodestar* in a gale—whenever necessary, and his speed of
movement had perhaps convinced her that here was a creature
of the plains rather than the forests, and she valued him the
more for that, had indeed been afraid to approach him until
the bushmaster had struck.

Then she had saved his life. For her own purposes. He was
determined never to allow gratitude to obscure the true facts
of the matter. It had not been easy. For three weeks he had
lain and shuddered, for not even her rapid and efficient
surgery had been able to prevent some of the poison entering
his system. In those three weeks, apart from caring for him,
she had built a shelter beneath which he could lie, to protect
him somewhat from the rain and the sun, and she had hunted
with a remorseless efficiency he had only appreciated when
able to accompany her. Using his knife, she had carved

herself a bow and arrows, and had rubbed two sticks together to make a fire on which to roast the fish she seemed able to shoot even when they were swimming in the rivers.

Clarity of mind had come only slowly as the fever had abated, but eventually he had realized that he was after all alive, and that he would continue to live. He had seen little of the sky, so dense had been the treetops which clustered above his head, but when he had been able to move and to see the stars from time to time, his seaman's skills had informed him that he had, in fact, come far to the north of Rio. He was on his way, and he had with him the best of all possible guides and companions, someone who might even know of his destination, and who would certainly be able to lead him to it.

All that was necessary was to make her irrevocably his, and he knew of only one way to do that. So it was necessary once again to wait, on his health and strength, in the meanwhile smiling at her and even stroking her on occasion as she crouched beside him to feed him. That she understood his intentions was certain, for she smiled back from time to time. She was as far removed from what he would normally have expected in a woman as it was possible to imagine, from her habits, which were instinctive and unashamed, to her remarkable cleanliness, for she bathed herself at least once a day, and as soon as he could move encouraged him to do the same. But she was most certainly a woman, and he had not known a woman in too long. Thus even her savagery, when she would return to him with her hands still wet with blood and coated in fish scales, or her primitive curiosity, when she would finger his penis and indeed his entire body with childish inquisitiveness, had slowly made her the more attractive in his eyes, as the easy accessibility of her naked body had made him positively yearn—until the day when he had been able to sustain an erection and had rolled her onto her back, to her alarm.

Here was a case for mutual concern and rivalry. To be possessed while lying on her back was to her both unnatural and delightful; once she had discovered that he neither intended to strangle her nor crush her to death, she had wrapped her legs around his thighs with the power and intensity of the snakes she destroyed with such ease. On the other hand, once he had allowed her to teach him the normal Indian method of copulation, and had known the marvels of feeling the woman's buttocks thudding into his groin, the joys of penetration farther than he had ever imagined possible, the paradise of being able to fondle her breasts as a means of propulsion rather than as merely a caress, he had wished for nothing more. His imagination had been quite overcome as he had allowed himself to consider Christina de Sousa on her hands and knees, yielding herself to him.

Here was a sudden spur toward regaining his fullest health, a reminder of why he was out here in this green hell at all, of what would be awaiting him on his return. His decision to go northwest meant nothing to Cali. One direction was much like another to her. She had found her man, and now that he was again mobile he revealed, in addition to being able to love her, an ability to learn forestcraft, which had certainly surprised and pleased her.

Probably the most important thing he had learned from her, however, was patience. In the forest, to attempt to hurry was to fail, and failure often meant hunger, or even death. Thus they seldom covered more than two miles in a day, sometimes spent hours standing absolutely still in shallow water, arrows strung to their bows, waiting and watching for an unwary fish to come within range. In the beginning he was too unskilled ever to shoot. He merely stood and watched, while Cali struck with deadly accuracy.

Other hours were spent in traveling merely half a mile. Jamey endeavored to follow the angle of the sun, having worked out his course by an examination of the stars the previous night. But since this often led them through the thickest undergrowth, where tangled vines seemed to stretch from tree to tree in a deliberate barrier, Cali would cast around to find a more practicable route, in the general direction he wished to go. These diversions were irritating, but he soon understood their worth, for they prevented the utter exhaustion which would follow even a brief attempt to hack his way through the trees and bushes which seemed to grow before his eyes.

To Cali's forestcraft he was also indebted for avoiding the more dangerous snares of the jungle, for learning when he was likely to find himself in the midst of a seething mass of red ants; where bushmasters and rattlesnakes were likely to lurk; in what circumstances a tree might contain a boa constrictor or, near water, the boa's even more deadly cousin, the giant anaconda, which, in addition to wrapping its coils around its victim, would then take that victim to the river to add drowning to its weapon of strangulation, being itself equally at home submerged. And from Cali he learned where and when it was practical to cross the various streams which continually barred their paths; when a stretch of apparently calm water might contain a shoal of piranha fish, tiny creatures whose mouths were filled with razor-sharp teeth and who attacked in hundreds, able to strip a bull tapir to a skeleton in minutes and a human being, according to Cali's gestures, much more quickly than that; and also where the alligators, some of which grew as long as twelve feet, were to be found basking in the shallows or on the mudbanks. Dawn and dusk were the best times for tackling these fearsome creatures, since they seemed to absorb all their energy from the sun and were therefore at their most dangerous in the middle of the day, when they lay in apparent somnolence on the river banks yet were totally alert to the slightest movement, which might mean danger or food. But when the sun was gone they became sluggish and, even if willing to respond, had little of the devastating speed and energy of their noonday basks.

In addition to knowledge of this nature, which eventually enabled him to treat with contempt the deadliest of forest creatures, there was her domestic lore to learn: the way she would, whenever they were delayed by rainstorms or swollen river, bake clay jars, burying them in the earth until they hardened, to hold water, or plait a hammock from a handful of vines so that they could avoid sleeping on the wet ground. Or her fetishes, which led her to crush certain berries in order to extract a red dye with which she would stain herself whenever she began to menstruate.

There was no part of the forest which ever appeared as new

or strange to Cali, and he was encouraged to wonder if she had heard anything of either the Amazon or El Dorado. But of course the names were Spanish, and she responded to them with bewilderment. And he soon discovered that if the forest and its animal and reptile inhabitants had no terrors for her, she was not prepared to risk an encounter with any human predator. Discovering on one occasion a scar on the trunk of a tree which had clearly been made by a knife, she had shown the nearest thing to fright he had ever discovered in her, had insisted they retrace their steps for several miles before taking him on a lateral march to avoid the possibility of encountering the people who had marked that portion of the forest as their own.

Keeping track of time was very difficult, because time had no meaning except in terms of seasons. Their progress slowed even more when the rains came. Then the rivers rose with frightening rapidity, and more than once they had had to swim for it. It had been in the last wet season, the third since he had left Rio, that they had found themselves marooned for several months on what had gradually become a very small island, with dwindling food supply despite Cali's skill at fishing. Thus it was with relish that they had attacked the tapir when finally the water had receded, and they had been able to make their way once again ever northward, toward El Dorado.

But as rainy season succeeded dry season and they continued to head patiently north, even Jamey began to doubt that El Dorado actually existed—if anything existed except forest, stretching on and on and on into the eternal future.

His faith was in the river. But he knew the Amazon would be a river such as he had never seen and could not truly imagine, rather than the succession of streams and swamps that meandered across this never ending plateau. But the plateau did end, and with extreme abruptness, as they became aware that they were descending, constantly, day after day. Now for the first time Cali became concerned. She had been born and bred—and for all she could remember of the epics sung to her by her mother and the great warriors of her tribe, her people had existed forever—on the high plateau. Here was a world she had not previously suspected to exist.

Jamey was delighted. This could only be a river valley. Now the European in him reasserted itself, and he drove them on, through jungle so thick not even Cali had any experience of it, in a steaming heat which had even her pouring sweat. It was again the dry season; it was not possible to conceive what this country might be like when the rains came. All around them was water, always flowing to the northeast. And in here the great snakes and the alligators seemed to demand a new perspective on size. Nor were there any human traces at all to be discovered. Yet here, he *knew,* he would find El Dorado.

And it was here, suddenly, that they came upon the river.

They had been hacking their way through some particularly dense undergrowth, tearing the vines apart with their hands—Jamey's knife was now whittled down to scarcely a blade and had to be preserved entirely for gutting fish and butchering game—wading constantly up to their ankles in mud and through matted rafts of fallen leaves, desperately seeking somewhere dry to use as an encampment for the night, when entirely without warning Jamey parted the last leaf wall and stared at water. It drifted by, immense and brown, moving, like everything else, to the northeast, certainly the largest river he had ever seen. Cali was so overcome, especially since she by now understood that this was what they had spent the past four years seeking, that she fell to her knees in an attitude of prayer.

And yet he was aware of a strange mixture of disappointment and relief, as well as exhilaration. Disappointment because while this *was* the biggest river he had ever seen, it was not the immense flood of water he had imagined—he had to remind himself that it was the middle of the dry season. And relief because since this river was not much more than a hundred yards wide, it was not an insurmountable barrier, although swimming it was clearly out of the question.

But they were here at last, and he was sufficiently overcome to sweep her from the ground and give her a European kiss on the mouth, which plainly pleased her. Now the end was truly in sight, for El Dorado, according to Sir Walter

Raleigh and those others who had dreamed, and listened to whispered Indian legends, was situated in the high country to the north of the Amazon, but yet close to the river. Once across . . .

It took longer than he would have imagined possible. In the beginning he decided to seek a ford, and they spent weary weeks moving first downstream and then upstream, without success. By now the heavy dark clouds of the wet season were gathering, and he reluctantly accepted Cali's repeated warnings that this was no place to be when the river started to rise. So back they went, retracing their steps, to find land high enough to preserve them from the waters and large enough in area to supply them with food during the long months ahead.

They very nearly drowned for their pains. The wet season here in the valley was like nothing they had supposed possible. It was not merely the rain, which was no heavier than it had been on the plateau, but the fact that all the streams and rivers which had proved so dangerous when flooding up on the plateau apparently deposited their foaming waters down here, cascading over slope and precipice, sweeping away entire gigantic trees in their mad rush toward an access to the ocean. Jamey and Cali hastily had to seek higher ground, leaving the river some fifteen miles behind them, and even so were more than once crawling out of danger with the water swirling around their waists.

Then once again it was necessary to wait, an exercise in patience which became extended far beyond his anticipation when Cali became pregnant.

It was not something he had considered. She was no girl, that had been obvious from the beginning. But it had been impossible to determine her true age. He thought she might have had children before, and had lost them in the upheaval which had made her into an outlaw. But in the four years they had been together she had never until now become pregnant. Perhaps she had used some contraceptive method which he had not understood, but having accepted his obvious decision that their quest was virtually at an end, had relaxed her precautions.

He was horrified, and became angry. However much she might suppose that in some mysterious fashion when they reached the City of Gold they would there take up residence and live happily for the rest of their lives, he was faced with the consideration of transporting all that wealth back to Rio. It was the first time he had actually considered the situation. It was the first time, in fact, that he had actually faced the fact of the journey that would have to be undertaken, the days and weeks and months and years which lay between himself and Christina.

Christina. There was a distant memory. And an impossible one, now. In all reason she could not have been expected to wait this long, would certainly be married to some high-ranking hidalgo, might even have returned to Portugal with her husband. Which was all the more reason, he swore, to make his fortune and reappear one day the wealthiest man on earth, to make her and everyone else realize that he had been no idle dreamer, that he had, after all, been a man who would succeed.

And then, he thought, if he still chose, he could seduce her away from her husband, and still enjoy her. Not even Christina de Sousa would be able to resist the lure of the wealthiest man on earth.

But it was not a dream which could be realized alone, and to his disgust Cali refused to move, even when the rain ceased and the waters started to subside. His anger grew, and he beat her, with absolutely no result. She merely curled herself into a ball, as best she could with her growing belly, and waited for his rage to pass. But proceed she would not, and she also made it perfectly clear, by drawing on the earth, that she intended to feed the child before continuing her journey. Not that her condition in any way interfered with her expertise as a provider. She was merely obeying certain natural laws which she had known all of her life, and preparing too for the future, spending her leisure hours in carefully plaiting together a basket which she apparently intended to hook over her shoulders, so that she could walk with the baby strapped to her back. Thus encumbered, she would be absolutely useless for conveying any large amount of gold.

Yet continuing on his way without her was inconceivable. Even in so simple a matter as locating the right sort of tree trunk to use as a dugout canoe, and then in actually creating the craft, he was entirely dependent upon her expertise. He had never before found himself so completely at the mercy of another human being, and as the waters receded and the ground hardened, he would walk away from her through the forest—there was no risk of him getting lost now, at least—until he reached a vantage point where he could look out at the great river, now once again reduced in size to about a hundred yards in width, and reduce himself to tears in frustrated mental agony at the thought of the time he was wasting when El Dorado already lay within his grasp.

It was while perched disconsolately in the lower branches of a tree, gazing at the slow-moving brown waters, that he one day saw a canoe coming downstream toward him. It contained but a single occupant, who was using his paddle to do nothing more than keep the craft in midstream, allowing the current to do the work of propulsion for him. But alike from his dress and his complexion, however it had been exposed to the sun, he was very clearly white.

Jamey found it quite impossible to believe his eyes. Here was a man who, far from being naked like himself, wore a broad-brimmed straw hat, a shirt and pants, and whose canoe was obviously well filled with various packets and boxes which suggested European rather than Indian goods. Here, on the Amazon? A thousand miles and more from the most remote outpost of civilization?

"Ahoy," he shouted, swinging himself to a higher branch and waving his free hand. "Ahoy," he screamed. "Over here, senor. Ahoy."

The man certainly heard him, for he twisted his head, laid down his oar, and picked up a musket in the same movement.

Jamey searched his memory for the few words in Portuguese he had learned before his departure from Rio. "Don't shoot," he bellowed. "Friend. From Rio de Janeiro."

The canoe was now quite close, and the man was laying down his musket in favor of a telescope, with which he examined the tree and Jamey himself and the bushes to either side. Then with a few quick strokes of his paddle he turned the boat in and, with a few even more forceful strokes, drove it onto the shallow mudflats which bordered the river.

That done, he laid down the paddle and again picked up his musket. "Are you truly from Rio?" he asked.

Jamey slid down his tree and stood on the bank with his hands high to show that he was unarmed. "I am, senor," he said. "Would you by any chance know any words of English?"

The man frowned at him. He was, Jamey estimated, in his forties, but this estimate was based partly on the white streaks in his beard and the leathery quality of his skin rather than any suggestion of dwindling vigor. His black eyes were sharp and quick, and there was no gainsaying either the force with which he had propelled his canoe or the steadiness with which he leveled his musket. Besides, there was the mere fact of his survival alone in this wilderness.

"A little," he said. "Then you are not from Rio? You are an English adventurer?"

"By no means, sir," Jamey said. "My name is Grant and I am from Rio, although, alas, some years ago."

The man's frown deepened, but he slowly laid down his weapon. "Grant?" he inquired. "Not James Grant!"

"The same, sir."

"By our Holy Mother." The man crossed himself. "But you have been supposed dead these past five years."

"I assure you, sir, I am very much alive," Jamey said. "And if you would happen to have a bottle of Portuguese wine or the merest suspicion of a piece of cheese, I would be eternally grateful to you."

"James Grant," the man said in wonderment. He leaped out of the canoe, splashed into the shallow water toward Jamey, recollected himself and returned to the dugout to fetch a bottle of wine, and then came closer again, arms outstretched. "Carlos Brazao at your service, Mr. Grant. Why, sir, all Brazil mourned your untimely fate, just as all Brazil will rejoice at the news of your survival." He pulled out the cork with his teeth. "This is poor stuff, sir, to be sure, as it has spent several months in that canoe, but it is none the less drinkable.''

Jamey held the bottle in both hands, took a long swig, and felt the heat cascade through his system, set his brain alight, make him feel twice the man he had been only a moment before.

When he looked back at Brazao he saw that the man was continuing to gaze at him in total astonishment.

The Portuguese flushed when he was discovered. ''My apologies, sir, but really, to consider your survival at all, to see you, naked and unarmed in this forest, by this river, why, sir, I am convinced that I am in the presence of a miracle.''

Jamey took another swig of the rancid wine, then slowly lowered himself to sit, his back against a tree. ''Tell me,'' he said, ''what they say of me.''

''Why, sir, only that your entire expedition was destroyed at the San Jacinto rapids. There was only one survivor, a man named Conybeare, an Englishman like yourself, and it was he brought the news of the disaster back to Rio.''

''We happen to be Scots,'' Jamey said dreamily. ''Coneybeare, eh? Good old Conybeare.''

''But that was five years ago,'' Brazao said, ''and a thousand miles to the south of here. My dear sir, it is impossible.''

''I set out to find El Dorado,'' Jamey said, ''and am not a man easily to be turned from my purpose. It has taken me a great deal of time to travel this far, but as you have observed and remarked, I am alone and unarmed.'' He saw no immediate advantage in revealing Cali's existence to this man. ''But now that I am actually seated on the banks of the Amazon, why, I calculate that I am about to complete my quest. As you, senor, have perhaps anticipated me.''

Brazao gazed at him for some seconds, then gave a short laugh. ''El Dorado. Yes, I have heard of the legend, and of your interest in it. Believe me, senor, it *is* a legend. As for the Amazon, *pouf*, it would be better surely to approach it by sea, regardless of the difficulties, than by an overland route such as this. Even without the disaster at the falls, and with a full expedition at your back, you would not have accomplished more than this in five years, with as great a distance yet to travel.''

Jamey stared at him. ''But I am here. Am I not?''

''Here? This is not the Amazon, Senor Grant.''

Jamey stared at him, a great weight seeming to clutch at his heart and pull it down to his stomach. ''Not the Amazon? But this is a great river.''

''Of course. Brazil is a land of great rivers. Farther north, indeed, the land is known as Guyana, which means the land of many waters. But the Amazon, why, senor, that is the mother and father of all waters. This river is called the Araguaia, and with the confluence of several other streams it becomes the Tocantins and debouches into the Atlantic at Belem.''

''Belem?'' Jamey gasped, his mind surging with hopeless anger.

''Exactly, señor. And if you have heard of Belem, you will know that in some circles it is regarded as situated on one of the mouths of the Amazon. Now this is not proven, to be sure. I have used this route many times, up and down these rivers. Never have I ventured into the sandbanks and shoals that lie north of the city. But at least by using Belem and this river, I have approached within what one might call striking distance of the mother of waters, following upon a month's sail from Rio de Janeiro. Not . . .'' he allowed himself a brief smile, ''. . . after five years wandering in the woods.''

Jamey kept his expression calm with a tremendous effort. ''I studied maps . . .''

''Maps,'' Brazao remarked contemptuously. ''Composed by learned gentlemen who have never set foot outside their offices. Let me tell you, senor, that maps are meaningless in this country. I do not suppose I have ever seen the Amazon. I have heard of it. I have talked of it, with Indians and with others like myself, who have traversed these waterways and these forests. Imagine this, senor. You have come a thousand miles from Rio de Janeiro, and you are in the Araguaia. You are only halfway to the Amazon.''

''*Halfway?*'' Jamey shouted.

''And you have traversed the easier half, senor,'' Brazao

continued. "You have crossed the high plateau. Well, that is a remarkable feat of endurance and determination, for a lone white man. What you must have suffered is written on your face. But ahead of you lies the Matto Grosso, the great forest, of which *no* man knows the truth. There may well be a City of Gold hidden within those leafy mansions. But I will tell you this, senor, you have accomplished nothing yet. That plateau you have crossed? There is another ahead, within fifty miles of this river. Those mountain peaks you have seen? There are higher yet in front of you. This valley? You will have to cross many such. And when you come to the Amazon, what then? El Dorado is north of it, they say. Have you any conception of the Amazon, senor? It is not a river. It is a moving sea, a vast brown waterway, with all the drawbacks of a river—the current, the sandbanks, the alligators, and the sting fish—but with the breadth and the volume of water of an ocean. No, no, senor. When you come to the Amazon, if you ever come to the Amazon, you will know it."

Jamey had a sudden urge to strangle the man there and then. His contempt no less than his experience and knowledge were equally odious. But he kept his temper with an effort and finished the last of the wine.

"So you would approach the problem in another way," he said.

"Of course." Brazao sat beside him. "Especially if I were Senor Grant, with the ear of the viceroy himself, and a stout ship at my disposal. I would first of all return to Rio and equip my ship for the rigors of an ocean voyage, but with certain extra features as well—great sweeps to combat the current, and a shoal draught to pass over the sandbanks. It is possible to make the entire journey from Rio in fine weather on an undertaking of this nature. It will not matter if you have to spend a day or two in port waiting for a favorable wind, eh?" He chuckled. "After all, you have spent five years in attempting to penetrate these forests."

Once again Jamey felt a surge of pure hatred overtake him. But this man was useful.

"Go on," he said.

"Well, senor, then I would make for Belem. Now, as I

have said, Belem is the mouth of the River Tocantins. But as you have heard of it, you will know that it is also a part of the coast where the sea is discolored with mud for several miles offshore. Now, senor, not all that mud can be brought down by the Tocantins alone. It is my belief that the area north of Belem is all part of the estuary of the Amazon, and that the great river has several exits, instead of just one. I know that it has been explored, and the exploration abandoned because of the sandbanks, the treacherous currents, which have brought many a good ship to grief. But senor . . ." again he chuckled, ". . . if you have been prepared to spend five years wandering in the jungles, you will be prepared to spend perhaps a year charting the estuary of the Amazon, eh?"

I shall kill this man, Jamey thought, if it is the last thing I ever do.

"Have you another bottle of wine?" he asked.

Brazao hesitated. "Another, certainly, senor. It was to help me on my way. From here it is yet six hundred miles downriver to Belem. Even with the current, that is a considerable journey. But since you are the viceroy's friend, and more than that . . . we shall drink it now. Very probably it will have gone sour in any event."

He waded through the shallows to his canoe, found the bottle, and returned again. Jamey watched the movement of the boat, the supplies that were obviously lying in the bottom. There seemed to be a great deal of them.

"And having discovered a way through the shoals, what then?" he asked. "How will my ship proceed upriver?"

"Well, senor," Brazao said, sitting down beside him once again and removing the cork from the bottle. "It is not as difficult as it might seem, at least in the early stages. Of course the river flows downstream, toward the sea, but sluggishly. With an easterly wind, and you will know that they are not so rare on this coast, it is possible to sail faster than the current. And once within the estuary, I have no doubt at all that there is deep water. I know something of the native tongues about here, senor, and I can promise you that the river is probably navigable, four, five hundred miles above the estuary."

"Five hundred *miles?*" Jamey asked incredulously.

"Why not, senor? All this country is on such a scale."

Jamey drank some wine. "You have traveled so much and learned so much, but you have never attempted such a journey yourself."

Brazao laid his finger on his nose. "Ah, senor, I dreamed, when I was young like yourself. I had read the books and heard the legend. But I . . . I have no such backing as yours. I came to Belem, and I struck upriver, because like you, I had no idea of the distances involved and foolishly supposed that by approaching the headwaters of the Araguaia I would also be approaching the headwaters of the Amazon. I sought my El Dorado, my friend. And never found a city of gold. But I found enough for my own needs."

"Enough of what?" Jamey asked.

Brazao gazed at him for several seconds. Then he said, "There is not only gold to be found in these forests, Senor Grant."

"But is there anything as valuable?"

"Not ounce for ounce, perhaps. But there are equally valuable metals, when you consider the ease with which they can be obtained." He got up. "I will show you, in confidence."

Jamey followed him through the shallow water to the canoe, and watched as the cloth was rolled back over the panniers beneath, to leave a mass of shimmering white grains and globules.

"Silver? By Christ . . ." He dropped to his knees, dug his fingers into the precious metal. *"Silver?"*

"There is a mountain of it, not a week's journey from this river, on the northern side."

Jamey rocked back on his heels. "But . . . how?"

"How? Oh, by accident, my young friend. As I have told you, I also searched for my El Dorado, in my time, many years ago. Then I found my silver mine, and I have used it ever since. It is a secret known to me alone."

"But . . . how do you find it, time and again?" Jamey asked.

Brazao smiled and winked. "I made a map." He tapped his chest. "It never leaves this pouch I wear about my neck."

"And you would share this secret with me?" Jamey asked.

"Ah, well. . . ." Brazao took back the bottle and drank. "I suspect that I have saved your life, Senor Grant. However well you have managed to survive these last five years, and looking at you I do not think it has been so *very* well, the jungle will get to you eventually. Now, senor, I will give you passage in my canoe down to Belem, and from thence you will obtain a ship back to Rio. I will tell you frankly, senor, that while I have managed to remove a considerable amount of silver from my mine over the past ten years, there is still a mountain of it waiting to be tapped. But I have lacked both the capital and the ear of officialdom, to remove it. For what would happen if I were to make my find known? Immediately the government would move in with its customs officials, and my profit would be reduced to nothing. But, senor, I will confess to you that as we have talked this morning, it has occurred to me that if I involved the viceroy himself in the ownership of my mine, well then all things might be possible. And since you are almost the viceroy's son-in-law—"

Jamey frowned at him. "The viceroy's son-in-law? How did you know of that?"

It was Brazao's turn to frown. "Well, senor, since your brother *is* the viceroy's son-in-law, father of his many grandchildren—"

"My brother?" Jamey shrieked.

"Did you not know, senor? My God, it must have happened after your departure. Oh yes indeed, Senor Jack Grant is married to the beautiful Dona Christina, and by her is a father three times over. Or was, when last I was in Rio. No doubt the happy family is increased several times since then. Well, sir, you can see that with such backing—"

"Jack? And Christina?" Jamey whispered.

"A lovely pair, senor. Well, rumors were not lacking, as you may well imagine. But then, as it was put about, your brother rescued the beautiful senorita from a watery grave, and who shall argue about that. . . ."

"My brother?"

"Is that not true, senor? It was certainly put about. And a

man who had accomplished so much may well be permitted to accomplish that much more.''

"You say they have children?" Jamey demanded. "The firstborn? How old would he be?"

"Well, senor," Brazao took refuge in his bottle. "A premature birth, certainly. That is what all true gentlemen believe, and I, sir, am a true gentleman. But it matters naught. The fact is, senor, that you are connected with the viceroy by marriage, and your brother has three fine ships at his disposal and the wherewithal to build others. Certainly he could supply one especially for such a voyage as you contemplate. And add to that a share in my silver mine, which will defray all possible costs, well, senor, you will understand the drift of my thinking.''

"My brother," Jamey muttered. "And Christina. And several times a father.''

"On the other hand, sir," Brazao said, studying Jamey's expression, "if you would prefer to follow your own cause, pursue your own mad quest, well then, sir, you have my blessing to be sure." He smiled. "I will even give you a piece of cheese to see you on your way. And if you wish it, a garment to hide your nakedness.''

Jamey gazed at him, all the hatred and frustration and anger and misery of the past five years bubbling within him.

"So, senor," Brazao smiled. "Will you come with me to Belem and thence to Rio? You can be my protegé, and I will make you a wealthy man." He chuckled and slapped Jamey on the shoulder. "I will make you the equal of your brother, eh?"

Jamey seized him around the throat.

Chapter 6

The sun, huge and red and round, peeped above the surface of the Atlantic Ocean, sending rosy fingers of light darting toward the western horizon, playing across the immensity of the sugarloaf mountain, turning the sand of Copacabana pink with the promise of another ecstatic day.

This was the time Christina Grant loved best. Looking out across the sea, she often imagined she would be the first to sight the *Lodestar* on her way home. She never had. But this would be an important sighting. Tomorrow was her birthday, and Jack had never missed one before.

She swept the horizon with her telescope, while her horse and her grooms waited patiently. But the sea was empty. She closed the telescope with a snap, turned her horse, walked it back across the beach. Tomorrow she would be thirty years old. An unimaginable age for a woman, and especially for Christina de Sousa. She seemed to have lived all her life before she had reached the age of eighteen. Since then her existence had been one of complete tranquility, of successful motherhood, of unfailing health, of happy wifedom—or perhaps, she thought darkly, contented would be a more appropriate word—of increasing wealth and popularity and worldly prosperity.

And of boredom? But this was not something she would admit even to herself.

She had become a matron, without realizing it. Marriage to a man like Jack Grant required a matron, a woman capable of matching his steadfast progress, through both age and challenge to a complete command of himself and his affairs. She had once estimated him to be the finest man she had ever known. She saw no reason now, after twelve years of marriage, to change that opinion in the slightest. Nor, she supposed, did anyone else. The upstart had become one of Rio's wealthiest and most respected men; for all his prosperity, for all his social stature, he yet insisted on commanding the flagship of his fleet himself, still thrice yearly made the voyage to Lisbon and back, content to leave his affairs in the hands of Arthur Conybeare and of his wife. Presumably there had been eyebrows raised at that. Perhaps eyebrows were still raised as she made her way to the shipping office every day, checked through bills of lading and orders, inspected cargoes herself, even climbing down into the nauseating bilges to kick rats and weevils aside as she examined timbers for evidence of deterioration. The emotion was pure envy, she knew. Envy that she, the girl they had all envied in the first place, for her beauty and her wealth and her fame, should not only have married well, despite the head shaking and the whispered comments, and not only been blessed with a regiment of beautiful children, and not only retained her wealth as well as her looks, but should also have been allowed by an indulgent husband to involve herself in his business affairs; this was really far too much for any single human being to enjoy, tied as most of her rivals were to their children and their backache, their termite-ravaged gardens and their listless servants, their vapors in the dry season and their influenzas in the wet.

She was the most fortunate woman on earth, certainly in all Brazil. So what devil kept crawling into the back of her mind, to suggest that she might wish to exchange it all if only her husband would once lose himself in a night of passion, and lower his head to kiss between her legs? But if such desires *were* inspired by the devil, then was she to believe that it was the devil, and not God, who had sent someone to fulfill such dreams, before immediately whisking him away again, to send him to a watery grave?

She had even supposed, after the fates of Miguel de Castro and Jamey Grant, that she was some sort of human black widow spider and that any man who sought to worship at that fount was doomed. Now she knew better. Or was it merely that Jack Grant could triumph over even a black widow spider?

She cantered toward the house, up the twisting drive of palms with pineapple plants at their roots, dismounted before the curved staircase, reins thrown to the waiting Negro groom, and climbed the steps with vigorous strides. The housemaids and footmen, all Negroes, gathered to greet her as she walked past them toward the chapel, and she gave them each a smile. They were her friends—sometimes, she thought, her only friends. She was an indulgent mistress who commanded the use of the whip only in extreme cases of insubordination or dishonesty. Some suggested that she might get more pleasure out of life in being more severe; such were the depths to which bored humanity would descend when placed in control of its fellows. But such a course was not for her.

Father Alfonso waited for her, as he had done every day for the past ten years. His expression was tired, even at half past six in the morning, due mainly to the nature of the confession he was about to hear, which would be meaningless. Father Luis had warned him of this when he had taken the position. "Dona Christina," the viceregal chaplain had said, "is at heart a heretic. She believes she has a special relationship with God and gives no more than lip service to the Holy Church. She will never tell you what she is thinking, even if it is sinful. And I can tell you, Father, that her thoughts are nearly always sinful."

Nor *had* she ever confessed her thoughts, however often he threatened her with eternal damnation. Once, indeed, in an excess of zeal, he had prescribed a whipping, with every intention of inflicting it on her lovely body himself. But she had merely looked at him, and the expression in her eyes had made him hastily change the penance to a dozen Hail Marys.

Since that day, when he had realized that she knew *his* secrets, he had been her devoted slave, however frustrating he found such a position.

Her confession completed, Christina climbed the inner stairs and marched along the gallery to her own apartments, surrounded now by her personal maids. The house remained quiet; there was little chance of the children being around at dawn. Perhaps, she thought wryly, she was also too indulgent a mother.

But it was this time of the day, indoors as much as out, that she loved most. Now the house was entirely hers—*her* house, which she had designed herself just as she had chosen the wood and listed the draperies and furnishings to be sent from Lisbon. It was her challenge to maintain it in its dark wood splendor, leading the daily battles against the termites that would gnaw away at the pillars and joists, the spiders—more often than not the great hairy monsters which the Indians called tarantula and whose bite could introduce a virulent fever—which gathered in the corners, the scorpions which lurked in the laundry baskets and amid her linen drawers, the cockroaches which prowled incessantly, eager to discover the slightest morsel of food left uncovered, and even the snakes which sometimes coiled their way up the various staircases when the ground outside became too sodden for comfort. It was a losing war, she knew. Even supported by a horde of servants, she was no match for the greater hordes of insects which assailed her. But it was a war she would not lose without a fight, and into which she had recently introduced a new and fearsome element, her seven cats, which, if by no means equipped to combat the ants, dealt with most other intruders with a deadly crackling of teeth.

But today the battle would have to be commanded by Antonio, her head butler. Today the mistress would be busy. Mother Luisa was coming out from Rio this morning with the final fitting for the dress she would wear tomorrow, for the day was to be spent at her parents' estate in the foothills of the Mantequiera mountains. Since his retirement as viceroy

six years ago, Pedro de Sousa had turned to farming on a
large scale, grew several thousand acres of sugar cane and
almost as many of tobacco, maintained a vast stable of horses, and pastured several hundred head of cattle. With his
wealth and his royal connections he remained the true arbiter
of Rio society, however much Rodrigo de Andrade might
now possess the authority as viceroy. And his daughter's
birthday, especially her thirtieth birthday, was not an occasion to be allowed to pass without an enormous celebration,
toward which at this moment no doubt everyone who counted
himself or herself anything in Brazil was solemnly trooping.

And for which her husband had not yet put in an appearance.

Christina sighed, and stood by the window to allow her
maids to strip off her sweat-dampened garments. From here
she looked down on the unending struggle to maintain a lawn
containing more grass than pitted red earth, on the shrubs and
flowers she had spent·years attempting to organize into the
topiaried paths she remembered from her childhood, at the
small army of machete-bearing boys and girls—the children
of her domestics—who squatted and chipped away at the
weeds which constantly threatened to obliterate the entire garden. Beyond this other eternal battle were the stables for her
horses, and then the slave barracoons, orderly rows of low
two-room huts, from whence those who tended the tobacco
plantation went out to work every morning. She saw no
reason why she should not be in business on her own account;
her tobacco crop was good, and was always sure of a place on
one of her husband's ships.

She felt blessed relief as the corset was at last removed and
she could feel the soft morning air, which blew off the land
until the heat again drew it in from the sea toward noon,
caressing her flesh. She turned away from the window to
scrutinize herself in the mirror, as she did every morning,
frowned at the red marks where the corset had pinched, at the
traces of prickly heat which gathered beneath her breasts. She
had put on weight over the past few years, and besides, she
had mothered and briefly fed four children. Yet unlike so
many of her compatriots, she had maintained herself with
utter determination, always wore a corset when abroad, lim-

ited her drinking to not more than four glasses of wine a day
and her eating to a single course except when actually enter-
taining. Thus the ravages of age and life in the tropics had not
yet assailed her noticeably. The impression she gave now was
one of voluptuousness, a word that would never have been
used to describe her in her youth. Judging by the evidence of
her various acquaintances, it was, alas, merely a stage between girlhood and obesity, but it was one she was determined to maintain for as long as was humanly possible. Thus
the spartanness of her diet, her insistence on long rides and on
being her own plantation manageress just as she was Jack's
head bookkeeper. And thus, too, her refusal to countenance
even the slightest flirtation, much less the affair which appeared to be so dear to the heart of every married woman in
Brazil.

These women could not understand such chastity, especially when practiced by the most beautiful woman in the
colony, and one whose husband spent half of every year away
from her side. The young caballeros who wrote her poetry
and gazed longingly into her eyes at supper parties could
understand it even less. Here was an utter delight going to
waste. It wasn't as if she hadn't given her husband the best
she had to offer—twelve years of love and four children.
Surely, their letters and poems whispered, it was time to grant
some other man the ultimate happiness, and even seize some
of it for herself.

The maids wrapped her in her dressing robe and sat her in
front of her dressing table to brush her hair. Now she could
study her face. She did not suppose that had changed at all,
was as serious and composed as ever she remembered. it. Her
would-be lovers thought her cold. But with the possible ex-
ception of Father Alfonso—who was in love with her himself—
there was no one in all the world, not even Jack, who
suspected anything of what went on behind those deep black
eyes. Least of all Jack. Theirs had been a continual love
affair, enhanced by his absences, and yet they had never,
throughout all these twelve years, progressed toward true
intimacy. She had no idea how to go about it, had never
considered that it would be necessary. Her schoolmates no

less than her duennas—even poor Aunt Malina, who was dead now—had outlined for her the true course of a Portuguese marriage. Her husband would be considerably older than herself, would introduce her to his version of sexual intercourse, which might be boring or vicious or perverted, according to the man, and by whom she would have her appointed number of children, after which she would be free to choose a young lover and teach *him* the arts she had suffered at the hands of her husband. It was, they had said, an inevitable process, like birth and death, and woe betide the woman who attempted to break the chain.

Marriage to a man only three years her elder had not been considered, and when she had been betrothed to Miguel de Castro her friends had been amazed and titillated, unable to contemplate what might happen when a *young* husband came to her bed. Well, she thought, they would be amused to know how little. Jack was a vigorous man, who certainly worshiped at the shrine that was her body. But because of his New England upbringing, in which, she had learned, sexual matters had been very much taboo, and because of his long absences, his love pursued an even, predictable, admirable, and wholly uninteresting path. He held her in his arms with all the passion of a man who loved, he entered her with gentle insistence, and never once in their marriage had he induced within her any sensation even approaching the touch of his brother's lips.

But since he did not know of that kiss, he did not know how much she yearned for a hint of that ecstasy she had known but once in her life. Nor was she in a position to tell him. She did not suppose, as she had feared in the beginning, that after twelve years Jack might still be jealously angry of something his brother had achieved and he had not. She simply had no idea how a woman went about telling her husband that she *knew* there was more to sexual intercourse than he had ever provided. Certainly not when that husband was Jack Grant.

There was no help to be had either. Mama would never have understood a desire like hers. She had no other true friends. To discuss the matter with Father Alfonso would be

disastrous. And while she enjoyed listening to the prattle of
the maids, and how they and their various men friends had
made "sweetness" the night before, and even from time to
time allowed herself a knowing smile, she was not about to
place herself in the power of a servant by inquiring just how a
man and a woman arrived at that happy state.

So why not indulge herself and take a young lover? There
was little risk of Jack ever finding out; the slaves would all be
delighted, and would certainly lend her their support. There
was, of course, the risk of being disappointed, and having to
start all over again. There was also the risk of syphilis. It was
as prevalent in all of South America as the common cold. But
this was a hazard most women seemed to be prepared to risk,
and most men positively to court—a lover without syphilitic
scars was scarcely to be considered a man, according to the
gossips.

There was also the simple question of being unfaithful to
Jack. She did not suppose morality entered into it at all. If it
did, there could not be a single Portuguese lady within living
memory, not excluding Queen Maria Anna, who could in any
way ascend to heaven. Rather it was a question of trust,
because Jack undoubtedly trusted her in every way—as the
mother of his children, as his business manager, as his lover,
and most of all as his friend. *He* might never be aware that
she had betrayed him, but would the knowledge of it not
affect *her?* And yet this point of view could be countered
with the suggestion that if she were to find a lover able to
awaken her senses as Jamey had done on that one tumultuous
night, she might prove a better mate to Jack than she had so
far been.

As for love, that did not really enter into it either. She
loved Jack as much as any wife could love her husband. She
was sure of it. Sexual passion, or lack of it, had nothing to do
with that. Again she was quoting from her many married
acquaintances.

But most important of all, taking a lover would mean, she
had no doubt, giving up her essential *self,* her independence
of mind. Jamey would have wanted her soul as well as her
body. She had known this at the time, and in the fervor of the

moment had been prepared to accept such a surrender. Besides, at seventeen, it had not seemed so important.

Jack had never asked so much of her. He had clearly been both delighted and relieved that she had not held him to his offer to make theirs a barren marriage, but had never encroached further upon her privacy. He shared his thoughts with her because it was his nature and because he trusted her. He had never demanded any confidences in return, had been content just to know she was *there*, waiting for him. A young lover, and certainly one who could bring her to orgasm, would want more. Worse, she might wish to give him more, in the ecstasy of the moment, the joy of afterward. So much sharing, in a relationship which very probably would be transient, was unthinkable.

Her maids were satisfied now with the straightness and neatness of her hair, and she was ready for the morning, in a simple house gown and with her feet bare. For if she insisted upon dressing better than any of her acquaintances when out of doors, within the house she sought coolness and comfort as much as they, did no more than reconcile it with decency. And it was time for the children.

So, once again, her delightfully wicked dreams were relegated *to* the sphere of dreams, no doubt to be resumed tomorrow morning. Unless in that time, pray God, the *Lodestar* made port.

The children's bedrooms stretched away from hers in reverse order of seniority, as she considered they might require her. Thus Anthony, her youngest at five years old, was in the room closest, and slept happily, his arms around a stuffed lion, his nurse rocking gently to and fro in a chair by the window. Like all her children, he was a healthy boy, giving every promise of being as tall as his father and as robust as well. She was undoubtedly blessed, which was but, in her opinion, another example of that mutual understanding and trust she enjoyed with her God, and which was not to be shared with any confessor.

Having been delivered of Anthony, and having spent seven years in either carrying or feeding, as was her duty as a wife and a Catholic, she had decided enough was enough. In this matter she *had* consulted Morella, the cook, a large black woman who was regarded in total awe by the rest of the slaves, as she was reputed to be a mamaloi, a priestess of the West African cult of obeah, witchcraft. This was both extremely un-Christian and very dangerous, because Portuguese law, while entirely lax regarding crimes against the person—even such offenses as rape and murder could be atoned for by the payment of a fine—reached back into its barbaric past in such matters as witchcraft, for which death was the only acceptable penalty for all concerned.

But in Brazil even this draconian law was seldom invoked; there was not a lady in a "big house" who did not rely upon her maids for contraceptive devices or, far more heinous, for love potions either to reject or attract the requisite man. Morella had had no difficulty in coming up with a tonic which, taken regularly, had certainly protected her mistress since Anthony's birth. In this, of course, Christina was well aware that she was not only dabbling in the occult but also breaking the Church's law on contraception. She refused to accept, however, that it could possibly be God's intention that she should go on bearing children until she died of exertion. There was too much left to be done with her life—if only she could discover what it was He had in mind for her. But that He had *something* in mind she never doubted for a moment. It was the rock upon which her entire existence was founded.

But Anthony, as her youngest, occupied a very special place in her heart. She stood above the bed for some seconds, smiling through the mosquito netting, before recalling that he too had a new suit of clothes to be fitted today.

"You'll wake him," she said to the nurse. "There is much to be done."

Inez, in the next room, was nine, a strange child, because while her three brothers were all dark-haired, as they should be with such parents, her hair, long and straight like her mother's, was streaked with red, an amazing phenomenon which was undoubtedly a throwback to some Scottish ancestor, and which redoubled her already burgeoning beauty—she certainly took after her mother in features. She was already up, sitting at her desk in her nightgown and drawing, which was her principal pleasure, while her nurse was remaking the bed and gathering the mosquito netting into its linen bag beneath the tent.

Christina never doubted that Inez was going to provide her with the companionship she presently lacked, when the girl was older. They already shared an indefinable intimacy of thought and mood, and the girl's artistic interest, and her very real talent, suggested that they would share an equal intelligence. But that was in the future. For the moment it was a relief that there were no problems to be considered regarding this one of her children.

"You'll not forget that Mother Luisa is coming out today," she said. "I expect her about eleven."

"Yes, Mama," Inez said, and turned up her face for a kiss.

William was eleven, and her son to his last drop of blood, smaller than the other children for his age, deeply serious, and as secretive as she had ever been. He sat up in bed reading an enormous volume of *Don Quixote*, profusely illustrated, which his father had brought back from Europe for his last birthday, and which Christina knew he had read at least once before from cover to cover.

"Time to get up," she said. "Come along, Billy. Mother Luisa is coming at eleven."

"Yes, Mother," he said patiently, and closed his book with a sigh. His grandfather was of the opinion, in view of his scholarly leanings, that he should go into the church. Only she and Jack knew better, in that only they knew that he was actually Jack's eldest child. They had determined, and promised each other, that James would always be regarded as theirs, and that legally he would be their firstborn, and she knew that Jack would never agree to *his* firstborn taking the tonsure. There were problems ahead in that direction, to be sure.

But none which could not be solved to everyone's satisfaction. She had never previously encountered such a problem, anyway, not even with James. She hesitated outside his door for a moment, because he, of course, no longer slept with a

nurse in the room. Indeed, he no longer possessed a nurse at
all, but instead a companion—as was normal with Brazilian
boys—a mulatto lad a year his elder who was required to
accompany him everywhere and see to his clothes and his
amusement. Jorge was a splendid boy, big and strong, the son
of a black woman who had been deserted by her Portuguese
sailor lover, a sober lad who was even able to cope with the
varied moods of his young master.

For James was, undoubtedly, Jamey's son. This was only
truly apparent to his parents, and possibly, Christina thought,
to his paternal grandmother, although *she* regarded it as a
happy family quirk. That he was small was no problem,
because his brother William was also small—clearly they
both took after their mother, the gossips were forced to
suppose. It was in his moods, his restlessness, his outbursts
of sudden anger, his wild dreams, that he made it clear he
was not Jack's child. Easily bored, he would certainly not
take kindly to being exposed to Mother Luisa's fussing for
very long.

Very gently Christina opened the door. The room was in
darkness since the drapes had not yet been drawn, and it was
obvious that James was still abed. She did not usually disturb
him this early; she did not usually disturb him at all, but left it
to him to decide when he would begin the business of the
day, as befitted the eldest son.

She crossed the room and drew the drapery, turned back to
face the bed, and felt her breathing constrict in utter consternation. Because of the warmth of the night, James had kicked
back his covers, and it was easy to see that beneath the
mosquito netting there were two naked bodies, and one of
them was black.

"Many happy returns."

"How lovely you look today, Dona Christina."

"How lovely you *are,* Dona Christina." This remark came
from young Henry de Carvalho, her cousin, who was the
most prolific of the writers of the sonnets which found themselves on her desk.

"You never age, my dear," said his mother acidly, taking

in the three children standing beside her with a glance. "James is not well?"

"No, James is not well," Christina agreed, with quiet determination.

"Poor child," Dona Isabella remarked. "And with his father away, and on such an occasion. . . ."

"Jack will be here, I am sure, Aunt Isabella," Christina said, keeping her composure with an effort. "There have been contrary winds, no doubt."

"No doubt," Isabella de Carvalho agreed, and continued on down the reception line.

"Dona Christina." Henry de Carvalho's brother, Thomas, kissed her hand and then her cheek. "We do not see enough of you."

"You are seeing me now, Thomas." Christina squeezed his hands and presented her cheek to his wife, Mary. Jack's sister had married well, at least publicly. Whether the marriage had been so successful privately was another matter. The American girl had lost a lot of her vivacity since moving into the Carvalho home, and clearly found her overbearing in-laws a little difficult from time to time. And what of her soldier husband, who had been Jack's best man at their own wedding? Thomas de Carvalho was not the sort of man to share. And his wife's face had taken on a haunted, apprehensive look.

But, Christina reflected as she kissed the two small children presented to her by their nurses, at least she had a family, so their marital relations could not be all that bad.

Flora Grant came last. Since her daughter's marriage, she had chosen to move to the de Carvalhos' estate rather than remain at the Copacabana one. She had never really approved of her daughter-in-law, Christina thought regretfully. But *she* had no regrets that Flora had moved, especially now. Her mother-in-law's Scottish rectitude had presented difficulties from the start; oddly, when she was behaving like a puritanical mother herself, she had no desire to share her problems with another. But apart from her inability to cope with what she regarded as the laxity of Portuguese morals—which, Christina supposed, might well account for a major part of Mary's

domestic discord, for Thomas was a famous man-about-town—
Flora was kindness itself. Now her face was contorted with
concern.

"Did you not say to Dona Isabella that James is ill?" she
asked anxiously. "I hope it is nothing serious?"

"A slight fever, Mama Grant," Christina said, holding her
close. "I consider it safer for him to remain at home."

"Well, give him my best love," Flora said. "I shall come
over to see him as soon as I can."

She passed on to greet the children, and then Don Pedro
and Dona Inez, and Christina was left to cope with the rest of
the guests. But these were not so close as family, and she
could smile in reply to their platitudes without giving them
her full attention. A slight fever, indeed. The boy was taking
after his father more and more, in every way.

Presumably she had reacted in anger for the very first time
in her life. Certainly she had never struck James before; her
hand still stung, and his cheek must be equally painful. Nor
had she ever ordered a juvenile to be flogged. But it must
have been Jorge's doing to have introduced the girl into
James's bed. Now she came to think of it, Jorge's mouth was
the slyest she had ever seen, his eyes the most liquid in their
changing expressions. Undoubtedly he had profited by playing
the pimp for his master, whether financially or by presuming
to bind his master's desires to his own ambitions.

Now he hung between the triangles. However, even in her
rage, Christina had not gone so far as to order the girl to be
flogged, for all that she was the eldest of the three, and
confessed to being fifteen. She had had the maids stretch the
girl across a table and had whipped her herself, expiating all
her wrath.

And why had she not whipped James as well, instead of
merely slapping his face in her outrage? He was at least as
guilty as any of the others. If he was younger, and more
innocent, she had to suppose that since he was a Sousa e
Melo *and* a Grant, he was also more intelligent. Certainly he
was more precocious. And what had it achieved? He had
merely gazed at her with those enormous black eyes of his,

his face utterly solemn and utterly closed. He had shown no emotion when she had made him come downstairs with her to watch the skin being torn from Jorge's back. And Jorge was not even a slave. She had acted quite illegally in commanding him to be punished in such a fashion. But no one was going to bring a charge against Christina Grant.

But what *had* it achieved, except her own self-satisfaction? She had left James at home, confined to his room, under the immediate care of both Father Alfonso and Antonio, the butler. But were either of them really capable of coping with James? If he truly wished to escape the house or, worse, wished to renew his amatory explorations, would either of them be able to prevent him? And she was here, thirty miles away, unable to do anything less than smile and be polite . . . and endeavor to control the wild surges of her mind and heart. Her life had never been free of crisis and looming danger, but they had always been *her* crises and *her* dangers. With those she had been able to cope, using her own strengths and her special relationship with God.

Or had she always been deluding herself? Did she really have such a relationship? Or if she did, had she not transgressed so often, confident in the justice of her own desires, her own demands, that she was at last being punished, and in the person of her son?

Or was she being totally absurd? Would it not be a good idea to discover if Thomas de Carvalho, for example, had ever taken a slave girl to his bed at the age of twelve?

And what had they done together? What *could* they do at such an age?

And what a predicament for a woman who had never faced any such problem before in her life. Where, oh where, was Jack?

She gazed at the last of the guests, her heart rolling over and over in sheer relief. Because there he was.

"Well," Jack said, "I doubt it is so serious a crime after all."

The maids had finally departed, having undressed their

mistress, and the two of them could at last discuss the situation. "I suppose when you were his age," Christina said tartly, "you were the rake of your village."

Jack leaned back in his chair with a smile and gazed at the magnificent black hair which had just been unpinned and released. He delighted in watching his wife being undressed, and after three months at sea, it was like sitting at the gateway to heaven. He would have wished that they were in their own bedroom, but whenever they visited the de Sousas, and especially on occasions such as this, they spent at least one night. He would also have wished that he was not quite so tired, but he had ridden the thirty miles from Rio as fast as he could to get here for her birthday, and since his arrival had not sat down until half an hour ago, when the guests eventually retired into the various chambers assigned to them. He had been more than just the husband of the guest of honor. He had been a guest of honor himself, because however much the Brazilian aristocracy disliked him as a parvenu, he was their surest link with the outside world, with that Europe which seemed so far away south of the Equator, and no one had been able to resist crowding around to learn the latest news, gain some inkling of the latest fashion, discover some new piece of gossip from the scandalous court of King Joseph I and his wife, Queen Anna Maria, and his favorite, Carvalho — Melo, the great marquis of Pombal, whose relatives formed such an important part of this very gathering.

He had spent not a moment alone with his wife, been allowed only a brief and very public embrace, before a few minutes ago. And then had discovered that his homecoming was to be blighted by a domestic crisis—if he permitted it. Having been married to Christina for twelve years, he knew most of her moods and attitudes, and he knew that now she was conscious of too strong a reaction, was merely seeking justification for what she had done, not, probably, in the whippings, but in forbidding James the pleasures of this enormous party. In reality, she required only his reassurance.

He knew her so very well. And yet the only blight upon the utter happiness of his existence was that he did not know her well enough. He had come back to her, as he always came back to her, like a young lover, his mind and his body inflamed with desire and even, since he was being honest with himself, with lust. Which was no crime, since it was directed at his wife. To have sat here and watched her being undressed by her maid, watched white shoulders being uncovered as she had stepped out of her dress, swelling breasts slowly emerge as her petticoats had been removed, splendid legs appear as the final chemise had been discarded, followed by tight, hard-muscled buttocks and magnificent pubic V, and to have waited while the corset itself had been unstrapped, and she could emerge naked, the most beautiful woman in the world, in his eyes, was what he had dreamed of throughout the voyage, for very shortly, when she had been perfumed and powdered, that body would become his.

But not entirely so. She slept with him whenever he wished it, which was every night he was in Rio, and she had mothered three children for him, all with every evidence of pleasure. But never with any evidence of lust on her own part, and certainly never with any ecstasy. No doubt women did not feel these things. He was not in a true position to judge, since she remained the only one he had ever been to bed with. But certainly the average wife had to be prepared to humor her husband's excesses of passion, in whatever direction they might lead. Only if his demands exceeded the limits imposed by Christianity or involved the risks of actual bodily harm could she possibly appeal to the Church for intervention, and there were few dared risk that step, for was not the Church ruled by men, and for men, with men in mind?

But, since he was Christina's husband by accident and by sufferance, he had never done more with her than enter and climax and withdraw.

And what was it he wished to do to her that she might refuse? Or worse, accept with bitter resignation?

She stood in front of him, her nightgown so sheer he could see the outline of her body beneath. Their intimacy, their marriage, was signified by his being allowed to watch her being undressed. But as she had always worn a nightgown, she always would; she had never slept naked in his arms. Was that so very difficult a request to make?

Because of that he had fondled her breasts no more than half a dozen times in his life, and that guiltily. To hold and squeeze her buttocks had always to be an act of supreme passion, an accident of orgasm—however carefully calculated beforehand; they had to be released the moment he appeared to recollect what he was doing. As for allowing his fingers to wander between those magnificent thighs, there was an unimaginable delight.

He dreamed of nothing more than this. He could not even contemplate some of the pleasures which other men claimed to indulge, whether by physical mistreatment of their partners or by using mouth or tongue for purposes clearly not intended by nature.

She stood against him, her arms around his neck, and kissed him on the lips. Over her shoulder he could see her in the mirror, standing on tiptoe, her ankles and calves emerging from the nightgown, her muscles little bunches of tension as they supported her weight. This was her prerogative and her pleasure, to welcome him home the moment the maid had left the room—he was sure of that—after which she was content to leave the proceedings to him.

He held her close, lifted her from the floor with his embrace, nuzzled her neck as their lips slid apart. Did he *want* anything more than the privilege of holding her in his arms?

He thought not. They had reached an intimacy of friendship, a closeness by nature of the secret they shared, and of the so many other aspects of life that they equally shared. To probe further, to uncover sexual fears and sexual desires which arose from and were best left in the pit of human consciousness, *might* be to transport them together into a new paradise. But it also might just plunge them into a hell of mutual revulsion, mutual distaste. His Scottish caution no less than his New England upbringing warned him to settle for the happiness he possessed, and not, like poor deluded Jamey, go in search of riches which were guarded by catastrophe. Not even when, like tonight, after three month's separation, he wanted her so fiercely that he felt he could crush her ribs against him in the fury of his embrace.

But oh, he thought, what would I give just to feel her, once, tremble with passion when in my arms?

"It's not just the . . . well, the thought of him, in bed with a black girl, and doing . . . well. . . ." Christina sighed. She lay with her head on his arm, her body against his. Since he had been away for a long three months, and since he still seemed to find her desirable even after twelve years, he had climaxed very quickly. But it always happened very quickly; she never even had the time to work up a sweat. And now it was back to the humdrum business of being a wife and a mother rather than a mistress and lover. "It's the thought of disease."

"Yes," Jack agreed. "And I think that is the line I am going to take. I'll have a long chat with him when I get back home. He's probably been hearing a lot of rubbish from young Carvalho about how a man who hasn't been poxed is only half a man, but I think I can convince him that it's too unpleasant a business to be endured at his age."

"Have you ever been poxed, Jack?"

"Not to my knowledge."

"Have you ever slept with a black woman?"

"I have never slept with any woman, my sweet love, except you."

"I suppose you'd say that anyhow," she remarked. But she believed him, and reflected that things might be so very different if he had. "Jack, I've been wondering if it might not be a good thing for you to take him back to Portugal with you on your next voyage."

"*Back* to Portugal? He's never been."

"You know what I mean. He could go to school there. Uncle Sebastian would be happy to have him in his house, I'm sure. And we'd know he was in good hands."

"I don't think that *would* be a good idea," Jack said.

She raised her head, propping it on her hand. "Whyever not?"

"A great many reasons, my love. First, twelve is a little young to be sent away five thousand miles. And if James is going to be sexually precocious, he can contract syphilis just as easily in Lisbon as he can here. Believe me."

"But in the care of Uncle Sebastian—"

"I haven't discussed this with your father yet, Christina, but I'm not sure that your Uncle Sebastian is going to be able to look after anyone except himself in the next few years."

Christina frowned at him. "Uncle Sebastian? But he is—"

"The most powerful man in Portugal. And has been for the past twenty years. Absolutely true. But he only holds his power by grant from the king. The marquis is no friend of Her Majesty's. And the queen mother loathes him."

"Well? It is not the ladies who decide governmental policy. And why should Uncle Sebastian ever lose the confidence of the king? He has made Portugal a force to be reckoned with. He has reorganized the finances and the army. He rebuilt Lisbon after the earthquake. He is gradually achieving a unified Brazil. He has sent the Portuguese flag all over the world. . . ."

He kissed her nose. "I know all of that. And so does all Portugal. Which is not to say that your uncle isn't the most hated man in the country. People are envious of his success just as they object to the way the government has its fingers in every pie. And you must admit he is not very good at winning friends."

"He is arrogant," Christina acknowledged. "All successful men are arrogant." She smiled at him. "You are not exactly humble yourself. But I still say His Majesty will never reign without Pombal."

"Absolutely true, in my opinion. The question is, how long will the king reign? Have you not been listening to the rumors from Lisbon?"

"I never listen to rumors from Lisbon, because they are always no more than rumors."

"Well this one isn't. His Majesty is a sick man."

Her frown was back. "In what way?"

"The worst possible. His brain is wandering. Sometimes he keeps his council waiting for hours, sitting at the table with him while he talks utter nonsense. It has proved impossible to keep it a secret. All the country knows of it by now. There is open talk of a regency."

"Which will surely be headed by Uncle Sebastian."

"By law, my darling, the regency must be headed by the queen, who would have the right to appoint her own ministers."

"My God." Christina sat up. "Have you told Papa of this?"

"I've not had the chance. But I intend to tomorrow. I don't think you have to worry about your family's position here in Brazil. They are no longer involved in the government. But I also do not think it will advance any of our children to send them back to Portugal at this moment."

Christina chewed her lip. "I can't remember Portugal without Uncle Sebastian in charge."

"Well . . . it isn't really your home anymore, is it? Brazil is your home. At least . . ."

She turned to face him. "There is something else?"

"It's a changing world, Christina. An exciting one. You know all the trouble and unrest there has been in America these last couple of years because of the duties and the Navigation Acts? The very reasons we had to leave. They even burned the *Gaspee,* remember? Now, if we'd thought to do that instead of running away from her—"

"They'd have hanged you," she pointed out.

"Maybe. Maybe the time wasn't right, then. Well, it is now. Just before I left Lisbon I heard the most remarkable story of how one of the East India men carrying tea arrived in Boston harbor to discharge her cargo and was boarded by an armed party of Mohawk Indians, who dumped all the tea in the harbor."

"Indians?"

"Well, they were disguised as Indians. But everyone knows they were Bostonians. Real Indians would have massacred the crew as well, and set fire to the ship. But the point is not the destruction of the tea. It's the reaction of the British government."

"They must be very angry."

"Hardly the right word. After all that's happened before, well . . . the rumor is that they intend to close the port of Boston, to quarter troops on the inhabitants, to make life in general as unpleasant as they can."

"They have the right to do that," Christina said. "And the power."

"They have the *legal* right, as things stand at the moment. Whether they actually have the power is another matter. And whether we will stand for it is another matter again."

"You?" she asked, turning on her knees.

"Well, it's my fight as well."

"You are talking about rebellion," she said, "against your government and your king."

"The English people rebelled against their king once before, when he became too obnoxious."

"It would be a disaster. Great Britain is the most powerful nation on earth."

"Yes, but it's a tricky business, fighting a war at three thousand miles' range. And do you suppose there aren't plenty of countries, all of those that lost to Britain the last time around, like France and Spain and Holland, who might be willing to help us?"

"Another great war," she said. "It is too horrible to contemplate. And you keep using this 'us,' and 'we'. You are not a New Englander anymore, Jack. You are a Brazilian."

"Well, darling, if it came to shooting, those are my people, my cause . . . why, do you know, it would mean that I could go back to Nantucket? *We* could go back."

"I don't want to go back to Nantucket," she said. "I don't want you to go either. For any reason. It will be rebellion. That will make you a traitor as well as a pirate. They will hang you if they catch you. I couldn't stand that, Jack." She held his hands. "Promise me you'll never go back."

"If they're fighting, my darling, against the British—"

"Promise me," she said.

He hesitated, then smiled and pulled her down on top of him for a kiss.

"It'll probably never happen," he said. "As you say, rebellion is a tremendous step to take."

* * *

He had not promised. That was the important thing to remember. And by judiciously suppressing most of the news from North America over this last year, he had not encouraged her to return to the subject. She was, in any event, more concerned with her family problems. For Pombal had not, after all, been driven from office, even though his patron, King Joseph, had been certified as a lunatic. For all the bitter enmity of the queen mother, there was always the possibility that the king might recover. But it would be idle to pretend that Portugal was a happy place.

On the other hand, he had consented to bring James to school here in Portugal the moment the boy was fifteen. That was still nearly two years away, and by then William would be fourteen. It was Jack's idea to bring the two boys together more, so that William's sobriety could restrain James's ebullience. This had not actually been discussed with Christina yet, but he was sure she would agree. She found the business of managing two growing boys, as well as the younger children, as well as the plantation, as well as the Rio end of his shipping business, a time-consuming occupation. But it was an occupation at which, despite her grumbles and pretended uncertainties, she excelled. She was the most complete woman he had ever known. He had no fears for her.

That was important, because for all the breadth of her character and her interests, she still did not truly understand the urges and ambitions and requirements that drive a man. To her, their life should be centered around their family and his success, and their own mutual admiration and respect. She wanted nothing more. He had been betrayed as a boy by someone he had called at least neighbor. His home had been wrecked, and it was possible to see in that fateful afternoon the causes of the deaths of both his father and his brother. He had turned his back not only upon New England, but upon everything British. He was a Portuguese hidalgo. She could not feel, as he did, the course of blood through his veins, a stirring of the mind and body reaching all the way back to his father's tales of Culloden, when the Highlanders had been

shot to pieces by the disciplined musketry of the redcoats.
Nor could she appreciate any desire on his part to go back and
fight, for a cause, an idea, simply because no matter how far
behind he had left it, it was still the cause to which he had
been born and educated.

If this rebellion ever came to pass. But it was going to do
just that, and now. The *Lodestar* lay at anchor in Cascais
Bay, some half dozen miles downstream from Lisbon itself,
in the very mouth of the Tagus. Ostensibly she waited for the
tide to enter the port, but she had already missed two tides,
because her master was waiting for more than that. And here
it was. A boat approaching from the shore, in the stern of
which he had discerned the features of Richard Adams, the
Boston merchant who had made his home and his fortune
here in Portugal, and with whom he had had many a long talk
over the past two years.

He leaned over the rail as the boat approached. "News?"
he shouted, using English so that his crew would not easily
understand what was being said.

"The best," Adams shouted, his face flushed with excitement. "There has been a battle at Lexington. The British
were beat, Jack, beat! We're raising troops in Boston, in
Philadelphia, in Virginia. We're going to fight."

"By God," Jack said, going to the gangway to welcome
his friend aboard. "And you?"

"I'm on my way back, by the first available transport. I
fought the Indians and the French—I've been offered a regiment." He squeezed Jack's hand, stared into his eyes. "The
first available transport, Jack."

"Of course," Jack said.

"I've been authorized to tell you that there'll be a frigate
for you to command, Jack. The most important post of all.
We'll only win if we can beat the Royal Navy. And there's
no sailorman with your experience or ability. A frigate, Jack."

Jack turned away to walk to the rail. It seemed to him that
he had been waiting all his life for this moment. A man-of-
war. To take on the Navy, and avenge his father's death. And
a great many other things besides.

If only he were not five thousand miles from Christina.

Adams stood at his shoulder. "Well, Jack? I must have a decision."

Jack raised his head and gazed at another ship, also at anchor. She was waiting for a wind and would then be making for Rio. He knew her captain well. And this *was* the decision he had been awaiting, all his life.

"You'll sail with me, Richard," he said, "in an hour. Just give me the time to write a letter."

Chapter 7

Christina stood before her mother-in-law, impatiently waiting for her to finish the letter.

"I just do not believe it," she said. "I have never heard of anything quite so absurd. A grown man, with a family to care for and a business to manage, a whole life to live, rushing off to fight like some schoolboy. It never crossed my mind that he would do anything so idiotic."

"Well," Flora Grant said, folding the letter, "I suppose it is his home. Was his home," she said hastily as Christina glared at her. "I know Brazil is his home now, but I suppose some ties go deeper than we think."

"He is taking part in a rebellion," Christina pointed out. "Your Americans may think they are fighting a war, but to the British they are rebels. If Jack is captured he will be hanged." She sighed. "Then I will be a widow and you be entirely without sons."

"I know, my dear," Flora said. "But there it is. There is nothing that can be done now. A ship can sail from Cascais to Boston far quicker than from Cascais to Rio. So if he left on the same tide as the ship bearing that letter—"

"He is probably already dead," Christina said bitterly. "Oh, I could scream."

Flora regarded her skeptically, as if unable to imagine such a phenomenon, and Christina flushed. "I must get back to town, Mama Grant," she said. "There is so much to be done. My God, so much."

And not a soul to help her, she realized as she sat in her phaeton driving to the Grant warehouses. She had expected that Flora would be at least as shocked as she was by such a madcap act, far more worthy of his brother than of a sober man like Jack. But, she was coming to understand, Flora had perhaps accustomed her mind to the fact that both her sons had been lost to her fourteen years before, and had never really accepted the Jack she had found again as the son she had known. She had settled far more happily into life with the de Carvalhos than in any relationship with the de Sousas.

She would have to manage on her own. But what a time for a husband to disappear, even if he did survive and come back to her. It seemed to her that her life, which up to two years ago had been entirely within her own control, had gone mad. She was aware of two vague but increasing menaces to the security of herself and her family: the business of constantly watching James, of wondering what he was doing whenever he was not in her sight, and of enduring the boy's resentment as well, for he bore grudges in a manner she associated more with his father's personality than his uncle's, and the equally worrying business of assessing what was happening in Portugal; it was all very well for Jack to assure her that her family would be no longer directly involved in any fall from power of Pombal, but even Jack had to admit that most of his considerable trading privileges had been granted by the marquis, and a good deal of his business arose because of his relationship with the most powerful man in the country.

To have to face these threats without Jack . . . did she, then, feel no other pang that she might never see her husband again? She was used to long separations, of course, but had never before doubted his return. And in her heart she did not doubt his return now. She dared not consider any other possibility.

But why, oh why, did he have to go in the first place?

Arthur Conybeare waited for her outside the warehouse. He had also received a letter, and had expected her to call.

"Well, ma'am," he said, helping her down, "I guess you're in charge now." He attempted a smile. "But I guess you have always been in charge."

She glared at him, swept into the office, and absently took off her hat, forgetting the immediate disruption caused to her carefully braided hair. "I suppose you wish you were with him," she remarked.

Conybeare shook his head. "I'm a little too old for fighting wars. Do you reckon he'll keep the *Lodestar* up there? He says he's been offered command of a frigate."

"When the frigate is ready," Christina pointed out, sitting behind the huge desk. "I think we may forget about the *Lodestar* for a few months, at best."

"It'll upset the schedule," Conybeare said.

"I don't suppose he has thought of that. When a man starts to prate about freedom, and a cause, and heaven knows what other nonsense, a shipping schedule, even his own shipping schedule, is not going to bother him very much. Where are the other ships?"

Conybeare gazed at the huge chart on the wall, with its colored pins. "The *Venturer* is in Lisbon now, or should be. The *Wayfarer* was diverted to Oporto, to load wines. The *Adventurer* sprung her foremast in a gale, you may remember, ma'am, and is in Funchal for repairs. The *North Star* should be back any day now; she was calling at Belem on her return voyage."

"She's here now," Christina said. "I saw her passing the narrows as I came down the road."

"Aye well, as you know, ma'am, the *Orion* and the *Plough* are here in Rio, refitting. That completes the list." He turned back from the chart. "I'd better get down there, if the *North Star* is in. Ma'am . . ." He twisted his hands together. "What are you meaning to do?"

"Do?" she demanded. "Why, what do you expect me to

do, Arthur? I shall continue to manage the shipping line until Captain Grant comes home.''

Conybeare opened his mouth, and then changed his mind and closed it again. But Christina answered the question anyway.

''And if he doesn't come home,'' she said, ''I shall continue to manage it until either James or William is old enough and ready to take control.''

Either James or William, she thought. It would have to be William. Not only because he was Jack's son, but because the thought of someone like James in control of all of this wealth was frightening. So, yet another potential problem had been landed in her lap.

''I'll come down to the dock with you,'' she decided. ''Captain Gomes may have some news of what is happening in America.''

She returned to her waiting phaeton. Conybeare preferred to ride, and walked his horse alongside her as they made their way through the streets, somnolent in the middle of the afternoon and yet beginning to buzz, as they neared the dock, with the excitement always generated by the arrival of a ship. The *North Star* was one of the newest, and by far the largest, of the Grant fleet, a brigantine, as were all Jack's ships. She supposed they were fortunate, she told herself bitterly, that Jack had always preferred to sail on the old *Lodestar* than on any of his newer and better vessels. But in that sentimental attachment to things past, she should have realized what was likely to happen in the future.

''Well, Captain Gomes,'' she called, as the ship was warped alongside the dock, ''have you news of the American war?''

''I have news, Senora Grant,'' the captain shouted. ''Great news. There has been a battle at Boston, and the Americans have been defeated.''

''My God,'' she said. ''*That* is great news? Have you not heard that Captain Grant has gone away to fight with them?''

''That I have, senora.'' The captain, satisfied that his vessel was secure, descended the ladder from the poop and saw to the running out of the gangplank. ''But, senora, at

least you will have his brother to help you until his return.''
He stepped aside to allow one of his passengers to reach the
head of the gangway, and Christina gazed at Jamey Grant.

Could it really be Jamey? Could it *possibly* be Jamey? But
even as her mind refused to accept it, her throat was constricting with a mixture of delight and fear, for if the skin, once
ruddy, was burned so dark as almost to suggest a mulatto,
and the mouth, even when smiling, as now, had come to
resemble a steel trap, and the body, so boyishly slender when
last she had seen it, had become so heavily muscled, even
when concealed beneath a suit, as to give his shoulders an
almost grotesque heaviness, there was no mistaking the eyes,
which glowed at her with as much fervor as ever she remembered, even if here too the experiences he had undergone
during the last fourteen years were clearly depicted. There
was no ebullience remaining in these eyes, but rather an
almost savage intensity. Every bit of which, she realized, was
directed at her.

"Jamey?" she whispered. "Can it really be you?"

"Jamey." Conybeare gave a shout and ran forward to greet
his old comrade. "My God . . . all these years we thought
you dead. When you were swept away—"

"I thought myself dead, Arthur," Jamey said, squeezing
his hand, but never taking his gaze from Christina. "Have
you no kiss for your brother-in-law?"

"Jamey. . . ." She presented her cheek, and he grasped
her chin to turn her head and kiss her on the lips. "Oh,
Jamey. . . ." If only she could think!

He realized her confusion and turned to clap Conybeare on
the shoulder. "It's good to see you again, Arthur. I'll be
down to talk over old times with you. But right now I have
much to tell Dona Christina. And no doubt she has a great
deal to tell me."

"I thought you were dead, Jamey," Conybeare repeated.
"You have to believe that. Those priests told me there was no
possibility of anyone surviving. They thought I was a miracle. That's the truth, Jamey lad."

"And I believe you, old friend," Jamey said, smiling at

him. "I'll tell you about it when I come back." He turned his smile on Christina and she felt a shiver run down her spine, but it was at least as much from anticipation as fear. "Will you not offer me a ride in your carriage?"

She recollected herself with an effort and smiled at Captain Gomes. "You'll take a glass of wine with me this evening, Captain," she said, "and tell me all your news. Of course you will ride with me, Jamey. There is so much . . ."

He handed her up, and she frowned at him; the thumb of his right hand was curiously misshapen, as if it had been crushed by some immense force. "I am anxious to see your children," he said.

She turned, still on the step. "You know of them?"

"I know everything about you," he said. "And much that you have done these past years."

She slowly lowered herself onto the seat. "All these years, and you have continued to stay away, letting us think you were dead?"

He sat beside her. "Well, I did not consider the time was ripe for me to reappear."

"And now you do? Your poor mother . . . we must go out and see her immediately. Mary will be overwhelmed."

He shook his head. "I will visit them later. It is you I wish to see." He leaned back to look at her. "To see my darling, darling girl. Or should I say woman? But you are my darling woman, Christina. You are the loveliest thing I have ever seen, and I have existed on dreams of you for fourteen years."

"Jamey . . ."

"But of course," he said, "you are married to my brother. Who has stupidly gone off to fight in a war. I sometimes think that since I was stupid enough to leave you also, we Grants must be demented."

"Is that why you have come back now?" she asked. "Because Jack is away?"

He smiled at her. "Not entirely, but I did suppose it might help you to consider the situation more impartially, so to speak."

"Consider the situation?" she asked, her heart suddenly

freeing itself from its constriction and commencing to pound. "What situation?"

He preferred to look out of the carriage at the houses and the people. "How this place has grown," he said. "I swear it has doubled in size since last I was here."

"Yes," she said absently. "What situation?"

"But not the beach," he said as they came in sight of the Copacabana. "And that is your house? It is quite magnificent. Jack has done well."

"Yes," she said. "Jamey—"

"We have all done well," he said:

"You have found El Dorado, then?" she cried.

"Ah . . . no. Not yet. But I shall. I had supposed you might be interested."

"Interested? My God. If only I could understand." She gazed at him. His clothes were of the finest broadcloth, and his cane was silver-topped, while there were silver pieces sewn into the brim of his tricorne hat. "You say you have failed in your quest after fourteen years, and yet—"

He squeezed her hand as the phaeton turned into the drive. "I will tell you all about it, my dear Christina. After I have met my son."

"This is your Uncle Jamey," Christina said. "You will have heard your father and me speak of him, children. He has returned after many, many years. Anthony. Inez. William. James."

Jamey ignored the three younger children and gazed only at James. Christina watched, waiting for catastrophe; there would have been no point in attempting to ask for any promises.

But he merely smiled, his mouth softening for the first time, and then gravely shook James's hand. "You are a handsome fellow, James," he said. "Tell me, where is your father?"

"My father has gone off to fight against the English, sir," James said.

"I would like you to call me Uncle Jamey," he said. "After all, I am your uncle and you have been named after

me.'' He glanced at Christina. ''That is a great compliment to
us both.''

''Then I *will* call you Uncle Jamey,'' James said. ''I am
glad that you have come back, Uncle Jamey. My mother has
often spoken of you.''

''Has she, indeed,'' Jamey said. ''Then I am doubly com-
plimented.'' He looked around him at the vault of the huge
reception room. ''And do you enjoy living in a great house
like this?''

James frowned at him. ''I have never lived anywhere
else,'' he pointed out.

''Then we must see that you never do,'' Jamey agreed.

It was James's turn to glance at his mother. ''But Mama
says I am to go to Portugal to school,'' he said. This time he
looked at William contemptuously. ''With Billy.''

''Indeed? Are there no tutors here in Rio?''

''Mama says it is best for us,'' William said.

''I am sure she will tell me why,'' Jamey said. ''You'll
leave us now. We have much to discuss.''

The children filed from the room.

''They are good, obedient children,'' Jamey remarked.

''After their fashion,'' Christina agreed.

Jamey once again looked around the huge room, and then
at the manservant who waited just inside the door.

''Now let us go somewhere private.''

Christina sat on the settee, her hands clasped on her lap.
''We can hardly be more private than here. No one will
interrupt us.''

''Then send that fellow away.''

''I would prefer him to stay,'' she said. All that was really
necessary was to preserve her composure, approach this crisis
in the way she had approached all the other major crises of
her life, in a spirit of calm and detached confidence. Had he
really meant to make trouble, he would have made it then.
Surely. ''There is naught to concern yourself with, if you
speak English. He does not understand it.''

Jamey gazed at the footman.

''But he will obey me,'' Christina said quietly, ''and is
quite capable of summoning assistance.''

"Do you, then, fear rape?"

"I wish to understand," she said. "After that, well . . . we shall have to see. Would you care for some wine?"

"Later." He sat beside her.

"I am grateful," she said, "for your forebearance, just now."

"Perhaps I also have much to understand," he said. "When I look at you, when I remember our night together, when I remember your promises . . ."

"I promised nothing," she said, and bit her lip, knowing that she had exposed herself to a riposte.

It came immediately. "You would not call yielding your body to me a promise?"

"Perhaps, to myself," she said. "But afterward I thought you dead."

"And married my brother, in some haste."

"I was pregnant," she said. "Would you have had me retire to a convent?"

"I am sure you did the right thing, as did Jack. But then, Jack has always done the *right* thing, even to rushing off to fight in this absurd rebellion. I observe, however, that you were not slow to mother a family for him as well."

Christina raised her chin. She was far safer angry, if that was what he wished. "I have no reason to offer you the slightest explanation," she said. "You were dead, I had my own life to live. Rather it is you who owe me an explanation. Fourteen *years,* with never a message?"

"Fourteen years," he said. He got up, walked to the windows, and looked out at the garden. "I sought El Dorado," he said. "I would not come back to you a miserable failure. For five years I wandered the forests, seeking El Dorado, seeking the Amazon."

"You walked from the San Jacinto rapids to the Amazon?" she asked in amazement.

"No," he said. "I have never seen the Amazon. Well, perhaps I have, or at least the mouth. I think I have. But I have never explored it. I am about to do so."

"You spent five years wandering the forests and did not even find the Amazon? How did you survive?"

He shrugged. "I became an Indian, you might say."

"But . . . what *of* the Indians? The climate? The snakes and alligators?"

"I fought them all, and beat them all," Jamey said. "Alone."

"For five years," she said. "Alone. I can see it in your face. But you say for five years, not fourteen."

"Ah," he said, and came back to sit beside her. "After five years of making my way north, through country such as you can never have seen, Christina, I came to the River Araguaia and realized that I was only halfway to my destination. But I was fortunate. The brave are always fortunate, Christina. Because there I met a man. A Portuguese adventurer named Carlos Brazao, who years before had set out on the same quest as I."

"And *he* had found it? El Dorado?"

"No. He too had found the jungles too immense. But like me, he was fortunate. He had found a silver mine not far from the headwaters of this Araguaia. An immense mine, Christina, inexhaustible in its wealth. This mine he offered to share with me."

Christina frowned at him. "Why?"

"Because there were difficulties. You know the government laws regarding bullion, the necessity to declare it all and pay duty upon it, the likelihood that the government will actually step in and take the mine for itself. Do you know, for ten years he had removed just a little silver at a time, taken it down to Belem in his canoe, smelted it into ingots, and stored it, buried beneath the yard of the house he owned there, without anyone knowing. And without ever spending any of it, except the little he converted into coin for his daily needs. Can you imagine, ten years, just accumulating wealth, with no clear idea of what he was going to do with it? But when he learned who I was, and of my relationship to the then viceroy— it was he who told me of your marriage to Jack—he offered me a partnership, if I could persuade your father also to join in our enterprise, and thus keep the mine and the silver between the three of us. Of course, I agreed. I was overwhelmed with joy at seeing a white man again, at realizing that I could regain civilization, at understanding that he was offering me untold wealth, just because there was too much of it even for him. We sealed our partnership there on the banks of the Araguaia, over his last bottle of wine.''

"Nine years ago," she said.

"Ah well, man proposes and God disposes, does he not? My friend Carlos Brazao contracted a fever only days after our meeting. I sometimes think that he was already in the grip of the disease when he met me, and perhaps this governed his actions. In any event, despite my efforts, he died. But his last words were, 'the mine is yours, Jamey Grant. I have no kin. The mine is yours. Make of it what you will.' ''

"Truly a noble man," Christina said, "as you must be the most fortunate one on the face of this earth. But still, what did you do then?"

"Ah," he said. "Well, at that time I intended to proceed as poor Carlos had outlined his plans to me. I continued down to Belem, for he had given me a map and instructions, both as to the location of the mine and as to the whereabouts of his house in Belem, where his ingots were hidden. At that time I had every intention of returning to Rio to involve your father, and to see you again, perhaps, and my son . . . but when I reached Belem I discovered that your father's term of office had been completed, that there was a new viceroy. And so I thought again. And besides, I concluded, why should I return to Rio, where I can only cause Christina pain and make my dear brother unhappy? Far better to continue my quest. But first, I decided to accumulate a somewhat larger store of capital. And so I returned upriver, and after some difficulty, I found Carlos's mine, and was amazed. It was, as he had described it to me, almost literally a mountain, or certainly a hill, composed entirely of silver ore."

"And so you did exactly as he had done, mined it secretly, and smelted it secretly, and stored it secretly, in Belem," she said. "And never confessed to a soul who you really were."

"Why, yes. All the while dreaming of you, but determined to return as I had said I would return, as a man of means. And now I am back."

"And I do not believe a word you have been saying," she said. "A mountain of silver, indeed. A Carlos Brazao. A secret store of wealth beneath the floorboards of a house in Belem. A man who would conceal his identity for nine years, from his family, and . . ." she flushed ". . . from the woman he loved. I would suppose that to me, at least, you could tell the truth, Jamey Grant."

He gazed at her for some seconds, glanced at the footman by the door, then opened his satchel, reached inside, and took out a small silver ingot.

Christina picked it up. It was certainly heavy enough to be real.

"You can have that," Jamey said. "I have plenty more." He smiled at her. "There are two more in this bag."

"But . . . you mean what you have told me is the truth?"

"Every word of it."

He was lying. She was sure he was lying. She could feel it. But she held in her hands the evidence that at least some of what he had said was true. She gazed at him. "And now that you have accumulated this fortune, what are you going to do with it?"

He seized her hands. "Christina, I am still going to find El Dorado. But it must be done by ship. I know that now. This is what I am seeking, here in Rio. A ship. One of Jack's ships. I came back to offer him the partnership I would have offered your father. But I understand that in his absence you are in charge of the company. Sell me a ship, Christina, and within a year I will make you the richest woman on earth. I know it."

She tugged her hands futilely. "A year? You would buy a ship from me to spend the rest of your life searching for some mythical city? Haven't you money enough?"

Yet she was relieved. He seemed to have accepted the situation. If only she could get over the feeling that it was all some kind of charade . . .

"It has to be from you, don't you see? I dare not reveal my wealth to anyone in the colony but you. The government would certainly learn of it, and . . ." He hesitated for a

moment, and a look she had never observed crossed his face.
". . . probably send me to prison. But Jack, or you, why,
you can arrange for the silver to be taken or sent to Lisbon
and smuggled in, and exchanged for goods or money."

"Yes," she said. "I see what you mean. But I do not
know that I can sell one of our ships without consulting
Jack."

"He is away fighting a war." His fingers tightened on
hers. "And it will yield you an immense profit, Christina. I
will give you half of what I find. I *know* it is there, and I
know how to reach it now. Carlos Brazao told me. It is
possible to navigate four, five hundred miles up the Amazon,
he said. Why, the whole river can hardly be longer than that.
No river can be five hundred miles long. I can sail almost up
to the headwaters and then strike across country. North of the
river the forest ends, and it is open land. Prairie. The going is
simple. And El Dorado stands in the middle of the prairie.
Waiting for the first man who can get there."

His eyes gleamed with a frightening intensity. His fingers
were like talons digging into her flesh.

"You are hurting me," she said.

Immediately he released her, and his face relaxed.

"You must give me time to consider," she said.

"Time," he said. "Of course. I have as much time as I
have money, Christina. Will you invite me to stay with
you?"

"I doubt that would be wise. You must go to see your
mother and sister. I think you should stay with them. They
will be overjoyed to see you."

"And if I were to stay here, you fear I might attempt to
suborn little James? Or do you anticipate I might creep into
your bed at night?"

She met his gaze. "I should not like to consider either
possibility," she said.

"You gave me your virginity," he said, "and mothered
my child. Do you not feel the slightest spark of love for me?"

"How can I?" she asked. "Even if I did, how could I
dare? For better or worse, fate has conspired to keep us
apart."

"For better or worse?" he asked. "You are not happy with Jack, then. Well, how could you be?"

She flushed. "I am very happy with Jack. Between us we have created more than just a family, a shipping line, an El Dorado of our own, if you like. We have created an . . . an entity. Us. We are man and wife, and father and mother, and business partners. And lovers."

"Now I may accuse *you* of lying. And you have no proof to offer *me*."

"I will prove it if I have to, Jamey," she said.

"And if I tell you that for fourteen years I have done nothing but think of you? That I have spurned all other women, have not even smiled upon one, out of my love for you? That you are my entire life, my universe, my reason for living, for being, for striving? That will mean nothing to you?"

"You could have come home nine years ago," she said.

"And then you would have accepted me?"

"Then I would have *believed* you, Jamey. There could never be anything more than that. I cannot believe that you have lived for fourteen years without a woman, just as I cannot believe that if you truly loved me the way you claim you could have spent nine years away from my side when you possessed the wherewithal to return to Rio whenever you chose. But whether I believe you or not, even whether I love you still or not, nothing can change our situation. You are proposing adultery, or something even more criminal. I am married, Jamey. That is the end of the matter, whether or not Jack is your brother.

"I understand your feelings for James, and I have no doubt that Jack will also understand them. But he is my child too, and Jack and I will be able to provide a future for him far more stable than could a father who proposes to spend the rest of his life in some absurd search for a nonexistent city. I would beg of you to understand that. But I will promise you this. If you wish it, when James grows to manhood I will tell him the truth of the matter, and he can then make his own decision regarding the three of us. I can offer you no more than that."

His lips curled. "And if I decide not to accept your so generous offer? Will you call me a liar to my son, and perjure yourself?"

"No," she said. "But I would beg you to consider. The boy has certain problems already. Would you make his life a misery?"

"His life," Jamey said, and got up. "A misery. I spent fourteen years alone and miserable. But the jungle was warmer than this. As I recall my Bible, the prodigal son was welcomed."

"As I welcome you. I am overjoyed to see you again, to know you are alive. But I welcome you as a brother, Jamey. I will not let you make criminals of us both."

"And will you sell me a ship?"

She chewed her lip. "I will have to consider," she repeated. "Give me the time to do that."

Was there ever a woman more bedeviled by fate? She stood at the window of her bedchamber and gazed out at the beach and the Atlantic rollers. How often had she stood like this, hoping for a first glimpse of the *Lodestar* returning from Lisbon. And what would she give to see it now. But now there was no hope at all of being able to share her problem. Oh, foolish Jack. Dear, sweet, bold, magnificent, but so foolish Jack.

Or was it merely that he trusted her, in every way? Trusted her to conduct her life as she would conduct his business— with the composure he adored in her, and presumed must rule even her emotions.

But her wilder emotions, her lust—he did not even suspect they existed. He had no idea that she had dreamed for years of a laughing, wayward boy with a gleam in his eye and a dream of achieving the impossible. Well, that boy no longer existed. But was the man not still more attractive, with the obvious power which rippled from those immense shoulders through to his fingertips, and which emanated from a mind which had experienced so much, survived for five years alone in the jungles of the Matto Grosso, and done so much else besides? Which he had not yet confessed to her. She only knew that he could not have spent nine years merely in smelting silver ore into ingots.

But the ingot lay on her dressing table behind her, to substantiate his tale.

And now . . . why not sell him his ship? Was it not an urgent necessity to have him leave Rio as quickly as possible? With Jack away, with her own tempestuous urgings ever present . . . Jamey could be the answer to everything she so desperately desired, and at times almost persuaded herself that she *needed*. Here was no callow youth, such as other women took for lovers, to whom she must yield her every secret, sure that he would share his triumphs with his friends. She would be yielding nothing to Jamey Grant because he already possessed all her secrets of that nature. Nor was there anyone for him to boast to. And most insidious of all, there would be no risk of disappointment. It was the touch of this man's hand, this man's lips, that had tormented her for fourteen years. Whatever secrets they might share in the future could only be an extension of the secrets they already shared.

All that was required was to allow herself to forfeit that trust. And Jack would never know. Or would he not have to know, by the mere fact that Jamey had returned, in his absence, and that she had sold him a ship?

That she had become his partner in some wild enterprise. Some illegal enterprise, too. Finding El Dorado might not be illegal. It would, indeed, ensure him immortality, assuming the city was actually there to be found. But removing the gold without paying the requisite duties on it was a different matter, and a refusal to grant the government equal shares in the source of wealth was a more heinous crime than murder, to Uncle Sebastian. Would Jack be prepared to involve himself in something like that when all his life since his father's death had been conducted in the strictest honesty?

Or was he more like his brother than she had ever suspected? He had certainly gone rushing off to take part in a most illegal war. She realized that the making of decisions was a more difficult matter than she had ever imagined. Her decisions in the past had always been passive ones, the decisions of survival. Even in managing the business for Jack, it had always been a matter of preserving the status quo, avoiding anything of a speculative or uncertain nature, sure that when Jack came home he would know what to do, without hesitation.

Oh, Jack, Jack. Why aren't your sails just peering above the horizon?

But they were not, and would not. She turned away from the window with a sigh, and gazed at the portrait of her father which hung on the far wall. Over the years she had drifted away from her childhood intimacy with Don Pedro. He was no longer in the best of health, and for all of his pretended interest in tobacco and sugar farming, he was undoubtedly bored since retiring from the viceroyalty.

But he was the only man she had ever known who possessed a vision and an openmindedness to equal Jack's.

She crossed the room in long strides and rang the bell for her phaeton.

Don Pedro Alonso de Sousa e Melo sat at his desk, smoking one of his own cigars, and regarded the young woman seated before him. It was a very long time since she had sat like this, talking to her father, turning to him for help. How often had he wished she would do so?

She was still the most marvelous creature he had ever beheld. And she was his daughter. His entire life had been dedicated simply to her prosperity and her happiness. He had only emigrated from Portugal in the first place because he had seen the misery in her eyes, for everything in Lisbon reminded her of poor Miguel de Castro. In the flying seconds that had elapsed while she had been swept away from the stern of the *Gloria Dei* and before she had been rescued, he supposed he must have doubled his age, and to her rescuer, and his brother, he had felt an overwhelming gratitude.

He had never seen any reason to alter that point of view, even if he still did not understand how he had so misjudged a man's character as that of Jack Grant. The fact of seducing a virginal girl of noble upbringing was, indeed, so out of character that it could only be explained by an overwhelming passion. And yet, that was irrelevant. To make Christina happy, Don Pedro thought he would have agreed to her marrying the devil.

A strange expression, he realized, as he listened to her dilemma. It was nearly midnight. She had left her children and her own warm bed to come riding out here as if the devil himself were behind her. Jamey Grant. The man who had saved her life, who had been at least as much in love with her as his brother—even more so, he decided, remembering the looks Jamey had directed at her during the weeks on board the *Lodestar*—and at the news of whose death she had been almost overcome with grief.

Surely this was an occasion for the ringing of the bells, for shouting her joy to the world, for inviting all Rio to a great ball to celebrate her brother-in-law's return . . . and certainly for *giving* him one of her ships, if he desired it, sure in the knowledge that Jack would be similarly overjoyed at discovering his only brother returned from the dead.

Not for galloping through the night in search of advice, when she did not really require it. He was merely someone to whom she could tell everything that had happened, and hope that by spelling it out for herself *she* might be able to reach a decision.

After fourteen years?

She had finished, was leaning forward, her elbows on the desk, her lovely face concentrated in its anguish, her lip red where she had bitten it, staring at him as if she would draw the vital response from the very depths of his brain.

Or as if what she had been telling him was nothing more than a novel, and she was endeavoring to make him understand the real truth of the matter. In which case his earlier supposition was wrong and she *was* asking for his help, in a direction she had not been able to put into words. She had been telling him something by just being here, by her actions.

"A difficult decision," he agreed, and got up to walk around the desk and pour two glasses of wine from the decanter waiting on the side table. He studied the back of her head while doing so. Christina. Fleeing as from the devil the man who had saved her life, and who might reasonably suppose that she would be his friend forever.

Who had perhaps once assumed much more than that? As the red liquid splashed into the crystal goblets, a lightning-quick revelation seemed to cut across his brain, leaving him for a moment quite stunned with the temerity of his own thoughts . . . and also with his obtuseness in not having understood before. He had not, after all, misjudged Jack's character, anymore than he had misjudged Jamey's. Any more than he had wondered how Christina's firstborn could possibly so resemble his uncle rather than his mother or his father.

Jack had played an utterly honorable role, as he would have expected. And Christina had been content, until the devil had so strangely reappeared, to tear her life apart.

Slowly he returned to the desk, standing beside her rather than sitting down, gave her the glass of wine and, as she raised her head to thank him, kissed her on the forehead.

"A difficult problem," he said again. "But I am grateful that you have come to me for advice. I shall not fail you, Christina. You have my word."

She squeezed his hand. "I knew you would not, Papa. I suppose you think it is absurd—"

"Not absurd," he said. "Not absurd at all. Now, as you are clearly exhausted, I think you should return home."

She frowned at him. "Return to Copacabana? But . . ." Always before when she had visited her parents, she had stayed the night.

"You do not wish to leave the children, do you, my sweet girl? Or to have the world know you came to me for advice? Why, I would even suggest you tell no one of your visit here tonight, and command your servants also to be quiet." Gently he raised her to her feet. "You can spend tomorrow in bed," he said. "And by tomorrow morning, I promise you I shall have decided upon the answer to your problem. I will bring it to you." He stared into her eyes. "I promise you."

"Yes." She looked a little bewildered. No doubt she had expected some recrimination, some condemnation. She did not really understand her own father, he supposed, or the depths of protective love which he felt for her, which he had always felt for her.

"Home and bed," he said, walking her to the door and pulling the bell rope to summon the maid who had accompanied her from Copacabana. "Bed. I will see you in the morning."

Another kiss, and she was gone. His Christina. The only thing in life for which he would give his life.

He closed the door and gazed at the rapiers which hung below the picture of the marquis of Pombal. But that would be senseless. Such a course *might* well cost him his life, without any guarantee that he would succeed in his purpose. In his fourteen years, which, as Christina had pointed out, could hardly have all been spent in the Matto Grosso, Jamey Grant might well have become an accomplished swordsman. Besides, he might refuse to fight a man old enough to be his father, and one he had once been proud to call a friend. The deed would have to be done by someone whose challenge was irresistible, or who would make himself irresistible, alike by presence and ambition and prowess.

He realized that he was plotting nothing less than murder. But would he not happily kill anyone who attempted to gain control of Christina? And was it murder to destroy a man who had died fourteen years ago? God had undoubtedly destroyed him for his crime against Christina. Only the devil could have plucked him from that river, just as only the devil could have sustained him, even supposing he had endured half of the experiences Christina had related. To deal with such a monster it was necessary to be absolutely ruthless, but also absolutely sensible. Jamey Grant's death could not *be* murder. He must die as a gentleman, defending his honor. But to accomplish that would mean taking his destroyer into the secret, now and forever.

He took a turn up and down the room, his hands clasped behind his back. Thomas de Carvalho. Of course. Thomas was the finest swordsman in all Brazil, and a member of the family, and a man absolutely trustworthy and absolutely dedicated to the fortunes of the de Sousas not less than the de Carvalhos. He was also a true friend and admirer of Jack Grant.

But as Mary Grant's husband, he was also Jamey Grant's brother-in-law, and surely Jamey had already revisited the de Carvalho plantation, been reunited with his mother and sister, and welcomed with all the hysterical joy that would have exploded on such an occasion.

Besides, could a man really be expected to kill his own brother-in-law?

Don Pedro stopped pacing and slowly raised his head. The far wall was decorated with a mirror, and he found himself staring into it, with the portrait of his great cousin looking over his shoulder.

Thomas might be the finest swordsman in all Brazil, but his brother was not far behind. And Henry was in love. If it was not painfully obvious whenever he and Christina were in the same room together, there were the rumors of the sonnets and love letters with which he apparently bombarded his beautiful cousin. And Henry loathed the Grants as utter upstarts, especially Jack, since Jack possessed the prize he so desperately desired. But if he was made to understand that Jack but shared her with his brother, that Jamey was the man who had first used her, that even, perhaps, she was planning to elope with her first lover, piqued at the way her husband had gone off to fight in a distant war . . . she had certainly been piqued, and Henry would have noticed it.

And Henry, when Don Pedro came to consider the matter, had a streak of iron anger lurking in his soul, which his more confident and genial brother quite lacked. Why, in many ways the two de Carvalho brothers strangely resembled the Grants. It was entirely fitting that the two younger brothers, who both so adored the same goddess, should find themselves face to face in combat for her love.

He pulled the bell rope and his butler, Fernando, appeared immediately.

"Have you any idea, Fernando, where Senor Henry de Carvalho spends his evenings?"

"Well, Your Excellency . . ."

"It is of no account which brothel it is," Don Pedro said. "But I must discuss a most urgent matter with him."

"I think I know where the young gentleman may be found, Your Excellency," Fernando said.

"Then saddle two horses and take me to him."

Fernando raised his eyebrows. "Now, Your Excellency? It is half past eleven."

"And we will not get into Rio before three. I am aware of that, Fernando. But the matter will not wait. Saddle two horses. And, Fernando—privily, eh? There is no one, not even my wife and especially not Senora Grant, who is to know of our little journey."

"Of course, Your Excellency." Fernando bowed and withdrew.

And Don Pedro stared at himself in the mirror. By dawn I promised you, my darling girl, he thought. It shall be settled by dawn. He looked at Pombal's face, over his shoulder. The marquis had a grim face, as befitted the dictator of all Portugal. But suddenly, tonight, those tight, harsh features almost seemed to smile in approval.

Jamey Grant dismounted from his tired mule outside the hostelry, stretched, and rubbed his backside. He was not used to riding, had selected a mule as being more docile than a horse, without recalling that its back was every bit as bony. But the double journey had been worth it. He could not possibly have spent the night in the de Carvalho household. The shrieks of joy and the sobs of delight, the way both Mama and Mary had clung to his arm, had been nauseating.

The fact was, he had forgotten what they looked like. He had even, until today, forgotten their existence. And even had he thought of them every day, he would not have recognized them. Mama was old, prematurely so, no doubt because of the heat and the climate. Mary was grotesquely fat, a too typical Portuguese lady, and a too typical Brazilian one in her frantic desire to learn what was happening in the outside world. And her children were also typically Portuguese, in a way Christina's somehow were not—fat little black-haired boys and girls, staring silently at their unknown uncle.

As for that husband of hers, with his twirling mustaches and his hand constantly dropping to his sword hilt—he had been far too reminiscent of the guards at the prison in Oporto, sufficient cause for the most instant and complete dislike. Jamey had promised to visit them again in a day or so, the moment the urgent business which he had explained was drawing him back into town was completed. As it would be. By tomorrow Christina would have made her decision, since there was only one decision she could possibly make. She dared not refuse him, however much she might guess the story he had told her was a complete fabrication. Because she knew that he could ruin her reputation and blight her marriage by a few words in the right quarter. She would agree to his demands.

He stamped up the steps and banged on the door. It was near dawn, and had been a long day. And yet he felt not the least tired.

What other demands might she not feel forced to agree to? He had not really considered the matter very deeply before yesterday. If it had been no lie to claim that he had often thought of her, as he had lain in his prison cell, or watched his hands bleed as he had worked on those endless roads to which convict labor was applied, and certainly that he had dreamed of her during those early days in the forest, before he had so stupidly tried to smuggle Brazao's silver out of Belem and been arrested, those had all been dreams of an unutterably lovely young girl, with all her life still in front of her. It had been that dream which had led him to strangle Brazao in a fit of maniacal jealousy, had then led him to abandon Cali and her baby. Christina, even a Christina married to Jack and several times a mother, had suddenly seemed very close. So close he had felt able to take his time, to make absolutely sure that Brazao had been telling the truth in his boastful contempt. Besides, it had been such a pleasure to be able to don European clothing, even if in a not very good fit, and eat European food, even if stale and worm-infested, and drink European wine, even if bitter.

Even the hard labor of paddling the canoe upstream again had been a pleasure, because Brazao's map had been so accurate and so clearly marked that it had been the simplest thing in the world to follow. It had seemed to him that his every dream was about to come true, that the five years wandering in the wilderness were at last being justified. And the mine had been there, just as Brazao had promised, a vein of silver as thick as a man's body, and as yet hardly touched. A perfect fortune. And even more, a promise of the other fortunes that were surely waiting to be claimed, here in the virgin forest. Of El Dorado itself.

Then haste had become imperative, and it had been his undoing. Haste, and perhaps a touch of conscience, because on his way downriver again he had seen Cali on the bank, her child in her arms, drawn hither no doubt by his disappearance of a few weeks before, searching for his body, perhaps, with the simple love of her people.

She had called out to him, in a long, wailing moan, and he had gone by as quickly as he could. Cali had no place in his future now. Nor could he convince himself that she would be any the worse off without him. She had saved his life, for her own purposes. Now he would take his life back again and return to a world of which she knew nothing, while she could continue to exist in the woods, which she knew so well, with her new toy to play with.

And Brazao's map had continued to be true and accurate. Belem had been exactly as he had foretold, at the confluence of at least two mighty rivers, with a maze of islands and water passages stretching a hundred miles and more, for all anyone knew, to the north. But the exploration of that estuary had been for the future. In Belem he had also found the house, shuttered in its owner's absence, and under the floorboards, the treasure trove of silver ingots, carefully hoarded. That alone had been a fortune. With that, his return to Rio as the wealthiest man in Brazil had ceased to be a dream, and become a reality—until they had searched his bags as he boarded ship. He had not been able to believe it was happening at first. No fate could be that cruel as to turn him loose in the foulest jungle in all the world for five years, bring him face to face with his dreams, allow him to touch it and hold it and plan for it, and then have it wrenched from his grasp. But silver smuggling was a grave offense in the eyes of the government. It was far more serious than murder; no one had asked any questions about how he had come to be living in a house built and owned by one Carlos Brazao.

Despite his despair and his raging fury, he had kept his head. He had not shaved his beard, and his skin had been burned so brown by the sun that it was difficult for anyone to dispute that he was actually a Portuguese named Jaime Moreno; his inarticulateness had been regarded as the obvious result of his years in the jungle. The temptation to declare himself Jamey Grant, to invoke the protection of the retired viceroy and famous Captain Grant, had been tremendous, but that too he had resisted, because he had not been sure that a *retired* viceroy could help him, and because *any* surrender would have meant the loss of his mine; with his seaman's instincts he had been able to imprint on his brain the map he felt compelled to burn. No one was ever going to learn of that. They had flogged him until blood had run down his legs, and they had used the thumbscrews until he had screamed, but he had not told them, and in time they had wearied of their sport, had settled for the confiscation of the considerable amount of silver they had found in his possession, and for trying and convicting him as a smuggler.

He had been sent to prison for eight years and returned to Portugal to serve his sentence. Eight years of existing alongside murderers and cutthroats, pimps and thieves, of laboring on the roads. Eight years of floggings and near starvation, of seeing men go mad from mistreatment and despair. But only eight years, to a man who had already spent five in the jungles of the Amazon. Eight more years in which to dream. But now the dreams had been entirely of revenge, and accomplishment. Of what he would do when he regained his silver mine, of what he would do when he found and plundered El Dorado. They had been dreams of violence and self-indulgence, never of love. There had been no room for such an emotion in the prison outside Oporto.

Within twenty-four hours of leaving prison, both the beard and the identity were gone, and he had emerged as Pedro Fernandes. He had made his way south to the Tagus, and had actually looked at the old *Lodestar,* riding to her anchors, had even supposed he could see his brother walking the poop. Then the temptation to shed Pedro Fernandes and become at last Jamey Grant had once more been overwhelming, yet still to be resisted. Jack was one of those who was his natural enemy, for did he not possess Christina? Jack was there to be destroyed, when he had regained his wealth.

As Pedro Fernandes he had undertaken the lengthy and tiresome business of emigrating to the New World as a seaman, of deserting his ship at Belem, and of making his way up the Araguaia once again, heart pounding as he expected to see Cali standing at every bend in the river, as he had expected to discover his silver mine looted by some more fortunate explorer. He had wept when he had found it exactly as he had left it.

But now he had learned sense as well as caution. Instead of smelting enough silver to buy the world, he had contented himself with smelting just enough to convince the world, when the time came, that he *could* buy it, no more than could properly be concealed in his clothing, together with some silver coins for everyday use. Besides, now that his plans were finally laid, when he had reemerged this time from the forest, it *had* been as Jamey Grant, reappeared after fourteen long years. No customs officer was going to search the long lost brother of the famous Captain Grant, son-in-law of the retired viceroy, especially since his long search had obviously been a fruitless one.

But there had been those, lurking in the waterside taverns, who had been prepared to believe his story that he knew where El Dorado was, who had been prepared to follow him, to obey him and carry out his instructions, especially when he had offered to pay their passages down the coast to Rio. For if his plans required a ship, and if it had seemed a fairly straightforward matter to obtain that ship from Jack, just in case Jack's name and influence might be required at a later date, he had no intention of sailing with a crew of devoted, honest men prepared to obey him only so long as he operated within the framework of the Grant Company. His men must be prepared to do what *he* required.

It was not until he had taken passage himself, having dispatched his advance guard and learned that his brother had departed to fight in the American war, that he had actually begun to think of Christina again. At first, he had thought of her only as being easier to convince than Jack, who had always possessed a streak of pessimistic realism. Revenge, however sweet, had then been going to wait on achievement. Seeing her again had almost made him change his mind. She was not the girl he remembered; she was incomparably more beautiful, more assured, even when confronted with her long lost lover. Infinitely more desirable. Infinitely more magnificent to consider as his, to do with as he chose. Infinitely more fascinating to imagine slowly shedding that composure, that arrogant security, that cold superiority, before the power and the passion, the crushing force of his lust.

Once again he was beset by dreams, when he had determined that for the rest of his life he would deal only in realities.

The door was opening and Senora Peixoto was smiling at him; she appreciated well-connected tenants who paid in silver coin. "Senor Grant, you have seen your mother? She is well? I did not expect you back this morning."

"Aye well, senora, there is much to be done. Even for the prodigal son."

"There have been some men here asking for you," Senora Peixoto said, watching him anxiously.

"Indeed? Are they here now?"

"No, no. I did not care for their looks, senor. I sent them packing. But one of them, a man called Alvares, he said you would wish to speak with them and that they would be at the Tavern of the Sea Spirit."

Jamey nodded. "I shall sleep for an hour, then I will go there to see them."

"The Tavern of the Sea Spirit is not a good place, Senor Grant. It is . . . well, of ill repute."

Jamey smiled at her and chucked her under the chin. "I will be careful, senora. But these men, they are my servants. I agree with you about their looks. But what would you? It is not always possible to choose handsome servants. Now I must rest. Will you call me in an hour?"

"Of course, senor. Of course. I . . ." She turned her head as there came a fresh banging on the door.

"They must have come back," Jamey said. "Ah well, I will see them now. There is naught for you to concern yourself with, senora." He went to the door, opened it, and gazed at Henry de Carvalho.

Chapter 8

The young man had been at his parents' house when Jamey had
called the previous evening and was thus instantly recognizable.
He had left almost immediately, pleading a prior engagement
in town; since he was wearing the same clothes that Jamey
remembered, although slightly disheveled, and was clearly
somewhat the worse for drink, it seemed likely he had not
been to bed at all. Yet both his eyes and his voice were clear
enough. "I have run you down, you abomination," he said.

Jamey looked past him at the two other young men, waiting
in the dawn; one of them carried a pair of rapiers. His own
brain was somewhat dulled by lack of sleep, but it came alert
very rapidly, while his entire body began to seethe with that
consuming hatred for the human race he felt whenever he even
suspected he was going to be opposed, whether verbally or
physically.

"You are drunk," he remarked. "You had best get home
to your mother, senor."

"Drunk? By God . . ." Henry de Carvalho pushed him on
the chest, sending him staggering back into the hall, and
stepped inside.

"Senors, senors." Senora Peixoto hurried into the hallway. "I will have no brawling."

"That is up to the American," said the first young man.

"We are here for his ears," said the second, also pushing into the house, and closing the door behind himself.

"Unless, Senor Grant, you would care to defend your honor like a gentleman," Henry de Carvalho said.

Jamey considered them. Undoubtedly they were callow, inexperienced children when compared with himself. But they were dangerous children in that they would all be accomplished duelists, and quite irresponsible in their attitude toward the shedding of blood, or even death. And they had been sent. There could be no doubt about that. By whom? It could only be Christina; the boy who wished to fight him was her cousin. His entire brain seemed to fill with a white-hot fury, but he spoke quietly. "I think you intend my murder, senors," he said.

"By no means," Henry de Carvalho said. "These gentlemen are prepared to act as our seconds, and as witnesses to the correctness of any proceedings which may follow. Allow me to present Jaime Vasconcellos and Rodrigo Nascimento."

The two young men bowed.

"And you are here to challenge me," Jamey said. "May I inquire your reasons, senor?"

"They are many," Henry said. "I do not like your face, I do not like your name, I do not like your appearance. I think you stink, senor. I do not like your past, and I refuse to contemplate your future."

"Those are all personal opinions, senor," Jamey pointed out, all the while staring from one to other of the young men, noting their expressions, the flush in Carvalho's cheeks, the way Nascimento kept lowering his gaze, the nervous twitch of Vasconcellos's nostrils, even as he estimated the strength of their shoulders and their legs. "You are entitled to your opinions."

"I have also made a resolution," Henry de Carvalho said, "to add your ears to my collection. It matters naught whether I remove them from your dead body or whether I remove them as you beg for mercy. I will have them now."

"Senors, senors," implored Senora Peixoto. "I beg of you—"

"Shut that woman up," Carvalho snapped. "Tie her to a chair and gag her."

"Senors," Senora Peixoto wailed as the other two seized her and sat her in a chair, tearing draperies from the windows to rip into suitable lengths to bind her.

"You will be paid," Carvalho said, "double what that cloth is worth, good senora. Just do not interfere. But you will also be a witness that I have challenged Senor Grant in an entirely proper manner." He stepped forward and slashed the back of his hand into Jamey's mouth.

Jamey's head jerked, but he did not move his feet. The blow completed his determination, however, to kill this man— or all three of them, as he suspected might be necessary.

"Well?" Carvalho demanded.

Jamey licked blood from his lips. "I know little of dueling," he said. "I have never dueled in my life."

Carvalho's smile was contemptuous. "We will teach you, Senor Grant," he said. "Very properly. Rodrigo."

Nascimento stepped forward, the two rapiers held by their blades and resting across his forearm, hilts toward Jamey. "You may take your choice of weapons, senor."

"Of *these* weapons?" Jamey asked softly.

"There are none finer in all Brazil," Nascimento said.

"No finer swords perhaps," Jamey said, still speaking quietly, "but Senor Carvalho has challenged *me*, therefore do I not have choice of weapons?"

"Bah, the fool seeks an issue with pistols. No doubt you hope for a misfire, senor. Well, let me tell you that our duel will continue until one of us is dead. Pistols matter naught to me. There is a case in my saddle bag, Jaime, and powder and ball." He smiled at Jamey. "I can assure you, senor, that they will *not* misfire, and that I am at least as accurate a pistol shot as I am a swordsman."

"I have no doubt of it," Jamey agreed. "But pistols are noisy, dirty things. Supposing you *were* to miss, senor, and since I would certainly miss, having never fired a pistol in my life, we would stand there banging away at each other until noon, disturbing the life of the entire city. No, no, senor, my choice is for weapons which are at once quiet and will certainly see the matter completed speedily and to your satisfaction." His voice hardened. "I choose knives."

The three men stared at him.

"Knives?" Nascimento said at last. "Only peasants and villains fight with knives."

For the first time Jamey smiled. "Would you not describe me as both a peasant and a villain, Senor Carvalho?"

"That is quite impossible," Vasconcellos declared. "Why, Henry has—"

"Not fought with a knife before?" Jamey asked gently. "Then he is but in the position I should find myself in if I were to pick up that rapier, senor. My heart bleeds for him, but after all *he* has seen fit to challenge *me*. I seek no fight with anyone."

"The man is being absurd," Nascimento said uneasily. "We had best withdraw, Henry, and reconsider the matter."

Carvalho chewed his lip.

"By all means do so," Jamey said, his voice growing even harder as his smile broadened. "You will forgive me if, while you consider, I leave the house? I have important business to complete, and besides, there is a certain publicity which must surely be given to this affair. Of Senor Carvalho's *consideration* of whether or not he dares fight a peasant and a villain."

His smile included them all but came to rest on Henry de Carvalho, who was still staring at him. The young man was taller than he and looked stronger, in his breadth of chest, the obvious muscles in his legs; since Jamey had not yet discarded his cloak, the enormous power in the hunched shoulders was not readily apparent.

"Bah," Henry said. "What difference does it make? A weapon is a weapon. Fetch some knives."

"I had no doubt that you would play the gentleman to the last, senor," Jamey said. "There are knives in my bedchamber."

"It is a trick to escape us," Nascimento exclaimed.

"I should not dream of it," Jamey said. "The bedchamber

is at the top of those stairs, and the door is not locked. *You* go and secure the weapons, Senor Vasconcellos.''

Vasconcellos hesitated, glancing at Carvalho, who nodded. He went up the stairs, and the room was quiet, except for the sound of their breathing, which had suddenly increased in intensity, Jamey realized, while poor Senora Peixoto's was positively labored. But he was hardly breathing at all. There could only be one outcome to the approaching fight.

Vasconcellos came back down the stairs with the two long, razor-sharp machetes in his hand. ''These are assassins' tools,'' he protested.

''On the contrary, senor, they are bushman's tools,'' Jamey said, ''intended for hacking down tropical forest. But they are sharp enough for our purpose. They can also be somewhat messy. Dare I suggest that we withdraw to the walled garden at the rear of this house? It would be a shame to spill blood all over Senora Peixoto's walls and furniture.''

The young men stared at him and then at each other. They were aware that in some unfathomable fashion they had lost the initiative, that they were as much in the hands of this man as ten minutes ago they had supposed he was *their* victim. Jamey obligingly went to the inner door, which led down a short flight of steps into the garden, opened it, and waited. Once again they exchanged glances, then they filed out into the uncertain dawn light. Senora Peixoto gave a moan of farewell.

Jamey closed the door behind himself, removing the key from the inside and locking it from the outside; the walls of the garden were several feet high, and there was no possibility of anyone leaving until he unlocked the door again, or of their being interrupted.

The three young men watched him almost anxiously as he came down the steps behind them. ''You'll allow Senor Carvalho to choose his blade,'' he suggested.

Nascimento held out the machetes, and Carvalho, after a moment's hesitation, seized one of the hafts.

Jamey removed his cloak and wrapped it around his left arm before taking the other machete. Carvalho stared at him; he was not wearing a cloak.

"Henry," Vasconcellos said, taking off his doublet and tossing it over. Carvalho glanced at Jamey to see exactly how it was done, rolled the small garment as best he could around his forearm. His confidence had entirely evaporated, but he certainly did not lack courage—not that that interested Jamey in the slightest. He was not here to admire, or even to condone. He was here to kill. His course of action, slowly hardening in his mind throughout the past twenty-four hours, was now clearly mapped in his mind. It was what his instincts were crying out for him to do anyway, which meant that there was no necessity to show the least mercy to these three arrogant puppies.

He smiled at Carvalho. "Are we ready, senor? You'll request your friends to stand back."

Carvalho nodded and Nascimento and Vasconcellos retreated, one to each side, Jamey noted, which only made them the easier to deal with, especially since Vasconcellos had absentmindedly retained both the rapiers.

Carvalho was regarding him hesitantly, not at all sure how to begin, whether to present his knife as he would a sword, or rely on agility. Jamey thrust his machete forward, and Carvalho followed his example. The ends of the blades touched for an instant, and Jamey retreated. Carvalho followed immediately, the instincts of the swordsman leading him to maintain contact between the blades before disengaging for a thrust. Jamey pivoted and struck downward with his cloaked left hand. Carvalho saw the blow coming and turned to parry, only to find his right hand trapped in the suddenly released cloak, which entirely muffled his blade. He gave an exclamation of anger and disgust, attempted to shake the heavy material free, but Jamey simply stepped around him and drove his own machete deep into Carvalho's back, thrusting upward then withdrawing the weapon in a vast spurt of blood which also then issued from Carvalho's mouth as he fell first to his knees and then to his face, gasping for breath, each pant a gush of blood from his throat.

"That was murder," Nascimento shouted. "You used your hand."

Jamey had picked up the other machete as well and turned

his back on the shouting but unarmed man, to face Vasconcellos, who stared at him as if he were seeing the devil, then dropped one of the rapiers to grasp the haft of the other. All too late. The second machete was already singing through the air, thrown with consummate accuracy, its point entering Vasconcellos's stomach just below the breastbone. He gave a choking gasp and also fell to his knees, bloodstained hands wrapped unavailingly around the blade.

"My God," Nascimento said, his voice almost a sob as he gazed at the execution in front of him. He backed against the wall, turned his head left and right, and fell to his knees as Jamey approached. "For the love of God, senor," he cried. "Would you murder me also?"

"That is my intention," Jamey said, and seized his hair to drag the young man's head up as he passed the blade neatly across the pulsing throat, almost severing the head from the body, then hastily stepping back to prevent the blood from soiling his boots. He bent and carefully cleaned the blade on the grass, wiping his bloodstained hand as well. They were all dead, except for Carvalho, and he clearly had only a few moments left to live. It was the neatest and quickest performance of his life, Jamey realized. Hitherto there had only been Brazao, whom he had killed with his bare hands, and the prisoner in Oporto, the first time he had used a knife. But that had been in the midst of a brawl, and had been an untidy business.

The pealing of the church clock reminded him that there was no time for him to admire his handiwork further. He thrust the machete into his belt, ran up the steps, unlocked the door, and went into the hall, locking the door behind him and again pocketing the key. Senora Peixoto stared at him with huge eyes. He smiled at her, went up the stairs, hastily repacked his two satchels and slung them over his shoulder, then came down the stairs again.

"I have left a silver coin on the table in payment for your services," he said. "Unfortunately I have to leave you in this sorry state, but you can be absolutely sure that within the next few hours someone will come along, if only to discover what has happened to my antagonists. They have, as you can see, been persuaded to allow me to go in peace, but I have considered it best to leave them locked in the garden for the time being. Senora, my thanks for your hospitality.''

He went outside, locking that door also behind him and again pocketing the key. Early as it was, there were people about, those whose business or duties required them to walk the streets and those who preferred to do so before the day got too hot. The three horses belonging to the young men waited patiently, secured to the rail outside Senora Peixoto's house, as did the hired mule he had ridden the previous night. He decided the horses might attract attention too soon for his advantage if they remained tethered in the street all day, so he released them, mounted the first, and led the other two toward the harbor.

At the Tavern of the Sea Spirit he dismounted, retethered the horses, and found that the publican and his son were already up, washing down the taproom and the steps. ''I seek the whereabouts of a Senor Alvares,'' Jamey explained.

''Of course, Senor Grant. Senor Alvares and his companions are in my house,'' the publican said. ''They said you would seek them. But, senor, they are all asleep.''

Jamey nodded. ''I will wake them. But I have a task for you, senor. These horses, as you may be aware, belong to Senor Henry de Carvalho and two of his friends. The young men, I am sorry to say, became so overwhelmed with joy at my return that they accompanied me to my lodgings last night and there drank themselves silly, so that I have had to put them to bed. Alas, I have business to attend to, and Senora Peixoto lacks the facilities for caring for horses. I would be obliged if you would take these unfortunate animals out of the sun and into your stables, and grant them some water and a bag of oats, until Senor Carvalho and his friends come for them.'' He tapped his nose. ''Which I doubt will be much before this evening.''

''Of course, Senor Grant, of course,'' the landlord agreed. ''I shall attend to it immediately.''

''I knew you would,'' Jamey said, and went up the stairs to the communal dormitory offered by the landlord for the accommodation of visiting seamen who preferred not to spend their nights in one of the town brothels. It was a large room, furnished with only a few cots but with a number of men sleeping on the floor. The stench was considerable, as was the noise of snoring in various pitches, but it took Jamey only a few seconds to identify the members of his group. He tiptoed among the sleeping bodies, touched Alvares on the shoulder, and caught the man's hand as he immediately sat up, knife at the ready.

Jamey shook his head to prevent him speaking and then jerked it to indicate that he wished to leave the room. Alvares nodded, threw back the blanket, and followed his master to the door.

"How many?" Jamey asked.

"There are twelve of us here, senor. Eight will arrive during this week."

"They will be too late. Twelve. Damnation! But we will have to manage with twelve."

"But, senor—"

"We cannot wait, Alvares. We must act today. I want you to wake the others and tell them to go down to the dock, to a vessel called the *Plough*. She flies the flag of the Grant Company and is almost ready for sea. You will stay with them and do nothing until I appear. You understand me?"

"Of course, senor, but . . ."

"I will explain when I return. I shall not be long. Perhaps two hours. You will wait, Alvares."

"Yes, senor."

"But I need someone to accompany me. Who?"

Alvares pulled his nose. "For help, senor?"

"Oh, aye," Jamey said. "He may have to break a few heads."

Alvares smiled. "I will fetch Caetano. He will break heads for you, senor. He will enjoy doing that."

Christina reached her house in a state of complete exhaustion and some concern. Her father had acted extremely oddly, not least in insisting she return home, but also in not immediately giving an opinion. She could not really understand what he needed to consider, since his emotions were not involved, and she had not confessed to him *her* emotional confusion.

She undressed, informed her butler that she would not be riding this morning, since she had already traveled some sixty miles in the phaeton during the night, and got into bed. No doubt Papa meant to go and discuss the matter with Jamey himself. That was the only conclusion that made any sense at all. But she could not see any good coming of it. In fact . . . she sat up in alarm. Jamey, if annoyed in any way, might even tell Papa the truth of the matter. She chewed her lip. Would it make any difference now? Papa could hardly have him arrested for a seduction carried out fourteen years before, even if he dared consider the publicity.

She lay down again, her heartbeat slowly returning to normal. But it was Jamey's unspoken threat of publicity that was dominating her thoughts. It was really impossible to contemplate the scandal, the effect it would have upon little James, already set to be a rebellious delinquent, upon Mama Grant and the Carvalhos, upon her own mother—for she had never been told the truth any more than Papa had.

She rolled onto her stomach, buried her face in the pillow. The sooner she agreed to let him have a ship the better. Even Jack would have to admit that it was the best thing to do. And there was no need for her to involve *them* in anything illegal. She would sell the vessel to Jamey, as he seemed to wish, and wash her hands of the entire affair.

Her agitation subsided, and she closed her eyes, immediately to doze. When she got up, she thought drowsily, she would dress and go down to the dock and tell Jamey her decision. Papa might be angry that she had acted without waiting for his advice . . . my God, she thought, rolling over and sitting up again, Papa would already be there.

She threw back the mosquito netting, pulled the bell rope as she got out of bed. "My riding habit," she snapped at her maid.

"But, senora—"

"I have changed my mind," she said. "I must get into town, and quickly. Tell Antonio to have my horse saddled. I will take a single groom. Haste, now."

The girl hurried from the room and Christina dressed herself, ignoring her corsets today in favor of a single shift beneath the somewhat heavy linen of her habit. Her hair had been loosened, and she contented herself with a quick brush before adjusting her tricorne; matching the habit, it was pale blue with a gold trim.

"Senora . . ." The maid stood in the doorway, fingers twisted together.

"Is all ready? I will come now."

"There is a gentleman to see you, senora."

Christina frowned at her as she picked up her crop. "A gentleman? At this hour?"

"The same gentleman who was here yesterday, senora."

"Jamey." Christina pushed the girl aside and ran down the stairs. Jamey was standing in the middle of the lower hall, accompanied by a large and extremely unpleasant looking man who had clearly not shaved in several days. But to her relief, her brother-in-law did not look particularly angry, or even excited. She slowed to a walk, and had her breathing under control by the time she reached the floor. "Jamey? I was about to come in to visit you."

"Were you, now?" he remarked. "Then I have wasted my journey. However, I will have the privilege of escorting you."

"But . . ." She stared at him, realized that he was not quite as relaxed as he had seemed at first sight; his eyes were like twin coals. "Is the journey not unnecessary now?"

"On the contrary, Dona Christina," he said. "It is more necessary than ever. Have you considered my offer?"

"Of course." She glanced at the big sailor. "Perhaps we should discuss it in private. There is an antechamber just there."

"But as I recall, you do not wish to be alone with me, Christina," he said.

"Well . . . things are different," she said, "now that I have had the time to consider." She led him into the antechamber and closed the door. "I have decided to sell you a ship as you wish." She turned to face him, her back against the window.

He gave a brief bow. "You are very kind."

"But it must be a straight transaction," she said. "I do not want any share in your enterprise for the Grant Company." She attempted a smile. "you will not have to divide your profits."

"Generous," he agreed. "I am overwhelmed. There is one small matter, Christina. I find it necessary to leave Rio this morning. Have you a ship immediately available?"

"Well . . . I shall have to see."

"I thought you had considered. Is not your ship the *Plough* ready for sea?"

"She is not yet loaded with cargo."

"But I do not wish her loaded with cargo, Christina," he said quietly. "I want her just as she is, and I understand she is already loaded with food and water."

"I do not think that will be possible," Christina said. "The *Plough* is already contracted, her cargo invoiced. I had thought of allowing you one of my ships that is on the way back to Rio at the moment. As soon as they dock, and are unloaded—"

"And I have just explained that I cannot wait that long, my dear Christina."

"But . . . yesterday there was no great haste. Or rather, only for my decision. And I have made that decision in your favor, Jamey. Surely we can drop this sparring and pretending. You shall have your ship as soon as it becomes available. I have given you my word. Now, let us have a cup of chocolate together and be friends."

She stepped past him toward the door, was taken completely by surprise when he seized her arm, fingers biting into her flesh with such force that she would have cried out had she not lost all her breath as she was spun around and pulled close against him, while in the same motion he used his other hand to draw the machete from his belt and hold it flat against her stomach, the point facing upward, between her breasts.

"You—"

"I have already used this knife to good purpose this morning, sweet Christina, beloved sister-in-law, mother of my child," Jamey whispered in her ear. "Dishonest, treacherous, murderous Christina. And it would give me the greatest pleasure to slit you from tit to toe.''

''You . . .'' She struggled to free herself, but was held too close. Her thoughts tumbled. She could not believe this was happening.

''You are hurting me,'' she gasped.

''I intend to, you little vixen,'' he said. ''Now listen to me. I am quite capable, with the help of Caetano, of destroying everyone in this house, and I shall, unless you do exactly as I say. Do you understand me?''

''You . . .'' She attempted to kick backward with her boot, but the effort came to nothing since it was hampered by her skirt.

''I wish you to ring that bell,'' he said, ''and command James to be brought to us here, fully dressed.''

The grip was slackening. She could step away, only to have him instantly at her side, the machete now resting against her back.

''You are mad,'' she said. ''Or drunk. Do you really think you can come here and manhandle me, threaten me . . . I will have you jailed.''

He twined his fingers in her hair and jerked her head backward with such violence that her hat fell off and she thought she had broken her neck. ''Send for James,'' he said, ''or by God I'll take an ear off right now.''

She stared into his eyes, her mouth sagging with pain and horror. Because suddenly she realized that this nightmare *was* happening, and that the man who was holding her was as far removed from the boy who had pulled her from the sea as it was possible to imagine. This man *would* kill, without compunction, as he claimed to have already killed this morning. And suddenly she believed him.

The grip on her hair was relaxing, and she could slowly straighten her head. ''The bell,'' he said.

She reached for it as if in a dream, gave it a pull, and listened to the distant chimes. She swallowed; her throat was hurting. ''He is your son, Jamey. If you harm him—''

''Whether I harm him, or anyone, is up to you,'' Jamey said. ''Now remember, when that door opens, my machete will be concealed. But I will kill both you and whoever comes, as well as every one of your children, if you attempt to play me false.''

Christina gazed at him, then turned to look at the door as it opened, ''Senora?'' It was Antonio himself.

Christina swallowed again. ''I wish to see Master James, in this room, immediately, Antonio,'' she said. ''Have him get dressed first.''

''Of course, senora.'' Antonio gazed at her in astonishment, and she realized that she must look a sight. Then he glanced at Jamey, gave a brief bow, and left the room, closing the door behind him.

''That was well done,'' Jamey said.

She turned to face him. ''What do you want of him? If—''

''You are hysterical,'' he said. ''I wish to say goodbye to my son. What could be more simple than that? I also wish the pair of you to accompany me to the docks. When your butler returns, you will order your phaeton.''

''The docks? But—''

''My dear Christina,'' he said. ''I cannot simply walk on board one of your ships and sail away. You will have to give the necessary instructions and command your watchmen, or whoever may be on board, to leave her.''

''You will sail her all by yourself?''

''I have a crew waiting to board her, the moment they are allowed to do so.''

''Well then, I will write you a letter to Conybeare . . .''

Jamey smiled at her, gently shaking his head. ''You will accompany me, dear Christina. You and James. I will sit beside you, and Caetano will sit beside James, and both your survivals will depend on your behavior. Do not fail me in this, Christina. And I am asking very little of you. Just a journey into town to see me on my way without any mishaps.''

''And then you will release us?'' she asked. ''And sail away, never to come back?''

''I shall never return to Rio,'' he said. ''I give you my word.'' His smile broadened. ''It would not be very wise, would it? As for releasing you, may I not ask for a last kiss before we part forever?''

* * *

There were only three watchmen on board the *Plough*. The captain and officers, as well as the crew, were all Rio men, who naturally preferred to sleep at home until the hour of sailing. The watchmen merely gaped at Christina as she commanded them to leave the vessel, and as they watched Alvares lead his people on board.

Christina felt like gaping as well. She stood in the shelter of the poop, for the sun was already high, with James beside her and Caetano behind them both, and watched the men, every one of whom she would have described as an utter villain, taking their positions and preparing to cast off. Once again she found it impossible actually to believe the evidence of her own eyes, the ache in her head and her throat and her arm. She had ridden into town as if in a dream, staring at James, sitting opposite her, next to Caetano. What the servants had thought she just could not imagine; she had only been relieved that Antonio, however mystified and displeased by what he saw happening, had been prepared to obey her, as always, without question. Now she wanted only to see the ship leave. Time enough to explain what had happened then.

She realized that Jamey had not yet paid her. No doubt this was his plan, and was why he had made her come down to the ship. As if she cared about the money. But she would send a warship after him. Of that she was determined. Her fear and her concern were slowly coagulating into anger. No one had ever treated her the way she had been treated this morning. And not even Jamey Grant was going to get away with it, if she had to have him hanged.

She glanced down at her son, wondered what *he* thought of it all. But he was clearly as bewildered as anyone, although he seemed to be enjoying his adventure. There would have to be explanations to him also, once they were safely ashore.

Jamey walked across the deck toward them. "There we are," he said. "All ready for sea." He looked up at the masts. "The wind is offshore. Couldn't be better. We'll just drift away from the dock, set sail, and be out of the harbor before anyone is the wiser."

"Yes," she said. "Well, I will say goodbye, Jamey. I shall

not forget what has happened this morning, and I can only offer to pray for your soul should you ever set foot in Brazil again, or come face to face with your brother. Say farewell to James. You will not see him again either.''

"Ah," Jamey said. "Now, as to that—"

"Ahoy there," came the shout from the dock. Jamey turned, and Christina stepped forward, to see Conybeare running down the road, accompanied by one of the watchmen and also by the captain of the *Plough*.

"Oh my God," Christina said.

"Take the boy below," Jamey shouted.

"No," Christina said. "No . . ." But the big sailor picked up James as if he were a sack and descended the companion-way, while at Jamey's signal another sailor came to stand beside Christina.

"You'll say not a word unless I tell you to," Jamey said, and went to the rail.

"Good morning, Arthur," he said. "What can I do for you?"

Conybeare stopped to stare at him, hands on hips. "Jamey? I could not believe it. What is the meaning of this?"

"Very simply, it means that your mistress has sold me this vessel," Jamey said. "And since I am in haste to put to sea, I am leaving now."

"Sold you the *Plough*?" Conybeare looked incredulous. "But she cannot have done so. The *Plough* is contracted for Lisbon, a week from today."

"Dona Christina is on board now," Jamey said. "Why do you not come up and speak with her? Only you," he said as Conybeare started up the gangplank and the captain made to follow.

Conybeare hesitated, then nodded. "I shall not be long. I am sure Senora Grant knows her own mind." He jumped onto the deck. "You spin a tangled web, Jamey."

"I am a man with things to do, Arthur," Jamey said, and escorted his friend across the deck toward Christina. "Arthur needs confirmation of your decision, Christina."

Christina opened her mouth, found that her throat was dry,

licked her lips. "I . . . I have sold Jamey the *Plough*, Arthur."

Conybeare frowned at her. "But, Dona Christina, there is contracted cargo waiting to be loaded. Our reputation will suffer."

"I am sure it is high enough to withstand a few shocks," Christina said, staring at him, willing him to understand. "In any event, the transaction has been completed, Arthur. So if you would be good enough to escort James and myself ashore—"

"I am sure Arthur would prefer to see the bill of sale," Jamey said.

"The . . ." She gazed at him.

"Yes," Conybeare said. "Yes, I would."

"It is in the cabin," Jamey said. "You'll come down as well, Christina."

"But—"

"And we are all in a hurry," he said, gripping her arm and forcing her toward the hatch. The steps loomed in front of her before she was ready for them, and she tripped, almost falling, and lost her balance enough to arrive at the foot of the ladder on her hands and knees, her mind teeming with frightened anger.

"Now hold on, Jamey," Conybeare protested. "You can't treat Mrs. Grant like a sack of potatoes." He scrambled down the ladder behind her and tenderly helped her to her feet. "I'm sure it was a mistake, Dona Christina."

"A mistake?" She looked up the ladder, at Jamey coming down, while the hatch swung to behind him. "He's gone mad. He's—"

"In there," Jamey said, and she saw that he held a pistol.

Conybeare saw it too. "By God," he said. "you are mad. What's this? Piracy? You'll not get away with it." He cocked his head as they heard feet pounding above their heads, and a moment later the squeal of halyards running through their blocks. "By God," Conybeare said again, "you've cast off." He ran for the ladder. "You let me up there."

"Stop where you are, Arthur," Jamey said, his back against the hatch. "It was your decision to come on board."

Conybeare stared at him, then glanced at Christina.

"He made me sell it," she explained. "And then . . ." It was her turn to stare at Jamey. "You promised to set us ashore. You—"

"I'll wring your lousy little neck," Conybeare bellowed, and ran forward. There was a loud report and a flash of light, and the confined space filled with smoke, while Conybeare gave a wailing cry and reared backward, to fall in a heap at Christina's feet.

For a moment Christina could not breathe, but without thinking she dropped to her knees beside the stricken man, to discover that he was already dead; the bullet, fired at such close range, had penetrated his chest and his heart. In a shock of disbelieving horror she raised her head and watched the hatch swing open as Jamey went out. She pushed herself up, ran behind him, and had her way blocked by another seaman, obviously just instructed by his captain. "Into the cabin," he said.

Christina felt the ship heel as the first foresail was set and began to fill with wind. She thought she could also hear people shouting from the shore, but they were drowned out by the orders Jamey was issuing as he took the helm, commanding his people to set the mainsail and to raise the ensign and house flags. In a few minutes he would be passing the forts, and must appear to be a typical Grant Company vessel putting to sea.

Not that the commandant of the fort would dream of firing upon one of Jack's ships in any event, unless . . . "Let me up," she said. "Stand aside."

The man grinned at her as he came down the steps. "Into the cabin," he repeated. "Captain's orders."

To her anger she discovered she was backing away before him, when she wanted to stand up and slap his face. "If you touch me . . ."

Her feet encountered Conybeare's body and she stumbled. Before she could recover, the man had seized her around the waist, opened the door to the great cabin, and bundled her inside. She staggered forward, found herself against the table, gasping for breath, raised her head and stared at her son, who was regarding her with wide eyes. He had never in his life seen his mother manhandled. Then his gaze drifted past her to the companionway—where Conybeare's body lay in a crumpled heap.

"That's Arthur," he cried.

"And he's dead," said Caetano, who was also in the cabin. "So you'd better behave yourself, eh?"

James turned his gaze back to his mother, who sat down on one of the bunks lining the bulkhead. Her knees would not support her any longer.

The sailor who had brought her in grinned at Caetano. "You can manage?"

"This pair? No trouble."

The man nodded and left the cabin, closing the door behind himself. Christina regained control of her breathing. "You are pirates," she said. "You are going to hang, all of you. Including your captain."

"In that case we've nothing to lose, lady," Caetano pointed out. "So you just keep your mouth shut or I'll put a gag in it. You, boy, sit with your mother."

A push sent James staggering around the table, and she hastily held his hand to make him sit beside her, putting her arm around his shoulder.

"Mama?" he asked. "What on earth is happening?"

"Your Uncle Jamey has gone mad," Christina said. "Quite mad. We shall have to humor him for the time being." She looked out the stern windows. The ship had turned, and she could see the dock and the people gathered there. It was too far to decide what they were saying or doing; they were certainly not taking any action, but rather discussing the strange events of the morning. By the time they did decide that something was wrong, the *Plough* would be out in the Atlantic. The brigantine's bottom was clean, since she had just been careened and scraped, and there was no ship in Rio that could catch her once she found herself a fair wind. Already, as Christina could make out from the stretches of shore appearing to either side, they were entering the narrows. They would have to humor Jamey for a very long time.

But what could he want with them? Her heart lurched as she realized there was only one thing he could want with them. He wanted a son, and he wanted . . . she bit her lip to stop herself from crying out.

He must know she would never agree to that. But would her refusal make any difference to a man such as Jamey Grant had become, who had just shot down his old friend in cold blood?

She gazed at Caetano. "Listen to me," she said. "Mr. Grant is mad. You must know that. He is turning you all into pirates. Your only hope is to disown him, take control of the ship, and put back to Rio. I will see that you are pardoned, that nothing happens to any of you. I will even reward you, and find you passages to wherever you wish to go. I give you my sacred word."

Caetano grinned at her. "Senor Grant is going to take us to El Dorado," he said. "That is better than a reward, eh?"

"You must know that that is only a dream," she cried. "A legend! There is no such place. Hundreds of people have died searching for it. Not one of them ever found it."

"We will find it," Caetano said confidently. "Senor Grant, he knows where it is."

"You . . ." She twisted her head as she heard feet on the companion ladder, followed by a scraping sound, and realized Conybeare's body was being removed. Then the door opened, and she gazed at Jamey.

"We're through the narrows and making north," he said, "with a fair wind. Would you not say that fortune is smiling upon our enterprise? Wait outside, Caetano. But stay close."

"Aye, aye," Caetano said, and closed the door behind him.

Christina drew a deep breath to steady her nerves. "Do you really suppose," she said, "that you are going to escape? You have committed murder. You have kidnapped me and my son. You have stolen a ship. Every man in the world will have his hand raised against you. You cannot possibly escape, Jamey."

He sat down opposite her, on the other side of the table. "I will escape," he said, "because only I know where I am going, in every sense. I think you should understand that, Christina. I also think that since we are embarking upon a new life together, we should arrive at a mutual understanding as rapidly as possible. I want you to tell James the truth, Christina. Right now.''

She gazed at him, trying desperately to think, to create some advantage, some bargaining counter with which to oppose him.

"Very well," Jamey agreed. "I will do so. You see, James, Jack Grant is not truly your father, nor is he truly your mother's husband. I am your father, and she is my wife."

"You . . . that is a lie," Christina snapped. "Jack and I were married before God, in a church."

"You and I, my darling, were married before God, in a bed, when you yielded me your virginity."

She glanced at James, who was looking from one to the other in amazement. "Must you do this in front of the child?"

"He's no child," Jamey said. "He's all but a man. Aren't you, boy?"

James glanced at his mother. "Mama considers me a child, sir."

Christina bit her lip.

Jamey smiled. "Well, mothers have a way of doing that. But I can see you're a man. And I need all the men I can find. You'll stand at my shoulder, boy. Will you be pleased to do that?"

"I—"

"He killed Arthur," Christina said. "Shot him down in cold blood."

Jamey continued to smile. "As I intend to kill anyone who gets in my way. To succeed in this world, James, a man must be strong and ruthless. Have you the courage to be strong and ruthless?"

"I . . . I think so, sir."

"I have no doubt of it. Together we shall make a fine pair. But no more of this 'sir'. I am your father. Believe me. Ask your mother."

James gazed at Christina, who felt her cheeks burn as they filled with blood.

"Tell him, Christina," Jamey said. "He has to know."

Christina sighed. "He . . . he is your father, James," she said.

The boy's eyes widened.

"So come and give me a hug," Jamey said. "I have never held you in my arms."

James gazed at his mother for a moment, then got up and went around the table to sit beside his father, whose arm went around his shoulder. Never had Christina felt so alone.

"It is not your mother's fault," Jamey said. "You should love your mother, James. Love her and respect her and honor her. She gave me her love, once, but then she thought me dead and so married my brother instead, while already bearing you. She is not to blame. There was nothing else she could do. Her only fault is in wishing to oppose me now."

"Oppose you?" Christina shouted. "Why . . . oh my God, the children. My children," she cried. "What is to become of my children?"

Jamey shrugged. "I am sure they will be provided for. They have grandparents. And even a father, who may eventually return to them. Do you care what happens to them, James? Did you ever really feel they were your full brothers and sisters?"

"Why . . ." James looked at his mother and flushed. "No, sir, I never did."

"Papa," Jamey said. "You must call me Papa." He smiled at Christina, at the tears which had started without warning and were rolling down her cheeks. "Besides, my dear, you are not too old to be a mother. I will give you other children."

"You? I would die first."

Jamey patted his son on the shoulder. "Caetano," he called, and the door opened. "I would have you take Master James and show him the ship. Explain things to him. He is your charge from now on."

"Aye, aye, Captain." Caetano waited.

"Off you go, James," Jamey said. "Your mother and I have things to discuss." He waited until the door closed again. "Such as the creation of a new family for you, eh?" He got up and slipped the bolt on the door. "I have waited fourteen years for this moment."

Christina pushed herself up, her back against the bulkhead. "I would rather die."

Jamey did not move. Instead he leaned back, to be more comfortable, and smiled at her. "Do you really believe that? Are you really going to abandon little James entirely to my schooling? Are you really going to give up all hope of seeing your children again? Of seeing Jack again, assuming you want to?"

She found herself panting. "Do I have such a hope?"

He shrugged. "While there is life, my sweet girl, there is always hope. And what are you so terrified of? Once I thought I made you very happy." His smile broadened. "I promise you that as a lover I am now vastly more experienced."

She stared at him, her heart surging. Of course he was right; she was not going to commit suicide. It was against her philosophy, her religion, her very character. But there was something far more insidious eating at her consciousness, the memory of that night, all those years ago, of all the dreams she had had since about this very man, dreams which, in the utter privacy of her mind, she had been able to indulge.

But which now had to be rejected, and certainly never suspected by him.

"You are a murderer," she said, taking refuge in facts.

"I am a man who will not be opposed," he said. "And what of you? Will you deny that *you* sought *my* death, sent that Carvalho boy and his two friends to make sure of it?"

She stared at him in utter consternation. "Carvalho?" she whispered. "Henry de Carvalho?"

"Your cousin, my dear, and the brother of Mary's husband. Out to slit my throat like a common assassin."

Her brain was spinning so that she couldn't think. "But—"

"Oh, I killed them," he said, smiling at her. "All three of them. It was like sending three house cats to destroy a jaguar, my lovely girl. But I do not think you have any right to call me a murderer."

Papa, she thought. It could only be Papa. Papa, who had

guessed the truth and thought to protect his daughter in the only way a Portuguese gentleman could consider.

Those poor boys. Sent to their deaths without a suspicion of the fate that was awaiting them. And the Carvalhos. And Mary and Mama Grant.

And herself. Because Jamey would never believe that she was not guilty.

"What I would like you to do," Jamey said, still smiling, "is undress for me. Take your time. I have never seen you undress, never *known* your body, Christina, except in the darkness. Show me your body, Christina."

She raised her head. "I shall not."

"Oh, come now. Are you not my wife, before God?"

"I am your brother's wife. I have sworn certain oaths, and I shall keep those oaths. If you take me, it will have to be by force."

He never moved. "Do you not suppose I will do that, my darling Christina? Do you not suppose I can bend you to my will, whenever I wish it? If I open that door, three of my men will be in here, happy to strip you, my darling girl, happy to hold your arms and feet and any other portion of your anatomy that I direct, while I do whatever I choose with you. Or I could take you on deck and have them all take part, and even, perhaps, share you afterwards." He sat up. "I am sure even James might wish to, after he has watched us."

She found her hands clasped around her throat. "Are you a *man*?" she whispered.

He leaned forward. "Aye, I am a man, who for fourteen years has slaved and struggled and starved, who has lain rotting in a prison cell, who has killed to prevent himself from being killed—who has *survived*, Christina, when every creature's hand was against him. I am a man who has learned that there is no God, no retribution, save that of being the weaker in a fight, and I have learned never to be weaker, and therefore never to fear. I will have you, Christina, every day for the rest of my life. I have made myself this promise, and I will keep it, as I have made all my other promises come true. If I have to torment you into surrender, then I will do that too. But you will surrender, because if you do not, *now*, I swear to you that within five minutes I will have you stretched naked on the deck above, and let every member of my crew sample you.'' His face relaxed, and he leaned backward. ''I am sure you will enjoy it much more within the privacy of this cabin, my darling girl. So, do as I ask and take off your clothes.''

Christina found that her fingers were already releasing the buttons at the neck of her gown. She knew that he could carry out his threat, and that her only sensible course of action was to survive, for as long as possible, and with as little harm or humiliation as possible, in order to revenge herself, and Jack, when the time came.

Her clothes fell to the deck, but she could not bend to pick them up. She wished to close her eyes, but the movement of the ship would make her giddy unless she could see. So she stared at the man instead, watching him slowly sit up again.

''Such beauty,'' he said. ''Such beauty, and you a mother of four. Come here.''

She hesitated, and then moved forward, around the table.

''You will have to sit down,'' he said, ''to remove your boots.''

She bit her lip, sat down beside him, raised her right leg to release the lacing on the riding boots, felt his fingers on her shoulders, gently stroking the flesh, slipping down her back, sending a shiver down her spine as they came around in front to stroke and then to cup her breast, to hold her nipple in a way Jack had never done.

The boot fell to the deck, and she gave a little sigh and started to lean back.

''There is another one,'' Jamey said.

She sat up again, and his lips followed his hands, kissing the soft flesh at her side, moving up to take the nipple between his lips, suck it between his teeth, but with utter gentleness, inducing the most delicious feeling. No one had ever kissed her breast before. She turned, kicking off the left boot, rising on her knees on the bunk so that her head touched the low deck beams above, sinking back onto her haunches as the man moved away from her, to undress himself, watching his enormous muscularity, the tan which was unaffected by his clothes, indicating the long years he must have spent naked, the surges of strength in every movement, the tremendous power of his aroused sexuality—and the terrible crisscross scar that disfigured his left thigh.

Then she was in his arms, rocking back and forth as their tongues sought each other, years peeled away in an instant, knowing only the utter passion of their embrace, working their bodies against each other, while his hands explored in a fashion she had never known, as he had touched her that first night, only so much more certainly, so much more knowledgeably. When at last he released her, she lay back, eyes wide, and legs spread as well, anticipating his entry, determined this time, if she was in any event to be damned, to remember every moment.

He smiled at her and lowered his face to kiss her, gently, on the lips. "There is something else I have promised myself for fourteen years," he whispered, and rolled her onto her stomach.

Presumably she *was* at last damned, because if God had meant these last few weeks as a trial of her strength, for which he had protected her and given her so much for so very long, then she had failed him utterly. And failed herself, and her children, and Jack.

She lay in her bunk, in the captain's cabin of the *Plough*, her body sliding gently to and fro as the ship rolled, equally gently, in the long Atlantic swell; the weather had remained fine throughout the voyage. Since they were not far off the Equator, there were no covers on the bed, nor did she wear any nightclothes. Even on deck she wore hardly more than her shift. Thus had her lover taken the carefully created barriers and privileges which she maintained between herself and the common herd and torn them to shreds.

He had done more than that. The removal of her defenses as a Sousa e Melo had been accompanied by a complete destruction of her defenses as a woman, or even a human being. She doubted he still loved her. In her five weeks aboard ship, including the two they had just spent sailing up and down the latitude of Belem, but out of sight of land,

waiting for the east wind, she had come to know him too well
to suppose that he loved anyone, even himself, when compared with his fascination with the yellow metal which he
supposed was the source of all power. As she had once
thought as a girl, she had never met a man more single-
minded in his determination to succeed, and the hardships he
had suffered since then had turned the dream of El Dorado
into more than the means to an end; it was now his only goal,
complete unto itself.

But love no longer entered into the dream. She was his as a
captive, and only his strength of mind and body stood between her and the hungry gazes of the womanless crew. But
she was also his as a woman. She had surrendered that first
day because there had been nothing else she could do. She
had determined that no matter what happened she would not
surrender her mind, her soul, her being. But could she now
live without knowing that he would return, soon, again to
take her in his arms?

He had shocked her, abused her sensibilities as he had
certainly abused her body, but in doing that he had also torn
away the veil of propriety in which she had always draped
even her most private thoughts. She had been incapable of
resistance. His fingers had stroked gently over her body,
seeking all the secret places whose delight was known to her
alone, from the soft down in her armpits to the crevices
between her toes, followed always by his lips, and gradually
she had approached that ultimate sensation of which she had
dreamed for fourteen years, only to discover that no dream
could measure up to the glorious reality, that her senses were
far more alert now than they ever had been then. She had
cried out in the sheer ecstasy of the moment, and found her
legs wrapping themselves around his neck before she could
stop herself.

But he was a man who had lived with the Indians, and had
discovered the delights of love the Indian way. Her slide
down the roadway to the hell of eternal pleasure had been but
beginning. She had imagined he was about to commit the most
hideous of crimes, at least in the eyes of the Church and the
law, and yet had been quite unable to resist him, had allowed

him to raise her thighs and adjust her to his own satisfaction, only burying her face in her arms so that he would not be able to look at her, or she at him. And had known a thrust, and a sensation, she had never supposed possible, made the more exquisite as his hands, instead of having to support his kneeling body, had been free to wander: to stroke and to caress, to massage and to manipulate.

In those few moments they had united two bodies and two desires into a loving such as she had always known must exist, but would never have supposed was possible for Christina Maria Theresa de Sousa e Melo, or Mrs. Jack Grant, a loving which had left her confused and ashamed, and yet desperate that it should happen again. And since it had happened again and again, even the confusion and the shame had dissipated, and she waited only, as now, for him to come off watch and send her once again soaring through the sky, as mentally drunk on too long submerged, and now too quickly released, sexual impulses as if she had consumed a case of wine every day.

And indeed wine had also played its part. For whenever she had felt sanity returning, it had been easy enough to secure a bottle and dull her senses. She remembered considering that the people of Brazil might be like shells, as were their houses, their imposing facades concealing a termite-stripped interior. Now she knew that such a description certainly applied to her. For fourteen years she had acted a role, that of the daughter of the viceroy, the darling of Portugal, the girl and then the woman who had survived catastrophe twice, or indeed, because of her illegitimate child, three times, by thrusting her chin at the world and the fates, by never surrendering. She had even carried that pose into her marriage. She had grown to love Jack, because he was a wholly admirable man, but she had denied him the utter surrender she now realized he must have wanted, had sought a partnership rather than a complete union.

And all the while her joists and her timbers, her very foundations, had been being eaten away by her own continually hidden desires, until now they had come bursting out, to leave her a drifting hulk, beyond the reach of reputation or personal pride, of family, or even of a husband she was only now learning to value at his true worth—beyond, too, the reach of the one son who had accompanied her upon this strange expedition in search of the headwaters of hell. He was his father's son, and he had accepted his father entirely. Jamey was his kind of man, and in the course of time, she had no doubt, he would be his father all over again. The instinct had been present in his character for too long, and was daily being developed—the dream of the City of Gold, the insistence upon might as the only right, the abandonment of all moral values in the worship of things that could be seen and felt and touched and spent. There was nothing she could do about it, at the moment. Even had she been in a position to exert any authority, James regarded her with contempt; knowing nothing of what went on in the captain's cabin, he considered her only a woman who, her props of birth and authority swept from under her, had taken refuge in her bunk and her wine bottle.

And was he not right? She could not even pray. That would have been a mockery. God had found her out and sent her whistling into hell with the dispatch He had once revealed to Lucifer.

Worst of all, she could not even love. It was not possible to love a man who boasted of his crimes, and whose crimes included the murder of her cousin and two other innocent young men, as well as one of her oldest friends. She could only lust, and feel her heart begin to pound, as the door swung inward.

Jamey threw her shift onto her chest. "You'll want to get up," he said, his face bright with excitement. "The wind's in the east at last. We're standing in for the Amazon."

The sea was brown, and to Christina, at least, terrifying, in that there was for the moment no land in sight. The crew had seen the brown ocean before, for they had all visited Belem, and yet they were excitedly apprehensive, every man clinging to one of the lower shrouds as they stared ahead. They had the utmost faith in their captain, who waited on the poop, his son and his woman beside him, not as yet taking the helm himself, but keeping a careful eye on the steersman to make sure he was following the precise compass course decided upon.

They were exactly on the Equator, and thus some hundred miles north of Belem itself as they followed the parallel due west. It was approaching noon and the sun hung immediately above the brigantine, sending its rays scorching downward with an almost human enmity, it seemed, burning faces even beneath the shelter of the straw hats they all wore, and scorching Christina's bare arms and feet as the deck turned hot beneath her and she could smell the tar melting in the seams. Where before she might have feared that she was being dragged down to hell, now she could no longer doubt that she had arrived there; sweat dribbled from her hair and made a river valley between her breasts—her shift was so damp it clung to her like a second skin, affording virtually no protection, but the alternative of going below and pulling on her heavy riding habit was unthinkable. Even her lungs seemed on fire as the breeze, behind them and coming out of the molten Atlantic, seemed to burn on its way down her throat.

And yet, amazingly, she, like the crew, had the utmost confidence in Jamey, in his skill as a navigator, his experience, and more than anything else, his own complete confidence in himself. If he was inspired by the devil, then he at least had no doubt that his mighty partner was watching over his shoulder. So she watched the brown water rippling away from the bows—the wind was fresh and they were carrying all working canvas—her instincts shrieking that there could not be more than a few feet of water below them, that at any moment they would come to a trembling halt, with enough force, no doubt, to pull the masts out of her, and leave them a stranded hulk, fifty miles from the nearest shore. But time and again she reassured herself with a glance at Jamey's face, the tight lips and the determined jaw, and the glow of anticipation in his eyes as he stared into the heat haze which shrouded the western horizon.

"Land ho," came the call from the masthead.

"Where away?" Jamey shouted, snatching his telescope.

"Dead ahead, Captain Grant."

Jamey leveled the telescope, swung it slowly left and then right, closed it again with a snap. "Shorten sail, Mr. Alvares," he said. "Take in the main for a start, and the fore-topsail. And have a leadsman stand by."

"Aye, aye," Alvares said, and sent his men scrambling aloft.

"Is it the river?" Christina asked, unable to contain her curiosity.

"It is an island, I think. But that is good. The estuary will be a mass of islands. It is our business to find a passage through."

She clung to the rail, stared at the trees which she could now see, appearing to rise directly out of the water, so low lying was the land. There were a great number of trees, but there was open water to either side.

"Land on the larboard bow," came another call from the maintop.

She ran to the other side and stood by Jamey as again he leveled his glass, and again she could see the trees, now forming a continuous line to the south.

"Alter course a shade to larboard," Jamey said.

"To larboard, senor?" Alvares inquired, coming aft. "That is the land."

"Those are two different sets of trees," Jamey said, handing him the glass. "There may be a passage in between."

"May, senor?" Alvares leveled the glass.

"That is what we have to find, Alvares," Jamey said. "Narrow passages between islands. We will not succeed by turning away from the first. Steady as she goes. Aim for the gap."

Christina peered into the distance. Certainly there was an opening between the two islands, if they were islands. Her heart began to pound, and she was aware of young James standing beside her, his hand instinctively seeking hers. This was a world beyond their understanding, and beyond the understanding of the crew too, she could tell as they exchanged glances. But a world in which, apparently, Jamey felt completely at home.

"Keep a sharp lookout," he called at the masthead. "Sing out at any sign of breaking water."

"At least take in some more sail, senor," Alvares begged. "If we hit at this speed—"

"Time enough, Alvares," Jamey said. "Time enough. We don't want to be out here after dark."

Christina watched the approaching land. Now the trees were tall, not more than three miles away to either side, she estimated. And now there were trees in front of them as well, and dry land, she was sure. She grasped Jamey's arm and pointed.

"Aye," he said. "But those in there are further off. If there is a channel, it will wind."

"Breakers," came the shout from above, the lookout's voice beginning to crack with excitement. "Dead ahead."

"Hand those square sails," Jamey shouted. "Bring her down to one foresail." He leveled his glass and Christina watched his face anxiously, but since she could make nothing of his expression she climbed into the rigging herself, to see better, and drew breath as she gazed at the line of white, seeming to stretch entirely across their course.

"Senor," Alvares begged. "For the love of God, senor, stand out. There will be other entrances."

"It's an on-shore wind," Jamey said. "Maybe twenty knots, probably less. Yet those are small wavelets, and brief. They don't stretch back. That bank has several feet over it, Alvares."

"You'll not attempt to cross," Alvares prayed.

Jamey swung the glass to and fro. "Two points to larboard," he told the helmsman quietly.

"To larboard?" Alvares screamed. "But, senor—"

"Quiet, man," Jamey said. "You'll frighten the crew. Start heaving the lead."

Christina squinted into the glare and could see what he was aiming at; the breakers came to an end and there was calm water before the trees were reached. Or was the water calm because there were only a few inches of it?

"By the mark ten," came the call from forward. There was

apparently still an incredible sixty feet of brown water beneath them.

Now the *Plough* was reduced to a single foresail, and had lost much of her speed, moving quietly and gently through the calm sea. And now the coast was close to either side, hardly three miles away, she estimated. As the breeze seemed to drop, she could smell the land, dank and unwholesome, a world of mangrove swamps and giant trees—and of what else? she wondered, recalling some of the tales Jamey had told her. A world in which a Sousa e Melo certainly did not belong except as Jamey Grant's woman, because it was a world he had made his own.

"By the deep six," the leadsman chanted, now indicating six fathoms, or thirty-six feet—one of the depths not marked on the leadline with cloth or leather, and therefore referred to as deeps. But that the bottom was shoaling fast was obvious to everyone.

"I'll take her," Jamey said, stepping to the helm. The breakers were almost alongside them, ripples of white water, and behind them even more sinister ripples which were not breaking at all, suggesting that the mud was very close. But in front of them was only slow-moving brown, and this was clearly the exit of some vast reservoir, in the tree trunks which came floating by, the weed and tangled vines which seemed almost about to check the vessel. The land to port was so close she could hear the forest sounds, a high-pitched whistling, then a series of chuckles followed by a roar which had young James once again clutching her hand and the crew spinning around in terror.

"That is only a monkey," Jamey said, never taking his eyes from the water in front of him. "Its shout is its only means of protection. There is naught to be afraid of."

They listened to a gigantic slithering sound, and slowly the *Plough* came to a halt.

"Aground," Alvares screamed. "Aground." He ran forward. "Drop that sail. Break out the boats. We must tow her off before she settles."

"By the mark three," the leadsman called in a bewildered tone; there was still eighteen feet beneath the waterline.

"Avast there," Jamey bawled. "You, Christina, take the helm."

"Me?" she cried.

He seized her shoulder, thrust her against the wooden spokes, "Just stop her swinging," he commanded, and hurried forward himself. Christina tightened her fingers on the wheel, felt the resistance as the rudder threatened to take control and send the ship sideways onto the mud.

"Get sail on her," Jamey shouted, driving the men at the shrouds with kicks and cuffs. "Everything she can carry."

"Sail?" Alvares asked, his voice thin with terror. "More sail, to drive her on?"

"More sail," Jamey said. "To drive her over. She's only just held. Keep her straight, God damn you," he bellowed at Christina.

She opened her mouth to protest, because not even he had ever cursed at her like that before, then felt the wheel begin to turn and desperately threw her weight on it to hold it steady. Young James came to help her, and between them, shoulder to shoulder, they got it amidships. By now the square sails were unfurled, and filling; the ship was starting to inch forward, but still with that dreadful scraping sound beneath the hull.

"Mad," Alvares moaned. "We are at the mercy of a madman. We will never get off now. We are lost in the Amazon. We will perish. We will—"

"For Christ's sake shut up and set this mainsail," Jamey shouted, himself heaving on the halyard. "Up she goes. All right, Christina, helm to larboard. Hard now."

Christina obeyed, pulling the heavy wheel around to her left, causing the ship also to turn left, while the sails, filling with the still fresh breeze, pushed her over on her side, lessening the draft even as she slipped forward. The scraping sound stopped, and the boat started to gather speed.

"Bring her back," Jamey screamed, running up the ladder to the poop to help. "Hard astarboard. Get sail off her, Alvares. Bring those down."

The men scurried to and fro, the sails were let fly, the

Plough lost way again and began to slip gently through the suddenly deep water, while the forest wall closed around them until the open sea itself disappeared and they might have been in a lake, surrounded by trees, by swamp, by animal noises, and by the stench of primeval forest.

Jamey squeezed Christina against him and kissed her on the cheek. "Drop that foresail," he shouted. "Let go the anchor. We're in, boys," he yelled. "We've crossed the bar."

Chapter 9

〰〰〰〰〰〰〰〰〰〰〰〰〰〰〰〰〰〰〰〰〰〰

"Steer two points to port, Mr. Cutter," Jack Grant told his first mate, raising his telescope, "and let go that bunting. Prepare to salute."

Heeling to the breeze, the *Lodestar* left Deer Island to starboard as she slipped close by Long Island, altering course to beat up into Boston harbor, her flag, a circle of thirteen white stars on a blue canton quartering a field of horizontal red and white stripes, fluttering proudly. In the same instant the yards of colored bunting were let go, and her six cannon, loaded with blank cartridges, began to boom one after the other, saluting the city which had launched the war and which was now celebrating the first real success the Americans had gained. Instantly the guns on the fort replied, smoke clouding into the spring air, while already they could hear the cheers of the people who flooded the waterfront, massed on Bunker and Breed's Hills as if they were reenacting the battle which had already become immortal.

"Brings a tear to the eye, Captain Grant," Lieutenant Cutter observed.

"Aye," Jack agreed, and thought how much more grand it

would have been had he entered here in that new frigate he
had been promised, and which was, alas, still a skeleton in
the Norfolk shipyard. His first months in this ramshackle
navy had indeed brought him almost to despair, left him close
to deciding to abandon the entire crazy venture, and return to
Brazil, and a Christina who must be awaiting his homecoming with a mixture of anticipation and righteous anger. Even
the enthusiasm with which he had been greeted, the delight
with which he had donned this blue coat for the first time,
polished his epaulettes and his sword, had very rapidly dwindled in importance when he had discovered that he was
expected to take on the Royal Navy in the worm-eaten old
timbers of the *Lodestar*. Of course they had converted her,
cut ports in her sides to mount six cannon, as well as a bow-
chaser with a range of well over a mile—and reminded him
that his business was destroying commerce, not engaging in a
regular battle. Yet it had been galling to have to cram on all
sail and run for his life whenever the smallest frigate appeared
over the horizon.

Still, he had stayed. These were his kith and kin, in a way
he had never been able to feel the Portuguese were, and
besides, they were fighting his war, a war in which, he was
proud to recall, he had caused almost the first shots to be
fired fifteen years ago. And however nonexistent their navy,
however absurd their army and its hope of success against
professionals who had proved themselves the best soldiers in
the world, at least one miracle had just occurred. The British,
incredibly, had evacuated Boston and taken their army to the
south. And with them had gone the Navy.

"Shorten sail, Mr. Cutter," he said. "And prepare to let
go."

The orders were given, and the crew hurried about their
tasks; on his arrival in America he had invited whichever of
his company so desired to leave the ship and find his way
back to his family in Brazil—only a half a dozen had wished
to do so, for most were rootless men who wanted only to sail,
and perhaps gain some prize money, while his numbers had
very rapidly been augmented by American volunteers, men
who knew the sea. He supposed the *Lodestar* had not been so

well handled since her original crew of Nantucket men had been split up to act as boatswains and mates upon the other ships of the Grant fleet. So now he could lean on the rail and watch with pride as the brigantine swung up into the wind, the sheets were let fly, and the anchor plunged into the clear blue water.

Instantly they were surrounded by boats of every description, from dinghies to coasters, their crews firing pistols and waving flags; the *Lodestar* was the first American warship to enter the harbor since the departure of the British fleet. And now, too, the boats from the shore were approaching, filled with dignitaries who would officially welcome them.

"Break out that gangway," Jack called. "Boatswain, you'll pipe our guests aboard."

"Aye, aye," came the call, followed immediately by the *coo-eee* of the whistle as the first of the gentlemen boarded the ship, red-faced and panting, but still hurrying forward with outstretched hand. Jack at once recognized Nantucket's leading merchant.

"Jack Grant, by God," John Atkinson called. "Why, boy, it's magnificent to see you again after so long, and on such an occasion."

"Well, it's great to be here, Mr. Atkinson, after fifteen years."

"Fifteen years, by God. Fifteen years. If you knew how I grieved to hear of the death of your father, Jack. . . . But your mother is well? Mary?"

"As well as they possibly can be, Mr. Atkinson." Jack eyed the clerk who was sifting through the letters in his satchel.

"Aye, they must be, down there with you." Atkinson chuckled, and clapped him on the shoulder. "You'll have heard we burned the *Gaspee*?"

"Indeed I did."

"She ran aground," he explained. "They were helpless. Ah, it was a splendid sight. You should have seen it." He turned to his clerk. "The letters, man. The letters."

"I have two here, Mr. Atkinson, for Captain Grant."

Jack took them, his heart pounding. But she would have

forgiven him. He could not imagine Christina ever remaining angry for more than a few moments at a time. He frowned. One was from his mother and the other from Don Pedro, unless Don Pedro had merely addressed the envelope.

"You'll want to read them," Atkinson suggested.

"Well . . . come below and take a glass, Mr. Atkinson." Jack ushered the merchant to the companion hatch, followed him down the steps into the cabin, and placed the decanter and two glasses on the table. "You'll pour for yourself?"

"Of course, Jack. Of course. You read your letters."

Jack sat down, hesitated, then slit Don Pedro's envelope first. He listened to the sound of the wine gurgling into his glass, and to Atkinson proposing a toast, absently raised the glass and drank, while his brain refused to accept what he was reading.

"You may believe," Don Pedro had written, "that this is the most difficult task I have ever had to undertake, and my life has not been an easy one. But when I say that your wife, and my daughter, the woman who I believe has always been to us both the most perfect example of her sex on this earth, has absconded from Rio, and with your brother, leaving behind her a swathe of mayhem such as you cannot imagine, abandoning her children, my dear Jack, I can scarce credit what this pen of mine is writing."

Jack finished his wine, and Atkinson, who was watching him carefully, hastily refilled the glass.

"The facts of the matter are, very briefly, that your brother, whom we had all supposed dead, suddenly reappeared in Rio, just a week ago."

Jack turned the page back, looked at the date, January 26, 1776—the letter had taken four months to reach him.

"Naturally we, the entire community, were overjoyed to receive him, except apparently Christina, who came to see me the night of his return and virtually confessed to me the entire truth of the matter which you so gallantly took on your shoulders fifteen years ago. I now understand that she was, in her own way, saying goodbye to me, but then I assumed she was asking for my help, and thus I dispatched three trusted friends, headed by Henry de Carvalho, to interview Jamey and obtain his true intentions. Imagine my horror and disgust when, the next morning, I was informed that your brother had left Rio in your ship the *Plough*, accompanied by your wife and his son James, and your man of affairs, Conybeare. You will remember that Conybeare was always a crony of your brother's, and in fact was desolated by Jamey's apparent death in the rapids of San Jacinto.

"I immediately took horse for the harbor, and called at the lodgings where Jamey had been known to stay, for there was no word of young Henry. It was necessary to break down the door, since it was locked and your brother had apparently departed with the key, and you will not credit what I found inside: Senora Peixoto bound and gagged and all but suffocating, and in the garden those three innocent young men, butchered by what I am told must have been a machete. Butchered, my dear Jack, like cattle. It was the most horrifying sight I have ever seen.

"I refused to believe that Christina could have been a party to such a ghastly murder. Nor do I believe it now. But that she accepted it afterwards seems unfortunately clear. Her servants inform me that your brother called at your house that morning, and it can only have been an hour or so after his dreadful deed, and that shortly after that she left with him and young James, accompanying him into town, while an hour after that she put to sea in the *Plough*, with young James, and, as I have said, Conybeare. Reluctant as I am to consider it of my own daughter, I am forced to the conclusion that when Jamey told her of his terrible act in killing those three young men, an act for which he would certainly have been hanged, she decided to abandon all, home and family and friends, and even her own children, to flee with him. Heaven knows where. I immediately persuaded the viceroy to dispatch a ship after them, but they had almost a twenty-four-hour start, and no trace of them has been discovered since their departure. The search will continue, but there is absolutely no saying where they have gone.

"Now, Jack, I wish you to know that I have taken it upon myself both to assume control of the Grant Company and also to step in as parent to your children. In this I am assisted not only by my dear Doña Inez, but also by your own mother. Flora will have written to you her own thoughts on the matter, but I can say that she is as shocked as I that her younger son can have become such a monster of destruction, or that my own daughter could condone his activities and indeed wish to spend the rest of her life with him. We can only hope that such a life will be mercifully brief.

"As for you, you must do as you see fit. Your home is here in Rio with us, where you have made such a successful career for yourself, and where your children and all the remaining members of your family are. Remember always that our hearts are with you, and that we can only hope and pray for your safe return, and your eventual happiness. Mine, alas, is ruined forever. Christina, as you will know, was everything to me. Every time I write her name I can feel my heart break."

Jack raised his head.

"Not bad news, I hope, Captain Grant?" Atkinson asked.

"Bad news?" Jack echoed.

"Good. Good. Because I have a great assignment for you. Now that the British have evacuated Boston harbor, and with it the entire northeastern seaboard, why, it is in our interests to rally as many of the islands as possible, as rapidly as possible, for the cause. Martha's Vineyard. Nantucket." He paused, smiled at Jack. "How would you like to sail back into Nantucket harbor, Jack, to claim it for America?"

"The channel lies dead ahead, Captain Grant." Cutter, an earnest young man who had dreams of making a career for himself in the navy—without at the present knowing which navy it would be—stood in the doorway to the cabin and twisted his tricorne in his hands. Like everyone else on board the *Lodestar* this past week, he was well aware that his captain was a man with much on his mind.

Jack had been staring out the stern windows. Now he turned to his first mate. "Any ships?"

"Not one, sir."

Jack nodded. "Then shorten sail and prepare to enter the

harbor. And have the guns loaded, just in case, Mr. Cutter. Solid shot, no blanks.''

''Aye, aye, sir,'' Cutter said with enthusiasm, and hurried back up the ladder.

This then, Jack thought, was supposed to be the greatest day of his life. To sail back into Nantucket harbor, in command of his own ship, in defiance of any price the British government might have put on his head, had been his dream for years, and he was honest enough to admit that it had been at least a part of the impulse drawing him to this struggle.

But there were going to be no great days for Jack Grant, ever again. Perhaps there never had been. Don Pedro might be unable to believe the evidence of his own eyes and ears, but Jack himself knew that he had never had Christina except on loan. In the circumstances he had been prepared to accept that, certain that it was a loan that need never be repaid, and to love her, knowing that she had never found true happiness in his arms.

Perhaps Don Pedro had expected him to go rushing back, abandoning commission and flag and cause. To what end? Even had she been kidnapped, it would have been futile. As Don Pedro had said, once they had put to sea, they could disappear, at least until they landed again. And Jamey, in command of a well-stocked ship, was enough of a seaman to sail right around the world, if he chose. The Jamey he remembered. What this new Jamey might be capable of beggared imagination. As for his children, at the moment he had no desire even to see them again, because they were far more her children than his. Even Rio itself was too closely associated in his mind with her—as if the entire world was not entirely associated with her, because whenever he closed his eyes, wherever he was, he would see her standing in front of him, just as whenever he breathed he seemed to inhale her scent, drifting on the breeze.

He stood up, placed his tricorne squarely on his head, buckled on his sword, and climbed the ladder. How splendid it would be if there was a British garrison on Nantucket and they had to fight their way into the harbor. To fight somebody, anybody, was the only way to alleviate the ice-cold fury which seemed to be holding his heart and lungs and belly in a vice.

A Union Jack flew above the harbor office. "What do you think they intend, sir?" Cutter asked.

The captain's face split into a smile. "Perhaps to fight, Mr. Cutter. Perhaps to fight. Fire the bow chaser."

The gun exploded; the ball screamed through the air and splashed into the sea only feet short of the docks. It was as if he had poked an ants' nest with his stick. People came flooding out of their shops and houses, abandoned the ships moored alongside, to stare at the approaching brigantine and to point, as they could make out the Stars and Stripes flying from her aftermast. Jack swept the shore with his glass to and fro, but could make out no redcoats in the sudden crowd which had gathered on the waterfront.

"Issue the men with cutlasses and pistols, Mr. Cutter," he said, "and preprare to go alongside."

Still he studied the shore, as memory came flooding back to him. Fifteen years since they had crept out of the harbor like the outlaws they had become. Lizzie Butler . . . but now was not the time to think of Lizzie Butler, even supposing she was still alive, or still living here. Now was not the time to think of any woman. He could feel a growing loathing for the entire sex slowly creeping through his system.

"The *Lodestar*," someone called from the shore as they approached. "By God, 'tis the *Lodestar*."

"Billy Grant's ship," shouted someone else.

"The *Lodestar*," they yelled.

"Sailing for the Congress. Down with that Union flag."

A burst of cheering broke out, as they came alongside, a hundred willing hands reached for their mooring warps.

"I remember him," shouted someone. "Jack Grant."

"Jack Grant." The name was taken up as the ship was secured and the gangplank run out.

"Are you mad?" Peter Butler called, clambering on board. "Are you out of your mind, Jack Grant? To come back at all, but to come back with that flag—"

"Peter Butler," Jack said, hands on hips as he advanced to the gangway. "By all that's holy." For the customs agent,

Lizzie's father, had hardly changed, except to grow more stout than ever, his face now a shade of deep purple, his movements heavy, so that he had to crawl down into the waist of the vessel, puffing and grunting. "I'd not thought to see you again."

"Nor I you, Jonathan. You're a fool, man. It's my duty to put you under arrest."

"Is that a fact," Jack said. "On whose warrant?"

"Well, sir, I do possess a warrant, issued by His Majesty and in the name of your brother and yourself and this vessel, on a charge of piracy. But I am also under orders to arrest any vessel entering this port and flying that flag. I'm sorry, lad, but there it is."

"Mr. Butler," Jack said, "I am right glad to see you again, and there's the truth. I look forward to having a conversation with you. But you'll not arrest me, or my people, unless you've a regiment of foot to dispose of. Look around you, sir. There are forty men on board this ship, every one armed and ready. There are four swivel guns mounted on those bulwarks, sir, and every one is loaded and will bring down a dozen of your people at a discharge. I have not come here to be arrested, sir. I have come here to do the arresting." He leaped onto the rail. "How now," he shouted to the eager crowd. "Have you not heard the news? The British army has evacuated Boston and fled south. Their Royal Navy has gone with them. Will the people of Nantucket not declare for the United Colonies? For the Continental Congress?"

There was a moment's silence.

"That is madness," Peter Butler insisted. "The Navy will be back. The army will be back. If you rebel now—"

"The Continental Congress," someone shouted, throwing his hat in the air.

"The Congress!" The cry was taken up. People flooded over the side to shake Jack's hand, embrace the crew, and shout their joy. The Union Jack was already on its way down the flagpole.

"Mad," Butler declared. "Mad. When the soldiers come—"

"We'll settle with you, for a start," someone shouted, and before Jack could stop them, six men had seized the protesting agent, lifted him from the deck, and tossed him over the side. He entered the water with a tremendous splash, while the crowd turned to seek his aides, who were attempting to disappear as rapidly as possible, only to be seized with shouts of vicious joy.

"Tar," the mob shouted. "Tar and feathers."

" 'Tis a riot we have started here," Cutter observed.

"Aye well, it is not my orders to fire into a sympathetic mob," Jack said. "But we'll do what we can. You'd better fish Butler out before he swallows the entire harbor."

Even from the poop they could hear the spluttering as the customs agent gasped for breath.

"Tar," the mob shouted, flooding off the ship as rapidly as they had flooded on, in search of loyalist victims. "Tar."

"And we'll not forget the females," someone bawled.

"Oh, aye," the cry was taken up. "We'll have the females. We'll have the Beresford bitch."

Jack swung around, seized a young man by the shoulder as he was about to step on to the gangplank. "Beresford? Did you say Beresford?"

The boy looked up. "Oh aye, Captain. Mr. Butler's daughter she is, and wife of a sea captain named Beresford. And a stuck-up bitch with it. Oh we'll stuff her ass with tar, that we will." He pulled himself free and hurried ashore.

For a moment Jack stared after the retreating mob, his brain a confused tumult of opposing emotions. He hated women. Of that he was sure. And there was no reason to suppose that Lizzie Butler, who had not even troubled to answer his letter, would be any better than the rest. Besides, she was now apparently Lizzie Beresford. Beresford? It could only be the same. The British lieutenant had sworn revenge, and he had obtained it in the most logical way he could.

In any event, Jack had no reason even to consider her. In marrying a naval officer she had made her bed just as irrevocably as had her father in deciding to continue as Tory agent. But Lizzie Butler being coated in tar . . .

He hurried down the gangplank.

"You'll need support, Captain," Cutter called, and half a dozen seamen doubled at his heels. At least part of the mob were already at the Butler house, only one street removed from the dockside. Here the locked front door had been pushed in, to the accompaniment of breaking glass from the windows as stones were thrown, and he heard a woman scream.

"Avast there," he bellowed, pushing through those who preferred to watch rather than participate. "This is no war against women."

He reached the shattered front door, where half a dozen men waited, stirring a pot of foul-smelling black tar. There were no feathers available except from the mattresses within the house, but that these were to be used was obvious from the down which was floating from an upstairs window, from where heartrending screams were issuing.

"Stand aside there," Jack shouted, and the men parted before his uniform and the authority in his voice. He stepped over the broken door, into the hall he remembered so well, and faced Phyllis Butler, as plump as ever, although her displaced mop cap revealed gray hair, being half pushed and half carried down the stairs, desperately attempting to fight off the men that surrounded her.

"To the tar," they bawled.

"Strip the bitch."

"Sport with her, sport."

Jack stood in front of them. The first man attempted to push him out of the way, and received a buffet which sent him reeling against the wall. The others halted, staring at the naval officer, and at the half a dozen brawny, and armed, seamen behind him.

"They're Tories, Captain Grant."

"You've no cause to help *her*, Captain Grant."

"Given herself airs, she has, these five years."

"She deserves a whipping, that she does. And *then* the tar."

"Jonathan Grant? Jonathan?" Phyllis Butler gasped. "Oh, Jonathan, *help* me."

"That I will, Mistress Butler," Jack said. "We're fighting for our freedom, lads. Freedom to live as we choose, tax ourselves as we choose. Not freedom to torture defenseless women. Stand back there, or I'll treat you as mutineers.''

His hand rested on the hilt of his sword, his gaze swept them. He had no fears for his back; that was well protected. And slowly the men holding Phyllis's arms released her.

''She's a Tory,'' they muttered, unable to meet his gaze.

''And she'll trouble you no more, as a Tory,'' Jack promised. ''I'm placing you under arrest, Mrs. Butler. For your own protection, you'll understand. You'll go to my ship, where your husband awaits you. Now tell me, ma'am, where is Lizzie?''

''Lizzie?'' Phyllis Butler blinked at him. ''You seek Lizzie?''

''There's a mob after her as well,'' Jack said. ''Is she not here?''

''Well no, of course not. Lizzie has a house of her own. Your old house, Jonathan.''

''My . . . by Christ.'' He swung around. ''You'll escort Mistress Butler to the *Lodestar*,'' he told his coxswain. ''Four of you. The other two come with me.''

He pushed his way back outside, kicked over the pot of tar, forced the crowd to part before him by the determination of his face and his movements, and ran along the street. Already he could hear the baying of yet another crowd, and a new set of screams, accompanied by the laughter of women. There had been few women at the Butler residence; their hatred was centered upon the wife of the naval officer.

He reached the gate, almost torn off its hinges. The front garden, always so carefully kept in his mother's day, had been trampled over, and the front door rocked back on its hinges. The garden was entirely filled with people, crowding against the door, peering through the shattered windows, laughing and cheering. Once again Jack had to hurl them left and right, incurring curses and angry looks, although no one would go so far as to retaliate against an officer. He reached the door and pushed into the crowded hall, every step a memory of his own boyhood. In here the crowd was as thick as outside, but the action was taking place in the parlor, and the doorway was a solid mass of people, so that he could not possibly get through. And yet he was drawn onward by the piteous screams from inside.

"Oh God." Lizzie shouted. "Oh God. I beg of you, sirs. Sirs, please . . . aaaagh."

Jack reached behind him, took one of the pistols from the two men who had accompanied him, pointed it at the ceiling, and fired. In the crowded, confined space, the explosion sounded like a cannon going off, and the white smoke momentarily blinded everyone. As they turned to discover the source of the interruption, their ranks opened and he was able to push through them, to gaze at Lizzie. Her face had so far been untouched, although there was tar in her magnificent golden hair, and he could see she had grown into a splendid woman, her full, somewhat coarse features suited by her obvious height, even when stretched on the floor, and her swelling figure, for she had been stripped to receive the bucketful of hot tar, which had been upended on her stomach and was now being spread over breasts and between legs, to the accompaniment of coarse laughter and even coarser jests.

These had also died at the sound of the shot. Jack reached behind him, had a fresh pistol pressed into his hand. "Release that woman," he commanded.

They stared at him.

"Release her," he said, "or I'll put a bullet through your brain." He stared at the man who held the skillet and was spreading the tar, and leveled the pistol. Slowly the wooden sliver slipped from his fingers.

"She's a Tory bitch, Jack Grant," he said.

"Oh God, it burns. Oh God," Lizzie whimpered. "Oh God. . . ." Then she raised her head. "Jack *Grant*?"

"And she married a Navy man," said someone else.

"Beresford. You remember Beresford, Jack. He remembers you."

"Jack?" Lizzie discovered that she had been released and attempted to sit up, only to lie down again, clawing at herself to remove the tar. "It *burns*," she screamed.

"A blanket," Jack snapped. "Quickly." He knelt beside her. "We'll take you to the *Lodestar*," he said. "We'll get it off."

She stared at him, tears flooding from her eyes. "Jack Grant," she whispered. "Oh, Jack . . ." Her head drooped backward as she fainted.

The longboat came into the side of the *Lodestar*, the boatswain's whistle sounded, and the watch lined up, smartly to attention, to welcome their captain and his first lieutenant back on board. Jack had decided to anchor off in preference to remaining alongside, to allow the Butlers some privacy from either stares or jibes, but he had had to play his part as a liberator and, with Cutter, return ashore to attend a civic function—with some trepidation, to be sure. Instead he had found that the merchants of Nantucket, who were now set to take over the government for the time being, in the name of the Continental Congress, were prepared to be grateful to him, not only for removing their Tory yoke, but also for preventing their first hours of independence from being stained by any excesses. Now the strains of "For He's a Jolly Good Fellow" continued to drift across the water behind him as he stepped down into the waist, saluted his men, and made his way aft.

Peter Butler was a lonely figure on the poop. His life and some of his dignity might have been saved, but he had lost his property, and obviously his income, at least for the time being; he even seemed to have shrunk physically.

"How is she?" Jack asked, climbing the ladder.

"Aye well, tar burns, you know, Jonathan."

"Is she in pain?"

"Discomfort, to be sure. But 'tis the humiliation of it."

"She'll never see those people again," Jack pointed out. "You must keep reminding her of that."

" 'Tis not those people, Jonathan," Butler said. " 'Tis any people. We've had to shave her, you understand. We've had to remove every bit of hair she has. There was no other way."

"My God," Jack said. "The poor woman. But may I see her?"

Butler hesitated, and then sighed. "Why, Captain Grant,

since we're on your ship, and doubtless owe you our lives into the bargain, you can see whoever you like."

It was Jack's turn to hesitate. But he recalled that Butler had always been a difficult man with whom to deal. He went down the companion ladder and knocked on the door of the great cabin.

"Who's there?" Phyllis Butler demanded.

"Jack Grant, Mistress Butler."

"Jack? Oh . . ."

"He's not to come in, Ma. He's not to," Lizzie cried.

"Put a shawl over your head, Lizzie," Jack said. " 'Tis not practical to hide on a ship this size."

There was a brief hesitation inside the cabin, and then the bolt was slipped and the door swung in. Lizzie sat up in the bunk by the stern window, wrapped in a blanket, and with another over her head. Her face was unmarked, except for a bruise on the cheek, but tears welled from her eyes.

"You know, then," Phyllis said.

"Mr. Butler told me. How do you feel, Lizzie?"

The tears furrowed her cheeks.

"Hair grows," he said. "And even burns disappear."

"The thought of it," she whispered. "Of those men—"

"Aye well, they're apologizing, to be sure." He gazed at her, unable to prevent himself from recalling the mental picture of her lying on the floor. Once he had loved this woman, had dreamed of taking her for his own. And instead, magically, he had come into possession of the most beautiful creature on earth.

But it had only been a loan, he thought, the bitterness welling out of his belly almost to contaminate his saliva. Only a loan.

And a memory which would tarnish any other relationship he could possibly create, for the rest of his life. As if he wanted any other relationship. As if there could ever *be* any other relationship, and especially with this woman, married to the man he hated more than anyone else in the world—except for his own brother.

Yet he was curious. "You'll permit me a word with Lizzie, Mistress Butler," he said.

Phyllis hesitated, glanced at her daughter, and then got up. "Of course, Jonathan. I'm sure you have much to discuss." She left the cabin, closed the door behind her, and Jack sat down in turn. Lizzie drew the blankets closer about her, almost lost control of the one acting as a shawl, and hastily retrieved it as it threatened to slide away and reveal the yellow down that was all that was left of her hair.

"Do you love him?" Jack asked.

"I . . ." She flushed, and then attempted to smile. "I've been married these eleven years, Jack. Does any wife still love her husband after eleven years?"

"But you loved him when you married him."

She shrugged. "It was the thing to do. Papa said it was the thing to do, Jack. You were gone . . ."

"I wrote to you."

"But what could I *do*, Jack? Pa was customs agent. I couldn't desert him."

"Unless you were in love."

"Well . . ." She pouted. "I've heard tell that *you* got married."

"Aye," he agreed. "So I did."

"He's a handsome man, Martin is. And a successful one. He commands a frigate now. He'll go far."

"In these waters?"

"Oh, aye. Keeping them clear of Yankee privateers." Her mouth made an *O*. "You'll not go looking for him, Jack? The *Eurydice* would blow you out of the water."

"Now, why should I go looking for a frigate, Lizzie? It's him said he'd come looking for me. Unless he feels he's already got his revenge."

She met his gaze, but her cheeks were pink.

"There're no children?"

She shook her head. "And you?"

"Four . . . I meant, three."

"Did one die?" she asked. "I'm sorry, Jack."

"Aye," he said. "One died. There's naught to be sorry about. 'Tis a strange world, Lizzie, that we should meet again like this."

"Yes," she said. "What . . ." She licked her lips. "What are you going to do? With us?"

"With you?"

"Well . . ." Her flush deepened. "We are your prisoners."

"Oh," he said. "Aye well, you'll have to be set ashore. My orders are to resume commerce destruction, once I hoisted the Stars and Stripes over Nantucket. I'll find somewhere safe to set you ashore."

"The Navy's as thick as fleas along the coast further south," she said.

"And you'd not have me hanged?"

She gazed at him. "No, Jack," she said. "I'd not have you hanged. Not after meeting you again, and you saving me from those brutes and all."

How unlike Christina she was. Instead of culture, pure peasantry, in speech as much as thought; instead of elegance, a heavy, fleshed earthiness; and instead of a closed, secret, impenetrable mind, an almost transparent kaleidoscope of desires and memories and emotions. And would she not, lacking any of Christina's graces, make a much better bedfellow?

Beresford's wife. There would be revenge turned inside out.

And then too would Jack Grant have revealed his true nature, which would leave him no better than either Jamey or Beresford himself. Perhaps then he would be able to hate himself as much as he hated everyone else.

He got up. "Then I'll take no risks, Lizzie. I'll set you and your parents ashore in Nassau. I'd meant to cruise the Bahama Passage anyway. 'Tis full of custom."

The first bar the *Plough* had crossed, momentous though it was to captain and crew, was only the first. There were other bars, row after row of sandbanks, around which Jamey, with consummate skill and to the bemused amazement of his men, guided the ship. And there were days of calm water, and even, when the wind was in the east, of good sailing, as they ran upstream over an area of water not less than four miles wide. If this is a river, Christina thought, then what are we to call everything else?

But even the river dwindled, compared with the forest. If it was difficult to comprehend a river so wide and so long and so deep and so *immense*, it was quite impossible to envisage what lay to either side, behind that unchanging wall of green and brown. It did change, of course. There were gaps and there were fallen tree trunks and there were tributaries, each one as large as any flowing water she had ever seen, including the Tagus itself, until at last they arrived at a confluence where each stream was similarly enormous, one making away to the south, the other continuing due west. Jamey chose the latter. El Dorado, he kept reminding them, was on the north side of the river, and after the trees had begun to thin, they reached open country.

Progress was slow. When the wind was in the east they sailed, and well, until running aground. When the wind was westerly or, as happened more often, had dropped right away, they either anchored, if the current was strong, or lowered the boats and towed her, the crew rowing, almost naked in the sun, while Christina steered and Jamey and Alvares kept a lookout, until they again ran aground. The groundings, which happened at least once a day, were seldom her fault; it was merely impossible to identify all the sandbanks that littered the river, often far enough beneath the surface to permit the boats to pass over them before reaching out to grasp the much deeper keel of the ship.

Then there were curses all around as she had to be towed off, and a new channel decided upon.

They anchored every dusk, as near to midstream as possible, because their first adventure at anchoring too close to the banks had cost them sleepless nights as they had been attacked by hordes of insects. But the stops were not only essential for restoring their exhausted muscles and their heat-stricken brains; by trailing lines all night, they could secure enough fish to feed themselves for weeks on end.

Fish were not the only living creatures they encountered. Now for the first time in her life Christina could see the alligators of which she had heard so much, basking on the mudflats close to the shore, and even, from time to time, the anacondas, the great water snakes which were reputed to attain lengths of forty feet and more and which could swallow a full-grown man with as much ease as she would consume a sweetmeat. Of game there was none, except for the monkeys which kept them constant company with their chatter. Monkey, indeed, made very good food, once they had overcome their repugnance at cooking creatures which, especially when dead, seemed so very human.

They encountered no human beings at all, and soon came to regard themselves as perhaps the last of their kind left on earth—supposing, she thought, that *they* were still human themselves. They existed in a world of endeavor, straining, sweating, cursing, stripped to their drawers or less, performing their bodily functions as it occurred to them, driven onward by their greed and the insatiable determination of their captain. She did not suppose she was much better, although she combed her hair and tried to wash herself whenever possible; there was no shortage of water, even if it was brown and opaque. Sometimes she wondered what they thought of her, and sometimes she knew, as she caught them staring at her, eyes seeming able to penetrate the by now sadly tattered shift, to reach her skin. She wondered, too, what they would think if they knew how little energy their weary captain now had for their rare couplings. Often she and Jamey did not even sleep in their cabin, but joined the crew on deck, praying for the sudden mind-deadening rainstorms which often assailed them at night, waking up with cries of joy as they turned their faces up to the water, feeling momentarily cool and clean and refreshed—only to be sweating as heavily as ever within an hour of the rain's cessation.

Only young James was truly happy. But remarkably, he was apparently enjoying even the heat and benefiting by having the least to do, able to indulge his hobby of clambering up and down the rigging, to her alarm at first, but with an agility clearly inherited from his father. And with a new respect for his mother, as he saw her taking part in the actual handling of the ship.

But what an amazing development, that Christina Maria

Theresa de Sousa e Melo should find herself standing on the poop of a ship, steering it up an empty river between walls of impenetrable forest, clad in only a tattered shift, her complexion, despite the straw hat which she never removed on deck, burned and peeling, her eyes wrinkling as she squinted time and again into the heat haze that surrounded them like a fog. She did not suppose her mother and father, or Jack and the children, would recognize her. But she dared not think of any of them, for as the days passed, she became ever more certain that she was destined to stay at the side of this ruthless, half-mad man until the ship rotted and they sank together into the depths of the Amazon mud.

"This is not possible," Alvares said at last. "When will the trees start to thin? When will we see this high land of which you speak, Senor Grant? We cannot go on forever. The sails are rotting. The ropes are rotting. The wood is rotting. This ship can never put to sea again; she would sink in the first gale. What are we *doing*, Senor Grant?"

"The trees will thin, eventually," Jamey replied. "And we shall come to the mountains. I made the mistake once before, of imagining this continent could be crossed in a matter of days. This continent is a matter of years. I wandered these forests for five years, Alvares, and only got halfway to where I am now. What is another year more or less?"

"For you, maybe, nothing," Alvares said. "You have your woman, and your son. For us . . . we have no women. Perhaps—"

"Perhaps one day I will put a bullet through your brain, Alvares," Jamey said. "And I shall do that if you ever so much as lay a finger on the senora's arm. You will have women. You will have all the women in the world, after we find El Dorado. It will not be long now." He glanced over his shoulder, at the telltale ripples they all knew so well now. "Larboard the helm," he shouted at Christina. "Larboard the helm."

"I'm trying," she screamed back, rolling the wheel to her left with all her strength, knowing the horrifying feeling of helplessness when there is no response, feeling the ship being carried sideways by the sudden surge of current which had taken her by surprise.

"Pull, God damn you," Jamey shouted, running forward to exhort the boats' crews. But they too were being swept sideways by the gush of water, and a moment later the *Plough* struck the bank with a shuddering crash, still moving backward, so that the giant trees became entangled in her masts, and with an even more heartrending tearing sound, they came down together.

Christina felt the wheel being wrenched from her hands. Endeavoring to hang on to it, she was hurled sideways and landed on her hands and knees, knocked full length by a giant branch which flailed along the poop. Dimly she heard screams and shouts, all overshadowed by the tearing, crashing, splintering cataclysm of the masts falling, taking with them all their stays and halyards, their sails and the gunwales on which they happened to collapse. She put her hands above her head, expecting every moment to be struck by cascading wood of one sort or another, realized that the noise had stopped, except for the bumping of the hull on the bottom and the shouts of the men, and that the vessel was still moving. Desperately she scrambled to her feet, saw that the current had pushed the bow of the ship right around while the stern was still anchored in the mud, and that one of the boats had been capsized as the towing warps had suddenly jerked away; the men were swimming desperately either for the bank or for the other boat, which was also drifting with the current, its crew bemused by the catastrophe.

"Get that anchor over," Jamey was shouting, regaining his balance and running forward. Alvares followed more slowly. Christina reached her feet in a paroxysm of fear.

"James," she shouted. "James? Where are you?"

"Here, Mama." He too had been bowled over by the force of the impact and was now getting up at the foot of the ladder. "I'll help Papa."

He started forward, and the *Plough* struck again, this time with a devastating crunch which seemed to come from the very keel up through the deck, and once again sent Christina staggering against the rail. Jamey, clambering over the mess of cordage and shattered spars which cluttered the foredeck, had to hang on for dear life while Alvares was again thrown full length.

"What's happening?" Christina screamed, knowing even before she asked the question.

Jamey looked aft, pulled himself up, drew his knife, and slashed the rope securing the anchor. It went splashing into the water, taking its vast chain behind it, but doing nothing to check the movement of the ship because the ship was no longer moving; instead she was rapidly sinking by the bow, with her stern still perched on the bank.

Jamey thrust his knife back into his belt and grasped the stump of the foremast. He looked at the bowsprit, already dipping into the fast-flowing brown water. "She's done," he said.

"Done?" Alvares asked. "Done?" he shouted. "We are wrecked, finished. I told you it would happen, senor. I knew it. You have killed us all."

"Nonsense," Jamey said, coming aft again. "She has brought us far enough. A thousand miles? Bah, no river can be more than a thousand miles long. We must be nearly at the headwaters. The headwaters, do you understand?" he shouted, seizing the stricken Portuguese by the shoulders and shaking him as a dog might shake a rat. "El Dorado cannot be more than a week's journey from here." He finished with a push which sent the mate reeling into the scuppers. "Now haste, if you would salvage anything from forward."

Christina watched him approach. "What *happened*?" she asked again, in a lower voice.

He shrugged. "That was a freshet, probably caused by heavy rainfall in the headwaters. And we have struck either a rock beneath the surface or one of those tree trunks, holing us like a spear." He climbed the ladder and stood beside her. The ship's angle was acute now, and they had to hold on to stand, while the river was already flowing over the foredeck. But the ship was no longer sinking; she was on the bottom. Alvares stood at the forehatch and gazed disconsolately into the crew's quarters, now a lake of swirling brown water.

"Can't be helped," Jamey said flatly. "She *has* brought us a fair distance. We'll get some gear up. Just what we can carry. Come along, boy."

"But what of the others? The boat?"

He pointed. The remaining boat was coming downriver behind them; it had picked up three of the six-man crew of the capsized dinghy. "They'll be disconcerted," he said, and grinned at her. "It may be necessary to knock some sense into them. Come on, boy."

He scrambled down the companion ladder, James at his heels. Christina held on to the rail and watched the approaching men. Some yelled and shouted, others wailed their fear, others rowed in grim despair.

"Lost," Alvares said. "Our bones will be picked white here in this forest." He climbed the ladder to stand beside her. "No man can survive the Matto Grosso." He crossed himself.

"That is nonsense, Senor Alvares," she said. "Captain Grant has survived it already. He will do so again. And us with him."

"Senor Grant is a *devil*," Alvares whispered. "He is not human. He never tires. He never sleeps. He scarcely eats." His fingers seized her arm. "Tell me this, senora. When he lies with you, is not his member cold as ice?"

Christina shrugged herself free in disgust, retreated as the boat came into the side of the ship and the men started to scramble up.

"We are wrecked," they shouted.

"Two men drowned."

"Eduardo vanished into the jungle."

"The ship is sunk."

"We are lost."

"We will starve here in this forest."

"We have been betrayed."

"There is no City of Gold."

"We are at the mercy of a madman."

"Avast there," Jamey bellowed, emerging from the companion hatch, two pistols thrust into his belt and a musket in his hands. "Are you men, or screaming children? We have lost our ship. Well, I will let you into a secret. I am delighted that she brought us this far. I expected her to be wrecked weeks ago. We have been fortunate. And we will go on being fortunate." He stared at them, and their wails slowly died, while they huddled closer to each other for protection.

"Now we have work to do," Jamey said. "We must remove everything that is worth saving from the ship to the shore. The north shore, my friends." He pointed. "Over there. Then we will commence our march. The great plains are not far away. The *savannah* is what the Indians call the plains, my friends. We are going to walk to the *savannah*, and El Dorado."

They stared at him.

"But I wish to be ashore by dark," he said.

"There is no El Dorado," someone muttered.

"You have tricked us," said another.

"You have brought us here to die."

"*You* walk to this *savannah*, this El Dorado," said the first spokesman. "You are used to walking the Matto Grosso by yourself, eh, Senor Grant? So you go. We will stay here." His gaze drifted to Christina. "With the woman."

The explosion of the musket took them by surprise. The ball struck the man in the face, from a distance of not much more than six feet, seeming to tear teeth and lips and nose and mouth apart, sending him crashing backward into the arms of his companions like a scattered rag doll filled with blood.

Jamey handed the musket to his son. "Reload that," he said, still speaking quietly, as he drew the first pistol from his belt. "I'll have no mutiny," he said softly.

The dead man fell to the deck; his blood ran into the scuppers. Christina could only grasp the rail in an effort to stop herself from fainting. But had she expected anything different? She had seen how ruthless he could be, at the time of Conybeare's death.

"I will come with you, Captain Grant," Caetano said. "I will walk with you to El Dorado."

"You will all walk with me to El Dorado," Jamey said. "I will leave only the dead behind."

*   *   *

It was easy to suppose the forest was a living creature, a gargantuan of insatiable appetite which had known all along that these foolhardy intruders must eventually become its victims, had waited with patient menace and was now swallowing them with every evidence of pleasure. After a night spent shivering close to the river, alarmed by every sound, every plop of hurrying water, supposing it was a monster come to assail them, they began their march at dawn. Within an hour all trace of the mother of waters had disappeared behind them, yet Christina was sure they had traveled no more than a few hundred yards. Before them stretched a seemingly impenetrable wall of close-packed tree trunks, reaching up and up, higher than she would ever have supposed possible in their search for light and sunshine; the space between the trees was packed with bushes and tangled vines, as thick as the ship's warps, every one of which had to be cut through, while their boots sank sometimes up to their knees in a mixture of soft earth and dead leaves, making every step a muscle-wrenching exercise.

Within an hour they were as wet as if they had been swimming. This was a liquid forest, where every leaf contained a small bathful of water. And as the sun rose, the heat turned the damp into steaming mist, which was not in the least cool, but rather warmer than the air, cloying and breathtaking.

And the forest was alive, in a way they had not supposed possible from the ship. The monkeys they knew of; here their chatter was ear-splitting. The snakes they suspected and feared, even if they did not actually see any. But never had they seen so many lizards, perfectly camouflaged to lie in the shade of leaf or branch, and yet betraying themselves as they scuttled away from the crashing, slashing, swearing approach of the humans; or so many spiders, hanging from enormous webs to brush against ear or cheek and send them reeling with exclamations of fear and disgust, or such a variety of birds, most quite unafraid, perched on branches immediately above their heads, only slowly fluttering to a more secure perch if they felt they were *too* close to these absurd intruders, regarding them with contemptuous pity, preening their brilliant

plumage and calling to their fellows in a tremendous variety
of whistles and notes; and above all, so many ants, proceeding up and down every tree trunk in long, thick columns,
content to pursue their own unceasing activity, but when
disturbed, seething in anger, and when dislodged, by careless
shoulder or swinging hand, stinging viciously wherever they
happened to land.

Never had Christina been so aware of the utter unimpor-
tance, the irrelevance, of being a human being, of the
arrogance of the human species, that they should suppose
themselves the most favored of God's creatures, when He had
also planted this teeming, vicious, cold-blooded kaleidoscope
of straining endeavor. Never had she felt so utterly crushed
by the desperate nature of their adventure, the certainty that
they did not belong here, that the forest and all in it were
aware of that, that they were surrounded by a deadly, brood-
ing patience, a knowledge that in time, in a very little time,
their flesh and their blood and even their bones would be
available to the watching eyes, the waiting teeth, the flicker-
ing tongues, which overlooked their slow progress. She could
only remember, as she watched Jamey's broad back and
flailing arm, for he led the march himself and worked twice
as hard as any other, that he had lived in this hell for five
years and survived. Without him they would already be dead.

And then it began to rain.

On board the ship the rain had always been welcome. Here
in the forest there was no shelter, no escape, no mercy. Their
very thoughts were obliterated beneath the huge *roar* of
crashing moisture, turning the muddy ground into a shallow
lake beneath their feet. Even Jamey had to call a halt and
huddle with them, squatting up to their haunches in mud and
water, heads bowed, and senses cowed by the continuous
heavy drumming.

But, as ever, he seemed undisturbed. He had experienced
this, too, before. Perhaps he had even had some instinct as to
how long it would last. Certainly, the moment it began to
slacken he was again on his feet, calling on them to follow
him, waiting only for a glimpse of the sun before setting his

course into another vast steambath, swinging his machete with tireless energy.

She struggled at his elbow. "We must rest," she gasped. "I am exhausted. We are all exhausted."

"No, Christina. We must get on. We are still too close to the river, and the wet season will soon be upon us."

You mean it isn't here already? She wanted to shout. But he had already turned away to resume his slashing, tearing progress. She watched, then, as he appeared to miss his footing, stumbled, and let out an exclamation which became a scream—a scream that was immediately drowned out by the most terrifying *hiss* Christina had ever heard.

"Aaaagh," Jamey cried, tumbling to the ground, desperately throwing his body away from the thick brown-and-red coil that struck at him with such deadly accuracy. "Kill it," he shrieked.

Christina had jumped backward, cannoned into young James, and lost her balance. They fell together, staring in horror as the bushmaster reared above them, forked tongue wisping to and fro, confronting them with a demoniac majesty, head swaying, body seeming to gather itself for another strike.

"Kill it," Jamey moaned, desperately trying to draw his own pistol.

The forest exploded into sound as Alvares, having pulled himself together, aimed and fired his musket. He was a good shot; the ball seemed to flick the snake's neck, half turned it, and before it could recover Caetano had rushed forward and with a swing of his machete sent its head flying into the bushes. Yet the huge body, some eight feet long and as thick as a strong man's arm, still moved, continuous muscular spasms undulating along its length as it slowly subsided into the earth.

"Help me," Jamey begged, his face twisted with agony as he writhed on the ground.

They gathered around, staring at him, and crossed themselves.

"Help me," he screamed at them. "Christina, I have only seconds. Help me."

She knelt beside him, gazed at the oozing perforations in his left calf; was it her imagination or was the flesh around the bite already turning black?

"A tourniquet," he gasped. "On the thigh. You must stop the poison spreading."

She looked left and right, her brain seeming to numb with the horror of her situation, and a leather belt was thrust into her hand. Quickly she passed it around his thigh, just above the knee, and drew it tight.

"Tighter," Jamey shouted at her. "Tighter." His entire face was contorting. It was horrifying to see blood separating above and below the belt as she thrust the barrel of a pistol through her knot and twisted it around and around to crush veins and arteries against the bone. When she was finished she was pouring sweat and gasping for breath.

"He will die," a voice said beside her. "It is a quick death."

"But very painful," said another.

"Papa," young James wailed.

"Jamey . . ." Christina begged.

He seemed to pull himself together with a tremendous effort. "Cut," he said. "Cut. Make a cross. You . . . Christina . . . *cut* me."

She looked around her, but none of the men seemed capable of moving. Her heart throbbed and her head was spinning. She picked up his machete, pressed it against the darkening flesh, watched only a trickle of blood emerge.

"Deeper," he commanded. "Deeper, for Christ's sake. To the limit of the fang."

She pressed in, her stomach rolling, then drew the knife out again.

"Now across it," Jamey said, his breath coming in rapid jerks. "For God's sake, hurry."

Christina held her own breath, turned the knife, and once again cut, making a cross on the tortured flesh.

"Now suck," he said. "Suck. Do not swallow. Suck and spit."

For a moment her stomach revolted. She thought she would

vomit, but she swallowed down the bile, reached for his flesh with her lips and her teeth, applied all the suction she could, and felt her mouth fill with an unspeakable bitterness. She jerked her head up and spat out blood and serum, and venom too.

"Again," he whispered, his entire body seeming to droop, "Again, for God's sake, Christina, again."

She sucked and spat, and sucked and spat, and sucked and spat, the entire forest seeming to revolve about her, the comments of the men no more than a distant humming in her ears. She was aware that young James was offering her a piece of cloth from time to time, to wipe her lips, and she knew she was spitting so hard she had no saliva left. But gradually the flesh around the bite faded from an angry purple to a bloodless white, and then became red again and began to spurt clean blood. She raised her head to receive fresh instructions, and discovered that Jamey had fainted, or sunk into the coma that precedes death; she could not be sure which.

But now her own scant knowledge of surgery could be used. She tore the skirt of her shift into strips to bind the wound, then released the tourniquet; instantly the white material turned red, but some loss of blood was preferable to the gangrene that she knew would follow too long a stricture.

She sat on her heels and gazed at him. He breathed unevenly, and his face was flushed. Certainly he had a fever, but he was alive—and now she knew what that scar on his thigh was, because it was an identical cross cut into his flesh. So he had been bitten by a bushmaster before, and survived. Then he would do so again. It was not possible to contemplate his death.

Others, however, were already doing it. Vaguely she became aware of the conversation behind her.

"He is undoubtedly dying," someone was saying.

"I think he is already dead," said another.

"Then we will all die."

"No," said another. "There is still the boat, moored in the river. Let us go back to her. There is no El Dorado, my friends. Let us return to the boat and go downstream."

"For a thousand miles?"

"It is better to risk that than to stay here and starve with him."

She turned on her knees. "No," she said. "He is not going to die. We have only to wait while the fever runs its course." She attempted to smile at them. "We shall remain here. We could all do with a rest, eh?"

They stared at her. She could feel their gazes scorching her skin, realized that her knees were exposed since she had torn away the entire skirt of her shift, just as the shift itself was hardly more than an extra layer of tattered skin, while the bodice had fallen open.

"We could take the woman with us," someone said.

"And the boy?"

"Not the boy," said another. "Leave the boy here with his father. Let them die together."

"But the woman? We *will* take the woman?" The man was anxious.

"Oh, we will take the woman," said the man who had first suggested abandoning Jamey. "But there is no reason why we should not enjoy her now." His mouth widened into a wolf's grin, and he started forward. "I have always known I would have her one day."

Christina pushed down with her hands to gain a crouching position. Desperately she looked from left to right. Alvares stood by himself, his face twisted in indecision; he still held an empty musket. Caetano was equally undecided, aware that this was a matter of life and death. He was armed with a machete, but a machete alone, even if he chose to defend her, was unlikely to stop the other seven men. And young James, kneeling a few feet away from her, beside his unconscious father, was helpless. He wore a pistol, and Jamey had made him practice with it during the voyage north, but she could hardly expect a fourteen-year-old boy to shoot anybody.

She was on the point of death for the third time in her life. But this time, unlike the previous occasions, she would need strength, of mind no less than body, beyond the passive determination to survive that had previously kept her alive.

Now she must *do*, in a manner she had never considered possible—and with no guarantee that either she or James would be alive at the end of it.

The man stood above her. "Now," he said, "senora, you are not going to fight me, eh? Because I will tell you this, if you scratch me I am going to strip the skin from your ass, slowly."

Christina threw herself to one side, rolling over Jamey's body. The man laughed, and turned behind her, then stopped as he saw her fingers wrap themselves around the haft of the musket, right hand sliding toward the trigger guard.

He grinned at her. "You'll not fire that," he said. "Not you, pretty lady."

The gun went off before Christina was quite ready for it. The weapon bucked in her hands and jarred her shoulder; despite her lack of aim, at that range she could not miss, and the ball took the man in the stomach, bringing him to his knees with a gasp of dying agony, his bubbling saliva already tinged with blood.

The shouts of the other men as they ran forward alarmed her, and she turned, swinging the musket at the full length of her arms to catch the first man across the head. Suddenly she was aware of a white heat in her veins, and pumping through her mind. She dropped to her knees as the second man came up to her, so that he tripped and fell over her, then she reached for Jamey's belt as she tumbled full length, to seize a pistol in either hand, rolling onto her back and firing, again at point-blank range, at the man who stood above her. Dropping the pistol, she changed the other to her right hand as she rolled again, listening to the explosion of another weapon and watching another man falling close beside her, half his head shot away, hearing the grunt of enraged effort and pain as Caetano closed with another of her assailants, machete pumping to and fro. Out of the corner of her eye she caught a glimpse of Alvares swinging his empty musket to deal someone a buffet across the back, and she fired her remaining pistol as she forced herself to her knees, away from yet another falling body.

With cries of fear, the three survivors crashed through the undergrowth as they fled, one still clutching his head, which oozed blood from the force of Alvares's blow. He tripped and fell to his hands and knees, then regained his feet and staggered after his companions, begging them to stop for him. Christina gazed at the scene of horror, with three men dead of gunshot wounds, and the other cut almost in two by Caetano's knife, sprawled on the ground with his blood seeping into the dead leaves. She gazed at Caetano himself, kneeling, drying the knife on a leaf, at Alvares, standing, staring at her, at young James, already reloading his pistol, and at Jamey, lying unconscious, half beneath the body of one of the dead men.

And then at herself, at the blood staining her shift, the powder burns on her hands.

Alvares was coming toward her now, slowly. No, she thought, oh God, no.

He paused in front of her. "Holy Mother," he said. "You are not a woman, senora, you are a devil from hell."

His hand moved, and she watched it, feeling a great weakness spreading upward from her chest to envelop her brain. His fingers came toward her, stroked her cheek, and she saw that he had removed another layer of black powder. "A devil from hell," he said.

His finger was wet. She realized that she was weeping, great tears dribbling down her cheeks, seeming to overflow from the seething turmoil that was her brain. She had not supposed it was possible to discover so much violence, animal as well as human, all within the space of half an hour, had not also realized how mentally exhausted she was by the events of yesterday, the shipwreck and the other four violent deaths. Eight men in two days, and Jamey a stricken wreck. And before that, nearly a year of unending effort, unending guilt, that she was not resisting her demon lover, unending distress at her present, and fear of her future.

But her future had arrived, and only she could surmount it. She raised her head, drew the back of her hand across her eyes to clear her vision, and looked at the two men. At this moment she was more in their power than ever she had been in the power of the other seven. But only for this moment. James had already reloaded his pistol, and now he had picked up her discarded musket and was carefully ramming a ball down the barrel to reprime that as well. And yet she did not think it would be necessary to fight again. Alvares and Caetano would not lay a finger on her. At least not for the moment. It must be her concern to maintain her ascendancy.

Wearily she pushed herself to her feet. "I think we should carry Captain Grant back to the boat," she said. "We cannot remain here in the forest without his knowledge to lead us, and it will be several days at least before he can do that again."

"They will have got there first," Alvares said, "and taken the boat."

"They ran that way." James pointed. "And the river is *that* way."

"That way," Caetano objected, pointing in yet another direction.

"There is no necessity for argument," Christina said. "We shall simply follow our own trail back. It is as simple as that." She picked up the belt which had been given her to use as a tourniquet, strapped it around her waist, thrust her two pistols and Jamey's machete into it. Young James retained the musket and his own pistol, glanced at his mother as Alvares started to recharge his piece. Christina shrugged. She could not stop him. But she would not surrender an iota of her command. "You must make a litter," she said. "Some kind of hammock. Caetano, you'll cut some vines."

"Yes, senora." Caetano plunged into the nearest thicket, began hacking at the bushes.

"Mama," James said. "There *is* no way back."

She looked around her, at the looming trees, the clustering undergrowth. As always, the forest seemed to have closed behind them like a door. And yet she was sure of the direction from which they had come. It was absurd to suppose she could have gotten lost in a morning's walk, and she was also sure that the river was only a mile or so away. She almost thought she could hear it, unless it was the whispering of the wind in the trees, far above them.

Alvares replaced the stopper on his powder horn. "Which way, senora?" he asked.

She chewed her lip, pointed. "That way," she decided. "Caetano, have you got those vines?"

Slowly Caetano came back toward them, backing through the bushes. Behind him came an Indian.

Chapter 10

Christina heard the sharp intake of breath from beside her, glanced to her right, and then to her left. Suddenly there seemed more naked brown bodies, more impassive brown faces, then there were trees.

"By Christ," Alvares whispered. "There must be a hundred of them. Senora—"

Christina's knees seemed to have turned to water, but she knew that now their worst mistake would be to reveal the fear which was obviously gripping the men as much as her.

"Stand still," she said in a low voice. "Hold your weapons, and stand still. Meet their eyes. We cannot kill them all."

They formed a little huddle around Jamey's body, the four of them, back to back. They had all heard tales of the forest Indians, of their cannibalism and their other habits; the priests dismissed them as bugres, the most unnatural of God's creatures. She listened to a voice wailing in the distance, begging for mercy in Portuguese. Alvares glanced at her. "They have the others as well, senora."

"Look to your front," she commanded, striving to keep

her breathing under control, gazing at the little men who were slowly moving toward them. They were painted with some kind of red pigment—circles around their eyes, crude lines down their cheeks and across their hairless chests. Otherwise they were absolutely naked, but all were armed, some with a kind of blunt-ended spear, the others with bow and arrow. Each with just a single arrow. Were they that accurate?

And they made no sound. That was the most terrifying thing about them.

But now they were parting, to let one of their members come closer to the huddled white people. He did not seem greatly older than any of his companions, and was quite as naked as they, wearing a similar paint—but around his neck there was a chain, made, she realized with a start of horror, from human teeth.

Slowly he came toward them, looking from one to the other, then down at the men lying on the ground. When he was six feet away from them he knelt beside the man shot by young James, half of whose head had been blown away. He dabbed his forefinger into the man's rapidly coagulating blood, held the finger to his nose, and then licked it, raising his head to stare at Christina again, with a frown. Then he gestured over his shoulder, and one of his people came forward, carrying what was obviously intended to serve as a knife, although it was made of bone. With this the man dug into the corpse's skin, several sickening thrusts which pushed up a sliver of flesh large enough to be gripped by the fingers. This piece of flesh he tore away, raising it to his nose to sniff before biting off a piece, and chewing, carefully and thoughtfully.

"Oh Christ," Alvares muttered. "Oh Christ."

"Stand still," Christina said, her mouth filling with bile. "For the love of God, stand still."

But if she had ever needed Him it was now, she realized, as the chieftain, for she guessed he was that, dropped the flesh and stood up, pointed at the musket in her hands, and held out his own hands. She shook her head. Obviously she had to meet him as an equal, for as long as possible.

He did not seem disturbed, instead made a gesture of holding the firearm to his shoulder. She realized that they

must have been watching throughout the battle, perhaps from
the moment they had come ashore after the wreck. And when
she did not immediately respond, he picked up his bow and
arrow, and the piece of discarded flesh. This he tossed to one
of his companions, who looked around, selected a tree about
thirty feet away where there was a suitable forked branch
close to the ground, and placed the flesh in the fork. The
chieftain raised his bow, sighted very briefly, and released the
string; the arrow sang through the air and struck the tree only
inches to the left of the flesh; its wooden barb could not
penetrate the thick bark and the arrow fell to the ground.

"Can you hit that, Alvares?" Christina muttered.

"I think so, senora."

"Then do so. For God's sake, aim true."

Alvares raised the musket, sighted down the barrel, squeezed
the trigger. White smoke clouded the air, and the piece of
flesh disintegrated, carrying with it a large chunk of bark to
leave the white wood underneath exposed.

A ripple of amazed alarm went through the watching Indians, and Christina hastily exchanged muskets with Alvares,
handing the empty one to James to recharge; she drew one of
her pistols.

The chieftain had turned back to stare at them, raising and
lowering his head as he followed the drift of the smoke. Then
he made another gesture, and there was a crashing of leaves
and branches as one of the three men who had run away from
the fight was half pushed and half dragged toward them; his
name, Christina recalled, was Veira,

"For the love of God, senora," he shouted, "do not let
them eat me."

He was brought to a halt, again some thirty feet from
Christina, and forced against a tree. Several vines had already
been cut, and these were passed around and around his body
and secured to the far side, to hold him against the trunk,
allowing him to move, certainly, but not to free himself.

"Senora," he wailed. "Senora, help me."

The chieftain pointed at the musket and then at the man,
and nodded.

Alvares glanced at Christina, who again shook her head.

The chieftain frowned at her and pointed at the bodies lying on the ground.

Christina nodded, and then moved her hand from side to side, firmly, hoping to convince him that she wished to have done with killing. He appeared to consider the matter for a moment, then made another of his quick gestures. This time one of his men came forward with one of the blunt spears, which he exchanged for the chieftain's bow. But now Christina saw to her surprise that what had appeared as a sort of pole was in fact a hollow tube, and that with it the warrior had given his chief a large dart, several inches long, made of wood, but probably dipped in some sort of a preservative.

The chieftain observed her interest, and his lips widened into a brief smile. Then he inserted the dart into the end of the tube, raised it to his lips, and turned in the direction of the sailor, who had stopped wailing for the moment. But now he gave a yell of alarm.

"Senora . . ."

"No one can fire a dart that far with his mouth," Caetano muttered.

"Senora . . ." screamed Veira.

There was a gentle *phut*, and the dart was suddenly sticking out of Veira's thigh. He looked down at it, struck dumb for the moment, and apparently not very seriously hurt—there was little blood.

The chieftain glanced at Christina and held up his finger. She could not understand him, looked from him to the blowpipe, and jerked her head as there came a dreadful wailing cry from Veira.

"Senora," he shrieked. "Senora . . ." The word died away, and he gave a choking sound. She watched his limbs seem to constrict, and his face turn crimson and then purple as he fought for breath.

"Poison, by Christ," Alvares muttered. "Poison."

"*Wourali*," the chieftain said, with a touch of pride. He pointed at the musket.

"Gunpowder," Christina replied, gazing at the dying man, feeling her skin prickling at the thought that such a fate could have been theirs at any moment during the morning, and could still be theirs at any moment. At last, she reflected, it had been terrifyingly quick; Veira had already lost consciousness, if he was not already dead.

And the chieftain still apparently wished another demonstration of the white man's powers. He pointed at the slumped body. "Gunpowder," he said.

Christina chewed her lip. But nothing could save Veira now, and it was possible that only another shot could save *them*. Besides, with so large a target she could prove her own superiority.

She took the recharged musket from James, placed the stock in her shoulder, drew a long breath as she sighted down the barrel, and fired. The smoke blinded her for a moment, but when she had blinked her eyes clear she saw that her ball had taken the dead man in the center of the chest, opening a terrible wound.

The chieftain ran forward to peer at the wound, accompanied by several of his men, who clustered around chattering at each other in low voices.

Christina discovered Alvares staring at her.

"There was nothing else I could do," she said.

"It was good shooting, senora," he said. "Do you suppose they will respect us enough to be our friends?"

"If they do not, then we are dead," she said. "We must *make* them our friends, no matter what it costs. And remember that they have probably never seen white people before. Take no offense, I beg of you, no matter what happens."

For the Indians were returning toward them, but this time laying down their weapons and advancing with outstretched hands.

"We must meet them," Christina commanded, and stepped forward, her own hands extended. It was the chieftain himself who approached her, first taking all her fingers in his, while he gazed at her, his head moving up and down as he took in all of her, as though realizing for the first time that she was a woman. When his eyes met hers again, he was frowning in mystification. Then, to her consternation, he put down his hand to seize his genitals and move them to and fro.

She shook her head, only then wondered if it might not

have been better to nod. But she had little hope of maintaining such a subterfuge for long, or even at all, she discovered, for he was pointing at her skirt, his frown deepening. She hesitated, chewing her lip, quite uncertain as to what would be best. But her instincts warned her that this man really wanted to be her friend, and that she could only benefit from such a friendship, while to reject him in any way, or attempt to be more mysterious than she really was, might be to throw away everything that she had already gained. Terribly aware that she was being watched by both Caetano and Alvares, as well as her son, she raised the skirt to her waist.

The chieftain slowly bent forward, and she realized that judging by the scant evidence of hair on his own body and those of his companions, he could never have seen a woman with such an abundance. She watched his hand begin to move, felt her entire body seem to become as light as a feather in an uncanny mixture of revulsion and anticipation.

"By Christ," Alvares growled. "By Christ . . ."

"Be quiet, and keep still," she said.

The chieftain raised his head at her words, and she forced a smile. A moment later he touched her, but hardly her flesh; he was interested only in the hair, in discovering whether it was some sort of a garment. Then he straightened, and in turn touched her long black tresses, allowing them to trickle through his fingers in delighted amazement, at once at the length of it and the texture. Gratefully she allowed the skirt to fall, only to discover that her ordeal was not yet over, as the chief pushed aside the remnants of her bodice to discover her other female attributes, and once again appeared to be totally mystified. As she understood. He could tell that she was not a girl; from the stretch marks on her belly he could also tell that she had had several children. Yet from her observation of the Indian women about Rio, she knew that her figure was at least as trim as that of an Indian virgin, still in her teens.

The chieftain stepped back, tapped himself on the chest. "Tupa," he said, pronouncing each syllable very distinctly. He pointed at the sun, shook his head, then pointed at the sky again, looked at her to make sure she understood that he was referring to the moon, and opened and shut his hands very rapidly several times. Clearly he could not count beyond the limit of his fingers, and equally clearly he was indicating that he was many, many moons old. Then he pointed at her.

She tapped herself on the chest. "Christina," she said, also dwelling on each syllable. Then she also opened and closed her hands several times rapidly. To make her point, she put her arm around James's shoulder, hugged him against her, and patted her abdomen.

The chief frowned, as if he did not believe her. But the resemblance between them was clear.

"James," Christina said. She pointed at Alvares. "Alvares. Caetano."

Tupa followed her carefully, looking from one to the other, his frown deepening. Then he pointed at her belly.

She smiled, and shook her head. "James," she said.

He seemed relieved and suddenly became very brusque, holding her hand and pointing into the trees, while his warriors retrieved their weapons.

"We'd best do as he suggests," Alvares said.

"We cannot leave these men here," she protested, and pointed at the dead men.

The chieftain shrugged, and pointed to the thin stream of ants already beginning to crawl over the first of the corpses.

"He's right, senora," Caetano said. "In a couple of hours they'll be picked clean."

Christina hesitated, but he was undoubtedly right. She sighed, and nodded. "But we'll have to carry Captain Grant." She pointed at Jamey.

Tupa shook his head, kicked the headless body of the snake, pointed at Jamey, and shook his head again.

"He's not dead," Christina cried, and knelt beside the unconscious man. "Look." She touched Jamey's nostrils.

Tupa stood beside her, pointed at the sun, made a gesture to indicate its falling from the sky, and shook his head again.

"No," Christina insisted. "He will not die. I sucked out the poison. Look."

She showed Tupa the scar on Jamey's calf, and the other on his thigh. But from the expression on his face, the chieftain had no idea what she was talking about. Again it was

easy to understand. Jamey had obviously learned the art of
surviving snakebite from the Indians nearer the coast, who
had come into previous contact with white men and secured
iron weapons. Here on the Amazon, where bone was the
hardest of their materials, the ability to make such a deep
incision was lacking, and thus these Indians must regard any
bite from a venomous snake such as a bushmaster fatal.

"He will not die," she said again, bit her lip as he continued to gaze at her, and then held her hand again and pointed
at the trees. It was necessary to risk antagonizing him. "No,"
she said. She touched Jamey's hand, then her own breast, put
her hands together, and held them against her face.

Tupa obviously understood her, for he sighed and indicated
with his finger a tear rolling down her cheek. But then he
shrugged and again shook his head.

"No," Christina said. She pointed at Jamey, and then at
the forest, and nodded vigorously. Then she tapped herself on
the chest, pointed at Jamey, shook her head, and sat down
beside him.

An almost European expression of irritation passed over
Tupa's face. For several seconds he regarded her, while she
met his gaze as squarely as she could, in spite of the pounding
of her heart. Then he shrugged again, and beckoned four of
his warriors to lift the unconscious man.

"You've made quite a conquest, senora," Alvares said.

"Yes," she agreed, and picked up her musket. She wondered what might be involved in maintaining it.

Even carrying Jamey's inert body, the Indians seemed able
to pass between the trees and vines without hindrance, hardly
disturbing a leaf, and moving at speed, having to halt every
few minutes to allow the white people to catch up. Christina
kept young James close to her side, while Alvares and Caetano
followed, casting fearful glances at their escort.

Christina did her best to reassure them. "Had they meant
to kill us," she pointed out, "they would surely have done so
already."

"They may be saving us for some sacrifice," Alvares
muttered.

"In which case," she said angrily, "we must just be

prepared to die as Christians.'' But at the moment the fear of death was less disturbing to her than the chieftain's interest in her, the way Tupa kept coming back to smile at her and stroke her hair; she could have no doubts that there was a crisis looming, even if, at the moment, she had no clear idea how to meet it.

As with everything else in this jungle, they came upon the village entirely without warning. One minute they were painfully clawing and hacking their way through the undergrowth, and the next they were standing by a rushing stream, undoubtedly on its way to join the great river, on the far side of which there was a large cleared area; close at hand were several huts—if they could be so called, for they were no more than troolie-palm roofs resting on uprights, lacking walls or doors—while at the back of the village, to her amazement, was a strip of obviously cultivated land, where women could be seen working. But these immediately abandoned their labor when they discovered the return of their menfolk, and accompanied by a horde of children of all ages, they came hurrying toward the stream to examine their remarkable visitors.

Having waded the stream, Christina was surrounded by naked women and children pinching her arms, prodding her back and thighs, seizing handfuls of her hair to peer at and even to suck. Young James was torn from her side and underwent an equal examination, as did Alvares and Caetano, although each of the three men, she observed, was not above doing a little examining of his own, as naked breasts and thighs were rubbed against their scanty clothing.

''Tupa,'' she shouted, as soon as she could catch her breath, and the chieftain immediately gave a loud whistling call, which had his people turning toward him obediently. Christina was able to sink to her knees in exhaustion, and watch while he obviously regaled the village with the story of the morning's adventure, referring several times to ''Christin-*a*,'' at which heads were turned in her direction, and equally obviously describing the terrifying effects of the strange weapons used by these equally strange beings. And once again Alvares had to demonstrate, shooting at a gourdlike

fruit the chief placed on a stick, and shattering it into a
thousand slivers, at which the women and children all took to
their heels and disappeared into the forest, from whence they
had to be coaxed to return by their menfolk.

Tupa now again indicated that he would like to have the
opportunity of firing one of the muskets himself, and again
Christina quite firmly refused, allowing herself a little panto-
mime as she indicated that the weapons had come to them
from the sky—and if he wished to believe that she herself
also came from the sky, she did not suppose that could be a
bad thing—and that only they were allowed to handle them.
For a moment he frowned at her, but she made herself meet
his gaze without flinching, and after a few seconds he turned
away, while Alvares wiped sweat from his brow. "By Christ,
senora," he said, "every time you and he argue, I think our
last moment has come.''

"And so it will, if we ever admit either fear or inferiori-
ty," she insisted, with a confidence she was far from feeling.
"I wonder how we may obtain some food?"

For the afternoon was now well advanced, and the sun was
beating down on the clearing; even the earth beneath their feet
seemed to be burning. The Indians apparently felt it also, for
without eating they departed to their various huts, where each
apparently had a hammock of his or her own, and proceeded
to go to sleep. But Christina observed to her surprise that the
sexes were strictly segregated; while the women and their
children, including all the males under puberty, divided themselves up among the smaller huts, the men went toward the
only large hut in the village, indicating that the three white
men should accompany them.

"No," Christina said, and held young James's hand, once
again patting her stomach.

Tupa replied by pointing at James's genitals, hardly concealed by the linen drawers which were his only remaining
garment. Certainly he was past puberty. Christina chewed her
lip, while James gently freed himself.

"You said we must humor these people, Mama," he pointed
out, and followed Alvares and Caetano.

Tupa meanwhile had seized Christina's hand and was leading her toward the only unoccupied hut in the village. She looked around her, discovered that she was alone in the center of the clearing with the chieftain and Jamey, who was commencing to move restlessly. Hastily she stopped, bringing Tupa also to a halt, for he was not much larger than herself, and pointed at the unconscious man, indicating the sun and then pointing at Jamey's uncovered head.

Tupa shook his head and made a dismissive gesture.

"No," she said, and stamped her foot. "He will *not* die if he is cared for." She pulled her hand free, folded her arms across her chest, and stood next to Jamey's body.

Tupa gave a sigh, regarded her for a few moments, then seized Jamey's shoulders and started dragging him across the ground. Immediately she helped him, and between them they pulled him under the shelter of the roof, where they found blessed relief. She had not realized how painful her eyes and her head had become from the unending glare.

She knelt beside Jamey, felt his forehead and his cheeks; he was terribly hot, but how much of that was fever and how much sunburn she couldn't be sure. But his lips were dry and caked, and she was thirsty herself. She stood up, pointed at the river, touched her mouth, and then pointed at Jamey.

Yet again she had to wait for the slow look of appraisal, then Tupa reached up to one of the narrow shelves formed by the solid branches laid across the tops of the uprights, to which the palm thatching was secured—and from which, she saw, the hammocks were suspended, at the moment tied up out of the way—and handed her one of the gourds at which Alvares had earlier been firing, only this one had been split in two; since it was entirely hollow, with a brittle, solid skin, it made a perfect little cup, lacking only handles.

She raised her head in delight, and Tupa smiled at her. "*Calabash*," he said.

"*Calabash*," she repeated, and hurried down to the water, where, after drinking herself, she carried a full cupful back toward Jamey, observing as she did so that Tupa was releasing one of the hammocks and arranging it with great care. She slowed as she approached the hut, and waited, but he seemed content with just one, and indeed now sat in it and smiled at her.

Carefully she knelt beside Jamey, raised his head to rest it on her knee, bathed his face, and then forced his jaws apart to pour a trickle of the water down his throat, all the while terribly conscious of Tupa seated in the hammock immediately behind her, slowly rocking himself to and fro. She needed to think, and to allow herself more time, so she made another journey to the stream, refilled the *calabash*, and returned to the hut, to give Jamey another drink. Now he moved, shaking his head without opening his eyes, and muttering, "El Dorado."

Gently she laid him back on the earth, arranging him as comfortably as she could. She would have preferred to be able to place him on some sort of a mattress, but she dared not risk the hammock, out of which he would certainly tumble.

Never had she felt so utterly alone. In fact, she realized, never before had she felt alone at all; even in the convent cellar she had been sure of the presence of God. Here in the jungle she was less aware of Him. Or was it because, over the past fifteen years, the umbrella of His protection had been slowly but surely replaced by the certainty of Jack's?

She could not think about that now, though. It was on Jamey's staying alive that she now depended for her own survival. Jack would understand that; he must.

And with that sudden injection of courage she could even face the chieftain, who was obviously interested in what the unconscious man had said.

"El Dorado?" he asked, pointing at Jamey.

Christina's heart gave a lurch. Was it possible he knew of the place? She nodded. "El Dorado?" And pointed to the north.

But the chief was clearly mystified. Christina bit her lip in frustration, then had an idea. She took off her gold wedding band, held it out. "El Dorado," she said.

The chief peered at the metal, took it from her fingers, smelled it and licked it, as was his habit, then pointed at the pistol in her belt, as if to ask whether the ring also possessed a destructive power.

She shook her head, took the ring back from him, and replaced it on her finger. Gold seemed to mean nothing to him. Yet he must have seen it, if indeed they were within days of the savannah and the City of Gold. The savannah! She determined to try again, once more pointed to the north. "Savannah?"

This time he frowned, surprised that she should know an Indian word.

"Savannah?" she asked again, her excitement rising.

"Savannah," he agreed, also pointing to the north.

She pointed at the sun, turned her hands outward. Tupa considered, then opened and closed his hands many times. Then he patted himself on the chest, shook his head, to indicate that he personally had never been there, and made the gesture of drawing a bow, before again patting himself on the chest and holding his hand above his head. She understood that the savannah was the home of very warlike creatures, who were considerably bigger than himself. But since he had never been there, that might very well be legend. And yet he had heard of it.

Once again she took off the ring. "Savannah," she said. "Gold?"

He pointed at her. "Savannah?" he asked.

She hesitated, but was determined to maintain her decision to tell the truth. She knelt and drew the rough outline of Brazil in the dust, with a deep, long line for the Amazon. "Amazon," she said. A dot to the north of the river. "Savannah." Another dot, far to the south. "Rio," she explained, and tapped herself on the chest. "Rio." She pointed at Jamey. "Rio."

Tupa was intrigued. He peered at the map for some seconds, then asked. "Tupa?"

She dotted next to the Amazon. "Tupa."

He smiled. "El Dorado?"

She indicated the savannah, watched him anxiously. But he was tiring of this game. "El Dorado," he said, and got out of the hammock to stand on her map, placing his foot exactly over where she had indicated him to be. "El Dorado."

She looked up at him, discovered that his interests had very definitely become centered upon satisfying his suddenly huge member, which was hovering immediately in front of her face. For a terrible moment she was again overwhelmed by a feeling of total helplessness, total surrender. This man alone stood between her and death; certainly, from the way they had disposed of Veira, she could not suppose that Christian ethics played any part in these people's thinking. And presumably, as they had been watching the brief battle between the white people, they judged them to be no different. The important point was that while the chieftain was obviously interested in the noise and power of their muskets, in the sharpness of their steel, in their pigmentation and their hair and their total strangeness, he was not particularly afraid of any of those things. His true interest, perhaps his fear of them, arose from the fact that she was totally different from any female he had ever encountered. She could understand that, quite apart from any sexual attraction, he must be considering that to couple with her might obtain for him some of her powers, even to firing the musket.

And the sexual attraction alone was obviously considerable. So why not surrender and do as he wished?

Except that she simply could not; she had never felt such complete revulsion. And besides, having conquered her, would he continue to be interested? Or would he then consider himself her master? Her instincts warned her that she had to maintain at least equality with this man—he might not be aware of it, but that was the only *true* difference between her and his women.

And yet equally she could not reject him out of hand, or even show concern at his offer; to anger him would mean all their deaths. Nor could she see any great value in reminding him that she was Jamey's woman; she had already indicated that, and it had not abated his ardor in the slightest. Besides, if she were to use that as a reason not to sleep with him, he might very soon discover her a widow. In some way she had to divert him and keep him diverted, at least until Jamey had regained his strength.

Until Jamey had regained his strength. She gazed at the chief, looked up at his smiling face, and slowly rose to her feet. It could be done, if she had the courage to maintain her position.

She pointed at Tupa's penis, then at herself. He nodded vigorously. She smiled at him and then sighed, allowed a look of utter dejection to cross her face. He frowned at her, stepped closer, and she hastily stepped backward. "El Dorado," she said, pointing at Jamey. It made a more impressive title than Jamey Grant. "El Dorado. Tupa, pouf. El Dorado . . ." She spread her arms wide, pointed to the sun, and then to the south, made a sweeping gesture.

Tupa's frown deepened as he gazed at the unconscious man.

"Christina," Christina said, and pointed to Jamey's thighs. "Christina. . . ." She clasped her hands together, knelt at Jamey's side.

Tupa made a growling sound, almost like an angry dog, and drew his finger across the air violently.

Christina leaped to her feet, conveying pure terror, gripped Tupa's arm, allowed him to come against her, shivering with fright as she pointed at the sky. "Bang," she said. "Bang, bang, bang." She pointed at the musket. "Pouf." Then the sky again. "Bang."

Tupa considered, in an obvious agony of indecision. But he had heard thunderclaps often enough. Yet he couldn't be given time to consider the matter. Christina still held his arm, allowed her gaze to drop to his member. "El Dorado," she said.

She opened and closed her hand several times. "El Dorado . . ." She flexed her biceps, squared her shoulders, patted herself on the chest. "El Dorado," she said, and kissed Tupa on the cheek. "Christina, Tupa."

The chief stared at Jamey; but already his ardor was starting to wane.

"El Dorado?" Christina begged. She pointed at the sun, opened and closed her hand, pointed at Jamey. "El Dorado?"

Tupa nodded. "El Dorado. . . ." He squared his own shoulders, threw out his chest, held up five fingers. "El Dorado."

"Five days," she cried. "That would be magnificent."

He smiled at her, raised his penis with his hand. "Tupa," he said. "Christina."

She retained her composure with an effort, smiled at him again. She had bought herself five days.

But only five days. There was a great deal to be done, as she managed to explain to Alvares that evening, when at last they obtained some food. Indeed the Indians put on quite a banquet, seated around a roaring fire which helped to keep off the mosquitoes, eating baked fish and a starchy, hard vegetable which they called *cassava*, and drinking a somewhat sickly white liquid, suggestive of milk with a strangely flat taste, which they called *piwarrie* and which also, she gathered, came from the cassava plant. Tupa, seated beside her, explained by means of his signs that the cassava liquid, in its pure state, was actually the basis of a poison every bit as deadly as wourali, but that properly diluted and fermented, it made their staple beer. And that it was fermented could not be doubted; within a very short space of time almost the entire village, even the children, were rolling about the ground in extreme inebriation, and she observed to her alarm and disgust that young James was in a hardly better condition; he must have decided to join the Indians as thoroughly as he could, for he had discarded the last of his clothing.

This only made their position the more untenable, their escape the more urgent. Caetano was indulging himself just as much as James, but she managed to catch Alvares's eye, and after an hour, when the Indians were happily oblivious of what was going on and were chattering to each other or wrestling or quite openly coupling, he crawled around to sit beside her. She was in the most difficult position of all, she estimated, for she had been given the seat of honor next to Tupa, who as he became more drunk had flopped against her, and kept trying to get his fingers inside her bodice. When she attempted to move he seized her around the legs and frowned so horribly she felt obliged to sit still.

"We must leave this place," she said to the mate.

"Indeed, senora. But how? We cannot leave, anyway, while the captain is injured." His eyes gloomed at her. "Or do you mean to abandon the captain?"

"I do not mean to abandon the captain," she said. "But I do not think we can remain until he is absolutely well again. The very moment he can move, then we must go."

"But, senora—"

"I know we cannot walk through the jungle, Alvares," she said. "We must use the boat. That is your first priority, tomorrow. This stream must debouch into the river. And the boat is moored in the river. I want you to find it and conceal it as best you can, making sure that you can find it again whenever you wish. It should not be difficult; it cannot be more than a few hours from here."

Alvares chewed his lip. "Will the Indians let us, senora?"

"We must go whether they will or not, Alvares," she told him, deciding against informing him of her bargain with Tupa, and the certainty that the Indians would *not* let them go. "You must see that we cannot remain here for the rest of our lives." She gazed at young James, now rolling on the ground with some Indian maiden—if the word *maiden* could possibly be applied to any of these utterly amoral creatures, she thought bitterly. "Soon we will be Indians ourselves."

From Alvares's expression, she guessed he was thinking that might not be the worst of all possible fates.

"Besides," she said, "don't you realize that we only survive by reason of our guns? If they insist on our proving that strength every day we shall soon run out of powder. And what then?"

Since he still seemed uncertain, she decided that it would not go amiss to add a little terror to his reasoning. "They are obviously cannibals," she pointed out. "You can see that. Look at the necklace Tupa is wearing. And I can tell you, Alvares, that they eat their victims alive. Can you imagine being tied to a stake and stripped of your flesh before your own eyes?"

He scratched his head. "But where would we go, senora, even if we reached the boat? There are not enough of us to row it against the stream. We could only go down the river."

"I certainly have no desire to go further upriver, Alvares."

"Then what of El Dorado?"

"There *is* no El Dorado. It is all a dream. It has never been anything more than a dream. Listen to me. The chief has heard of the savannah. He has even, somehow, come into contact with the Indians who live there. But he has never heard of El Dorado. Nor has he ever seen gold before. Can't you see that if there is any sort of communication between these people and those to the north, they would have had to know what gold looks like, if those northern people had ever used it?"

Alvares chewed his lip. "But downriver . . . senora, downriver there is government, and your father's people. And no doubt your husband as well. They will hang us all."

"No. Listen, Alvares." She held his hands, having to allow Tupa to fondle as he chose, but he was by now so drunk his eyes were shut. "I give you my word, my sacred word as a Sousa e Melo, that if you and Caetano help Captain Grant and James and me to get down the river, you will be pardoned by my father, and more, I promise you that my husband, whenever he returns to Brazil, will reward you most richly. As I am sure my father will do also."

He gazed at her a moment longer, then nodded. "I will find the boat, senora."

For all his villainy, she felt she could almost kiss him with sheer relief. But, she reflected, there really had been no other decision he could come to. He could see as well as anyone that to remain here would be to die. Now it was just a matter of waiting. She debated having a word with young James, but it was far too late for that; he had passed out. Besides, their intention would be safer kept just between herself and Alvares. Instead, she disengaged herself from Tupa, gave Jamey another drink of water and bathed his forehead, then rolled into her hammock. She felt more confident than she had been for a long time, and more her own mistress. For a year she had been dragged along behind Jamey. Now she was in control, as always before she had been in control. It was only necessary to continue dissembling, and keep Tupa happy, and attend to Jamey's health, until he was well enough to travel.

Next morning she was up early, expecting to see a total shambles, but to her amazement the Indians were also about, despite the vast quantity of liquor they had consumed, and were already busy with their daily tasks, the women either working in the fields or baking clay pots or weaving hammocks and fish nets, the men assembling to depart for the hunt. In this they expected the white men to assist them with their guns, but since they also expected Tupa to lead them, she was promised a relatively peaceful morning, although Tupa had apparently instructed two of the women to stay by her side and assist her as she required. She could not help but wonder if they were his wives, and if indeed they would show any hostility to her, but they seemed delighted with their new responsibility, kept fingering her or Jamey's hair and giggling to each other as they watched her attempt to make him swallow a gruel she had concocted from the remains of the *piwarrie* together with some crushed manihot flour, or as she repeatedly bathed his forehead in an attempt to bring down the fever. Clearly they thought she was wasting her time, and when she looked at the terrible scar on his calf she was inclined to believe them. She could only take comfort from recalling that he had survived such a snakebite before, and that Tupa had stated that he would be dead by sundown, now more than twelve hours in the past.

He *would* get well, she kept telling herself. He would recover, and then . . . she chewed her lip, staring at the bearded face. She might be able to persuade her father, and even Jack, not to prosecute. She would never be able to persuade them to forgive him. And he would be a shattered man, forced to accept that he had lived all his life in pursuit of a senseless dream.

If only she could make herself hate him. That she did not, could not, love him was certain. The boy who had fascinated her was long lost in this savage, brutal, single-minded, and utterly selfish man, who had stolen her from her husband and from her children—and who had appealed to some utterly primitive streak in her own nature. But she could never hate him, either, not after sharing this past year with him. But it was a year she knew she would be happy to forget once she could return to Jack and her children—as a nightmare which had yet been terrifyingly exciting. And which had made her understand her true nature. Surely her marriage to Jack could only benefit from such a self-examination. And surely she could make him understand that.

In the jungle, so far from the least suggestion of civilization, it was a simple matter to rationalize, to realize that only the essentials mattered. And to believe that others would realize that too.

When she heard the men returning later, she hastily scrambled to her feet. Their chatter told her they were excited, as they flooded across the stream waving their bows and their blowpipes. Christina ran toward them, searching for James, and found him and Caetano walking with Tupa, and in turn hurrying toward her as they saw her approach.

"Mama," James shouted. "Alvares . . ."

She frowned at them, an icy hand seeming to grip her heart. "What has happened?"

"Alvares, senora," Caetano said. "He led us toward the river. We did not understand why he insisted upon going there until we found the boat. It was still there, senora, still tethered to the bank."

"Yes," Christina said. "But what *happened*?"

"The Indians were all interested," James went on, "never having seen a European-built boat before, and Alvares indicated that he would show them how it worked. He got in, cut the painter, and rowed away."

"Rowed away?" Christina shouted.

"The Indians tried to stop him, and he hit one of them so hard across the head with his pistol barrel, he opened the man's skull," Caetano said. "Killed him stone dead, senora. The others tried to shoot him with their bows and arrows, but by then he was out of range."

"He just rowed away, Mama," James said. "Just rowed away."

Her stomach seeming to be filled with molten lead, Christina turned to face the chieftain.

Amazingly, Tupa did not seem the least bit angry, or even concerned by the morning's incident; certainly he did not suspect that she might have had any part in it. The death of one of his people he accepted as a matter of course, and Alvares's escape he regarded as of no importance whatsoever; he considered the river as the roadway to hell, as he expressed most convincingly by gestures. He was far more interested in showing her the large collection of teeth he had removed from the corpses they had left behind, the ants, as intended, having picked them clean during the night.

Christina smiled, and pretended to be as delighted as he, while her thoughts tumbled. Very likely he was right, and Alvares, by himself, would not survive the journey downriver. But either way, his departure with the dinghy had shut them in this leafy green prison as certainly as if he had slammed a door and slipped the bolt. She had painted the futility of their quest for El Dorado, the dangers of their situation, far too well, and she had not painted the likely rewards he might receive for his aid well enough.

She looked at Caetano, who was still waiting indecisively, and then at James, who had already wandered off, seeking the girl with whom he had coupled the night before. Remaining here was impossible; she was certain it was only the other Indians' acknowledgment of Tupa as their chieftain that had kept them *all* from attempting to get their hands on her. If he were to lose interest . . . but his interest only presented other problems. Its only blessing was that he was prepared to keep his word that he would help Jamey recover. During the afternoon he prepared some kind of a paste, with which he smothered the now inflamed cuts, and he also produced an evil-smelling liquid which he indicated she should pour down Jamey's throat. This she was not prepared to do until she had established that the great sun, who was Jamey's immediate and only superior, would never permit her to give herself to *any* other man were his protegé to die. Tupa reassured her by drinking some of the syrup himself.

Jamey's medicine administered, there was nothing to do but wait and pray—she was not quite sure for what—and watch the Indians at their work and their play. And despite herself, she found them fascinating. During her sojourn in Rio and her visits to the immediate neighborhood around the capital, where the tribes had long been subjugated, converted to Christianity, and exposed to the miseries of European diseases and European alcohol, she had formed the conclusion, held by all the colonists so far as she knew, that these were the most degraded and useless of God's human creations, indolent, careless, amoral, unpredictable. Well they were certainly amoral, in every possible sense. The women were the workers and the bearers of children; the men seemed to be at least as much pleased to copulate with each other as with the women. Yet it was all so natural, so much a part of their everyday life, that disgust was pointless; her concern was entirely for young James, who for the moment was only concerned with the enormous amount of naked female flesh with which he was surrounded, and in the enjoyment of which she dared not interfere.

Morals apart, she very rapidly discovered the Indians to be a delightful people. They were dangerous, in the sense that they were hardly more than overgrown children. If they did not injure, or even kill, each other in their interminable wrestling matches, it was obviously because they considered themselves as belonging to one family—which she supposed they very probably did. And perhaps they were well aware that they were managing to exist in the middle of the most hostile of environments, where every creature's claw was directed to their destruction. Thus they regarded death as an everyday concomitant of life, wasted no time in tears or even in burial or cremation, but rather abandoned the corpses to be destroyed by the ants, and then returned to obtain the teeth and such bones as could be used for the manufacture of knives or arrowheads; she soon realized that they were not habitual cannibals.

At some stage, she understood, they had come into contact with other human beings, very probably the people from the savannah, and had learned that humans, too, could be their enemies. But they were not instinctively antagonistic, as they had proved in their welcome of the white people, however terrifying was the thought of their quite casual destruction of Veira, entirely because they had formed the correct opinion that he was an enemy of their new guests.

Thus they lived a self-contained, inward-turning life, and very industriously. Not a day passed but the men went hunting and fishing, and every day the women tended the cultivated field and went about their labors, which included the never ending battle against the encroaching jungle. They all indulged in an afternoon siesta, and every evening they got themselves drunk on *piwarrie*, but she could not discover any difference in this mode of life to that practiced by the white men of Rio.

They enjoyed smoking as much as drinking, for tobacco grew wild in the forest, and it was a remarkable sight to see almost the entire tribe, women as well as men, seated in a row puffing at the rolled leaves. They also enjoyed playing games. There were trees in the forest which, when the bark was cut into, emitted a thick, sticky white liquid. Rolled into a ball and dried, this liquid solidified into a light missile which, when tossed against a hard surface, would spring back. They called it *caoutchouc*, and delighted in chasing it back and forth with small branches stripped from the neighboring trees.

Their religion appeared to be nothing more than an accumulation of fears and superstitions. They allotted life to everything, and where it could not be physically defeated it was regarded as a superior, or even a god. They had no doubt that the sun she indicated as her own god was the most powerful of them all, and associated with the heavenly body the powers of thunder and lightning. But hardly inferior was the great river, which never changed and which was death to venture upon, and of course its handmaidens, the alligators and the big snakes. The jungle was equally full of terror, and yet this in no way deterred them from venturing forth. Life was there to be lived, however much of a gamble it might be.

And above all, they were healthy. She had in fact never come across any people with less evidence of illness. She had accepted that the truly ghastly diseases, like leprosy, had come from the old world, but the Indians of the coast had also been riddled with consumption, had died of influenza or even the common cold, and had certainly been the most rabid carriers of syphilis. Here there was no such thing as a runny nose, and she could not imagine any of these people ever spitting blood, while there was not a syphilitic scar to be seen, for all of the unceasing carnality with which she was surrounded. Could it be possible that these diseases too had been imported from Europe, instead of the other way around?

It occurred to her that despite all the horror of the past year, she would not have missed such an experience as this; perhaps all life on earth had once been equally simple, before men had become ambitious and greedy. But she came back to reality with a jolt as she found Tupa watching her, with his slow, anticipatory smile. Again the urge to surrender, to become an Indian herself, crept over her consciousness. But at least it was not a decision which would have to be taken until Jamey had recovered. And on the third day, miraculously, he opened his eyes.

Tupa was as pleased by Jamey's recovery as she was; he patted himself on the chest, and then held his genitals and shook them at her. She indicated that their bargain waited upon Jamey's regaining all his strength and health, but he did not seem concerned. He gave her more of the evil-smelling medicine, and suggested that within another week she would be in his hammock—a fact she decided to keep from Jamey for the time being.

Jamey's consciousness was accompanied by an almost complete lucidity of mind, although of course he could remember nothing of what had happened from about five minutes after he had been bitten. He listened with utter amazement as she told him what had taken place over the past few days.

"Truly," he remarked, his voice still weak, "you're quite a girl, Christina." His fingers slid over her arm and found her own fingers, to give them a squeeze. He looked around him at the village, and the men, just returning from their morning's hunt. And at James and Caetano, as naked as any of the savages. "And you mean no man here has attempted to claim you as his own?"

"Well . . ." She stood up as Tupa approached.

Jamey said nothing then, merely smiled at the chieftain and accepted his medicine with a grimace, but that he was quite capable of estimating the situation he revealed that evening, when she sat with him as the Indians indulged in their carouse. "I wonder," he said, "that you have not asked your friend for some information about El Dorado."

"I have," she said, and told him of her conversation.

He listened without conviction. "Of course it is there," he said. "Raleigh knew of it. So do the Spanish explorers. It is just further off than we supposed. Everything in this benighted continent is further off than we supposed."

"Jamey," she said, "Tupa knows of the savannah. Surely—"

"It *must* be there," he said, half to himself. "I have spent half my life . . . my God, half my life. . . . It *must* be there." His tone was almost desperate. And yet, the sooner he came to terms with the truth, the better for them all.

"It isn't, Jamey," she said. "I showed him my ring and he did not know what it was. If there was gold anywhere north of here, he would have to have seen it before."

"And what else has he seen before?" Jamey asked, his fingers suddenly tight on hers.

"Nothing," she said, "of what you mean."

"You expect me to believe that? I know how a man looks at a woman when she is his."

She sighed. "He anticipates such an event," she admitted, and explained her subterfuge.

When she had finished, Jamey lay back to gaze at the palm roof above his head. "So they think I am a God," he said.

"No. They think you are a chieftain protected by God."

"And more powerful than their own."

"I'm not sure about that," she said. "I do not think Tupa accepts that. He recognizes you as an equal, possessed perhaps of a certain magic because of our gunpowder. But he reasons that if you were truly a supernatural being, then you would not have succumbed to the snakebite at all."

"Then as soon as I am able to move, I must convince him, and all his people, that I am indeed supernatural."

"You must be careful," she said. "They are very strong, very agile. And we have only a small supply of powder and ball left to us."

"And besides," he said, "you are looking forward to having to pay your forfeit."

She raised her chin. "It was a bargain," she said, "which I am prepared to keep. As he has kept his, by restoring you to health."

"Then the sooner I am *fully* restored to health, the better for us all, do you not agree?" And he closed his eyes.

Clearly he was considering a plan. She could only hope and pray that he would not endanger all their lives in some madcap scheme. But the next day he seemed relaxed and thoughtful.

"El Dorado," he said. "There was a dream."

She looked at him suspiciously. But he sounded as if he had genuinely accepted what she had told him. "Only a dream, Jamey," she said. "It was never more than that."

"Oh, aye," he agreed. "I think you are right. Having come this far, to discover there is not even any knowledge of gold . . . you have to be right." He pushed himself into a sitting position, revealing again the amazing speed of his recovery, and gazed at the Indian women going about their tasks. "But what a thorny trail I have trod all these years, seeking a dream." He glanced at her. "And have dragged you over, as well."

"I cannot pretend to understand the workings of God's will," she said.

"God," he remarked in disgust. "There is no God, Christina. Only men. And men's wills. Which can lead them into some strange paths."

She feared a mood of despondency even more than one of arrogant ebullience, and endeavored to set his mind to more practical subjects. "What do you propose we should do?"

"Do?" Now he watched the warriors, returning as usual with their baskets filled with fish. "Even assuming we could cross the river, do you suppose you could walk back to Rio? It is nearly two thousand miles through the jungle.''

"No," she said. "I could not walk back to Rio."

"Well then, do you suppose we could strike north and make for the coast?"

"I doubt we would succeed there either."

"So there is your question answered," he said bitterly. "We are marooned here as securely as if we had been cast away on some desert island."

"Jack will come for us one day," she said.

"Jack? Do you really suppose Alvares is going to go to Jack? Even if he survives?"

"No," she said. "No, I do not suppose that."

"Well then? No one else has any idea where we have come."

"Jack knows you seek El Dorado," she said. "He will seek us, up the Amazon."

"*You* are the one who is dreaming. And supposing he does find us one day, will not his first action be to hang me?"

"No," she said. "I would not permit it."

"Ah, you have forgiven me for all of my crimes."

"Forgiven you? I doubt I can ever truly do that, Jamey. But we have adventured so far, and survived so much, I could not stand by and see you die."

"What a comfort you are," he remarked, his bitterness seeming to increase. "And in the meantime you are content to remain here."

"I do not see that we have any alternative," she pointed out. "And besides, there can be many worse places than this village. Indeed, Jamey, I think I would be hard put to name a *better* place. Here is food, and health, and contentment. . . . Why, supposing you *found* El Dorado, could you buy anything that is not here? Anything of true value?"

"El Dorado," he said. "You would compare this mud heap with El Dorado."

"Yes," she insisted. "There is no wealth in the world that could buy you what you have here already. This *is* El Dorado, Jamey. All the El Dorado any man will ever find."

"And you have an Indian chieftain for me to share you with, just to pass the time."

"If that is what fate decrees, Jamey. You will not want for my companionship. I promise you that."

He stared at her for several seconds, then lay down and closed his eyes. "I am not very good at sharing," he said. "Either my dream or my woman."

By the seventh day he was able to move, although he needed a stick upon which to lean, which was cut for him by young James. And with returning health, his humor improved as well. He became quite cheerful, passed the time of day with both his son and Caetano, smiled at Christina, and seemed to go out of his way to cultivate Tupa. Christina was enormously relieved to see him accepting their fate, for the one thing she feared was a jealousy-inspired clash between him and the chieftain; but then she started to worry that he was going too far the other way, when she saw him actually handing one of the two muskets to the chieftain and indicating how it should be fired.

"The gunpowder is our only source of superiority," she said. "I am sure you make a mistake. Once he conceives that we are no better than he—"

"We are to share," Jamey pointed out. "You have told me so. Therefore we will share. We may have to spend the rest of our lives with these people. We will only accomplish that by playing absolutely straight with them. As you have been doing." He smiled at her, and left her profoundly disturbed; she had seen that crooked smile before, too often.

But the following afternoon he proved that he meant what he said, by actually charging a musket and letting Tupa use it. The chieftain was delighted, although his first shot screamed toward the sky, his second all but killed one of the women, who ran into the woods shrieking with a mixture of fear and amusement, and his third thudded into the earth only feet from where he stood. It all seemed a terrible waste of powder and ball to Christina, but Jamey was patience itself, and helped the chief to aim and level, explained that the ability to fire a musket was granted by the great sun, and that for true accuracy a special prayer was necessary, which he then proceeded to offer, kneeling on the ground and muttering the most absurd mumbo jumbo, which was followed with the keenest interest by the Indians, and especially by Tupa, intent upon aping his mentor's every action.

If it was a joke, Christina thought, it was a cruel one. If, as she decided was far more likely, it was some sort of a plan, she could not fathom what he intended. But in any event, she was more concerned with her own coming ordeal, for there could be no doubt that Jamey was almost fully restored to health—a fact that was not lost upon the chieftain, who that evening at dinner insisted upon removing her bodice altogether and holding her breasts in his hands to display them to the tribe, at the same time indicating that on the morrow he would claim the sun goddess for his own. She retired in some confusion, quite unable to meet Jamey's eyes, and totally uncertain as to her own feelings in the matter. On the one hand there could be no argument that Tupa had behaved honorably, upholding his side of their arrangement to the last, and was quite content that she should be recognized as a superior being prepared to bestow her charms upon the head of the tribe. But on the other she could not help but conceive of herself as a sort of human sacrifice, and besides, might he not discover she was less than the overwhelming experience he anticipated?

Next morning she went with the women to the stream as usual, for they were the most remarkably clean people she had ever met, and bathed morning and evening; today she took particular care with her toilette in anticipation of what was to come.

When she returned to the village, Jamey was sitting in the shade of their hut, whittling a piece of wood.

She attempted conversation. "I suppose," she said, "since you no longer need your cane, you should go hunting with the men."

"I shall do as I choose," he said. "After all, I am a great chief. You have told them so."

"I think these people expect to be led by example rather than exhortation," she suggested.

"As I intend to do," he said, "when the moment is right. Perhaps now."

For the men were returning. Christina drew a long breath and retired to her hammock, because there could be no mistaking Tupa's intention as he marched toward her, as aroused as she had ever seen a man in her life.

Jamey got to his feet slowly, but moving with a catlike grace she had observed before. A sudden band seemed to constrict about her chest; she could put no name to it, but she knew she was about to witness a tragedy.

"Jamey," she said, sitting up.

He ignored her and stepped away from the tent, directly into Tupa's path. The chief merely smiled at him and endeavored to step around him, again to be blocked. This time he frowned.

Jamey pointed over his shoulder at Christina, then at the chief. Tupa nodded, his frown fading. Jamey pointed at Christina again, and then at himself. Tupa merely smiled and held up his right hand, the first two fingers crossed, clearly indicating that from now on they must share her. Jamey shook his head, and Tupa's frown returned.

By now the fact that the two chieftains were having a difference of opinion had become obvious, and the other men, as well as the women, were starting to gather around the hut, attempting to follow the conversation with twisting heads and grunts of concern or mutual information.

Jamey was pointing at the sun and then at himself, patting himself on the chest and flexing his muscles. Not to be outdone, Tupa, as might have been expected, did the same, to indicate that he considered himself entirely Jamey's equal. More, he pointed to the wound on Jamey's leg, and then to his own unmarked flesh, and gave a derogatory smile to indicate that *he* had never fallen a victim to any of the forest monsters.

Jamey ignored this sally, pointed at the sun again, and then at each of them in turn, and while Tupa nodded vigorously, Jamey shook his head with equal energy and slowly pointed first to himself, nodded, and then at Tupa, and shrugged. His meaning could not be mistaken; there could only be one chieftain in the eyes of the sun.

Christina found herself almost unable to breathe; Jamey was in no condition, despite his miraculous recovery, to face the chieftain in hand-to-hand combat. But of course he would not have to, for at least part of his plan was at last revealed as he indicated the muskets. She bit her lip to stop herself from crying out, because Tupa had revealed a steady eye and a real ability to learn. She could understand that Jamey's pride would not permit him to share with the chief, but this seemed to be deliberately risking death when it was not at all necessary.

Certainly Tupa was quite content, and appreciated the point that Jamey was putting across—that since it was the sun that gave them the power to use the muskets, it would be the sun that decided which of them would survive the coming conflict. The Indians also, with all the irresponsible delight of children in any kind of contest, clapped their hands and whistled with anticipation.

Caetano held the muskets, and now he presented one to the chief and the other to Jamey. Once again Christina was consumed with a certainty of approaching tragedy. She wanted to interfere, and dared not at this stage. She could only sit in her hammock and watch them as they took their places.

But Jamey was playing an even grimmer charade than she had anticipated. For as Tupa prepared to level his musket, and Jamey to level his, Caetano, obviously briefed during their conversation of the previous day, stepped forward with two pieces of grass and indicated that in matters of this nature it was necessary to draw lots for the first shot. Now she realized what was happening; the poor chieftain was being set up for an execution. In a bound she left her hammock, ran outside into the hot afternoon sun, and halted in sheer amazement: it was the chief who had drawn the long straw, Jamey the short. She could not believe her eyes, that Jamey was actually allowing a perfectly fair contest when it would have been so easy to cheat, that he was actually going to accept the first shot, that he was in fact committing suicide, giving her to the chief and giving his life away as well. It was not credible.

The Indians were delighted, and increased their hullabaloo,

while Tupa, obviously enjoying himself, carefully settled his
feet in the dust and leveled the musket. Jamey, for his part,
laid down his weapon and held out both hands toward the sun
as if in prayer, then folded them on his chest, his face
composed, staring at his opponent. Tupa returned the gaze for
some seconds, and then squeezed the trigger.

The flash of light and the explosion were accompanied by
the inevitable puff of smoke which entirely enveloped the
chief's head for a moment. Christina stared at Jamey in
horror. But the chief had missed. What was more, his ball
had missed even the Indians, who had carelessly grouped
themselves behind the white man. In that instant she knew
what had happened, understood that she was, after all, wit-
nessing a murder. Her throat went dry as she saw Jamey
smile and slowly bend to pick up his musket, while the chief
stared in absolute horror, unable to comprehend how he had
failed to hit so large a target. She had to cram her hands into
her mouth to stop herself from crying out, from blurting the
truth. But she dared not. Were the subterfuge to become
known, the Indians would probably tear Jamey limb from
limb, and Caetano, as well, since it was he who had loaded
the muskets, and probably young James as well, and perhaps
even herself. She could only watch as Jamey carefully aimed
his piece, as the weapon exploded in another cloud of smoke,
as Tupa spun around with the impact of the ball in his chest
and fell full length to the ground. The Indians gave a low
moan of concern.

Jamey turned to face them, completing a circle, the musket
held high, pointing at the sun, and slowly they came forward,
to hold his hands, to acknowledge him as their chief. And
when he indicated that they should remove Tupa's body and
cast it into the forest, they obeyed without a murmur. The sun
god had spoken.

Only then did he come toward her. "You murdered him,"
she said. "You had Caetano load his musket with blank shot.
He was kind to you, he saved your life with his medicine, and
in return you murdered him."

"I told you," he said, "that I am not a man to share. But I
will rule these people well. El Dorado. Yes. I think you may

be right, my darling girl. There is no place on earth like this. Here we have everything. And from this moment we also have absolute power. Sometimes it is necessary to be brutal, even criminal, to achieve something worthwhile. We shall rule these people well, Christina. As this is to be our home for the rest of our lives, then shall it also be our kingdom, our empire. Yours and mine. For the rest of our lives.''

''Or until Jack comes,'' she said.

Jamey smiled at her. ''Jack will never come,'' he said. ''And if he does, why, he will have an Indian nation to contend with, *my* Indian nation. They'll not hang the king of the Amazon, Christina. Not even Jack will manage that.''

Chapter 11

"There's a sight for you, Mr. Cutter," Jack said, handing his telescope to his first lieutenant. " 'Tis not something I had ever hoped to see."

The *Delaware* frigate had left Kiptopeke, at the extremity of Cape Charles, well behind and was creeping around the shallow Middle Ground toward Cape Henry, the bottom lip of the entrance to Chesapeake Bay. And in front of her in the cove just west of the headland, known as Lynnhaven Bay, there waited eight enormous men-of-war, every one at least a second-rater with upwards of seventy guns to dwarf even the big American frigate, and every one flying the fleur-de-lis of France.

The date was the second of September, 1781. Jack found it incredible to remember that more than five years had elapsed since he had sailed the old *Lodestar* into Nantucket Harbor, or indeed that this war had now lasted more than six years. Six years of cut and thrust, of disasters like White Plains and Savannah, of victories like Saratoga and Bennington. Of determination, as signified by the Declaration of Independence which had turned a rebellion into a war, and of growing violence, as the desire of France and Spain and Holland to avenge past defeats had spread the conflict over the entire world. And for him, it had meant six years of legalized piracy. The *Delaware* had been especially built for just that purpose, larger and more heavily armed than the British frigates, which were usually employed on commerce protection, able indeed to tackle anything afloat short of a line of battleship. In her he had been able to vent all the anger that continued to consume his being, had earned himself a reputation for ruthless daring in cruises that had taken him from Cape Cod all the way back down to Barbados, seeking and destroying. And running, whenever heavier metal hove above the horizon.

In many ways, he supposed, this continual frustration had helped to keep burning the flames of his resentment that life should have cast him, almost from the day of birth, in so ignoble a role. He commanded a vast machine dedicated entirely to destruction, with forty guns and two hundred skilled and eager fighting men, every one an experienced seaman, and yet the prospect of ever being *able* to fight, or being permitted to fight, had for five years remained nothing more than a dream. In the western Atlantic it was the battle fleet of the Royal navy that ruled supreme, and his orders had always specifically forbidden him to engage *any* British warship. The infant Navy of the United States had no ships to spare for deeds of derring do which might, or might not, be successful; those feats were reserved for John Paul Jones, in his *Bonhomme Richard,* on the other side of the ocean.

Nor had the frustration been his alone, because however General Washington and General Greene might time and again rally their forces, now augmented by the French volunteers under Count de Rochambeau and the marquis de Lafayette, however many battles they might win, they knew, as did everyone else, that ultimate victory for the Americans, which could only be achieved by driving the last British or Hessian soldier from the continent, could never be theirs as long as the Royal Navy commanded the seas and could transport men at will, either from Europe or up and down the continental seaboard. Thus for the past year all the efforts of both the French and American governments had been directed at uniting the French West Indian fleet and the French Atlantic fleet, off the Carolina coast, for just long enough to gain a decisive superiority. And surely, Jack thought, that moment must be close at hand, in the presence of these eight battleships, anchored at the mouth of the bay that was the lifeline to the British general Cornwallis, entrenched at Yorktown.

But only eight ships?

"There will be more, Captain Grant," said Count de Grasse, frowning down the length of his enormous, sharp nose at the weatherbeaten seaman in front of him. "I can tell you that Count de Barras is also on his way to the Chesapeake, with another twelve ships. Then we shall see, eh?"

"Indeed we shall, Your Excellency," Jack agreed, looking around him at the snowy white decks, the blue-jacketed marine band drawn up on the quarterdeck, the rows of huge cannon, and the masses of pigtailed seamen who filled the waist of this tremendous vessel. He had never actually been on board a ship of the line before. It was impossible to suppose that anything could stand against so much power. But the British had even more ships of the line, and they seldom lost a battle.

The admiral began to walk up and down the quarterdeck, hands clasped behind his back. Jack hastily fell in beside him. "I do not have to tell you the importance of this rendezvous, Captain Grant," de Grasse said. "You are aware that Lord Cornwallis has adopted Yorktown, just fifteen miles away up the York River, as his main base?"

"I am, Your Excellency."

"But perhaps you are not aware that he is now surrounded there."

"Surrounded, Your Excellency?"

"Oh, indeed, By a remarkable feat of cooperation and speed and secrecy, our Count de Rochambeau and your General Washington have united their armies and marched with desperate haste across the head of the peninsula. Cornwallis is shut in, and by a superior force."

"But he still has the sea," Jack protested.

"Quite so. And we have information that a large British

fleet is on its way here, not only to relieve the garrison, but also carrying with it enough men to ensure, once they are landed, that Cornwallis will be able, if he chooses, to fight his way out. Captain Grant, my orders are to prevent that fleet from entering the Chesapeake.''

''With eight ships, Your Excellency?''

''Ah, there you have it. I must attempt to avoid an engagement until the arrival of Count de Barras. And yet, I must repeat, my orders are plain. I must bar the British from this inlet even if it means my own destruction. So, Captain, you will understand how pleased I and my captains are to see you. We entirely lack frigates of our own. You will be our eyes, Captain Grant. Do you understand?''

''I do, Your Excellency.''

''Well then, sir, as soon as you have watered your ship, I would like you to proceed to the north and cover the area between here and Cape May. I must know the very moment that the Royal Navy approaches. The very moment, Captain Grant.''

''I shall not fail you, Your Excellency.''

''Indeed, sir, it is not me you would fail. For I will tell you this, Captain. If the British fleet cannot reach Yorktown, then it is my belief that Lord Cornwallis will not be able to sustain the siege for more than another fortnight. And if Lord Cornwallis were to be forced to surrender, Captain Grant, Great Britain will have been defeated, at least here on the continent of North America. That is as certain as it is that the sun will rise tomorrow morning. So, sir, it is not merely the fate of my battle fleet that is in your hands. It is the fate of the United States themselves.''

''Sail ho.''

Jack choked down the last of his breakfast and joined the rush of officers up the companion ladder to the poop. It was just dawn, and after two days of beating up the coast, the *Delaware* was now running back to the south, and the French anchorage, before the light northeasterly breeze. Three days, and not a Union Jack in sight. Surely, he thought, Barras will be here by now.

"Where away?" he called at the masthead.

"On the port quarter, sir," came the reply, and instantly half a dozen telescopes were leveled over the taffrail.

"I see her, sir," called one of the midshipmen. "A frigate, I think."

"A frigate it is," Jack agreed. "And another."

"And another, sir," Cutter pointed.

"Hm. Three frigates. They could be looking for the French, or just on patrol."

"Or they could belong to Count de Barras's fleet," Cutter suggested.

"You'll wear ship, Mr. Cutter, and we'll stand toward them until we can make an identification of their colors," Jack decided. He had nothing to fear from even three British frigates, if he kept a reasonable distance; he would escape them easily when he decided it was time to run.

The *Delaware* came around as her sheets were hardened in, but in the light wind it was a slow process, watched by Jack from the break of the poop with a critical eye.

"Captain," Cutter called.

Jack joined his lieutenant at the rail and followed the direction of his pointing finger. Three more sails had appeared over the horizon. Jack leveled his glass, frowned. "Those are two-deckers."

"Yes, sir," Cutter agreed. "And there are three more behind."

"Six," Jack said thoughtfully.

"And two more a shade to port," said another officer.

"And some more over to starboard."

"Twelve, by God," Jack said. "That has to be Barras."

"Two more, sir," called the masthead.

"Eh?" The glasses were leveled.

"Fourteen."

"No, fifteen."

"Sixteen."

"And two makes eighteen."

"And there's another one."

Jack studied the approaching fleet. His own sails would be in sight by now; the distance was not greatly over ten miles.

And there were nineteen battleships, together with a frigate screen, bearing down on him. There was no longer any question that it could possibly be Barras. Rather was it, he suspected, the squadrons of both Admiral Graves and Admiral Hood.

"Put about, Mr. Cutter," he said. "All sail now. Shake out those royals. We are going to need all she can do."

"Aye, aye, sir," Cutter agreed, hurrying forward to give the orders.

So once again, Jack thought, we are running away, but this time in pursuance of our proper duty as the eyes of the French fleet—although he did not really see that Grasse stood a chance with his eight ships against nineteen British.

But already land was in sight to the southwest.

"I'll have a signal up, boy," he said to his midshipman. "Enemy in sight, and then nineteen. Have you got that?"

"Aye, aye, sir."

"Right away, then."

He watched the signal flags climbing the shrouds, and returned to the taffrail to study the British. They had dropped back. But they would be coming up all the time. He estimated they would be at Cape Henry just after noon.

Now he could clearly see the French fleet, still at anchor as he had left them three days before, and he could make out their pennants, so they could surely make out his.

"Signal acknowledged, Captain," Cutter called.

Jack leveled his glass, watched boats rowing to and fro. He could imagine that there was the most tremendous hubbub in there. But Grasse had to obey his orders and come out and fight, just as he had to stand in and receive *his* orders. Frigates had no place in a fleet action, but Grasse would want him close by for carrying messages and dispatches.

"At last," Cutter commented as the first anchor began to come out of the mud. Jack glanced at the sun; it was after ten. And behind him the British were still standing on, the van, flying the red ensign of Admiral Hood's squadron, now drawing clear of the main body; their frigates had prudently pulled aside since the enemy was in sight. The British, in their haste, had not as yet waited to form line of battle, but in

Jack's opinion, with their superb gunnery they were more dangerous in a melee than in a standard ship-to-ship conflict.

"Message from the flagship, sir," said the signal midshipman. "Message reads, 'Thank you, and God speed.' "

Jack and Cutter exchanged glances.

"That sounds like a man determined on suicide," Cutter remarked.

"Aye," Jack said, "Well it is suicide, I reckon, opposing eight to nineteen. Even if they were better handled."

For the French were making very heavy weather of getting under way, tacking to and fro inside the headland, relying more on the ebbing tide than any seamanship to find themselves clear of the land.

"Ah well, bring her around, Mr. Cutter. We'd best stand off." And watch a massacre, he thought. So Cornwallis would be relieved and the war would drag on—unless the destruction of their fleet would so discourage the French that they might seek a separate peace, and leave the Americans in the lurch. But there was nothing he could do. He had the hands piped to dinner, but remained on deck himself, watching the ships behind him and to his larboard now, and watching, too, the British frigates which were on a parallel course with the *Delaware*, some five miles to the north. They were upwind of him and therefore possessed the vital weather gauge—it was up to them whether or not they wished to make a separate issue of it. He thought he would rather enjoy that.

"Mind you, sir," Cutter remarked, "I don't see too much spirit about the British either. It's definitely not Rodney in command."

"Well, we know Rodney's in the West Indies," Jack said, once again leveling his glass. But he saw what Cutter meant. Instead of continuing on their way to smash into the slowly forming French, the English van had altered course, to form line ahead themselves, parallel with their enemy. They were intending to fight a textbook battle after all. Not that he supposed it could make a lot of difference, except that they were wasting a great deal of time; it was already nearly two o'clock.

"There they go," Cutter said.

The lead ships on either side were belching white smoke; the sounds of the explosions only reached the distant frigate some seconds later.

"It'll be hot work," Jack agreed. "I reckon we can stand back toward the head of the French line, Mr. Cutter. There may be something we can do."

"Aye, aye, sir." Cutter turned to give the orders. "Captain," he said, and pointed.

Jack saw that the three British frigates were bearing down on him.

"By God," he said. "They *are* out for blood, after all."

"Shall we run off, sir?"

Jack bit his lip. He had received no instructions from the American navy, except to put himself under the orders of Count de Grasse for as long as was required. And Grasse had given him no specific orders either, other than to find the British fleet, which he had done. But certainly he was no longer just a commerce destroyer at this moment. He was a fleet frigate, and if he could cripple or destroy the British frigates he would be doing Count de Barras, at the least, a power of good, while if he was sunk or taken himself, he could no longer do Count de Grasse any harm.

He closed his telescope with a snap. "Wear ship, Mr. Cutter," he said. "Let's have ourselves a battle of our own."

The rumble of the drum reverberated through the ship, summoning the crew to battle, bringing the gunners to their stations, the powder monkeys to theirs, sending the marksmen into the mastheads and the surgeon into his cockpit, while the officers gathered on the poop beside their captain to watch the now rapidly approaching enemy; the tremendous cannonade going on a few miles to their west was forgotten in the tension of their own approaching conflict.

"Three to one," someone muttered. "Long odds."

Jack was continuing to study the three frigates. "Not so long, Mr. Hannaby," he said quietly. "Now, gentlemen, here is what we shall attempt. You'll observe that the first Britisher, the smallest of the three in fact, has pulled out ahead, and that the two larger ships are about three miles astern of him, with the largest of all in the rear. This is to our advantage. We shall make direct for the van ship and give her a broadside. A single broadside, gentlemen, which must do as much damage as possible; I want those guns double-shotted. If we can bring down a mast she will be useless for the rest of the battle. That will shorten the odds to two to one, and if we then alter course fractionally to starboard, it may well be possible to exchange broadsides with frigate number two before the big one can see us clearly enough to fire. That is our plan, gentlemen. To your stations. And shoot straight."

They saluted and went to their positions.

"You make it sound so simple," Cutter remarked.

"Aye, well, it is, in theory. It's the practice of it causes the trouble." Jack smiled; his entire being seemed to have caught fire in anticipation of the coming minutes—for so long he had wanted to fight. "But they *have* made it easier for us. Alter course two points to starboard, helmsman."

"Aye, aye, sir."

The bow swung around, so that the American ship was pointing directly at the lead Britisher. Now the *Delaware* was as close to the wind as she could manage; to point more directly would have been to put her in irons, causing the sails to flap uselessly. So if the first British ship had the sense to bear away, he realized, his plan would be negated from the start. He could not follow her directly, and to waste the time to come about would be to give the other two vessels time to reach him together, while if he allowed his first target to remove herself out of range, then she would be free to rejoin the fight at a moment of her own choosing.

But the Royal Navy ship held on, bluff bows throwing white water to either side, sails billowing before the wind. Jack smiled grimly; no Navy man was going to turn away from a scrap with someone regarded as an inexperienced rebel.

"Range two miles, sir," Cutter said.

"Very good, Mr. Cutter. Steady as she goes."

Cutter glanced at him, chewed his lip, and looked forward again; a moment later the British bow chasers exploded, causing plumes of water to rise out of the sea about a hundred yards to starboard of the *Delaware*.

"Good shooting," Cutter said. "They'll have the range next time. Distance three thousand yards, sir."

"Steady as she goes, quartermaster," Jack said, studying the remaining Britishers. Having discerned his tactics, they were cramming on all possible sail to get to the fight in time. Once again he smiled; slowly but surely, the second ship was pulling away from the first. The biggest Britisher obviously had a foul bottom from too long at sea without a refit. They were fighting this battle exactly as he would have wished it.

Cutter was still watching their nearest antagonist. *"Antigone,"* he read through his glass.

"Twenty guns, sir," said the signal midshipman, ready with his Navy list. "Captain James Morton."

"A bold fellow," Jack commented. "And . . . there, by God."

The bow chasers had fired again, and with a screaming crash that seemed to shake the *Delaware* from stem to stern one of the balls struck forward, sending splinters of wood flying into the air, followed by the screams of the wounded.

"That *was* good shooting," Jack said. "Damage report, Mr. Cutter." He was looking at the foremast; to be dismasted now would be disastrous. But it seemed steady enough.

"Aye, aye, sir," Cutter said. "Range two thousand yards."

Which was one sea mile. Jack nodded. "It'll take them five minutes to reload those chasers. Prepare to fire your starboard broadside."

Cutter ran down the ladder into the waist, leaving Jack alone on the poop, except for the signal midshipman and the helmsman immediately below him. Now the frigate was only fifteen hundred yards away, and her bow chasers must be almost ready again. But she considered herself close enough for a damaging broadside and was starting to bear away. He must beat her to it.

"Steer four points to larboard." He snapped down the open hatch and went to the break of the poop, his midshipman hastily thrusting the speaking trumpet into his hand. "Light your matches," he bellowed.

Slowly, ever so slowly, the *Delaware* came around, while Cutter hurried aft.

"No serious damage, sir," he reported. "Struck on the larboard side just aft of the chain plates. Bulwark stove in and three men hurt."

"Very good, Mr. Cutter,"Jack said. "Fire," he shouted.

The *Delaware* had turned away fractionally faster than the *Antigone,* and had gotten her broadside in first. Smoke billowed up from the gun decks and the ship heeled beneath the force of the explosions and the recoils. Officers climbed into the lower rigging to see what they had done, and gave a cheer, immediately taken up by the gun crews, as the smoke cleared and they could see the tremendous result of their efforts. The double-shotted guns had swept the British ship from bow to stern. They were so close they could see the shambles on deck, with the poop entirely cleared save for scattered bodies, and the wheel shot away, so that the ship had turned further to larboard than had been intended, and her own broadside, which now exploded, screamed uselessly past the American's stern. Even as they watched, the foremast trembled and came crashing down in a welter of sails and cordage.

"That was well done, sir," Cutter said, regaining the poop.

"Not *so* well done, Mr. Cutter," Jack said, "seeing we've twice her fire power. There's still a lot to do."

The second frigate was only three miles away now. She had realized that she was too late to assist her colleague and was in an overexposed position herself, and so was taking in sail in an effort to slow and let her larger sister catch up.

"Three points to starboard," Jack said. "Bring her back, quartermaster. Bring her back. We must close that fellow."

"Aye, aye, sir."

Jack moved to the break of the poop and looked down on his exultant seamen, busily reloading the starboard guns, while the port gun captains waited eagerly for their chance. He watched the three wounded men being carried below. The first of many, he thought sadly.

"Inside three miles, sir," Cutter estimated.

Now the British ship was definitely alarmed, having had the opportunity to inspect the damage done to the *Antigone* by the American guns. Instead of holding on her course, she suddenly altered to starboard, taking her across the bow of the *Delaware*, while still out of range.

"The devil," Cutter said. "We'll have one on either side."

"Which won't do, Mr. Cutter," Jack agreed. "Come to larboard, quartermaster. Four points. That'll do."

The two ships were now on a converging course, both sailing west toward the drooping afternoon sun, and toward, too, the battle between the main fleets, still shrouded in clouds of smoke; Grasse was apparently giving as good as he was receiving.

"Prepare to fire, Mr. Cutter," Jack said, handing over the speaking trumpet.

"Aye, aye, sir," Cutter acknowledged.

Jack stood at the starboard rail, watching the slowly approaching English ship, which now fired her larboard broadside, but while still at extreme range. The sea between the two ships became a maelstrom of churning white as the balls fell short.

"Steady as she goes," Jack said without turning around, and squinting to pick up the enemy's name. *"Penelope,"* he said to his midshipman. "Look it up, Mr. Lucas. Look it up."

"Thirty guns, sir," Lucas replied. "Captain Thomas Trowbridge."

Now they were less than two miles distant, and the *Penelope* would be reloading as quickly as she could.

"Prepare to go about, Mr. Cutter," Jack said quietly. "But first, now, fire your starboard broadside."

"Fire," Cutter bellowed, and once again the ship exploded into reeling, booming noise.

"Good shooting, Mr. Cutter," Jack said. Several of the balls had struck home, and he estimated that more than one of the British guns had been dismounted, although no serious damage had been done. "Now come about," he shouted. "Haste. Bring her around. Helm hard to starboard."

The quartermaster spun the wheel, and the *Delaware* swung

up into the wind as the *Penelope* fired her second broadside.
But instead of an entire ship the British cannon now found
themselves with only the American bow at which to aim; once
again their shot fell helplessly into the sea, while the *Delaware* continued to swing, until she had come right about,
presenting her still double-loaded larboard broadside, and at a
range of hardly more than a thousand yards.

"Fire," Jack told Cutter.

"Fire," the lieutenant bellowed into his trumpet.

The captain of the *Penelope* had realized his danger and
was attempting to minimize it by turning away. The maneuver was carried out quickly and skillfully and yet not in
sufficient time, for the *Delaware* was still presented with the
enemy quarter—the stern and some thirty feet of larboard
topsides—at which to aim. Jack drew his breath as the balls
smashed through the stern windows, upended cannons and
cabin furniture, sent men screaming to their deaths, while
abovedecks they had slashed across the poop, scattering
officers like ninepins. And now the mizzenmast came down.
Once again the Americans could afford to cheer, as they
sailed by, so close they could see the angry faces of the Navy
men, shaking their fists in defiance. The *Penelope* was by no
means crippled, but she would need another hour before she
could get back into the fight.

"Reload," Cutter was shouting. "Reload. There's the big
one yet."

She was now coming into view as they emerged from
behind the smoke-wreathed *Penelope,* and only just over a
mile away. "*Eurydice,*" Jack said to his midshipman.

"Aye, aye, sir," the midshipman said, busy with his refer-
ence book and pad. "Thirty-six guns. Commanded by Captain Martin Beresford."

Jack's head came up in a mixture of consternation and
sudden savage delight, even as he realized that his larboard
guns, those facing the oncoming frigate, were still unloaded,
while to come about to present his starboard guns would be to
bring himself under fire once again from the *Penelope*. But to
bear away, when he was already downwind, might cost him
the victory he sought; the British would have time to regroup

and make repairs long before he could come back up against the wind.

He would just have to accept a broadside.

He hurried to the break of the poop. "Haste with that reloading, boys," he said. "And keep your heads down."

The *Eurydice* had altered course to larboard, and now he watched her sides disappear behind the cloud of white smoke. Instantly he was surrounded by an immensely hot cloud, and felt his ship shaken as if by a giant hand. Noise billowed about his ears and he instinctively ducked as from above his head there came a giant cracking sound. He looked up, expecting to see the entire mizzen on its way down, but it was only the topmast, although that was serious enough.

He turned to look aft and gazed in horror at Lucas; the boy had lost his head and lay in a crumpled mass, blood pumping from the great arteries in his throat. Cutter was also on the deck, but he was endeavoring to get up, staring in bemusement at the stump which had been his left arm.

"To the poop," Jack shouted, stopping to regain the speaking trumpet. "Go below, Mr. Cutter. Haste now."

Two marines were already waiting to assist the officer, and Jack hurried forward again, to stare down at the wreckage which was the waist of the ship. But the *Delaware* was a long way from being crippled. He saw that three of the larboard guns had been thrown off their carriages, scattering their crews and in one instance lying across a gunlayer, drawing the most terrible screams from his tortured throat, while the mizzen-topmast had fallen into the waist, making things look much worse than they actually were.

He raised his head, watched the *Eurydice,* just emerging from her smoke cloud, heard the cheers of her crew drifting down on the wind, raised the trumpet to his lips, discovered they were too dry to use, and had to lick them violently before he could shout his orders. "Fire," he commanded. There were still fifteen guns left in the larboard broadside, only one less than the *Eurydice* commanded even when undamaged. And the range was very close.

Smoke clouded his nostrils, and he lost his footing on the blood-wet deck and slipped to his knees as the ship trembled.

Then he was up again and back at the rail. "Mr. Hannaby," he bellowed, "I want that wreckage cleared. Over the side with it. Mr. Mortimer, issue cutlasses and pistols. Quartermaster, hard alarboard. Hard, man, hard."

The quartermaster spun the wheel, and the *Delaware* came up into the wind, within three hundred yards of the Britisher, where they in turn were removing the wounded and clearing up the rigging brought down by the American shot.

Turned into the wind, the *Delaware* was now in irons, traveling forward only by the momentum of her recent speed. But the *Eurydice* was also traveling forward, her sails still filling, and the two ships were closing rapidly.

"We have to be quick, lads," Jack called to the marines and sailors hastily assembling beneath him, cutlasses drawn and bayonets fixed. "We must have her before those others can get back to her." He looked aloft. "Marksmen, fire at will."

The first musket immediately spoke from the main-top, and was followed by the rattle of the others from forward; those unfortunates who had been in the mizzen-top had crashed to their deaths with the falling spar.

By now the Britishers had realized his intention, and orders were being given to bear away. But it was too late. The ships were too close to avoid each other, and the British alteration of course to larboard only made the maneuver neater than it would otherwise have been; instead of meeting head on, the two vessels merely glided alongside each other making a ripping sound as protruding gun muzzles and ports were torn aside by the thrusting timbers, which was a great relief to Jack; the British larboard broadside had not yet been fired.

But it was too late for Beresford to remember that now. The grappling irons were already flying through the air, securing the ships alongside each other, and the Americans were clambering over the bulwarks, having the advantage of height so that they could fire downward and then jump behind their missiles. Jack leaped from the poop into the chain plates, scrambled upward, faced a red-coated marine armed with a musket and bayonet, but avoided the initial thrust and swung his sword sideways with all the force he could manage. The flat of the blade caught the Englishman's head and tumbled him right over the side into the sea. Then Jack was clambering onto the forecastle, temporarily deserted, and looking down into the waist where the main conflict was taking place.

But the Navy men were outnumbered, and were being forced back, despite the exhortations of their officers. Jack gazed across the confused melee at the poop and saw Beresford staring at him. Then he was sliding down the ladder and fighting his way aft, belabored by cutlasses and defending himself with his sword, attempting not to be delayed, arriving at the foot of the ladder to the poop deck out of breath and bleeding from a thrust in the arm.

"Jack Grant, by God," Beresford said from above him. "Jack Grant." His lips drew back in his wolf's smile. "I always said we'd meet again."

"And you were right," Jack said, starting up the ladder, to check as Beresford's right hand came up, holding a pistol. He sucked air into his lungs and threw himself forward, reaching the top of the ladder and sliding along the deck as he listened to the bang above him, then slicing his sword sideways to catch Beresford's legs. Beresford stumbled and cursed, retreated, dropping the empty pistol and changing his sword to his right hand.

Jack reached his feet, inhaling slowly and carefully, getting his balance under control. It was then he realized that the noise of conflict had almost ceased from behind him.

"Your ship is taken, sir," he said. "I'll have your sword, Captain Beresford."

"You'll take it," Beresford shouted, and leaped forward. Their blades clashed and Jack was forced backward by the fury of the Englishman's assault. This deck too was slippery with blood, and Jack's shoes skidded to bring him to his knee. Hastily he brought up his sword again to meet Beresford's continuing thrust, ducked beneath the blade seeking his throat, and saw his own sword point rip into the blue tunic in front of him, thrusting on with the force of the charge until their faces were within inches of each other, as Beresford in turn came to his knees.

His mouth opened, and then closed, and then opened again. "God damn you, Jack Grant," he said, and died.

Slowly Jack withdrew the bloodstained blade, pushed himself to his feet, and found Hannaby at his side. "Are you all right, sir?"

"Aye," Jack said. "I'm all right. Strike that flag, Mr. Hannaby and set the Stars and Stripes." He staggered to the rail, more exhausted, emotionally as well as physically, than he would have thought possible, and looked out at the afternoon. The *Penelope* lay about half a mile away; she had once again got herself under control and was coming about, but she was on the same side as the *Eurydice* and could not immediately fire. Further off, the *Antigone* was still drifting, still desperately trying to rig a jury mast to come back up into the wind.

Jack looked to the west. There the action had also ceased, at least for the moment, the French having borne away and the British . . . he squinted into the setting sun, the British were also turning away, to the north, preparing to beat. Preparing to decline a further battle? He could not believe his eyes, especially when they had such superior numbers.

Hannaby gripped his arm. "Look there, sir. Sails. Coming up from the south."

Jack picked up Beresford's telescope and stared at the approaching fleet. It was flying the fleur-de-lis. Barras had arrived, as the British admiral had obviously observed. The French would retain command of the Chesapeake. And Cornwallis would be forced to surrender.

And the war would be won. For a moment he could not believe it.

"What now, Captain?" Hannaby asked.

Jack closed the telescope. "Assign a prize crew, Mr. Hannaby," he said. "And then let's cast off and get under way again. There are two more ships waiting to be taken."

Chapter 12

≈≈≈≈≈≈≈≈≈≈≈≈≈≈≈≈≈≈≈≈≈≈≈≈≈≈≈≈≈≈≈≈≈≈≈≈

Jack Grant kicked sand from his shoes as he left the beach and walked up the slope to Bay Street. He stood with his hands on his hips, gazing at the ramshackle wooden buildings that lined, unevenly, the hill; only sixty years ago Nassau had been the headquarters of every pirate in the western hemisphere, from Avery to Teach. Then it must have been a prosperous, if raffish and violent, community. In the years since Captain Woodes Rogers had driven the pirates away, and hanged those who tried to assert their rights, it had declined into a shantytown of derelict fishermen and desultory cotton planters, who were not above supplementing their living, it was said, by judicious wrecking of the many vessels that made use of the New Providence Channel to the north.

Of legitimate trade there was almost none. Behind him, in the vast natural harbor formed by the breakwater of Hog Island just a mile away, the only ship of any size at anchor was the *Lodestar,* with the flag of Portugal flapping from her masthead. Once again he was plain Jack Grant, owner of the Grant Company. And the six years in between might never have been. But they had happened, and had left their mark on this outpost of British imperialism, just as they had on his own mind; the Bahamas was the ultimate refuge of large numbers of Tories driven from the mainland by the American victory. Most of these had come from the southernmost of the now independent thirteen colonies, and had sought to continue their cotton-growing activities in the larger Bahamian islands such as Eleuthera. Those from New England, with skills more in the direction of services rather than agriculture, had gathered here.

He paused beneath a palm tree, nudged a sleeping black youth with his foot. "I seek a man called Peter Butler," he said.

The boy scrambled to his feet. "Oh yes, Captain," he said. "Oh yes. Mr. Butler's bar does be up Union Street."

He pointed, and Jack flipped him a copper coin before continuing on his way. Was his heart pounding? He was not terribly aware of it. He had no real idea of the reception he would receive, or why he was here at all, delaying his voyage south by yet another week when there was so much to be done.

He supposed he had mellowed. On that single tremendous day off the Chesapeake, he had expelled much of the frustrated anger that had gripped his mind for too long. And of course, common manners demanded that he call upon Beresford's widow and explain the circumstances of her husband's death. But after that . . . he was forty years old, she thirty-nine. He had supposed, if he *ever* were to feel like embarking upon another romance, that it would be with some girl half his age. So probably he was not seeking romance at all, but merely the comfort of a woman's arms, some solace to soothe the bitter midnight hours when he dreamed of Christina.

But Christina was surely dead by now.

He opened the door, stepped inside, and gazed at the man behind the unpolished wooden bar. Peter Butler wore neither coat nor cravat; his shirt—obviously unwashed for several weeks—was open to the waist. Although he was indoors, a straw hat was perched on the back of his head, and he chewed an unlit cigar. He had put on even more weight, and wheezed. "What'll it be?"

Jack looked left and right; he was the only customer. "You've ale?"

"I've got cane rum," Butler said.

"Well then, cane rum." He went to the bar. "You've a short memory."

Butler blinked at him. "Jonathan Grant, by God." He shook hands. "The hero, I've heard tell."

"I'm on my way south," Jack said. "I thought I'd call to say goodbye."

Butler filled two glasses with the pale liquid and brushed them together. "Then I'll drink to your health, even if I hate your guts."

Jack smiled, "For winning?"

"Oh aye. And for marooning me on this Godforsaken island. Still, it's better than a hanging or a bucketful of tar. I've become a philosopher. But you've not come all this way to see me, I'll wager." He stumped around the bar, opened a back door leading to an empty yard, and bellowed, "Lizzie."

"She's here, then?" Jack said stupidly, because now his heart *was* pounding.

"Where'd you expect her to be?" Butler finished his drink and poured himself another. "She has her Pa to look after."

"But . . .Mistress Butler?"

Butler peered into his drink, and used his thumb to extract a dead fly. "Gone," he said. "It was the heat. She couldn't stand the heat. See who's come to look us up, Lizzie."

The back door had opened, and Jack gazed at Lizzie Beresford. In strong contrast to her father, Lizzie had not put on weight, indeed had lost some, he estimated. Her golden hair was loose and windblown, and her feet were bare; she had not expected company. But Lizzie Butler, widow of a captain in the Royal Navy, a beachcomber?

She seemed to sense his incredulity. She flushed as she put up her hands to attempt to restore order. "Jack? Jack Grant? Oh my God." She made to step backward, and he caught her hand.

"Jack Grant, Lizzie."

"Oh, I . . ." She glanced at her father, who gave a guffaw.

"He's come to see you, Lizzie. All this way. Now, why should he have done that?"

She licked her lips and gazed at Jack again. "But . . . the war . . ."

"Is all but over, Lizzie. There's no fighting anymore. Just bickering around a conference table. So I've resigned my commission. I've got the old *Lodestar* back, and I'm sailing her south to Rio. My home."

"Rio." Once again the quick flick of her lips. "We heard . . . how you were a hero, Jack. Taking three Navy frigates in one day."

"I was lucky. But then you'll also have heard—"

She nodded. "Six months ago."

Jack drew a long breath. "I killed him, Lizzie."

Her mouth formed the round *O* he remembered so well.

"It was a fair fight, and I called on him to surrender. His ship was taken, anyway. But he refused."

"Aye well, he would, that one," Butler remarked, pouring himself a third drink.

Lizzie sat down, hands clasped in her lap. "And you came to tell me? That was noble of you, Jack."

"I thought, maybe . . . that we might have things to discuss." Did they? he wondered, his resolution suddenly fading. But had it ever even been a resolution? He only knew that the ending of the war, of living for something beyond himself and greater than himself, had left him emotionally drained, and able to understand for the first time just how much he had lost, just how little he had to live for. Thus he had drifted here because, like him, she had been cast adrift herself. They might be able to share, since they had a common background, and a childhood spent together. Certainly, to attempt to pick up the ruins of his life in Rio by himself would be impossible.

She raised her head. "To discuss, Jack?"

Now he could feel himself flushing, could feel the blood pumping through all of his arteries, because Lizzie Beresford was still a handsome woman, and it had been too long.

"He wants to take you upstairs, Lizzie girl," her father shouted. "Upstairs. You go ahead. I'll mind the bar. He'll have money in his pocket."

Lizzie got up, her lips tight. "Is that what you came for, Jack?"

"That?" He stared at her. But he had come for that too. Even if he could not believe she could have become a whore, he had come for that. "I'd like a word," he said.

She walked away from him, opened the back door, and went into the yard. Jack hesitated, glanced at Butler, and then followed.

"Mind you're generous," Butler called after him. "Coin is hard to come by in this pest hole."

Jack blinked in the sunlight, and saw her climbing the outside staircase at the back of the house. There was a faint breeze which fluttered the hem of her skirt as high as her knees. And suddenly he was entirely controlled by his desire for her, realized that he had wanted to take her to bed since the day he had rescued her from the mob. As he had wanted to take her to bed more than twenty years ago, when he had supposed he loved her. He could not believe that it was about to happen.

Even if she was a whore?

He climbed the stairs behind her; the door at the top was open. Inside there was a bed, with just a blanket over the torn feather mattress, and a washstand with a chipped china ewer and a cracked basin; there was no slop bucket—obviously the waste was just thrown out the window. A chest waited in the far corner, some clothes draped carelessly across it. There was no other furniture in the room, and no mosquito netting either, he observed.

"You don't have insects in Nassau?"

"Some." She sat on the bed. "Sandflies, more than mosquitoes. And no net is going to keep out sandflies."

"That's true enough." He sat beside her, wondered what came next, and tried to control the questions which battered at his mind.

"I only see gentlemen," she said, looking at the door. "Planters, government people. Only gentlemen, Jack." She turned. "There was no other way to *live*. Can you understand that?"

"No," he said, "I cannot understand how this has happened. Did Beresford leave you nothing?"

She sighed. "I have received nothing," she said. "We have had nothing, for more than a year. And then Mama was ill. . . . I have to live, Jack. Pa has to live. So . . . I have to ask for a gift."

"What do you require?"

"That . . . that depends on the gentleman. If . . . if he isn't generous, I don't see him again. But in your case . . ."

She did not understand him. But perhaps she was past understanding any man. "Since I'll be gone on the next tide, anyway," he said, "I can afford to be mean." He hardly recognized his own voice.

"You'll never be mean, Jack Grant."

Her lower lip was trembling, and she was close to tears. He wondered if he was not close to tears himself. What a crooked path is this life of ours, he thought. I sought only the love of the most fabulous creature on earth; and became a millionaire— although it cost me what I wanted. Lizzie had married for security. As the wife of a Royal Navy captain she could have expected at least a genteel comfort for the rest of her days, and had instead wound up a whore on a desert island, with a drunken father to support.

"What do you reckon to earn in a year?"

She raised her head. "I've only been at it for four months, when money stopped coming from Martin."

"Well then," he said patiently, "what have you earned these four months?"

She shrugged. "Six pounds."

"Eighteen in a year, maybe. You manage on that?"

"Living's cheap in Nassau."

"Well then," he said, "I've forty pounds in coin on board the *Lodestar*. I'll give it to your pa. That's more than two year's living. And I'll see to it that he gets more every year."

She frowned at him. "But—"

"I want you to come with me, Lizzie. Not your pa. Just

you. He can get someone in to cook for him. Just you. I want you to come with me to Brazil."

"To Brazil? With . . . with *you*?"

"Aye," he said. "To Brazil. With me."

"Land ho," came the call from the main-top, the voice faint in the aft cabin of the *Lodestar*. Jack Grant opened his eyes and immediately closed them again. It could only be the sugarloaf; he had the utmost confidence in his navigation. He had equal confidence in Cutter, who would not disturb his captain unnecessarily. The cannonball which had ruined his first mate's hopes of a career had done him a great service, he reflected sleepily; he could have searched the world and not found a more faithful servant—except that once he had supposed that of Conybeare. Was his entire future to be twisted by the past? Well, there could be no doubt that the big man had always been an omen of bad luck. Let him be bad luck to Jamey, now. If they still survived.

And if Christina still survived? But those were thoughts which he would never permit again. Instead he held the woman in his arms yet tighter, allowed his fingers to stray down the arch of her back to her buttocks, slide around in front . . . he could touch this woman as he chose, because she was only a woman and not a Sousa e Melo, and because she came to him without reservation. He had, in a sense, bought her; there was no loan involved here.

Now she stirred in his arms. "Someone called," she murmured.

"The lookout. We have sighted Brazil."

"Brazil?" She sat up, hair tumbled, then jumped out of the bed and ran to the stern windows. "I don't see it."

He smiled at her enthusiasm. "That's because it's in front of us, and you're looking aft, Lizzie. We'll be there in good time. By this evening, if the breeze holds."

"Brazil." She came back to sit beside him; unlike Christina, she slept naked. Her body overflowed with sheer femininity, from the heavy, sagging but so comfortable breasts to the great pout of her belly to the surprisingly firm-muscled thighs betwen which he loved to lie. "I am so excited."

She gazed at him, her lips slightly open. He wondered if she loved him. They had spent five weeks together now, and they had been as blissful a five weeks as he had ever known. Here at last was a woman who wished only to please *him*, whom he could neither shock nor be shocked by. Whether or not she loved him was irrelevant. She was his, just so long as he gave her food to eat and his body to love.

A far more relevant question was whether or not *he* loved *her*. Well, was she not everything he wanted in a woman? She was voluptuous and attentive and passionate and completely uninhibited. And there was no suggestion of superiority, such as he had always felt with Christina, no fear. Was he, then, admitting that he had always been afraid of his wife? There was a strange confession for a war hero and a successful merchant. Still, he *was* afraid of her, because he had worshiped her, because to him she had always *been* a superior being, and he had lacked the courage or the knowledge to bring her back to earth.

Whenever he tried to decide whether or not he loved Lizzie, he wound up thinking of Christina. No doubt that was the answer. But did love enter it for him either? Here he had found contentment, and all the loyalty he could ever expect from a woman. He would be a fool to look elsewhere. And yet, for all the weeks that they had sailed south, one vital question, which no doubt was uppermost in her mind, had never been brought out into the open. It could hardly be postponed any longer.

"It is exciting," he agreed. "It could be the most exciting country in the entire world."

"And it's yours," she said.

"No," he said. "I belong to it. And you shall belong to it too."

"I want to," she said. "Oh how I want to."

"You do understand," he said, "that I can't marry you, for the moment. I do not know where my wife is, whether she is dead or alive. The Church insists on seven years. Well, it is not far off now. But we must wait those seven years."

"I do understand," she said. "I had not expected to become your wife."

"You shall be my wife," he promised, "in all except name. And as soon as you can have that too, why, then shall you have it."

"You're generous."

"No," he said. "Not generous. I want your loyalty. Give me that, and you shall never have reason to question me."

"Well then," she said, "how can I be otherwise than loyal to you, Jack Grant, who has raised me from the very dust to be at your side? I will be loyal. I swear it."

He took her face between his hands and drew her forward for a kiss on the mouth.

"Then are you as much wife to me, Lizzie Beresford, as ever I have had a wife," he said. "And so shall you be mother to my children. On this you have my word. And now . . ." he tossed back the covers and leaped out of bed ". . . get dressed, and come on deck, and look at Brazil. Your home, now and forevermore."

Jack handed Lizzie down from the carriage and they turned to face the house. "What do you think of it?"

She stared up at the facade, the three stories rising one above the other, the marble outer staircase and patio, and looked from left to right, in utter bemusement, at the excited servants and slaves. But then, he had been equally bemused by the way Rio itself had grown and obviously prospered during his seven-year absence. He had been delighted to see the two vessels alongside flying the Grant Company flag—the blue of Scotland combined with the green and red of Portugal, the whole crested with the golden lion rampant—and now he was even more delighted to see his own house again. But for Lizzie, the whole event was obviously too much to be taken in, from the splendor of the bay, to the realization that he was, after all, a wealthy shipowner, to the cheers of the crowd which had only just understood that it was indeed Captain Grant returned after so long an absence, and now to the magnificence of the house. He had to hold her arm to help her up the stairs, to check himself at the sight of his mother, waiting at the top.

"Jack?" she asked, her voice thin. "Jack, is it really you?"

"None other, Mother." He took her in his arms. Her hair was snow white, and she was a thin, pale memory of the woman he remembered.

"Jack," she said, resting her head on his chest. "Oh, Jack."

"Lizzie," he said. "You remember Lizzie Butler?"

Flora Grant blinked at the woman. "Lizzie?" she asked. "But—"

"A great deal has happened these last seven years," Jack said. "I'll explain it all." He stepped past his mother and his mouth opened in amazement for he gazed at a girl who might have been Christina herself as he first remembered her, except for the extra height and the spectacular streaks of red in the dark brown hair. "Inez?" he asked. "Is it really Inez?"

"Papa," she said, and was in his arms. Behind her waited a boy who must be twelve or thirteen, who was big and curly-haired and craggy-faced.

"Anthony?"

Then he too was in his father's arms.

"What of Billy?"

"He is in Portugal," Flora Grant explained.

"Portugal? But—"

"Don Pedro said it was best, Jack. He means to send Anthony too, as soon as he is sixteen."

Jack tousled the boy's hair. "And do you want to go?"

"It will be an adventure, sir," Anthony said. "Is it true you took three British frigates, sir?"

"We'll talk about it." Jack faced Lizzie, his arms still around his children. "This is . . . Aunt Lizzie," he said. "She will be staying with us." He gazed at his mother.

"Lizzie," Flora said, taking her hand. "Lizzie Butler. If you can make Jack happy, then are you welcome. More than welcome."

They went inside together, where Antonio and the servants were lined up to greet their master. "God, but it's good to be back," Jack said. "I can promise you, Mother, I shall go roaming no more. That is my resolution. Home I am and home I'll stay." He sat down in the great drawing room, legs stretched in front of him, while his mother and children, and Lizzie, stood in front of him, and Antonio hovered in the background. "I think you should show Aunt Lizzie the house," he said to the children. "You too, Antonio. I'd like a word with Mrs. Grant."

"Jack—" Flora began.

"In a moment, Mother. Off you go. I'll see you all at supper." They left the room, laughing and chattering to the still wide-eyed Lizzie.

"Now then, Mother," he said, "come and sit beside me. And tell me."

Flora sat down cautiously. "There is not much to tell. Your company prospers. Don Pedro has been handling it, you know. In fact, since the death of Dona Inez—"

"Dona Inez is dead?"

"Well . . . the strain, I suppose. She was very unhappy, Jack."

"Aye. And Don Pedro?"

"Thrives. He has aged, of course. But he has kept busy. Apart from the plantation and the shipping line . . ." She drew a long breath. "All goes well. Mary is in splendid health, as are the children. Thomas is now colonel of his regiment and commands the garrison. All goes—"

"Well," Jack agreed. "You are repeating yourself. And there is no news?"

"News?" She stared at him, color fluttering in and out of her cheeks.

"You know of what I speak." He held her hands. "And there *has* been news. I can see it in your face."

"News? Oh, Jack . . ." Tears welled in her eyes.

"They are dead. Do not dissemble with me, Mother. They are dead."

"Oh, if only . . ." She turned her head at the sound of voices and boots in the hall. "Don Pedro. Oh, thank God."

Jack got up to face his father-in-law. Don Pedro's hair was also entirely white, as much of it as he retained, and that was no more than a fringe over his ears. But he came forward, arms outstretched, with all his former vigor. "Jack. This is the happiest day of my life."

They embraced, and then held each other at arms' length.

"You hardly seem to change. You have seen the children?"

"All except Billy."

"Ah, yes." Don Pedro went to the sideboard to pour them all a glass of wine. "I thought it best. It is too parochial, too *colonial* . . ." he attempted a smile ". . . for a young man to spend *all* his life in Rio. Flora did not agree with me. We had a rare quarrel, I promise you. But I talked her into it in the end."

"Aye well, I'm sure you acted for the best, Don Pedro," Jack said. "Now tell me of Christina."

"Of . . ." He gazed at Flora, his eyebrows raised.

"I . . . I have told him nothing," Flora said defensively.

"Don Pedro," Jack said evenly, "I wish to know. Now."

"Yes." Don Pedro sat down and gazed into his wine glass. "You received my letters?"

"*A* letter, six years ago."

"I wrote others."

"They never reached me."

"Ah. Yes. Well, of course, there has been a war. A great war. A—"

"Don Pedro," Jack said. "I wish to know of Christina."

"Yes, well . . ." Don Pedro sighed. "There was a man. Alvares was his name. He appeared in Rio, more dead than alive, several years ago. He claimed to have been your brother's mate on board the stolen ship."

Jack frowned. "Jamey's mate? And he came to you?"

"With what a tale, Jack. He claimed that your brother had abducted Christina, murdered Conybeare, and forced them to undertake an exploration of the Amazon—"

"Abducted her?" Jack asked. "Abducted Christina?" His voice rose. "But you told me—"

"I told you what I, and everyone else in Rio, assumed to be the truth. How could we assume otherwise, in view of the facts? And we still do not know how much of what this man Alvares said is the truth. A great deal of it is quite unbelievable."

"You mean you did *nothing*?"

"Of course I did something. Hear me out, Jack. You asked, and I am telling you."

"I am sorry," Jack said, and sat down. "Continue." He dared not allow himself to think, to feel, to do anything, for the moment, except listen.

"Well, this Alvares had a strange and terrible tale to tell. Of the abduction and murder, as I say. Of how they found an entrance to the river, if that can be believed. Of how they sailed up that river for a year. Can you believe such a thing, Jack? A year, up the same river?"

"Go on," Jack said.

"And of how they were eventually wrecked, and took to the forests. Then, he said, Jamey was bitten by a huge snake, and there was a mutiny. He claimed Christina herself sucked the poison from Jamey's leg, and then, with the help of him and young James and another man, fought the mutineers and killed them all. Can you believe that?"

"Go on," Jack said.

"And then, he claimed, they were taken prisoner by a tribe of savage Indians. It is then, he says, that Christina told him to make his way back to the river, where the one remaining boat from the *Plough* was moored, and escape, to bring them help. Can you believe that, Jack? If Alvares could escape, then could they not all escape? Anyway, he claimed to have done as she asked, and made his way downriver. But he too was wrecked, and had to wander the jungle for more than a year before he found his way to Belem, and thence to Rio."

"And you did nothing," Jack said, "because you did not believe his story."

"What do you take me for, Jack? Of course I did everything I could. I went straight to the viceroy, who placed Alvares under arrest. After all, if even a part of what he had told us was true, he was a self-confessed pirate and murderer. Then I begged the viceroy to commission an expedition, but he refused."

"Refused?"

"Well . . ." Don Pedro sighed. "Things have changed, as you are no doubt aware. It was just about that time that the marquis quarreled with the queen and was driven from office. He died last year. Did you know that?''

"I had heard,'' Jack said. "I do not see that the marquis of Pombal has anything to do with it.''

"It is easier to get things done when one is related to the first minister in the land,'' Don Pedro explained quietly. "But the viceroy put forward some strong arguments as well. According to Alvares, Jamey died of the snakebite, or was certainly dying when he left. He says the Indians were sure of it. That would have left Christina and young James and this other sailor. And he was reporting what had occurred *two years* before he reached us here. Two *years*.''

"But Christina had been well when he left?''

"Well? Yes.'' Don Pedro's face twisted.

"Tell me,'' Jack said.

"Alvares suggested that the chieftain of this tribe of savages— cannibals, he called them—had chosen Christina as his wife.''

Jack stared at him, while Flora gave a sob.

"His *wife*?''

"Well, his woman, at any rate. Two years before we knew of it, Jack.''

"And thus you abandoned her.''

"I . . . I did not, Jack. I commissioned a ship and a volunteer crew and sent them up the coast.''

"You did not go yourself?''

"How could I? The news had proved too much for dear Inez, and she was quite prostrate. She died of it. Then there was the plantation, and your shipping company. . . .'' He sighed. "Had you been here. . . .''

"Yes,'' Jack said. "Had I been here.''

"And besides,'' Don Pedro said, "what good would I have been? I am an old man, and I know nothing of the sea. Or the jungle.''

"And you regarded Christina as already dead, since she had been bedded by a cannibal.''

"That is not true, Jack. That is unfair.''

"Aye. You have my apology. But your expedition did not find her, in any event.''

"I doubt they even entered the river. They said it was impossible."

"But . . . did not Alvares accompany them?"

"Alvares was in prison."

"But—"

"The viceroy would not give him permission to go on a private expedition. He had been sentenced, and it was decreed that he must serve his sentence." Don Pedro's shoulders sagged. "Anyway, what does it matter now? The expedition failed. Christina is most certainly dead by now."

"Or has been living as the wife of a cannibal chieftain, waiting, and praying, for her rescuers to come."

"That is not even thinkable," Don Pedro said. "It is . . . we do not even know that *anything* Alvares said was the truth."

"Aye," Jack said, and got up. "Where is this man Alvares now?"

"I have no idea. Perhaps he is still in prison. That was a long time ago."

"As you say," Jack said, and went to the door.

"Jack," Flora said, "there is nothing you can *do* now."

Jack closed the door behind him.

"Alvares, Alvares, Alvares." Slowly the prison governor turned the pages of his register. "Joachim Alvares. Would that be the man you seek, Senor Grant?"

"I do not know his first name," Jack said. "He would have been imprisoned several years ago."

He was almost afraid to breathe; even in the governor's office the stench of unwashed bodies and untreated sewage clung to the air. Living was difficult enough as a free man, in this heat and surrounded by interminable hordes of insects, with a clean bed to retire to in the midday sun. He did not see how anyone could survive a week in this pesthole.

"This is the one," the governor said. "Joachim Alvares. I remember. He was condemned for piracy and abduction and murder. Or at least being an accessory to those crimes. He was sentenced to life imprisonment at hard labor. He was fortunate not to be hanged."

"I would like a word with this man."

"A word?" The governor allowed himself a grim smile. "But you cannot, senor."

"Why not? Can't he speak?"

"He is dead, senor."

"Dead?"

"Oh indeed, senor. He died within a year. No one lives more than a year in this prison, senor." Another grim smile. "Except me."

"Dead," Jack said. "In a year." He got up and put on his hat. "As you say, senor, he was lucky not to have been hanged."

He went outside, inhaled some relatively clean air, mounted his horse, and walked it down the track leading back to the town. The sun was now at its highest, and he could feel waves of heat coming at him from the ground. And this was Rio. He could not imagine what it might be like two thousand miles farther north, on the Equator.

On the Amazon. What could life have been like for her— the most marvelous creature on earth, who had been brought up as the pampered darling of the Portuguese court, had never moved without a servant at her heels, never worn anything rougher than the best linen next to her skin, never allowed herself to be seen in public without her appearance being utterly flawless?

The fault was his, the guilt of what had happened was his, for leaving in the first place. Had he been here . . . but he did not know that. Don Pedro found it more convenient to suppose that Alvares might have been lying about the abduction, about the murder of Conybeare. He preferred to believe the tale, if only to reassure his battered pride. But even if he had been here, might not Christina have gone off with her first love?

And even if she had been kidnapped, she had lived with Jamey for a long while before his death. And it had been she who attempted to save his life by sucking the poison from his wound. That had been no act of hatred. Whatever she had felt in the beginning, she had been reconciled to her fate, before the end.

His hands curled into fists as he walked his horse up the drive to his house.

But still, Christina. All that beauty, all that composure, all that intelligence, at the beck and call, the whims and the lusts, of a cannibal savage. No matter what she had done, what she had accepted, she did not deserve such a fate, could not be abandoned to such a fate.

No doubt she was dead, for how could a white woman survive in such conditions? Thus, common sense reminded him that he had adventured enough, that he had sworn never to roam again, and caution told him he had neglected his business and his children too long already. But if she *was* alive, his Christina, no matter what it had required to survive. . . . He whipped his horse up the drive to his house, and drew rein in a flurry of dust. Scarcely noticing the phaetons and carriages that waited at the door, he ran up the steps and burst into the crowded hall, looking left and right in bewilderment.

"Jack, oh Jack." Mary threw herself into his arms.

"Jack." Thomas de Carvalho stood behind his wife to shake Jack's hand. "We came as soon as we could."

"Captain Grant." The new viceroy was also waiting to shake his hand. "I have heard so much about you, cousin, that I am delighted at last to make your acquaintance."

"Cousin?" Jack squeezed the strong fingers.

"His Excellency is Don Luis de Vasconcellos e Sousa," Don Pedro explained. "He is my second cousin."

"And you may imagine how grieved I am at the news to which you have returned," Don Luis said. "Believe me, Captain Grant, if there were anything I could do—"

"You can lend me your support, Your Excellency," Jack said.

"My support? Why, sir, you have that."

"And your official sanction for an expedition up the Amazon." The others fell silent.

"You intend to go up the Amazon?" Don Pedro asked finally.

"I do," Jack said. "And immediately. There are two Grant ships loading in the harbor now."

"And contracted for delivery of sugar and tobacco to Lisbon," Don Pedro protested.

"Well, they will have to be unloaded again," Jack said. "There are some things more important than trade."

"But . . . your wife is assuredly dead," Don Luis said.

"I do not know that, Your Excellency, any more than you do."

"But . . . those are uncharted waters," Don Pedro protested. "It would be suicide."

"My brother found a way through, Don Pedro," Jack said. "I can hardly do less." His smile was grim. "I taught him all he knew about navigation and seamanship."

"It would still be madness. Your men will never follow you."

"I shall call for volunteers," Jack said. He looked around the room. "Indeed, I do so now. This is a Portuguese lady we seek. Who will accompany me to find her?"

They stared at him and looked away when his eyes met theirs.

"You said . . ." Flora Grant bit her lip.

"I must ask to be absolved from that promise, Mother. It would be impossible for me to stay here, not knowing whether Christina is alive or dead." He found himself staring at Lizzie. "You must understand that."

"I understand that she is your wife," Lizzie said quietly, "and has a prior claim upon you."

"Lizzie," he said, "you will stay here with Mother. I will be back. I promise you."

"And if she comes back with you?"

He gazed at her, then sighed. "You will never want. You have my word, Lizzie. I *must* go. I will go."

"I will come with you, Papa," Inez said.

"You? That is absurd. I may be gone a year."

"Why is it absurd? Next year I will be eighteen. Mama was no older when you married her. And do you not suppose that if we succeed in finding her she will *need* me?"

Jack stared at her. How like Christina she was. How determined and how confident.

"I should like to come as well, Papa," Anthony said. "I do not want us to be separated again."

My children, he thought. How could I ever have left them? Once again he surveyed the room. "Well then," he said, "it seems that it will be us three."

He turned to leave, was halted by an exclamation from Thomas de Carvalho.

"Not just three, Jack. I will go with you."

"You?" Don Pedro cried. "You are commandant of the garrison."

"I resign my position."

"My God," Don Pedro said. "But—"

"I will come with you, Captain Grant," said another young man.

"And I."

"And I."

Jack felt tears springing to his eyes as he looked at the fervent expressions on the faces, the drawn swords.

Don Pedro gazed at his cousin. "What are we to do?"

"Do?" Don Luis said. "Why . . ."

"You cannot possibly give official backing to such a hare-brained scheme, Your Excellency," declared a stout, red-faced man, glaring at Jack. "This madman would empty Rio of its every defense."

"Hm," the viceroy said. "Hm. I tell you, gentlemen, that Her Majesty, as she discussed the situation with me just before I left Lisbon, is extremely concerned at the Spanish encroachments into our territory. What do we see in the south? The Spanish lay claim to the Banda Oriental, despite our occupation. What do we see in the west? They cross the Paraguay River and creep ever eastward. And what of the north? This is the most uncertain area of all. We lay claim to the Amazon basin, show it as ours on our maps. The Spaniards lay claim to New Granada, as they call it, and send its boundaries ever southward. No one knows where is the point where the Amazon actually rises, where it goes, where it spreads. But I will tell you this, senors, the first nation actually to establish an armed post on the river will have possession. I have been debating this fact for some time."

Jack stared at him, unable to believe his good fortune. "You mean you will support me, Your Excellency?"

"I mean, Captain Grant, that if you seriously intend to explore the Amazon and proceed up it as far as possible, then I will refuse to accept Colonel de Carvalho's resignation and instead place him in command of a company of regulars, with orders to accompany your expedition, both to protect it and to establish a Portuguese outpost wherever he may think convenient."

Jack seized his hand. "Then, sir, am I ever in your debt."

Don Luis smiled. "I hope to be in yours, Captain Grant. Now go with God, and find your wife. If it is possible."

Chapter 13

The mist, as usual in the early morning, was thick and clammy, lying over the forest like an immense blanket, but reaching even below the giant trees to smother the very ground. The two women might have been utterly alone in the world, for they stood, ten feet apart, up to their ankles in the gently rushing water, bows at the ready, arrows strung, and some twenty feet from the bank, where the trees had already faded to uncertainty.

The pair made a strong contrast to each other, despite their superficial resemblance. Both had black hair falling almost to their thighs. Both were brown-skinned. And although one was old enough to be the mother of the other, the fact was not readily apparent. Yet it would have taken only a brief second glance to realize the essential differences between them. The girl's hair was thick and heavy; it hardly moved in the soft morning breeze. The woman's was fine, and drifted away from her back. The girl's features were thick, and dominated by the thrusting jaw, the high cheekbones; the woman's features were delicate, with small, flared nostrils and pointed chin. The girl had a long and yet stocky body over short, muscular legs; she already had a tendency to sag, from breast to belly, and her complexion was the color of copper. The woman possessed long, slender legs, and a relatively short body; and if her breasts, at thirty-nine, were no longer as high as they once had been, they remained full, and her complexion was a remarkable golden brown, illustrating the long hours, and indeed years, she had spent in the sun, but also a continual reminder that for the majority of her life this skin had been carefully protected from the slightest blemish. And she wore a short apron, which reached from just below her navel to just above her knees, while the girl was naked.

Yet they were clearly equals at forestcraft. For having stood, facing each other, motionless for almost an hour, while the mist swirled about them and gradually dispersed before the heat of the sun, they released their arrows in the same instant and stepped forward in the same instant, with complete confidence, leaving the sandbank to plunge up to their thighs in the swirling brown water, slinging their bows and reaching down together, shoulder to shoulder, to lift the big fish into the air. What it was, Christina had no idea. The Indians called it *lukanani*, and it was certainly very good to eat, while its size made it an invaluable source of food for the entire village, even if it also made it, when still flapping against her chest and attempting to wriggle through her fingers, the most difficult to manhandle to the shore.

But at last they made it, panting and laughing, stumbling to their knees as they deposited the dying creature on the ground and waited for it to gasp its last.

"Good," said the girl. "It's good, Kita?"

The name was as close to "Christina" as any of the Indians could manage, however they tried. And they were anxious to try, just as the girl was now anxiously waiting for Christina's approval. For was she not the queen, the woman of the mighty *cacique*—or supreme chieftain—El Dorado?

Christina smiled. "It is good, Lala." This was another approximation, she supposed, although the Indian language certainly contained no names, or any words, of more than two syllables.

They knelt beside the dead fish, withdrew their arrows, and

cleaned them on the grass. Then Lala lifted the fish into her arms, stood up with an effort, and waited for Christina to lead her into the trees. She would not be able to carry the twenty-pound weight all the way back to the village, but she was prepared to do the major part of the work—Christina was not only El Dorado's woman, she was also Lala's mother-in-law. This girl, in fact, who could hardly be more than eighteen years old, had made Christina a grandmother, twice. To her knowledge. But Billy would now be twenty, and Inez eighteen, and it was not impossible that there were other grandchildren as well.

She parted the leaf screen which kept reforming in front of her, and her eyes flickered from side to side in constant watchfulness—eyes that once would have filled with tears at the mere memory of her children's names, much less a consideration of what they might have become. But she had not wept in some time. She was dead to them. That much had become obvious more than two years ago. Perhaps she had, without truly realizing it, set a time limit on her rescue.

She had now been here seven years.

So, either Jack had been killed in his crazy fight for independence, or he had decided, on his return to Rio, that it was futile to come looking for her. Which made very good sense. Either way, she did not doubt that her children had been well cared for by their grandparents. As Sousas e Melo, who were also Grants, they would never want, would lack only a mother's love and guidance as they embarked upon adulthood. And besides, what would they make of their mother now? If she had never been quite able to remove the last of her clothing, as young James and Caetano had so readily done—a modesty the Indian women accepted as quite natural, for they suspected her to be a supernatural being herself—she knew she would find it difficult ever again to accept a corset or a dozen petticoats just as she knew it would never occur to her to seek shelter when it rained, or to allow a day to pass without bathing twice, at least, or without setting forth to secure her food with her own hands.

Behind her, Lala sank to her knees with a sigh of exhaustion, and Christina hastily relieved her of the fish, holding it in both arms against her breasts as they resumed their walk.

It was not as if she lacked a family of her own. Lala had parted the last leaf screen, and they were wading the shallow stream which led to the clearing, where the sight of the large fish in Christina's arms brought the women and children racing from their various tasks to congratulate the two huntresses and examine their prize. She supposed all of them, the mothers as well as their progeny, were as dependant upon her as if she had borne them all; if during her first two years here she had been the pupil, nevertheless she had found it simple to dominate their minds.

But if she had learned to love them all, she was increasingly, frighteningly, aware that she was the oldest woman in the tribe—for they did not seem to live much beyond the age of thirty-five, their primitive medicine leaving most illnesses fatal—and there were new responsibilities to think of. Her grandchildren were Zak—for the hard *J* was beyond the Indian tongue—now age four, and Ciss, another Indian abbreviation, age three. That Lala had failed to produce any more was obviously due to young James's drifting attentions, for polygamy was irrelevant in a society where every woman was the property of every man—a tendency Jamey refused to condemn, since he practiced it himself. Only the great Kita was immune, prohibited from contact with any man but the equally great "El Dorado."

Jamey had finally accepted the fact that there *was* no El Dorado, after sending several search parties to the north in search of information, and perhaps had even absorbed her concept that there could be no City of Gold superior to this eternal paradise they inhabited, but he was also determined to be master of as much of it as he could manage, and the seven years of his primacy in this tribe had been years of increasing conflict and conquest. But perhaps he had done nothing more than pander to the innate desires of the people who called him lord, and who followed him with unswerving loyalty, the more so since he had brought to their tribal wars a mind well read in the military arts and quite unaffected by the various taboos which afflicted their enemies. In place of the missile skirmishes with arrow and dart which were all the tactics the Indians had ever practiced in the past, he had armed his men as well with wooden clubs, shaped like African knobkerries, with which he had taught them to charge home after an arrow volley, to the invariable discomfort of their opponents. These skirmishes, which had extended his authority up and down the river, had not been particularly costly in human lives, for the neighboring tribes quickly bowed to the superiority of a warlord who so obviously came from another world.

But his successes had not made him any easier to live with. If she still yearned for his touch, she also welcomed his lengthy absences when he and young James went on tribute-gathering expeditions, and when she could be her own woman. She counted herself fortunate that Jamey had not been able to fulfill his promise and make her again a mother, a fault she assumed was in him, since he had not become a father by any of the Indian women either. But much as she missed her other children, the thought of first of all being crippled by pregnancy, and then having to carry a child at her breast for upwards of a year, in these surroundings, was quite unimaginable.

"Is good," remarked Poot, who, both as Tupa's woman in the past and as Caetano's woman in recent years—she was not especially comely, and was larger than the average Indian woman, but was apparently a source of great comfort to her husband in their hammock—had arrogated to herself the rank of deputy chieftainess. Now she pointed at the *lukanani*, already being gutted preparatory to roasting on the fire. "Is good."

Christina nodded, "Yes," she said. "Is good." She gazed at her friend, frowning, as she heard the distant notes of a whistle. "They're back."

The older women had heard it too, had abandoned their cooking and other tasks to stare at the forest, awaiting the return of their men. It had been Jamey's idea that whistles should be used as a means of communication, to inform the various branches of the tribe that it was friends approaching—as if, Christina thought, any Indians on the upper Amazon would dare attack El Dorado or his people.

His success had been the more amazing because it had been

accomplished almost entirely by his mental power alone. Of course, the magic of gunpowder remained always at his disposal, but only just so, since he was reduced to hardly more than a dozen charges. But he had used his sun-given supremacy so skillfully, and to such effect, in the early days that it was hardly ever necessary to demonstrate it nowadays. Now his people followed him because he *was* El Dorado, because he never failed them, because he had made them the greatest tribe on the river. He had even removed their ancient fear of the water, and indeed his campaigns were all conducted by canoe, to the terror of his enemies. The returning army would now be landing their dugouts, exhilarated at once by victory and by their mastery over this immense element they had worshiped for so long. Their newfound sophistication had spread throughout the tribe. Certainly the women ran across the stream with utter confidence, sure that they would be welcoming another successful expedition.

Christina followed more slowly. It was at moments like this that *her* confidence reached its lowest ebb, until she learned that Jamey and her son had returned safely. Jamey laughed at such fears.

"Even if young James and I were to die tomorrow," he would say, "you have naught to fear. These people love you, where they only fear and respect me. You will be their queen forever, no matter what happens to the rest of us."

His mind moved only in well-rutted channels, could conceive of life only in terms of fear and respect, and a love which should be a combination of both. He could not understand that she might weep at the death of her son merely because he was her son and not, more importantly, her support and protection. Nor could he conceive that she might weep over *his* dead body. He still considered her his prisoner, the woman he had abducted and made his own, at the cost of everything she had previously held dear. Well, she *was* his prisoner. There could be no argument about that. But he was still the most substantial thing in her present life.

So now she waited, heartbeat slowed rather than increased, watching for the first sight of the men hurrying through the trees, allowing herself only the faintest sigh of relief as she made out first of all the height of Caetano, and then both Jamey and her son, walking together, surrounded by triumphant warriors. The men carried baskets of manihot flour and fruit, of dried tapir meat, and less willing spoils as well, for Jamey insisted upon a human tribute from those tribes which he forced to acknowledge his supremacy. His reasoning was perfectly simple. By claiming half a dozen young boys and half a dozen barely nubile maidens—why half a dozen, Christina often wondered? Did he compare himself with the minotaur?—to be brought up as their own, he not only weakened the neighboring tribes, but also increased the strength of his, as well as ensuring a constant variety of fathers and mothers for his people. But the human tribute could never be convinced they were not destined for some ritual sacrifice. These boys and girls crossed the stream with fearful glances, shrank away from the advances of their new compatriots, and most of all from the woman of whom they had all certainly heard, and who, by reputation, they feared nearly as much as her terrible mate.

Christina could only do her best to reassure them by smiling and holding out her arms, while she stifled a frown as she observed, walking beside Jamey, an adult man she had never seen before. Her heart seemed to constrict, because sometimes Jamey did bring back other chieftains, men who had refused to accept defeat and *had* been condemned to a dreadful, lingering, sacrificial death, either by being cut to pieces while still living, or even worse, being staked out to be eaten alive by ants. Either death the Indians took very seriously, for it was a matter of honor to meet such a fate without a word of complaint.

She completed her welcome of the girls and boys as quickly as she could, sent them into the village, and reached for her husband. "Jamey . . ." She embraced him, reached past him to kiss young James, and continued to stare at the man. "Why is he here?"

Jamey laughed, and gave her a squeeze. "Because he has news, my love. Remarkable news, if it is true. He claims to have seen European ships on the Amazon."

"Oh my God," Christina said.

Her knees felt weak. But hadn't she known it might happen one day, however dim the possibility had become? Hadn't she *wanted* it to happen?

She looked past them into the trees, as if expecting to see white men hard on their heels.

Jamey laughed again, and threw his arm around her shoulders as he walked her up the slight slope toward the huts. "They are some days away yet, my love. But we must prepare. That's why I brought Pelo along."

The Indian had followed them up the slope. Now he paused to look around him, as if wondering what made this tribe the greatest on the river, when they apparently lived the same as everyone else.

"He comes from ten days from here," Jamey explained. "Ten days through the forest. That would be at least twenty by the river upstream. Anyway, the ships were halted when he left them. Anchored for several days already, he says."

"Ships? You mean there is more than one?"

Jamey spoke in an Indian dialect. "Tell the queen what you say, Pelo. How many ships?"

Pelo held up three fingers.

"My God," Christina said. "Surely he means canoes?"

"Show the queen what these ships look like, Pelo," Jamey commanded.

Obediently the man squatted and drew in the dust, with his forefinger, the very rough outline of a ship. But judging by the elevated bow and stern, and the two masts he gave each one, there could be no doubt that they were oceangoing vessels.

"Are they Portuguese?" Christina asked, heart continuing to pound.

"Flag," James said. "Show the queen the flag."

Once again Pelo drew in the dust, a square flag divided into two. He touched the outer half, and then pointed at the green forest wall surrounding the clearing. Then he touched the inner half, opened his mouth and put out his tongue, and touched it in turn.

"Red and green," Jamey said. He looked around him, for by now almost the entire village had gathered, the women

having been told by their men of the approaching fleet.
"Well, it's not so surprising, after all."

"But *three* ships," Christina said.

"That's quite an expedition," young James agreed. "But
you've nothing to worry about, Mother. They won't beat
us."

"For heaven's sake," she said. "Is that all you can think
about? Why should they *want* to beat us? They're exploring
the Amazon. Surely they are." She stared at Jamey. "You
don't think it could be Jack?"

"No I don't," he said. "Jack would have come long ago,
if he was coming at all. But it doesn't matter whether it's
Jack or not. We must prepare for their coming."

"Yes," she agreed, looking down at herself. "I must find
some clothes. We all must. Well, you and young James,
anyway."

Jamey smiled at her, the smile she knew so well, and had
learned to fear so much. "No need for clothes," he said.
"The only members of that expedition who are going to see
you, my love, are the ones we bring here as prisoners, and
you'll be the last thing they *ever* see. You can allow them that
last treat."

She stared at him. "You . . . you're not going to *fight*
them?"

"If I have to, certainly. And I don't see how it's to be
avoided. I've given instructions for the tribes down the river
neither to show themselves nor to interfere with the ships in
any way. But the wreck of the old *Plough* is still visible in
parts—her cannon, anyway. The ants haven't been able to eat
those. So they'll know we came ashore here. They'll start
looking here. So what I've done is—"

"But don't we *want* to be found?" she cried. "Isn't that
what we've prayed for, these seven years?"

"*You* may have prayed for that, my love. I'm in the
unhappy position of facing a hanging."

"Oh, surely—"

"Surely nothing. I've committed too many crimes ever to
be forgotten."

"But . . ." Desperately she wracked her brain for arguments. "They're not *looking* for us. There has to be some straightforward explanation. Pelo says they've anchored for several days and sent their boats out to row up and down the river. That must mean they're charting it."

"Doesn't make any difference. They'll still know there's been a European ship up here when they see those cannons. Believe me, my love, I've thought about ways of moving them, but we'd need a block and tackle, since they're half in and half out of the river. These vines just aren't strong enough."

"So they'll see the wreck of a ship," she said. "They may even guess it has to be yours. But they're explorers. They'll be overjoyed to discover white people here, especially in a position of authority. Wouldn't *you* have been overjoyed if Tupa had been a white man, able to understand you and help you? Even if you did know he was a criminal?"

Jamey smiled. "It would have been helpful. I'd still have killed him to get control of the tribe."

"Maybe . . ." she gazed into his eyes ". . . maybe these people aren't quite so—"

"Vicious?"

"I was going to say ambitious."

"Any man who fits out a three-ship expedition to come up the Amazon has to be ambitious. And that's all irrelevant. Even if it is simply a colonizing expedition, we don't want it here."

"But . . . don't you ever mean to make contact with the outside world?"

"Not if I can help it, Christina. You showed me what this place was, remember? You pointed out that we could never find a better El Dorado than this. Would you ruin it all?"

"Of course not. But—"

"What do you want from these people? Beautiful clothes, fine jewels? Can you possibly be more beautiful than you are now, as naked as the day you were born? Can any jewels even equal the marvels of your eyes, your nose, your lips, your breasts?"

She could feel herself flushing.

"So you desire a glass of wine? What's wrong with *piwarrie*?

The effect is the same. Do you miss a feather mattress? Your hammock is the best bed you can ever have. Do you still dream of your children? They have forgotten you by now. Besides, have you not children enough right here?''

She sighed. "I suppose you are right, Jamey.'' She attempted a smile. "If it *is* just an exploration, then all we have to do is keep out of sight, even if they do land after they find the *Plough*. They'll soon go away again.''

"And come back again,'' he pointed out. "If we let them. They *will* wish to plant a colony.''

"Then—''

"I created an empire here,'' Jamey declared. "A golden empire. I founded it for us, and after I am dead, for James, and then for Zak. I'm not going to give that all away. And can you imagine what would happen if I did permit it? You've seen the Indians near the coast, where the priests and the do-gooders have been able to get at them. They've become drunken layabouts, incapable of living. They're riddled with European diseases, a degenerate race. Would you wish that on these people? Your people?''

"No,'' she said. "It will be up to us to make sure that civilization comes slowly.''

"It is up to us,'' he said, "to make sure that civilization does not come at all.''

"You can't *stop* it,'' she cried. "Not now. It's here, now, anchored down the river. You can only come to terms with it.''

"I *can* stop it,'' he said. "I have already laid our plan. I have instructed the people downriver not to show themselves, as I told you. Not even if the Portuguese land. I have also required them to send their best warriors up here to us, and I have sent messengers upriver to summon aid from there as well. There are three ships. I estimate about forty men on each. One hundred and twenty men. I shall muster not less than that, and I hope more.''

"But . . . you mean to *fight* them? To fight European weapons?''

"Nonsense. European weapons are useless in the jungle. The jungle is *our* weapon.''

"All right," she said, and realized her breath was coming in short gasps. "So they land and you manage to kill a few of them. Then they retreat to their ships and sail away. But they'll come back, Jamey. They'll always come back, with more and more men and guns."

He shook his head. "No they won't. Not if the expedition disappears without trace."

She stared at him. "You can't kill them all, Jamey. Not a hundred and twenty men. You can't even *think* of killing them all."

Jamey smiled at her. "Every last one, my love. If you're interested, I'll tell you how I propose to do it."

The sailors had erected a canopy over the poop, using the sails, which were hardly ever set these last few weeks; Jack preferred to have the ships towed, after carefully reconnoitering each ten miles of river to map the sandbanks. Thus the poop became the pleasantest part of each ship, protected both from the heat of the sun and from the pounding raindrops, which, in the absence of any wind, fell absolutely vertically; it was possible to stand at the taffrail and watch the rain falling six inches away without getting wet.

Inez Grant spent a great deal of time watching the rain. There was not much else to do, but she also found it fascinating. She had known nothing like it before. First of all the sun would disappear as if someone had drawn a blind across the sky. A moment later the first drop would fall, sounding like the rap of a knuckle on the deck forward. Then the thuds would become continuous, merging together in a staccato beat, both on the deck and on the canvas above their heads, so mind-deadening as to preclude thought; the wall of almost solid water isolated each ship from the others, from the forest on either side, almost from the very river in which they lay.

The rainstorms that came every day between eleven in the morning and two in the afternoon, whenever the sun's heat had sucked enough moisture from the vines and the forest, were the best part *of* the day. The rest was a heat-induced misery, rendered worse because she had so little to do.

In the beginning, certainly when they had first entered the

river, she had imagined herself to be in an artist's paradise, her only concern that the dozen sketching blocks with which she had equipped herself before leaving Rio would prove absurdly insufficient. For three months she had spent almost every daylight moment with pencil in hand. Here was a world which neither she nor anyone else on board, except possibly the half-caste Indian boy they had recruited in Belem, and who claimed to know the Matto Grosso, had even suspected to exist.

He himself had provided a delicious subject. He did not know his age, but Father had estimated him to be about seventeen. His heritage was plain to see, for if his features were pure Indian and he was by no means tall, his legs were relatively long and his hair was surprisingly fine, and unlike a pure-bred aborigine, he possessed hair on his face and chest and armpits, a fact she saw instantly, for he never wore more than a pair of trousers—a habit the crews soon learned to imitate.

His Portuguese was limited, and it was impossible to discover whether he had ever known his father or if his mother had merely happened to encounter some wandering white man in the fastnesses of the forest. In any event, she was apparently dead, but had possessed enough acumen to direct her son to that white man's world in which he already had a toehold. In Belem he had worked at a variety of labors, but as he had explained, his heart had remained in the jungle, and the moment he had heard that the famous Captain Grant was seeking anyone with a knowledge of the great rivers and the forests that surrounded them, he'd hastened to volunteer his services.

His name, as near as it could be translated into Portuguese, was Cal.

Inez guessed her father had been somewhat disappointed in him up to now. He had never been on board a ship before, had been lost in wonder at the huge masts, the way the sails were set and altered, the workings of the rudder, just as he had been bemused by the swivel guns each ship mounted— the largest muskets he had ever seen. Thus, he had so far spent the voyage rather as a fish out of water. But that he

knew the forest was unquestioned, and he would come into
his own whenever the expedition took to the land, which
would be, Father said, whenever they discovered some sign
of humanity. They knew the Indians were there, because
Alvares had told Grandfather so. But so far they had not
found any.

This continual expectation, and continual disappointment,
was now affecting them all, but herself, she thought, most of
all. For nearly a year now she had hardly drawn a line. In the
beginning she *had* been fascinated by Cal, by his changing
expressions, and most of all by his reflective moods, when he
would spend hours just gazing over the bulwarks at the forest
screen, his expression varying from a sad contemplation to an
almost savage intensity. Undoubtedly there were memories
clouding that half-European, half-Indian brain which would
be worth uncovering, if it were possible to do so. But it was
not possible. Cal kept his thoughts to himself, and regarded
her, especially, with something akin to fear. He had never
been in close proximity to a white woman before—they were
rare in Belem—and he clearly found her too strange to be
accepted, the more so as, unlike everyone else in the fleet
except the priest accompanying them, she refused to make
any concessions to the climate, still wore two petticoats and
stockings every day, following her instincts, which warned
her that, however uncomfortable, it was preferable than a
surrender to the jungle, from which she considered there
could be no recovery, especially for a woman.

But there had been a limit to how many times Cal could be
sketched, just as there was a limit to the number of trees, the
number of alligators, the number of monkeys, that could be
sketched. The most formidable aspect of the river and the
jungle, she had early realized, was the unchanging monotony
of it. Each day at anchor was exactly like the last—for
Father, as was his nature, was proceeding slowly and with the
utmost caution, and for every day the fleet moved upriver
they spent another day anchored while the boats reconnoitered—
and the same could be said of each day when they were under
way. Often, indeed, it was difficult to convince oneself that

they were not making their way up exactly the same stretch of river as two days before. Certainly all time seemed to merge into one long struggle, against heat and damp and insects. That it was well over a year since they had left Rio was on the one hand incredible and on the other absurd, for Rio was a world that seemed to belong to her distant past, or even a previous existence.

The rain was stopping and she turned back from the rail, carefully and deliberately arranging both mind and features into a good-humored smile, because she owed them all, and especially Father, that much. However much she might privately be appalled at this enormous chunk that was being taken out of her life, when she could have been enjoying balls and receptions in Rio, when she might even have become betrothed—she was not far from nineteen and she had no doubt that most of her contemporaries were married by now— Father had warned her that this voyage would take at least a year, and she had been happy to accept that at the time.

Of course he was aware of her despondency. He was aware of the low state of morale that pervaded the entire fleet, and attempted, by means of feasts and sporting competitions, wrestling matches, climbing matches, swimming matches, and rowing races between the various boatcrews, to make the unending journeying acceptable. Certainly he worked as hard as any man on board, and harder than most. On stationary days, such as this one, it was he who commanded the reconnoitering boat, while the other officers and the majority of the men rested. And she could tell that disappointment was probably having a greater effect on him than on anyone else. It was *his* wife they sought. And her mother. But having observed the jungle at first hand, Inez was no longer sure she *wanted* to find her mother. Perhaps, she sometimes thought, Father has also grown uncertain whether an attempt to return any woman to civilization after she has spent eight years in this green hell, could be other than cruel.

Yet he would not give up, until he had either found her or gained positive proof of her death. In that determination, so characteristic of his family, he was perhaps fortunate. She worried even more about men like Hal Cutter, at this moment climbing the ladder to join her on the poop. For if the forest frightened them all in its totally hostile immensity, what must be the feelings toward it of a man whose left arm had been severed just above the elbow? Hal, with his experience added to a quick and thoughtful brain, remained an ideal shipmaster. There was no one, after Father himself, she would sooner trust to navigate her out of trouble, be it shoal waters or a gale. But he must know that if he were ever to be pitchforked into a situation where survival depended on physical strength and agility, he would be helpless.

Yet he had a ready smile and unassailable good humor, at least when in her company.

"You show sound sense in remaining on deck during the rain, Dona Inez," he remarked. "Our decks have been so opened by the heat that the water comes straight through. I am soaked. And you are dry."

"Not anymore," she pointed out. For the forest was already beginning to steam as the sun reappeared, and in place of teeming water they were entirely surrounded by a white mist. "I really am sorry for poor Father, caught out in it."

He stood beside her at the rail. "They should have returned by now."

"Do you fear for him?"

"For your father? Not I, senorita. Jack Grant could sail into hell and out again, with all its devils busy shooting at him."

"Would you not say that is exactly what he has done?" She smiled. "Into hell, at least."

"And out, when he decides it," Cutter said, and pointed. "Here they come." He frowned. "And excited, by God."

Inez peered into the mist. The boat was certainly coming downriver very fast, the men bending their backs with a will, Jack Grant standing up at the tiller.

"Father," she shouted. "You've found people?"

"Better than that," he called in reply. "We've found the *Plough*."

*   *   *

Jamey Grant gazed past the leaf curtain at the ships. He was not alone. The entire river bank was lined with his warriors, concealed behind the green, preserving the secrecy of their presence by remaining absolutely still—and all watching him at least as intently as they watched the ships. Here was something entirely beyond their experience, and beyond, too, the limits of their imagination. Certainly they understood that out there were beings like El Dorado himself, who, if not entirely supernatural, possessed the supernatural powers which had made El Dorado their *cacique*. Thus their ability to withstand the coming invasion was based upon his lack of fear or even apprehension about the outcome of the approaching conflict.

He would not disappoint them, because he *felt* no fear of the approaching conflict, not even as he stared at the men who paced the decks of the three ships, who rowed the boats for a closer look at the few gaunt, termite-ridden timbers and the rusting gun barrels which were all that remained of the *Plough*, and as a slow suspicion began to solidify in his mind; the ships were all brigantines, and in addition to the flag of Portugal drooping lazily in their sterns, they flew another flag, a flag in which the red and green of Portugal shared the blue of Scotland.

He glanced at Christina, standing beside him, and she raised her head. "Jamey—"

"Aye," he said. "These are Grant Company ships."

"Then—"

"Aye," he said again. "Look on the poop of the lead vessel."

Now he watched her, instead of the ships, as she squinted into the distance. Because he knew what she was looking at.

"That's Jack," she whispered. "Oh my God. That's Jack."

"Aye."

"You said he wouldn't come now. You said . . ." Her voice suddenly faded in the quick catch of her breath, and he looked back at the ship and frowned at the girl who had just climbed the ladder to the poop and was taking off her straw hat as the afternoon began to cool, to reveal a fluttering mass of copper-brown hair.

And with her there was a boy, not far from the age young James had been, eight years ago, when he had started up this river.

"That's Inez," Christina said. "Inez . . . and Anthony. Inez and Anthony." Her voice rose, and she reached forward to part the leaves.

Jamey threw one arm around her shoulder, pulling her backward at the same instant as he used his other hand to hold her mouth and prevent her from crying out. Desperately she twisted in his arms and kicked in an attempt to free herself.

"Help me, damn you," Jamey snapped at his son, and young James hastily scooped his mother's legs from the ground. Meanwhile Jamey had signaled with his head, and the entire Indian army silently began to withdraw from the bank. "If you scream," Jamey said into Christina's ear, "so help me, I'll kill you." He and young James had carried her several yards into the forest, and now he signaled his son to release her. James set her feet on the ground, and Jamey slowly took his hand away from her mouth.

She stared at him with enormous tragic eyes. "Those are my husband and my children," she said.

"Not anymore," he replied.

"But . . . you can't fight them now," she begged.

"It's more necessary than ever to fight them," he pointed out, "because it *is* Jack. He's come looking for you, and he's not going to give up until he finds you. And if he finds me he'll hang me." He gazed at young James. "You understand that, boy?"

"Yes, Father."

"And do you have any wish to see your father hanged, to be taken back to Rio and sent off to Portugal?"

"No, sir. My home is here. These are *my* people."

"Indeed they are. When I'm dead you'll be their king." He clapped his son on the shoulder. "You're prepared to play your part?"

"I am, sir."

"It'll be difficult to convince your Uncle Jack," Jamey warned.

"I'll not fail you, sir."

Christina caught his hand. "For God's sake," she cried, "your brother and sister are out there."

"*Half*-brother and -sister," Jamey said.

"Your flesh and blood," Christina implored. "You can't see them killed. Jamey, if you have ever loved me at all, you cannot do this."

He smiled at her. "I had not intended to, my love. However foolish Jack may have been to bring his children upon such a venture, he'll hardly take them into the forest. I give you my word that when we take the ships, neither Inez nor Anthony will be harmed." He gave her a squeeze. "They'll live here with us. I'll find some handsome young brave for Inez, and some pretty little squaw for Anthony. How does that sound?"

She stared at him. "You can't be serious. Inez is a Portuguese lady."

"Weren't you a Portuguese lady? Who was prepared to share her all with Tupa?"

"To save *your* life."

"Nonsense. You were anticipating it. And if I'd died you'd have moved into his hammock without the slightest hesitation. The girl will enjoy it."

Christina's shoulders slumped. "And Jack?"

"Ah, now that's a different kettle of fish. I doubt he'd settle here. He'd keep dreaming of you, since he's come so far to find you. Besides, he must hate me as much as I hate him." He held her arm to urge her through the trees. "Let's get back to the village. Tomorrow is going to be a busy day."

She glared at him, then made her way through the trees. He walked immediately behind her, watched her shoulder blades peeping through her hair as she walked, the rippling muscles in her thighs and calves, in their latent power, typifying the superb athlete that she had become. Even after eight years of possessing her utterly, he still found her beauty irresistible. In its ownership, not less than the omnipotent power he wielded as El Dorado, was all his happiness centered, and he was a happy man—happier at this moment, he thought, than ever before in his life. It was not merely the thought of actually fighting for his kingdom that was exhilarating, or even the prospect of at last ending the nightmare that had haunted him for all these eight years, of eliminating the only man he both hated and feared. It was at least partly the certainty that for all her submission she would betray him if she could, was almost certainly already planning to do so.

He knew her too well, could read her eyes and her expression as easily as he read the forest. She had never *given* him her love. She had surrendered again and again, submitted again and again, because survival was the mainspring of her character. But Jack remained her husband. He did not doubt she would have planned her desertion—knowing that it must involve *his* execution—even had her children not been involved.

Knowing this merely made his possession the sweeter, his foiling of her plan the more amusing. She sat beside him as usual as they ate—an immense feast, this, for no fewer than one hundred and sixty warriors squatted around the fire—and smiled at them as he repeated his commands for the morrow, making sure that each inferior chieftain knew exactly what was required of him. This was in itself exhilarating, for never had he commanded such a force, and such an excited, confident force as well. The Indians adored fighting, regarded it as an enormous game. And now they were going to fight and defeat these strange beings from another world. They did not doubt it for a moment. El Dorado had willed it, and El Dorado was never wrong. Besides, his plan was so simple and so foolproof, there was not a man who could not grasp it and know it must succeed, however afraid they remained of the ships themselves.

The meal finished, Christina bade good night to her son and her husband and retired to her hut, where Jamey joined her after giving his last instructions to his own people. To pull her out of her hammock and make her kneel before him on the ground was more pleasurable tonight then it had been for months. He knew she could not resist his lovemaking, but in addition, this night she was more responsive than usual. Another indication that she was prepared to humor him before abandoning him.

Passion spent, he lay in his hammock with her in his arms, her head against his cheek. She appeared to fall asleep immediately, her long lashes drooping over her magnificent eyes, her breathing regular. He was ready to enjoy the game, moved restlessly for some time, only slowly appearing to subside, to lie still at last, and wait for her to move, with the utmost caution, carefully swinging her legs out of the hammock, settling them on the ground before easing her weight away from him. Then he could open his eyes and watch her tiptoe across the hut, and stop with a gasp of frightened dismay as she found herself facing the warrior he had instructed to wait for her.

The dawn mist still clung to the river as Jack conferred with Cutter and the captain of the other two ships on the poop of the *Lodestar*. Cal and Inez and Anthony were also present, with Thomas de Carvalho, in command of the soldiers, and Father Alfonso.

"Thus far everything in Alvares's story has proved correct," he said. "It is here my brother was wrecked, and here he took to the forest with the remnants of his crew, making north. But according to Alvares, they were taken prisoner by the Indians on the very first morning. How far would they have traveled in one morning, Cal?"

"Not far," the boy said. "It is not possible for white men to travel far in the forest in one morning."

"So the Indians must be close by," Cutter suggested.

"They are watching you now," Cal said.

Jack looked at the impenetrable green wall on the far side of the river. An entire Indian army could be concealed there, he knew.

"Will you be able to talk with them?" he asked.

Cal nodded.

"So how do we make contact?" Thomas de Carvalho asked.

"It is hard," Cal said. "They will wish to fight you, to kill you."

"That's why you're here," Jack explained. "To tell them

we have not come to fight. We have come for my wife and young James, if they still live. Or for news of them, if they are dead. There are a great many of us, Cal. More than any Indian tribe, surely. They will not attempt to fight so many men. It is just a matter of being able to talk with them."

"It will be hard," Cal said again.

"Look!" Anthony said suddenly. He had continued to watch the forest while the men had talked, and now he pointed. "There's one of them over there, signaling to us."

The crews had seen the man too, and began crowding the bulwarks, waving and shouting. Jack stared at the trees and at the Indian, who was also waving his arms in a very European manner as he tried to attract their attention.

Cal had also noticed. "That is not like an Indian," he said.

Inez glanced at him and found herself holding Hal Cutter's hand in excitement.

"Launch a boat," Jack snapped. "Six oarsmen. I'll take the tiller."

"It could be a trap," Carvalho objected.

"We must speak with that fellow, Thomas. But load and run out the guns, just in case." He slid down the ladder into the waist and vaulted over the gunwale to join the boat which was already waiting alongside. Without instructions from him, the crew had armed themselves with pistols and cutlasses, and when he looked back up at the ship, Inez was leaning over with his own sword and pistol.

"Be careful, Papa," she begged. "Take Cal."

"I'm bringing that man back," he pointed out. "Cal can talk to him then. Give way."

He watched the north bank in an agony of fear that the Indian might have disappeared, but he was still there, a splendid sight, for he was quite naked and was most powerfully built, with a well-proportioned body, and oddly soft black hair, worn in the Indian fashion, to be sure, in that it was cut in a fringe over his eyes and around his ears, but entirely lacking the stiff immobility common to his people.

But his face . . . his face was entirely European and strangely familiar in its craggy features. As the boat came into the bank, Jack experienced an almost painful throbbing of the heart.

"Father?" Young James said. "My God. Father! I could not believe my eyes."

Jack leaped out of the boat and splashed ashore to embrace him. "James? It's unbelievable. It's. . . ." He held him at arm's length to look at him.

"Get me away, Father," James said. "They'll know I've escaped by now. They'll be following. Please, Father."

"But . . . your mother . . ."

"She waits for you. But it will be difficult. And bloody." James looked over his shoulder at the jungle. "Please take me to the ship, Father."

"Climb aboard." Jack followed him into the dinghy. "Give away." Unable to contain his excitement, he waved at the ships. "It's James," he shouted. "James Grant."

The gunwales were still crowded, and he could make out both Inez and Cal staring at them. He realized Inez had never seen a naked man before.

"And throw down a pair of breeches," he called.

Cutter was waiting as they came alongside, and the garment was handed down. James looked at it in amazement.

"You're back to civilization now," Jack said with a smile.

James pulled on the breeches, then swung himself on board, and stopped to stare at Inez, standing at the break of the poop. "Inez?" he whispered. He bounded forward, to scramble up the ladder and take his half-sister in his arms. "Inez. But . . ." He stepped back to look at her. "You're beautiful. Just beautiful. And Anthony . . ." He slapped the boy on the back. "My God, after so long."

"After so long," Inez said. "To see you looking so well . . ."

"I'm a warrior," James said, with some pride. "They made me a warrior."

"And Christina?" Jack had climbed the ladder behind him.

"Mama?" Inez begged. "Is she? . . ."

"She's alive. And well. You must believe that."

"But she is also an Indian," Jack said, his face hard.

"No, Father. She has resisted them to the utmost. That is why they keep her a prisoner, at all times."

"And what else?" Jack asked.

"Well, she . . . there is a chieftain named Tupa who claims her as his woman."

"Tupa," Father Alfonso said. "That was the name given by Alvares."

"Aye," Jack said grimly. "We have heard of Tupa. Tell me, boy."

James sighed, his shoulders suddenly sagging. "You must forgive her, Father. There was nothing else she could do. There was nothing any of us could do. After they killed my father . . ."

"You knew he was your father?" Jack asked. "And yet you call me by that name."

"You *are* my father," James insisted. "You have always been my father. My real father . . . he kidnapped us, Mama and me. He treated Mama worse than Tupa ever has. He . . . he deserved to die. But then there was nothing we could do. I was only a boy then, and we were the only survivors."

"Alvares spoke of a man named Caetano," Carvalho said.

James glanced at him. "They killed him too, Uncle Thomas," he said. "There were only Mama and me left. But we never gave up hope. We knew you'd come for us one day, Father. We didn't really expect Alvares to bring you . . ." He looked around him.

"He didn't." Jack said. "Alvares is dead too, and I stayed away too long. My God, I stayed away too long."

"But you are here now, Father," James said eagerly. "You'll get Mother out of here, and you must forgive her, Father. You must. If you knew how she wept when she heard there were ships coming up the river—she knew it had to be you. Tupa beat her for weeping."

"Forgive her?" Jack asked. "What do I have to forgive her for? 'Tis she must forgive me, for deserting her. For allowing this to happen. We are here to rescue both of you, if you will tell me how."

"I will lead you to the village," James said.

"They'll know we're coming," Carvalho objected. "They'll attempt to stop us."

James's glance was scornful. His whole demeanor had suddenly changed, obviously at the thought of avenging himself, Inez thought. But how handsome he had become, how strong. How determined.

"I did not suppose you had come this far," he remarked, "to turn back at the prospect of fighting a few Indians."

"We did not," Jack agreed, "although I had hoped to avoid bloodshed. But will they not murder your mother, or at least carry her off into the jungle, as we approach?"

"I do not think so," James said. "You must remember that these Indians have never encountered white people before, except us, and because of the mutiny and my father's snakebite, they found us very easy to defeat. I am not pretending you will not have to fight. But I do not think they will evacuate the village, because they will be sure they can stop you."

"And will they not?" asked one of the captains, Jaime Gomez.

"Hardly. Tupa does not command more than seventy warriors. You must have twice that number of men, in three ships."

"Which have to be manned," Cutter pointed out.

"By half a dozen men each," James said. "The Indians will never attack ships. They are terrified of them." He gazed at Jack. "I cannot believe you will not face Tupa down, Father."

"I came here for that purpose," Jack agreed. "We'll mount an expedition. One hundred men, Thomas. You'll see to their arming. Muskets, pistols, and cutlasses. How far to the village, James?"

"A good distance, Father, We will not get there before dusk."

"Aye. Well, do not expect us back before tomorrow, Hal. You'll keep the guns run out and double-shotted, though. And you'll bring the boats back to the ships after we have been ferried ashore. Any questions?"

"May I come with you, Father?" Anthony asked.

Jack shook his head. "You'll stay with the ships." He smiled at the boy. "You have to look after your sister. But you'll come with us, Cal."

The half-caste had been standing quietly by the taffrail, but Inez had noticed that he never took his gaze from James's face. Now he made no immediate response.

"Well, boy?" Jack asked. "That's why you're here, to guide us into the forest. So now we'll have two guides. That will be useful, for so large a body of men. You'll not be afraid?"

Cal seemed to awaken from a deep sleep. "Cal come," he agreed, and pointed at James. "He stay with ships."

"Eh? No, no, Cal. He comes with us. He knows where the Indian village is."

"Cal find village," Cal said.

"Who *is* this?" James demanded.

"A guide we found in Belem," Jack said.

"He's not even a pure Indian," James pointed out. "What does he know of the forest?"

"He claims to have grown up in it," Cutter said.

"I doubt that," James said.

"Nevertheless, we'll take him," Jack said. "You're coming with us, Cal."

Cal nodded. "Cal come, is good. *He* come, is bad."

"I do believe he's jealous of you," Cutter remarked with a grin.

"I don't care much for him either," James said.

"You're both coming, and that's final," Jack said. "Squabbling at such a time is absurd. I'll have none of it. Now we are wasting time. Issue the weapons, Thomas, and let's get to it."

Inez stood beside the half-caste boy. "Why do you not wish my brother to go with you?" she asked.

Cal's eyes gazed gloomily at her. "Is bad," he said. "Is bad."

"Ship men have come," the Indian said. He stood before Jamey and Caetano and the other chieftains, his eyes glinting past the paint with which he had adorned his cheeks.

"How many boats?" Jamey asked.

The warrior held up three fingers, and then three more.

"Three boats," Jamey said. "Each landing three times. Say a dozen men a time, that's over a hundred. There can't be more than twenty left between the three ships. Young James has done well. Now, Caetano, you know what to do?"

"I take twenty men," Caetano said, "and harass their march."

"Just enough to keep them busy," Jamey said. "They'll expect it. But, remember, attack from the west. James will be leading them away from the village, but if they should attempt to charge you, I wish that to be away from the village as well. Keep it up until dusk, and then you can abandon them. We'll have taken the ships by then."

"Aye, aye," Caetano agreed. "We could take all of them, Captain."

Jamey grinned at him. "You'll take all of them, but after we've burned the ships. There'll be enough to go around." He slapped the big sailor on the shoulder. "Off you go."

He walked up the gentle slope toward the village, and Christina. She stood just within the shade of the palm roof, watching him. The mingled anger and humiliation with which she had returned to the hammock had disappeared, and her face was once again composed. Only the slight bunching of the small muscles of her jaw, the ebonylike flintness of her eyes, revealed her smoldering anger. But it was a controlled anger, as her entire approach to life was controlled by her brain rather than her emotions. Of all the women he had ever met—and most of the men, too—she was the most capable of coming to terms with what situation she found herself in, from being isolated in the flooding cellar of a wrecked convent to being left pregnant by a lover supposed dead to having to take off her clothes and live like an Indian. But that instinct made her the more dangerous, however more enjoyable it might make thwarting her, time and again.

He smiled at her. "I will say goodbye, for the time being. By the time I return, all your fears will be dispelled."

She gazed at him. "I have no fears."

"Well then, you will have the pleasure of being reunited with your two children."

"To watch them being abused."

"Whether or not they are abused is up to them," Jamey said. "I propose to offer them a life as members of my people. The best life in the world. It is up to them to accept it. Now I must leave. You will remain here with the women. Pelo will also stay to watch you." He glanced at the Indian, who remained squatted on the earth behind the hut.

Christina also glanced at the man, her face twisted with contempt.

Jamey grasped her wrist, bending her arm up so that she winced with pain. "Now you listen to me, my darling girl. I don't know what ugly scheme is roaming through that deceitful little mind of yours, but this is my life you're playing with, and I swear to you, if you attempt to play me false again, I'll stake you out."

She met his gaze without blinking. "You are hurting me," she said.

Slowly he unclamped his fingers, and watched her rub her wrist. Perhaps she did not believe that he would condemn her to so terrible a death. Staking out was the Indian method of execution for their most desperate enemies; since he had become *cacique* he had employed it only to destroy those defeated chieftains who would not swear allegiance. The unhappy man had his anus packed with honey and was then staked out over an ants' nest. It was then up to him, as a brave warrior, to die without screaming his agony as his bowels were eaten away by the sugar-hungry ants. Few succeeded in dying with the dignity their honor demanded.

But Christina, although forced like the rest of the women and children to witness the executions, had never taken part in the laughter and jeering the others had indulged in, and indeed had often remained throughout the ceremony with her eyes shut. And no doubt her mind as well.

He suddenly realized how much he hated her. She found him physically attractive, and physically satisfying. Therefore having to submit constantly to what many a woman might have considered rape had never been hardship to her. But she had given nothing in return, not even a glimpse into her mind. This had never occurred to him before. He had supposed she was his victim, but the facts were quite the reverse. *She* had taken from *him* what she wanted, and then been able to close her mind to everything else.

Perhaps he even *wanted* to stake her out, to hear her screams, to watch her die in the most horrible fashion. Except that she would then *be* dead, and he would never again have the pleasure of maltreating her. She understood that, of course, which was why she could respond to his threat with such contempt.

Undoubtedly she *was* planning something, all over again.

With a sudden inspiration he snapped his fingers. "Pelo."

The Indian rose to his feet and silently approached them.

"You have done well, Pelo," Jamey said in the Indian's tongue. "You have watched Kita well. I am proud of you. I shall reward you."

Pelo waited with a quiet patience worthy of Christina herself.

"For this day, until I return," Jamey said, "I give you Kita as your woman." He smiled as he heard Christina's sharp intake of breath. "Use your time well, Pelo. Kita returns to me when I come back."

At last Pelo showed some reaction. His flat mouth broke into a grin.

"You . . ." Christina bit her lip. "I will give you my word," she said in Portuguese, "that I will not leave the village. You cannot permit this . . . this animal to possess me."

Jamey laughed. "I think the idea is quite fascinating. Besides, I do not accept your word. I do not think I can trust it." He clapped Pelo on the shoulder. "I will return by sunrise tomorrow. Use her well, Pelo. Use her well."

"I hate you," Christina said very quietly. "I loathe you, Jamey Grant. And once I saved your life."

"As I saved yours, my darling. I have no debt to you." He walked away from her to where his warriors were waiting, bows and blowpipes at the ready. Ceatano and his twenty-man decoy force had already left.

On the banks of the stream Jamey looked back. Christina stood as he had left her, watching him. But Pelo now stood beside her, fingering her hair.

Chapter 14

═══

The last of the warriors vanished into the trees, and the village was quiet. The women went about their usual tasks, unconcerned with the blood that would shortly be shed. To them, this was no different from any other day, the attack on the white men no different from any other campaign undertaken by the great El Dorado. They had no doubts as to the outcome.

But they all knew how Kita had attempted to desert them. No doubt they were surprised that El Dorado had not beaten her for her treachery. Now they all watched her surreptitiously, both to prevent her from again attempting to escape and also out of curiosity, for if they had not overheard what El Dorado had said to Pelo, they could calculate its gist from the suddenly possessive air he had assumed. Certainly there was not one of them, not even Lala, whom she could turn to for help. Jamey might have been right in prophesying that if both he and young James were to be killed they would transfer their allegiance to her, but that had been before last night. Now she had suddenly become an alien.

"Now," Pelo said, lifting her arm to pull the hair in her armpits. Like all the Indians, he was more fascinated by her

hair than by any of her female attributes. "Now I shall use
you as my woman. El Dorado has said it."

She glanced down at him; he was certainly ready for it.
And she doubted she would be the victor in a wrestling
match. Yet she was not aware of any fear, or even of any
great repulsion. Jamey meant her to be punished, to be humil-
iated, but this was just a man.

Thus far have you come, Christina Maria Theresa de Sousa
e Melo Grant, she thought, from the rustling silks and satins,
the studied manners, and the hypocritical innuendo of your
drawing room in Rio. But the question was, *how* far had she
come? Last night her reaction had been almost instinctive. Jack
was here at last. He had come for her, and he had brought
two of her children. She had not considered whether he had
truly come for *her*, or whether he was merely going through
the necessary motions dictated by European chivalry—or worse,
whether he merely sought revenge. Certainly he must know
that the Christina who had for years been in the Amazon
jungle would bear little resemblance to the artificial creature
who had been his wife. He might even, as she had always
hoped and prayed, believe that it might make no difference to
him, but the reality of it would not become apparent until she
was his again, when it would be too late for either of them to
change their minds.

And after so long she was even, suddenly, uncertain as to
what would be her own reactions to returning to civilization,
to Jack's bed. Could she ever remain there, lying supinely on
her back, having known for eight years the excitement of
Jamey's embrace, the utter uninhibitedness of living like an
Indian? Thus she had allowed herself only to recognize that
Jack was here, with over a hundred white men, as well as her
children, and that Jamey intended to kill them all. Warning
them had been the only course to be considered.

But now she had had twelve hours to reflect, and to allow
herself to be overwhelmed by her doubts. Jamey did not mean
to kill either Inez or Anthony, and if she doubted they would
be prepared to accept life as Indians, especially, in the case of
Inez, as an Indian squaw, they would eventually have to
accept it. Nor could Jamey really mean to kill Jack, surely

. . . as if she could possibly risk that, with her knowledge of Jamey's character! But the fact was that to go to Jack now, to warn him, to enable him to turn the tables on Jamey, would be to destory the Indians, whether immediately by steel and lead, or slowly and more horribly by drink and disease. She had grown to love and admire these people . . . but out there were her husband and her own people.

Was it even possible to warn him? By now he and his men had been lured into the forest by young James, leaving their ships virtually undefended, certain that those floating castles would never be attacked by primitive Indians, quite unaware that those Indians were directed by a European brain. And once Jamey had the ships, Jack and his men, floundering through the forest, would be as dangerous as the bushmaster after it had lost its head.

She became aware that Pelo was on his knees before her, examining her intimately. He was as irritating as a chigger, a tiny insect which was fond of burrowing into the flesh of the toe and which had to be prised out with a knife.

"Now," he said, indicating that she too should kneel. "I am to use you."

"I have not bathed," she said. And when he frowned at her, she explained. "White women do not kneel with men except after bathing." Before he could protest, and since he had momentarily released her, she stepped past him and moved with long strides toward the stream.

What to do? To attempt to warn Jack and to fail would be unthinkable; she did not really believe that Jamey would go so far as to kill her, much less stake her out, but he would certainly punish her, and he might inflict that unthinkable fate on those of his enemies he took alive and force her to watch. He was entirely at the mercy of his own impulses, his own desires; like the most omnipotent of Eastern potentates, he recognized no law, moral or physical, save his own.

Which was why, she suddenly realized, he had to be stopped, no matter what the risk. She almost shuddered with the implications of her earlier doubts. He was planning nothing less than the deaths of more than a hundred men, as he had planned the deaths of hardly less than that during the past seven years in establishing himself as king of the Amazon.

But what she was proposing to do would almost certainly end in his death, either in battle or by the rope, and this was equally unthinkable. No less than Jack, he was the father of one of her children, and he had been her lover for eight years . . . and no one could doubt that however bloody his methods, he was adored by his people. He had provided the strength and the authority they so badly needed—they were the happiest people she had ever known. Nor could she doubt that Jamey was equally devoted to them. He might regard every one of them as his to do with as he chose, but his attitude to them was the same as she might regard her arms and legs, her fingers and toes. It would never cross her mind to consider any of them refusing to accept a command from her, just at it would never cross her mind to make special provision for their individual well-being, but at the same time she would never deliberately harm any of them, and every bit of food or drink or rest she enjoyed was devoted to their good as well as to the rest of her body.

Jamey was not merely the brain of these people. He was the heart and the will as well; without him they would surely dwindle into nothing.

If only that point of view could be put across to Jack before the conflict between the brothers reached open warfare.

She became consumed with urgency. And with getting rid of Pelo, who had followed her to the stream.

"You wash," he said. "Quickly."

He was still decidedly anxious. And they were still being watched by the women. She shook her head. "Kita washes there," she said, and pointed to where the stream debouched from the trees, at the edge of the village clearing.

Once again she set off with long strides, listening to Pelo hurrying at her heels. But now he was becoming impatient.

"You are my woman," he said. "For this day, you are my woman, Kita. El Dorado has said this. If you do not kneel with me soon, I will beat you."

Christina stepped into the shallow water and sank to her knees, and the stream flowed around her waist. She turned to face him, and realized that she had accomplished the first part of her plan—they were concealed from the women.

"Yes," she said. "You must beat me. I am better after I have been beaten. You must beat me with a stick."

He gaped at her, but partly in delight. He had never expected her to be so compliant.

"I will fetch a stick," he said, and waded past her to enter the forest. Christina immediately dug her hands into the water, located a large stone, stood up, and followed him. He heard her behind him, stopped, and turned, even as she drew a very long breath and swung her arms, the stone held between her hands.

The blow caught Pelo across the side of the head, sending a shock of savage pain right up Christina's arms into her shoulders. But she reflected that it had hurt Pelo more. He fell to his knees, and then onto his face. Hastily, she knelt beside him, turned him over to make sure he was still breathing, then raised her head and found herself looking at Poot.

Christina was aware only of pain, and of exhaustion. The knuckles of her right hand were split and dripped blood, and the stone had eaten into her palm as well, leaving it red and angry, while her brain seemed to have collapsed. The long tension of yesterday and last night, the equally long agony of indecision, had combined to leave her as weary as if she had run several miles, just as the realization that it was not yet over made her want to lie down at Pelo's side and close her eyes, and hope that when she woke up again the entire nightmare would be ended.

But to do that would be to condemn Jack, and a hundred others, to death. She drew a long breath, again tightened her aching fingers around the stone.

"Is bad," Poot said, parting the leaves to come toward her. "El Dorado going to *beat* you." She knelt beside the unconscious man. "You hit like a man," she remarked, and suddenly realized that having hit that hard once, Kita was quite capable of doing it again. Hastily she rose and turned as Christina swung her arm again, biting her lip against the anticipated pain. But Poot saw the blow coming, stepped away from it, and as Christina carved empty air, Poot moved behind her and kicked, with nerve-shattering accuracy, her toes catching Christina on the back of the right knee, and bringing her down with darts of agony racing up her thigh.

She fell onto her back and gazed up at the Indian woman, who was smiling at her. "Is good," Poot remarked. "I beat you myself."

Christina swung her left leg sideways like a scythe—her right leg was still incapable of movement. Her ankle crashed into Poot's calves and she in turn fell over. Christina sat up and forced herself forward, driving her still pain-paralyzed right leg into motion, straddling Poot's body as she tried to rise, forcing her down again with the pressure of her thighs, staring into the dark eyes. She still held her stone, could end it now—but Poot was an old friend.

Poot recognized the indecision, reached up and seized Christina's breasts, squeezing with fingers and nails, bringing an involuntary gasp of agony from Christina's lips, dragging her forward even as she attempted to twist free of the thigh embrace. Christina struck down, left and then right, felt the fingers relax as they lost their strength, gazed in horror at the blood trickling from Poot's nostrils, dropped the stone, and lowered her head to press it against Poot's chest and make sure she was still breathing.

But she was definitely unconscious, with two huge bruises starting to form on her face and nose. Now, Christina realized, she had burned her boats. No matter what happened now, she could never live in this village again. Only success counted now. She pushed herself up, gave a last glance at the two people on the ground, and ran into the trees.

She headed west; this was the direction young James had been instructed by his father to lead the white men, away from the village. She had no doubts about finding them; a hundred armed white men hacking their way through the jungle would be audible for a considerable distance, and she could travel much faster than they and without any fear of encountering Caetano and his little band, since Jamey had commanded them to get to the west of the invaders, further to distract them from the village.

After years of acting the savage, she no longer found the

thorns and drooping branches any hindrance to her progress. The soles of her feet were like leather, and the sweat which coated her body allowed it to slide through all obstacles where clothing would have been continually snagged. Only her hair, drifting behind her, was occasionally caught on a dangling branch, to be freed by a quick shake of the head.

She moved like an Indian too; she did not lift her feet more than was absolutely necessary, in the interests both of quiet and of preserving her energy. She looked immediately in front of her, continually on her guard against seething ants' nest or lurking snakes, able instantly to decide where such deathtraps were likely and where was obviously safe, just as she could tell at a glance which fallen tree trunks were firm enough to step on and which would immediately crumble beneath her feet, with the attendant risk of a sprained ankle. But for all this concentration upon what lay ahead of her, she was also continuously scanning the trees and bushes to either side, always alert for the slightest sign of danger, utterly confident that unarmed though she might be, in her speed and her understanding of the habits of every creature she might encounter, she was as safe here as ever she had been in her own drawing room at Copacabana.

The suggestion brought her to a sudden halt. After today, she would never be allowed to roam any forest again without an escort. Nor would she ever again use the forestcraft of which she was so proud.

She stood absolutely still, another forest-learned accomplishment, scarcely seeming to breathe as she reflected. But her head jerked when she heard the rolling notes of a musket volley ripping through the jungle, and arising, she estimated, not very far in front of her.

She moved forward again and now heard other noises, shouts and curses, while now she too had found the path taken by the white men, easily discerned from the broken branches and boot-crushed leaves, and marked suddenly, and terribly, by the body of a man, his face suffused and contorted, the poisoned dart still protruding from his shoulder.

Now the shouting was very close. Christina eased her way through the trees and suddenly found the white men immediately in front of her, forming a vast circle, she estimated, although she could only see the curve of it, some twenty men, facing the jungle, half hastily recharging their pieces, the others awaiting the order to fire, while the powder smoke still drifted above them into the trees. But that their reply to the darts and arrows of the Indians had been nothing better than a gesture of defiance was proved by the fact that they obviously could not even see her, though she was no more than twenty feet from them.

On the other hand, it would require only one nervous finger on a trigger to bring her down, and she did not doubt every finger in that beleaguered circle was nervous.

Slowly she sank to her knees, then eased her body forward to rest on her elbows. Then she called, as loudly as she could, "Jack! Jack Grant!" and threw herself flat on the ground.

As she had anticipated, there was an immediate response, a crash of fire which sent leaden balls whistling above her head, ricocheting from tree trunk to tree trunk; one spent ball actually fell beside her with a sinister thud.

But behind the musketry she heard shouts. "Hold your fire," someone called.

"That was a European voice," said someone else, and her heart began to pound as she recognized it as that of Thomas de Carvalho.

"That was Christina," Jack said.

Cautiously she raised her head, to look at him. Jack! A somewhat leaner man than she remembered with hair graying at the temples and a face hardened by warfare and anxiety. But still the man who had taken her life from the depths of despair and given it happiness and purpose. She rose to her knees, and then to her feet, parted the leaf barrier, and stepped through.

Jack Grant gazed at the woman who emerged from the trees in front of him. Since he had heard her voice, he knew it had to be his wife, just as the face before him belonged to Christina. But could that golden brown, superbly muscled body possibly belong to Christina? After so many years in the treacherous Amazon, she was even lovelier than the girl who had so strangely come to his bed over twenty years ago.

"Do you not recognize me, Jack?" she asked.

"Christina," he said. "My God, Christina." Suddenly he realized that every man in his command had gathered to stare at the wondrous apparition which had appeared from the forest. "To your posts," he shouted. "Have you forgotten we're surrounded? Face the trees. Christina . . ." He whipped off his shirt and gave it to her. She looked at it for some seconds, then shook her head.

"Time for that when I am again your wife, if that can ever be," she said.

"Christina . . ." He made to step forward, stopped as he heard Thomas de Carvalho and young James hurrying behind him.

"Christina?" Thomas gasped. "But . . ." He stared at her.

"Mother?" Young James was equally amazed, but also alarmed.

"Seize him," Christina said, pointing to her son. "Do not harm him, but seize him."

"Young James?" Jack cried. "But, Christina, he brought us news of your captivity and is guiding us to the village where you have been held captive."

"Seize him," Christina repeated. "Quickly!"

James had suddenly turned and run for the forest, but fast as he was, Cal, who had followed him from the far side of the defense perimeter, was even faster, and threw himself forward and grasped James's ankle to bring him heavily to the ground. James twisted and struck at him, then lay still as he found himself surrounded by several men.

"Don't harm him," Christina said again, "but bind his arms to make sure he cannot escape."

"I don't understand," Jack said. "He is your son, and he was taking us to your rescue. He had no idea you had already escaped. My darling Christina, will you not put on my shirt? It really is unseemly for you—"

"Think of me as an Indian, for now," she said. "And James may be my son, but he is also Jamey's son."

"Jamey?" Carvalho demanded. "But Jamey is dead."

"Because *he* says so?" Christina pointed at young James. "Jamey is very much alive, and by this afternoon will have seized your ships."

They stared at her in disbelief. Even Cal seemed struck dumb with the implication of what she was saying.

"Don't you understand?" she cried. "It is all a trap. It has been a trap from the very beginning. Jamey knew you were coming days ago. He planned your destruction days ago. He knows that without your ships you can never survive in the forest. These people who you think have been attacking you, they have only been pretending. There are no more than twenty of them. But there are more than a hundred Indians, led by Jamey, planning to attack your ships under cover of today's rainstorm."

"By God! But what can we do?" Jack said.

"We must get back to the river as quickly as possible. There may yet be time. Time at least to strike a bargain before the ships are destroyed. The village lies on our way. If we capture that, we will be in a strong position."

Jack frowned at her. "But these men who have been shooting at us—"

"There are only twenty of them," she said again. "And if we march back to the river they will attempt to stop us and we will be able to defeat them." She sighed. "I will show you how to make your musketry effective against them. When you fire, aim low, for they will be crouching or lying on the ground."

"A bargain?" Carvalho was also frowning. "What have we to bargain with?"

Christina pointed at young James.

"But . . . he's your son."

"He is also Jamey's most precious possession," she said. "And are not my other son and my daughter on board one of those ships? Your children as well, Jack. Listen to me. Jamey has founded an empire here. He has conquered up and down the river, and he rules the Amazon as king. But it is *his* empire, and he plans that young James will inherit it and continue his work, not that it should revert to the savages. There is your strength. Does not Portugal lay claim to this land without ever taking possession of it? If you were to offer to confirm Jamey as governor of the Amazon, for him and his heirs, to forgive him for his crimes and allow him to come and go as he pleases, in return for abandoning this war and acknowledging Portugal's superiority, why, the matter would be resolved at a stroke.''

They stared at her, even young James, while his hands were tied by the seamen.

"Bargain with him?" Carvalho demanded at last. "Confirm him in his stolen rights? The man is a red-handed murderer. The blood of my brother stains his every action. And many others. What of the good fellows who have died this morning?"

"And what of all the rest of you, once the ships are burned?" Christina shouted. "Can you not understand? You have been outwitted, defeated. You are lost in an element of which you know nothing. You have no *chance* but to forgive him. But to attempt to make some good come out of all his evil."

Carvalho glanced at Father Alfonso.

"It is what the viceroy would wish," the priest said.

Carvalho looked at Jack.

"And do I also forgive him his crimes against you?" Jack asked quietly.

"I would beg that of you," she said. "He does not regard them as crimes, for reasons you know as well as I."

"He was always your first love."

"He was my first love," she said. "But not my last, Jack. I will come back with you, if you wish it."

"And if I pardon my brother."

"There is no other *way*," she said.

"It is hopeless, in any event," Captain Gomez said. "Your son will hardly guide us now. How *do* we get back to the river?"

"Cal will be able to guide us," Jack said. "He knows these forests. Eh, boy?" He turned, frowned, and looked from left to right. "Where is the half-breed?"

The sailors looked at each other in consternation.

"Deserted us, by God," Carvalho said.

"The moment he realized our situation," Father Alfonso said. "Truly, these people are not to be trusted."

"Then we *are* defeated," Jack said.

"*I* will guide you," Christina said. "Do you not suppose I know this forest as well as any Indian? We have wasted too much time. Only haste will help us now." She glanced at the cloud-hidden sky. "And tell your men to keep their powder dry."

As she spoke the first raindrops fell.

"Will we hear, do you think," Inez asked Cutter, "if they engage the Indians?"

"Not until the rain stops," he said, standing beside her at the rail to gaze at the pouring water; they could not even see the far bank. "But they won't be able to engage anyway, not in this. Their powder will be useless."

"Then *they* are useless," Anthony said, with a shiver.

"Your brother will know how to keep them out of trouble," Cutter said confidently. "He must be almost an Indian himself, after this long."

"Yes," Inez said.

Cutter glanced at her. "You have not seen him for eight years. Do you find he has changed too much?" Cutter asked.

"As you said, Hal, he is almost an Indian himself. Look!" Her voice suddenly squeaked with excitement. "They're coming back."

They stared into the watery mist, could dimly make out the shapes of several boats approaching them.

"But . . . ." Anthony looked over the rail, where the ships' boats lay alongside, half full of rainwater.

"Those are canoes," Cutter snapped. "Canoes, by God." He ran to the forward rail. "All hands on deck," he bawled. "To arms." Desperately he drew the pistol from his belt and fired it into the air. The explosion sounded flat in the rain-smothered air. Then he seized Inez by the arm and thrust her toward the companion ladder.

"I can fight them," she gasped. "You'll *need* me." Apart from the three of them, there were only five men on board the *Lodestar*.

"They'll not board," he said. "Your brother said no Indian is going to board a ship. But they'll have arrows. Take Anthony and stay below."

Inez hesitated, but she had been brought up to believe that in matters of violence, men must know best. She held Anthony's arm and pulled him to the hatch.

"I want to stay," he protested. "I can shoot a pistol."

"There'll be no pistols in the melee," Cutter said. "Not until the rain stops." He stood at the rail, biting his lip as he watched his men emerging from the forehatch. A single cannon shot might win the day, but no match would stay alight in these conditions.

Inez opened the hatch, thrust her still protesting brother down it, and pulled it shut behind herself. Immediately they seemed to have entered the interior of a drum, as the rain pounded on the deck above, obliterating all other sounds.

Anthony hurried through the great cabin, found that he could see nothing through the stern windows, and opened them. Together they gazed at the *North Star*, which was the next vessel, no more than fifty yards away, riding gently to her anchor and completely surrounded by canoes, from which naked brown-skinned men were clambering over the gunwales.

"James said they wouldn't board," Anthony said.

Inez looked down and saw a canoe immediately beneath the *Lodestar*'s counter. "Anthony," she screamed, "help me."

They slammed the windows shut in the same instant as they heard feet on the companionway. They turned, gazed at several Indians, and, at their head, Jamey Grant.

Inez recognized her uncle immediately, despite the fact that she had seen him only once in her life, when he had visited the house on his strange reappearance in Rio eight years before. But since that event had been immediately followed by the disappearance of her mother and her elder brother, his appearance had remained carved on her memory, even when she had supposed him dead. Now she knew instinctively who this naked, brown-skinned man was, and also knew instinctively that he meant her no good.

She had stepped backward at the sight of him, found her

thighs against the table. "Uncle Jamey?" she said. It was half a plea, and was instantly regretted as he smiled at her.

"Aye," he said. "And you'll be Inez." He ignored Anthony as he came toward her. "My God, you're a lovely little thing. You look like your mother." He stretched out his hand, twined his fingers in her hair. "But she never had hair like this."

"Uncle James . . ." She turned to pull herself free, and his fingers tightened. She could feel her eyes widening as little slits of pain raced across her forehead. "Uncle Jamey . . ."

"If you hurt her—" Anthony shouted, grabbing at Jamey's arm, to be swept away by a swinging fist. The boy fell against the bulkhead, and was immediately seized by two of the Indians, who had remained in the doorway. "Let me go," Anthony shouted, and he was dragged toward the ladder.

Jamey spoke a language unintelligible to her, without turning his head.

"Please don't harm him," Inez gasped. "Please, Uncle Jamey."

"I don't intend to." Slowly the grip on her hair relaxed. "I was just telling my people not to kill him with the others."

"The others? My God. Hal!" She tried to reach the door, and he twined his fingers in her hair again, bringing her up with another start of pain.

"Hal?"

"Mr. Cutter. The mate. You've not harmed him, Uncle Jamey? Have you?"

"The mate? Not the one-armed cripple?" He grinned at her. "Well, well, soft on him, are you?"

"Please let me go," she said, determined to keep calm.

"Soft on a one-armed cripple," Jamey said contemptuously. "You're not for him, Inez. You should be a queen. You're Christina reborn."

The fingers relaxed and she could breathe again.

"Hal is my friend. He is Father's friend. Father . . ." She stopped, staring at him.

"Oh aye," he said. "A friend of your father's is no friend of mine, Inez. They're here to hang me."

"No," she said. "How could they be? They think you're dead."

"Now they'll know better. But they're not going to hang me, anyway. I'm going to hang them." He smiled again. "Well, maybe I won't hang them. I've more interesting ways." His fingers curled around her chin. "But not you, my sweet Inez. Never you. You're to live with us. You'll like that."

"Like that? Live here?" Desperately she tried to think, but a bloodcurdling scream sounded from above her.

"In the name of God—"

He smiled. "Just my people enjoying themselves. I told them to enjoy themselves. Maybe that was your friend Cutter. I don't think he was killed in the assault."

"Hal?" she gasped. "All right," she cried. "I'll live here with you. Just spare Hal's life. Spare all their lives. Please, Uncle Jamey."

Another scream cut through the afternoon.

"You can't bargain with me, miss," Jamey said. "You're staying here whether you want to or not."

"I won't," she said. "I'll kill myself. I swear it."

He gazed at her for some seconds. "I believe you would, too," he said at last. "Oh you're Christina's daughter all right, except that she had more sense. All right, Inez. If I spare this Cutter's life, you'll stay up here with us, willingly?"

"Yes," she said. "I swear it, Uncle Jamey. But not just Hal's life, all of them."

He grinned at her. "Just like your mother. Always giving orders." He took her hand and dragged her to the ladder and up it, into the pouring rain. They emerged forward of the awning, and for a moment she couldn't see as water flooded her face, soaked her gown, brought her hair down in tumbling ruin.

Desperately, she blinked, and gasped with horror as she saw that one of the crew, stripped as naked as the men who surrounded him, had been hoisted by one ankle from the deck by means of a trailing halyard, while the Indians cut at him with their bone knives. Blood streamed down his body along with the rain, and washed his face as he gasped for breath and moaned his pain. To her horror Inez saw that he had already been castrated, and had lost several of his toes.

"Please," she begged. "*Please*, Uncle Jamey."

He said something in the Indians' language. The warriors looked at him, obviously disappointed, but not prepared to disobey. The rope was slashed and whipped from the mutilated ankle, and four of the Indians picked up the moaning man and threw him over the side. A last despairing scream ripped across the afternoon, followed by a splash.

"You promised," Inez shrieked.

"He was dead anyway," Jamey pointed out. "I was only saving him from further pain. Here are the people to interest you."

Hal Cutter, Anthony, and three more of the crew stood forward, also surrounded by Indians. The other man lay beside them, his head a mass of blood where he had been struck by one of the knobkerries with which all the Indians were armed. Inez had to bite her lip to stop herself from screaming again.

"The senorita has interceded for you," Jamey explained. "Especially for you, Cutter. I hope you're properly grateful. Now let's get to work." He spoke rapidly in the strange language. Inez watched him disappearing down the hatch, followed by several of his warriors. But there were still more than twenty on deck.

"We must *do* something," Anthony said. "We can't just stand here."

"Inez," Cutter said. "Are you all right?"

She didn't want to look at him. Her senses were still too shocked by what had happened. She couldn't grasp that it was her own uncle who had just caused a man to be murdered, so hideously, and in whose power she and all the others now found themselves. She turned away from them, found herself against the gunwale, and looked down at the brown water rustling past the hull. She expected immediately to be dragged back by the Indians, but no one seemed concerned that she might jump overboard.

Would it not be best to die? Far better than to remain a prisoner of these people. Except that Mother was also a prisoner, and seemed to have survived. And anyway, if she might wish to die, there was no saying Anthony or Hal did. She could not abandon them.

In any event, it was too late. Jamey reappeared on deck, shouting orders in the Indians' language. He seized Inez around the waist and swung her over the side and into a waiting canoe. She watched the Indians swarming down the topsid, watched Hal and Anthony and the others also being tossed into the boats, then looked up at the *North Star* as they came under her stern. She had not really considered the other ships in the trauma of what had been happening on board the *Lodestar*, but now she realized that they had both also been taken, for only Indians looked down at her.

"Hold your breath," Jamey commanded at her elbow. She obeyed, and seemed to lose all her senses as from behind her there came an ear-shattering explosion. The blast caused the canoes to rock dangerously, and was certainly far greater than anything anticipated by the Indians, who set up a tremendous chattering. Inez twisted her neck to look over her shoulder at the *Lodestar*, her decks torn to pieces by the blast, her masts and furled sails on fire, already settling by the head.

"One down, two to go," Jamey said. "You stay here. I won't be long."

He swung himself up onto the *North Star*. Inez realized that the rain had stopped, as if the very clouds had been dispersed by the force of the explosion. Instantly the sun came out, causing the forest to steam, and their sodden clothes as well.

Indians were climbing down the side of the *North Star* to regain their canoes, chattering amongst themselves, followed by Jamey, once again shouting orders. Clearly he had set another powder train. And here, she realized with a shock of horror as he sat down beside her, there were no white men being evacuated.

Se opened her mouth to protest, and was stopped by the sound of a pistol shot.

They turned their heads to look at the far bank, and the white men who lined it, either kneeling or standing, every man with a musket to his shoulder.

"You'll surrender, Jamey," Jack Grant called, "or I shall fire into you."

Jamey stared at his brother for a moment, then turned back to look at the ship he had just abandoned. "Paddle," he shouted, forgetting himself and using Portuguese, before changing into the Indians' language. The warriors dug their paddles into the water, the canoes surged away from the side of the doomed vessel, and the *North Star* exploded. This time they were much closer, and the blast enveloped Inez like a heated embrace. At least Jamey's canoe stayed afloat; several others were capsized, throwing the panic-stricken Indians into the water, where it was immediately evident that they couldn't swim.

Inez looked from boat to boat in terror, trying to spot Hal and Anthony, and gasped with relief when she saw them both unharmed, although their captors had been so shocked by the explosion they had abandoned rowing and were drifting with the current, downriver to the one remaining ship, the *Venturer*. The *North Star* was burning fiercely and already sinking, in company with the *Lodestar*, which was now disappearing into the brown water with an immense sizzle.

The Indians on the *Venturer* were setting up a tremendous chatter, but across the water Jack's voice could be clearly heard.

"Choose your targets," he commanded. "There are white people on those canoes. But bring down anyone who tries to board the *Venturer*."

Instantly several muskets spoke, powder smoke clouded the bank, and more than one Indian gave a cry of pain and fear; one man tumbled right out of his canoe and into the water.

By now the entire Indian fleet had clustered in the shelter of the *Venturer*, trying desperately to paddle to the south side to get the bulk of the ship between them and the terrible muskets. But several more were hit before they found shelter, and from their clamor it was obvious they were appealing to Jamey to save them. He shouted back at them, then seized Inez by the hair and pushed her toward the gangway.

"Get up there," he snapped. "Quickly."

She hesitated, but the expression in his eyes was so dreadful she clambered up, to pause in amazement, for the Indians who had taken the ship were all sheltering beneath the bulwarks, crawling to and fro.

"Over there," Jamey said, pushing her aft. "Mount the poop."

Slowly she climbed the ladder, terribly aware of the bullets which were still thudding into the hull of the vessel.

"You there," Jamey bellowed from behind her. "Jack. Hold your fire. I've Inez here, as you can see. And Anthony. I'll slit their throats."

The musketry died, and Inez was pushed to the rail.

"Harm a hair of her head, Jamey," Jack called, "and I'll hang young James from this tree."

"Listen," Christina shouted. Inez could see them both now, although she found it almost impossible to recognize her mother in the deeply suntanned woman with the bare legs who had advanced to the very edge of the bank. "You can't win, Jamey," she shouted. "Jack's men have taken the village. He has taken all your women and children prisoners. And Caetano's force has been defeated. Caetano himself is dead."

"Your doing," Jamey snarled.

"Yes," she said. "My doing. You'll not massacre all those people, Jamey. Burn that ship and we'll execute all our prisoners. Young James as well."

"You?" he sneered. "You'll execute your own son?"

"Can you risk it?" she answered. "Can you risk the possibility that you have taught me too well? Can you risk my speaking this same message in the Indians' tongue?" She paused to let the threat sink in. Inez watched her uncle's face working in his anger. "They care for their women and children, Jamey, even if you do not," Christina said. "You cannot win this war, but if you'll listen to me, you need not lose it either."

There was another pause.

"Speak," Jamey said.

"Jack has the power to confirm you in your position. He will make you governor of the Amazon, with a pardon for all your crimes. The position will be hereditary in your family.

Young James will inherit. All you have to do is swear allegiance to the Portuguese crown, and give us that ship in which to leave.''

"Us?" he demanded.

"I will accompany Jack," she said. "With *all* my children, except for young James, as he is more your son than mine."

"You," he said, "think to dictate to *me*? I have this ship. When I burn it, you will all be helpless. You will all die. You threaten to kill young James? Does that concern me? I have Inez here beside me. She will give me all the sons I need, to succeed me, to perpetuate my dynasty. I need no blessing from some distant king. *I* am the king here. King of the Amazon."

"Don't be a fool, Jamey," Jack said. "Don't you suppose there are other expeditions fitting out at this moment to come up the river? Do you imagine you can fight all the rest of Brazil? Do you imagine your Indians will follow you when Christina tells them you have permitted the massacre of their families? For so help me God, unless Anthony and Inez are returned to me within the hour, I will execute them all. Do not doubt that."

Jamey stared at his brother. Inez could see the conflict raging in his mind, between sheer common sense telling him to accept the offer as the best he could possibly expect, and his innate arrogance and *anger*, at being thwarted in the slightest degree. She realized that all their lives hung on the whim of a man who was not entirely sane. And suddenly only she could force his hand.

In his anger, and his interest at what was being said to him, he had released her, and even half turned away from her. She took a long breath, leaped onto the gunwale, and threw herself into the river.

She struck the water with a tremendous splash and went under the surface, desperately trying to hold her breath. She could not swim, was prepared to die, aware that she was breaking her promise to her uncle, but was equally sure that he had no intention of keeping his word either, and that he would use his possession of her to force her father to surrender. She did not even expect ever to reach the surface again, and was surprised when she suddenly found herself gasping for breath, and already some twenty feet from the canoes.

Instantly she sank again, but not before she had become aware of a storm of musketry, and a hail of shouting. Now, she thought, as her lungs started to hurt and stars to float before her eyes. She could hold her breath no longer, and now was the time to end it.

But as she inhaled she was seized by the shoulders and jerked back to the surface, gasping and spluttering, opening her eyes to gaze at Anthony, who had apparently followed her example and jumped out of his canoe. And Anthony swam like a fish. But there were other men in the water as well, brawny Portuguese seamen who had hurried to the rescue of the drowning girl and were now pulling her and her brother to the safety of the bank, and the arms of her mother, standing up to her waist in the water.

"You've nothing to bargain with now, Jamey," Jack Grant shouted. "Don't be a fool, man, surrender."

"I've four white prisoners here," Jamey retorted. "I'll gut them before your eyes."

"No," Inez whispered, her head against Christina's shoulder. "Hal is there. He mustn't be killed."

Christina frowned at her. "Hal?"

Inez felt her cheeks burning. "Father's mate. Hal Cutter."

"No harm will come to him," Christina promised. "Your uncle is clutching at straws."

"And see the same thing happen to your son?" Jack went on. "You've got everything you want, Jamey. Accept it and call an end. You can even represent it as a victory to your people. I'll supply you with enough powder and ball to reestablish your superiority for a hundred years. Listen to me, Jamey. Stand on the gunwale and wave your arms, and I'll order my men to withdraw and let your people ashore in peace. You can tell them your magic forced us away. But it has to be done now."

They stared at the *Venturer*. It looked deserted. Inez could understand what was going through Jamey's mind. Once he stepped onto that gunwale, he was exposing himself to a treacherous shot, the very thing he would do to an enemy.

But he knew his brother too well. As they watched, they saw him slowly emerge from behind the bulwark, climb onto the rail, and wave his arms.

"It goes against the grain." Thomas de Carvalho leaned back in his chair before the table in the great cabin of the *Venturer* and brooded at the half-empty glass of port. "The man is a murderer several times over, a villain, a scoundrel, utterly ruthless—"

"In fact, Thomas," Christina said, "the ideal character to create a Portuguese empire along the Amazon and defend it, even against the Spaniards."

Thomas glared at his sister-in-law. It was their first night out of Belem, and thus the first night in which they had managed to sit down in any comfort, for on the voyage down the Amazon, the *Venturer* had been carrying nearly three times her normal complement. But at least the voyage downriver had taken only a fraction of the time it had needed to work up against the current, and now the surplus crews had been off-loaded, to await the ships that Jack would send up the coast for them. Tonight, for the very first time, Christina supposed that the adventure was over. For some of them. It was over for Inez, resolutely determined to forget that last terrible day. As it was over for her brother Anthony, seated beside her.

And it should have been over for Thomas de Carvalho. But he had brooded on the inequity of leaving his brother's murderer not merely unpunished but even enhanced, all the way down the river. It went, as he repeated endlessly, against the grain. Now he returned an angry stare to meet her smile, then drained his glass and got up to go on deck.

"You should not tease him so," Jack said. "He feels, perhaps correctly, that our attitude might be different if it were not Jamey involved."

"Would it be different?" she asked.

He returned her gaze. "I do not think so. I hope not. We are here to build a great empire. Sometimes it is necessary to use tainted materials, if those are stronger than any others we have to hand.''

And is it over for you, Jack Grant? she wondered. Can it ever be over for you, any more than it can be for me? They had shared nothing since leaving the Indian village. There had been no opportunity, in the overcrowded vessel, even supposing they had wanted to. But now the opportunity was at hand. Tonight, for the first time in nearly nine years, they would spend a night by themselves. Could she go to his arms without seeing Jamey in front of her? And could Jack ever forget that she had lived for eight years as his brother's woman? But could either of them even contemplate the future together if they did not succeed in banishing these memories?

She gazed across the table at Inez, who immediately flushed. Inez flushed whenever she found her mother looking at her. It could not merely be continued embarrassment. Inez had a secret, which she betrayed every time she looked at Hal Cutter. And suddenly Christina saw in her daughter's predicament a means of at least denting the wall of ice that seemed to surround Jack and herself.

''I wonder if you would excuse us, Anthony, Father Alfonso,'' she said. ''I have had so little time to be alone with my daughter. I would take it very kindly.''

''Of course, Dona Christina,'' the priest said. ''Come along, Anthony. We'll practice our knots.'' He was delighted, for this was the first indication that she was intending ever again to behave like a Christian lady. Although she had attended religious service every Sunday, and even gone to church during the stop in Belem, she had neither given confession nor received communion, and to his strictures that she was endangering her soul had merely replied, ''You must give me time to think, Father. If my soul is really in danger, I'm afraid the damage was done several years ago.'' He found this a difficult point to answer. Now he ushered Anthony to the door and waited for Hal Cutter, who was getting up with some difficulty.

''Sit down, Hal,'' Christina said. ''I am sure any discussions we may be going to have concern you equally.''

The young man flushed crimson, and looked to Jack for permission.

"Eh? Oh, indeed," Jack said, clearly mystified by the whole thing.

Hal sank back into his seat, now casting an anxious glance at Inez, who gave him a reassuring smile.

"Yes, Mama," she said.

"And you, Hal?"

"Well, Dona Christina . . . I doubted that a one-armed cripple, with no prospects and less money, would be acceptable, or I would have spoken before."

"Do you love my daughter, Mr. Cutter?"

"I do, Dona Christina. By God, I do."

"And has he *no* prospects, Jack?"

Jack had at last realized what was going on. "Indeed he has, my dear. Command of the next Grant Company vessel to be launched—we are going to have to undertake quite a ship-building program, you and I, Hal, seeing that we have just lost two."

"Well, then . . ." Christina leaned across the table to squeeze her husband's hand. "The Grant Company itself started with no more. Now kiss me, my dears, and then go on deck to plan your future."

"Oh, Mama . . ." Inez threw both her arms around Christina's neck. "You have made me the happiest girl in the world."

"As you have made me the happiest man, sir," Hal said.

"Aye well, it is the effect you have on each other that truly matters," Jack said. "Now be off with you."

The door closed. Christina picked up her wine glass, looked at it, and put it down again.

"That was generous of you," Jack said. "But Cutter is a good fellow, brave and loyal."

"They love each other," she said, and raised her head.

"And that is all that matters?"

"I think so."

"Did you love Jamey?"

She shook her head.

"But you were determined to survive."

"Yes," she said. "But it was not as hard as you suppose. Jamey . . . well, he was, and is, a fascinating man."

"You told me so a long time ago," he said. "Well, long may he and his prosper. If he has always used methods I could never consider, he has also always shown great determination." He attempted a smile. "One day, no doubt, he will receive his just deserts."

"Are you also bitter that you did not hang him?"

"I suppose I am."

"Jack . . . I came with you, I betrayed Jamey to you, because . . . because I love *you*." She bit her lip for he did not immediately respond.

"Despite all?" he asked at last.

"I must ask your forgiveness, and ask you, too, to forget everything that has happened to me. I am still young enough to be your wife . . ." She flushed. "In every way. I apologize for my brown skin, my heathen ways. No doubt my complexion will improve with care, and my morals also, with practice."

"You, improve?" he cried, and seized her hand. "You are the loveliest creature I have ever laid eyes upon, and the best. When I said 'despite all,' I was thinking of *my* crimes, my desertion of you, without which none of this would have happened. And there is more . . . I have told you of Lizzie Butler . . . she waits for me now, in Rio."

Christina squeezed his fingers. "Then I must learn to share," she said softly.

"No, no, never. Lizzie understands it is you I love. She understood the minute I announced I was going to find you. I wanted you to know that I have not been faithful."

"And I am happy that you found some solace in my absence, my love. But you cannot just cast her aside."

"Nor will I do so. She has no family save a wreck of a father. I would like to make her an allowance for the rest of her life, and a house in Rio if she wishes it, or a passage back to the Bahamas if she prefers that."

"Jack, she has doubtless been more of a helpmeet to you this last year than I have been throughout my life. She

deserves anything you can spare her. It is I who must learn to
be once again Mrs. Jack Grant.''

"No," he said, and took her in his arms. "I want you as
my wife, but as Kita equally with Christina.''

She moved her head back to look at him. "Do you understand what you are saying, Jack? Kita is an Indian. She will
shock you, perhaps make you hate her.''

"That could never be," he promised. "I think that perhaps
I was never truly able to love Christina de Sousa e Melo as I
wanted to love her, because she was as far above me as is the
sun. But I want to love her, with all my heart, all my soul,
and all my body.'' He kissed her on the lips. "Perhaps it may
be possible for me to love Kita that way, where Christina
remains a dream.'' His cheek was against hers, his lips
against her ear. "If Kita would but teach me to do so.''

Christina smiled into his hair. After more than twenty
years, she thought, now have I at last found the man I married.
"Kita," she whispered. "would be happy to teach you everything she knows, my dear sweet love.''

Jamey Grant stood on the banks of the Amazon River and
looked from the slow-moving brown water to the flagpole,
carefully embedded above the flood limits and set in an area
cleared of trees and bushes.

"After all, it is a proud flag, Father," Young James said.

"A symbol of our defeat," Jamey said bitterly.

"That is not so, Father. Of an honorable peace. The Indians certainly think so.''

"They like the pretty colors. They like to feel they have
dealt with the white men as equals. They will tell the story
of how they burned the two ships for the next ten generations.''

"And they will continue to deal with the white men as
equals, Father.''

"You must always keep out the priests, boy. You'll have
seen what they did to the aborigines by the coast.''

"I'll rule this land as you have done, Father," James
promised. "But I see a great future for it. I see towns, cities,
and ships plying up and down the river.''

"When you are king," Jamey said. "Or viceroy, or governor."

"It is just a title," James said. "But you'll be ruling it yourself for years to come."

"Aye," Jamey said thoughtfully. He turned away from the bank and began to walk toward the village. The pair of them were quite alone in the dusk. The Indians were still celebrating; the noise of their chanting and laughter drifted through the trees. "You'll not hold it against me that I bargained with your life, that I threatened your brother and sister? It was all bluff."

"I understand what you had to do, Father."

"Aye," Jamey sighed. "You've a sight too much of your mother in you. And now I need a woman. There's none in the village I fancy. I'll go upriver tomorrow." He slapped his son on the shoulder. "She'll not have your prospects, boy. You are my heir, and Zak is yours. We have been granted this land in perpetuity." He laughed. "There's a pun for you. There's . . ." His words ended in a sudden gasp, and young James, walking just in front of him now, turned in alarm, to see his father sink to his knees, breath bubbling from his lips in bloody froth as he fell to his face.

James stared at Cal. The half-breed's long-bladed knife was dull with blood where he had driven it through Jamey's back into his lungs.

"You . . ." James took a step forward, halted as the knife came up. Then he dropped to his knees beside his father, turned him over, and cradled the pain-stricken head in his arms. "Father," he said. "Father."

Jamey Grant opened his eyes, focusing with difficulty, and looked from his son to the boy who had just killed him. "You . . ." The word came out in a welter of bloody froth.

"My name is Cal," the boy said. "I have sought you from the day I buried my mother, after she had died of a broken heart."

"Your . . ." Jamey almost smiled. "My God," he said. "Those were good years. Aye, good days. You did your duty, boy. You did your duty." His eyes closed, and then opened again. "El Dorado," he said. "I knew it, once."

His eyes closed again, and the froth ceased to bubble.

James looked up. "You'd best kill me too," he said, "whoever you are. Because I swear to God that I am going to kill you."

Cal stared at him for several seconds. Then he said, "He deserved to die, for what he did to my mother. Hunt me if you will. I have nothing more to do with your life, and by the evidence of what you have just been saying to your father, you have a great deal. God go with you, *brother*."

He turned and vanished into the trees, leaving James staring after him.

55